ADDITIONAL PRAISE
THE BLACK HOUR

"*The Black Hour* is the rarest of mysteries: one that wants to keep you turning pages in a cold sweat, suspecting every character you meet of both the best and the worst motives; and also one that has something complicated and important to say about the forces that impel us toward death . . . and life. It's an extraordinary debut, marking the arrival of a major new voice in literary suspense."

—Christopher Coake, PEN/Bingham Award–winning
author of *You Came Back*

"Lori Rader-Day's debut *The Black Hour* is the perfect thriller—smart, tense, and foreboding. Every page left me hungry for the next."

—Clare O'Donohue, author of *Life without Parole*

"In her debut psychological thriller Lori Rader-Day joins the ranks of Barbara Vine and Sophie Hannah. Examining the deep complexities of damaged people, she teases and tempts the reader as she leads to her harrowing conclusion."

—Terry Shames, author of *The Last Death of Jack Harbin*

"So often, mysteries set in academe are populated by ivy-draped eccentrics with a terminal case of the cutes. Lori Rader-Day's Rothbert U. is anything but cute: the atmosphere, for faculty and students alike, is ruthlessly competitive and mistrustful. Her characters, beginning with Amelia Emmet, are complex, capable of surprising both themselves and us. Like Barbara Vine [Ruth Rendell], Rader-Day is as interested in the *why* of evil things as in the *who*."

—Jincy Willett, author of *Amy Falls Down*

"*The Black Hour* is a brilliant suspense debut, rich in psychological nuance and the cold, terrifying places where our worst fears—and darkest desires—reside. Let's hope this is only the first of many from this talented newcomer."

—Lynne Raimondo, author of *Dante's Poison*

"Lori Rader-Day captures the angst and envy lurking behind every campus doorway. . . . Most impressive about this suspense debut: the unfolding tale of how easily an individual can goad another into hatred, suicide, or murder."

—Susan Froetschel, author of *Fear of Beauty*

THE BLACK HOUR

A NOVEL

LORI RADER-DAY

SEVENTH STREET BOOKS®
AN IMPRINT OF PROMETHEUS BOOKS
59 JOHN GLENN DRIVE • AMHERST, NY 14228
www.seventhstreetbooks.com

Published 2014 by Seventh Street Books™, an imprint of Prometheus Books

Cover image by Matt Frankel
Cover design by Nicole Sommer-Lecht

Inquiries should be addressed to
Seventh Street Books
59 John Glenn Drive
Amherst, New York 14228
VOICE: 716–691–0133
FAX: 716–691–0137
WWW.SEVENTHSTREETBOOKS.COM

18 17 16 15 14   5 4 3 2 1

Library of Congress Cataloging-in-Publication Data

Rader-Day, Lori, 1973-
    The black hour / by Lori Rader-Day.
        pages cm
    ISBN 978-1-61614-885-0 (paperback)
    ISBN 978-1-61614-886-7 (ebook)
    1. Women college teachers—Fiction. 2. Teachers' assistants—Fiction.
3. College teachers—Crimes against—Fiction. 4. Psychological fiction. I. Title.

PS3618.A3475B57 2014
813'.6—dc23
                                                                2014003653

Printed in the United States of America

For Greg

PART I

CHAPTER 1
AMELIA

My lungs clawed for air as though I were drowning. I stopped, hunched over my grandmotherly cane, gasping. The curved walk up from the parking lot stretched out before me longer than I remembered, steeper. This is how it would be. Every task more difficult than before. Every step a public performance.

That's when I heard the camera.

I'd been expecting someone, hadn't I? One of the lawyers, a campus cop. I always expected to be watched now. Why else had I parked not in the handicapped spot in the faculty lot but the one just next to it?

The guy with the camera was too young to be a lawyer or the police. His hair punked, his chin smooth. The student press had provided my welcoming committee.

What did I look like to this kid? From a distance, ignoring the cane, without the zoom lens, maybe I could pass for a student. A grad student. My hair swung loose and long. I'd made an effort. After ten months on the couch, I'd pulled out the good shampoo, the high heels, *lipstick*.

The cane, though, wasn't fooling anyone.

"Did you get a shot up my skirt—" I couldn't chase down my breath. I readjusted my bag across my chest. "—when I was digging myself out of my car? Did you get that? Pulitzer stuff."

He lowered the camera, paying close attention to his lens.

"You're not the one who claimed to be my nephew in the emergency room, are you?" My face felt hot. Through the zoom lens, clutching the swan's neck of my cane, I wouldn't look anything like a student. Dark circles under my eyes. Shaking hands. Maybe the photographer couldn't see that I already regretted the heels. Maybe he wasn't really looking. "Or are you the one who prank calls me at two in the morning? Don't get me wrong," I said. "I'm up. The pain's good for that."

He looked now.

"Get my good side, OK?" I posed, both hands on the cane, chin lifted toward the lake. It sat like a blue jewel on the horizon. A beautiful day to rise from the dead.

The camera stayed silent.

"What? Are you waiting for me to drop my clothes so you can see the—"

I'd been looking forward to this day and had planned an early arrival to avoid a few stares. Hoping to get one minute with my old life before the new one caught up with me.

"Here's what I think," I said, continuing past his spot against the ivy and on to the front door of Dale Hall with what I hoped looked like dignity. "A restraining order isn't the best way to start your career."

I reached for the door. An electrical charge shot through my belly, my hip, down through my leg. A crushing bolt of lightning I couldn't predict and couldn't control. I was on fire. Out of the corner of my eye, I saw the photographer raise his camera.

I launched myself through the pain and into the lobby.

The kid didn't follow. No one came running. I took my time, clutching the cane and fighting for the surface. At last I felt the ground steady under my feet. After a few shuddering breaths, I could smell the deep musk of Dale Hall: wood paneling, dusty books, and disinfectant that never quite reached the corners. It was a smell more than a hundred years in the making. Home. Only one place in the world felt more inviting than this spot, and that was the small, drafty room upstairs that served as my office.

I lurched toward the elevator, then stopped.

I had taken the elevator, able-bodied, many times. But the path to the elevator would trot me past the glass doors of the dean's suite, past his gossiping assistant, and through an open atrium, where my clicking and clacking would only be magnified.

To my right, the staircase rolled out like a tongue, a taunt.

At the summit, just up there, lay the scene of the crime. Peering up into the darkness, I felt a cold finger of fear slide down my spine.

The dark hall, a hand rising—

No.

I'd begun to think of my memory as a high shelf at the back of a closet. I couldn't reach everything, no matter how hard I stretched. When the shelf of memory wobbled, I righted it by force.

There were twenty-five or so stairs, and then one more after the landing pivoted. That was all. A physical challenge, sure, but how hard had I fought, only to have a few stairs stop me? I could do this. I had to.

I positioned myself at the first step and took stock.

Up, lead with the good leg, the physical therapists had said. Down, lead with the bad. I didn't like thinking that half my body had turned on me, but who could blame it? I took a first gentle step with my right leg, no problem, then positioned the cane and pulled the left—bad—leg up behind, only to be met with a pinprick of outrage deep in my gut. I eyed the next step like a foe.

We'd make it a game, the cane and I. Right leg, weight shift, cane-tap up, left heel up, *ouch*, weight shift, right again, repeat. I lost track of the game and stopped to rest. I glanced over my shoulder. I'd climbed four steps.

Below, a young man stood watching.

A different kind of electricity shot through me. I noticed his heavy backpack, his empty hands. A student. I'd always liked the students. You had to, or none of it was worth it.

I didn't have to like them anymore.

I went back to my climb, suddenly understanding why the dean hadn't wanted me to return.

Jim Perry, his bushy white eyebrows like a pair of hamsters shading his eyes, had come to see me at home a week ago. An unexpected visit, me still in the sweatpants I'd worn for three days. I didn't look like I had it together, but I promised him I did. The university would offer me retirement, he announced, as though I'd won an award. With a settlement and health benefits. I needed those. "Amelia, you should take more time to get over this," he said. He'd already called it *the accident*. "We want to see you healthy. We want to see you well."

In other words, they didn't want to see me at all. Retire? I'd only received tenure two years ago, only been handed my PhD a handful of years before that. An academic career was supposed to be long and steady. A marathon—though the metaphor stung—where you ran hard and long, and at the finish line your peers gathered around you with precariously full wineglasses and seethed with jealousy. No more teaching. No grading. No advising earnest graduate students. No more obligations beyond your own research interests. The ultimate tenure.

But you had to earn it. You had to run the marathon, or you were just unemployed.

I took a deep breath and leaned into the next step. I could not believe how many stairs there were to the second floor. I had enough time to think about architectural trends, the ascent of the modern style. Short ceilings, manageable flights of stairs—what was wrong with squat, one-story buildings? Nothing. I loved this building, loved the wide stairs worn with footsteps, the smooth wooden rail I clutched to pull myself up. Even at first sight, Dale Hall had seemed to me a venerable finish line. Not bad for a girl from the sticks, for the hardship case who'd gone to a state university and only by the grace of full funding. Not bad, and highly unlikely. That first year at Rothbert University, I'd hardly relaxed, certain that someone would pull out the rug. But I'd earned my post and then tenure to keep it. I'd be damned if they were going to take it from me.

Though just now I'd have given it all away to work in one of those sprawling suburban junior college malls instead of this relic.

A hesitant footstep sounded behind me. I clung to the railing, leaving plenty of room to get by. Whoever it was hung back.

"OK," I huffed and waved them ahead with the cane.

"Good morning, Dr. Emmet." The kid from below caught up with me, his hair flopping into his eyes. Of course. They'd all know me now.

"Do you need—"

"OK," I said.

His quick shoes hurried ahead and around the corner.

What did I need? I needed to take the elevator.

Right foot up, cane-tap, left—*oh, jumping Christ that hurt.*

What would happen if I couldn't make it up the stairs, if I could not force my body to finish what I'd started? I was more than halfway now, but sweating and deaf to everything but my own ragged breath. All the worries came rushing up to greet me. I might never walk without the cane. I might never live without that bolt of lightning through my gut. I would never carry children. I had trouble imagining in which universe I would ever again hope to have sex. Doyle's face came to me, but that didn't help. I was alone, damaged. Old fears I thought I'd pushed away roared back. Never good enough. Now that everyone was looking, I couldn't hide it.

Step by excruciating step, I rose toward the landing, glaring at the last riser. Cane-tap, and now there was a pause, a brace against what was coming, *goddamn heel up*—and the searing pain in my hip and through my pelvis, so much pain that I wanted, just for a while, to lie down and give up.

My boss wanted it. Maybe they all did.

"I didn't do anything wrong," I'd said the morning Jim came to talk me out of my life.

Like everyone else I'd heard from while I was in the hospital or on leave, like the insurance detectives and the kid's family's lawyer who wasn't supposed to contact me but tried, like all of the reporters and the bottom-feeding curious who had no real excuse to want to know what happened. Like the voice on the other end of the line most mornings at two. Like everyone else, the dean thought I must have done *something*.

Something unspeakable. Something so bad no one could think what it could be.

"What could have caused that kid to . . . did you even know him?" Corrine had asked. When they finally let someone visit me in intensive care, Corrine was the only person I wanted. Even she, my officemate and best friend, couldn't make sense of it. "What *happened*?" she kept saying.

Highly medicated, I'd hardly managed Corrine's name. I could barely speak, barely think. I couldn't tell her.

I couldn't tell anyone why that kid had shot me.

I didn't know.

The landing. Cane-tap, pause. The last step might buckle me, but I had come this far. I had come to—drumroll—the second floor.

It didn't seem like much, but the roar of my bones and belly assured me it was something. Even weak and gnarled, I could climb a few stairs. I could get to my office. I could work.

Of course I'd never be able to get back down. I'd have to wait until everyone else had left so I could take the elevator. Tomorrow, the next day, the rest of the academic year? I couldn't begin to think about the life ahead of me.

At the very least, though, I had a life to dread.

I turned to face the hallway, and there, leaning against the wall outside my office, his back to the stairs, was a man. My brain supplied the image—a *hand and gun rising out of the dark*—

It couldn't be.

What about the second explosion? And the open hand, like a flower, on the carpet? The hand that was not mine. Memories rushed at me but didn't link up.

My heaving breath roared in the silent hall. I collapsed against the handrail, waiting. If someone had come to finish what the student before had started, I couldn't stop it. I was too weak to do this, all this, again.

The man turned. It was the kid from the stairs.

What was in his backpack? What was that look on his face? Shame, stealth, a resemblance.

The moment passed. His features rearranged into uncertainty.

"What?" I panted.

"I was hoping to, uh, catch you."

"Not moving that fast. What do you want?"

He glanced away. "I think you're my advisor."

"Your advisor?" I tried my weight on the cane. This last step was Kilimanjaro. It was Everest. Who's to say I wouldn't fall? Someone somewhere had already placed that bet.

"Your *advisor*." I mopped my forehead with the back of my hand. "If I were you, I'd have mixed feelings about that."

CHAPTER 2

The kid shot me outside my office. He was not my student. He was not my lover. He was not my enemy.

I had never taught him. I had never advised him. I had never *met* him.

This was the part no one believed. The police nodded and used words like *indiscriminate*, but the doubt was palpable.

The reporters questioned my story. They wrote articles that made other people question my story. Calling it *my story*, for one thing, as though I were not stationed in the intensive care unit at all but rather up in my writer's garret, spinning tales. Using *alleged* in strategic phrases. The student press—they were brutal. They didn't allege. They published purple prose memorials online to the sanctity of the campus—sometimes remembering to mourn the kid, too—and let anonymous comments do the accusing.

Nothing like this had ever happened at Rothbert. This could happen at other places, but not at dear, venerable Rothbert. The administrators, the trustees, quite a few people, in fact, would have felt happier if they'd simply never heard of me again.

I don't know what they all thought—that I baited a troubled kid, drove him insane with sex or quid pro quo grading practices, and then suffered the only outcome that made any sense? Got what I deserved? *Asked for it?* That was a phrase I'd come across more than once in the comments section of the student newspaper's website.

The kid waiting at my door shuffled his feet.

"You're not from the *Rothbert Reader*, are you?" I said. I managed the last three feet to my office door without succumbing to the television static playing at the edges of my vision. Pale, light-headed, drenched, shaking. I must have looked like I'd survived something. I must have looked just the way they'd expected me to.

"I'm from … the sociology department?" The student's look of doubt grew deeper, concerned.

He reached for his backpack—

I held out a hand to stop him. I hated backpacks. I hated the dark. I hated loud noises. I hated students. I hated my hatred and my paranoia, but they were deep. I hadn't found the bottom.

"You're probably in the right place. Can you get the door?" I pulled out the key ring and held it out. If he thought the request strange, he didn't let on. He took the key and unlocked the door, putting his shoulder into it. On the wall next to the door two brown plastic plates had been mounted, my name and Corrine's etched in white, and underneath them, a bin attached where students left late work and notes pleading for deadline extensions. The kid held the door, but I made him wait while I swept the bin. Some gum wrappers, nice. An errant Rothbert University business card. From Psych Services, great. Ten months gone and the welcome I get: trash, an offer of psychological assistance, and a skittish grad student.

To his credit, the kid flinched only a little when I brushed past him into my office.

Now. Now I was home. I had loved my office from first sight. From first dirty-window, bad-lighting, cracked-plaster sight. My and Corrine's office had the same high ceilings I'd lamented not ten minutes before, gorgeous to me now that I wasn't climbing their height, and tall windows that opened up on the lake. If you pressed your face to the glass, the tiny Chicago skyline lay twenty miles or so down the coast. When I sat at my desk, I felt as though I had done something right in my lifetime.

I flicked on the light and stumbled for the solid corner of my desk, displacing a stack of mail waiting for me. I'd have a backlog of e-mails and voice mails, too. The kid bent to pick up the mail.

"Don't worry about it," I said. "You can sit down." I leaned my good hip on the corner of my desk and used the cane to keep balance. I swung my bag over my head and onto the floor. "What's your name?"

"Nathaniel Barber."

The student watched me get settled but didn't say anything. He finally helped himself to the guest chair. Good boy.

"Did Dean Perry send you?"

My voice was sharper than I'd meant it to be, and the slap showed on the student's face. "No."

"You're new? Just starting the program?"

"Yes."

"So how am I your advisor?"

"I talked to Dr. Woo."

Ah. There it was. "Dr. Woo sent you to me. Today." I looked at my watch. "Before nine a.m."

"He said you might need some help."

Again with what I might need. "Did he now?"

J. Benjamin Woo and I had started at Rothbert the same year, reached tenure together. Which he couldn't stand, because I'd gone to a state school. He could barely utter the words *state school*. He had a year on me now.

The kid's knee started to bounce. "Dr. Woo said there might be an assistantship. Or a TA position?"

I took a closer look at Nathaniel. *Nathaniel*. Not Nathan. Not Nate. Unwrinkled clothes, clean-shaven. His backpack was all zipped up, and so was he. Just that one swipe of unruly hair across his eye, and now I could see that it was not an affectation as much as a bad haircut. He was too wide-eyed to be anything but sincere.

I sighed. My conspiracy theories and I needed to part ways.

"Bring me your resume and a copy of your transcripts. I don't have any idea what I need yet, but there might be something."

He nodded sagely, but I saw the childlike excitement as he reached for his backpack again. Of course he would have the paperwork with him. I watched his hands closely until he'd retrieved a sheaf of papers.

The only high-functioning enthusiasm I'd seen in the last year belonged to the lawyers, the reporters, and the nosy civilians at the grocery store when I could finally leave my apartment. I could think of a lot of reasons, unsavory reasons, why a student might seek me out right now, today, first thing. "What's your research area, anyway? Anything pre–World War I, you have to go back to Dr. Woo."

A flicker of concern crossed his face as I shifted my weight on the desk and found a knot of pain waiting for me. I might have made a noise. Nathaniel watched me pant it out. "I'm sort of . . . Prohibition," he said. "Through Great Depression."

I'd been having one of those myself. Or I'd start another, if I didn't get off this desk and into my pain meds. I glanced uneasily at the bag at my feet, a terrible fear landing with a thud in my gut.

Had I left the bottle on the bathroom sink?

Once the thought was in my head, I couldn't think of anything else. The pills—large orange pills made of magic and moonbeams that gave me the courage to be alive for another few hours. Orange, fluffy clouds on which I could rest my weary body.

The silence in the room had grown long. "Sort of?" I said.

"Well, I'm interested in poverty and—are you OK?"

"Sure. Of course. Why not?"

He leaned over his backpack again, unzipped one of the pockets, and pulled out something. I couldn't be anxious—my nerves jangled five-alarm, already fully engaged. The image of the bottle of pills on the bathroom sink clawed at me. I wouldn't make it. I wouldn't make it, even if I took the elevator and didn't mind who the hell saw me. Even if I could *run* all the way home.

Nathaniel held out his hand. In his palm sat a little plastic packet of folded tissues. "You're crying."

I swiped at my cheek.

He flicked a tissue out of the pack and handed it to me.

"Poverty and what?" I said, my voice strangled and whimpering, the mewl of a kitten. I hated myself, I really did. The pills, orange. On the sink.

He watched me sniffle into the tissue, and there it was again: the barest flash of something shifty and unexpected on his boyish face. It could have been discomfort. I was breaking down in front of him— who would want to be a part of that? But I didn't think that was all.

"Out with it."

"Crime," he said at last. "That's my focus. Particularly violent crime."

"That's my favorite, too," I said through clenched teeth. I was pleased to know Woo's game at last but distracted to the point of delirium.

The pills. If they were at home, I'd need some assistance. And even if. And even if they were in the bag, here in the bag. Even if. I would need help. Lots and lots of help.

"This assistantship," I said, gripping the edge of my desk. "It might be a little different than what you expected."

CHAPTER 3

The boy genius found the pills in my bag and dropped two fat specimens into my trembling hand. There was a bottle of water on my desk from the last time I'd sat there. I didn't stop to think that the cap had been off for nearly a year. I washed the meds down with whatever was in the bottle and stood against the desk with my eyes closed, waiting for the pills to take me somewhere I could stand to be.

"Do you need—"

"Please shut up," I said.

I heard him stowing my bag behind my desk, then his retreat to a safe distance. He stood there for what must have seemed to him a long, silent time. From my perspective, that time raged with white pain pulsing under my skin. At last the pills started to chip away at the maelstrom. I could feel the desktop under my good hip, my fingers tight on its edge, and my good foot solid on the ground.

When I opened my eyes, the kid was gone. I had crumpled the business card from the bin in my fist. I pitched it at the trash.

The door was closed, the prim pack of tissues left behind. I had no idea how long I'd stood there, or if Nathaniel would ever return.

The thing was, I wanted the door open.

I hadn't come all this way to sit alone in a dusty office. All this way, and not just up the stairs and down the hallway and before that, the long walk from the parking lot. *All* this way.

My mind snapped like a rubber band back to the last time I'd been in this building, the rush of the dark red carpet coming to meet me, then—snap—forward to waking up in a white room and a man's hand lying heavy on my chest. I'd never figured out whose hand that was.

Someone who believed in God might say it had been an angel or Jesus himself, that the white room was heaven. But the white room was only a corner of the ICU, and the hand probably belonged to the nurse's assistant named Gordy who sometimes came down and watched *The Price Is Right* with me after I moved to a different floor. Maybe Gordy shouldn't have been touching me, but I hadn't minded. It had already been a while since a man had laid a hand on me.

And then the memory faded, the weight of the hand lifting.

The pills had done their good deeds. I could stand and tap to the door. For a second I thought I was locked in, but no, just the usual difficulties with the heavy, sticking door compounded by my inability to put any muscle into it. Finally it squawked open, and I stood in my doorway with no one at all to witness how far I'd come.

It was too early for students. If they were awake, they were in class trying to keep their eyes open and their text messages hidden. And the faculty—even the early risers weren't rushing into the first day of another year. The only people around were those of us too eager. Nathaniel, to get his assistantship settled. Me, to sneak in without a news crew escort.

In the quiet hall, all the other doors were shut. I had remembered the second-floor hall as a dark place, more of a natural place to be assaulted, but that wasn't true. The walls glowed a creamy butter yellow, and there were some nice frames filled with bright playbills from student theater productions, black-and-white campus scenes, and tinted photographs of long-gone classmates. Truly, I didn't remember any of it.

I concentrated on the frame across the hall from our door. Surely this was one I'd remember. The painting featured a dewy, soft-focused young woman. She was pretty, with pastel pink lips and her hair pincurled into a '40s-specific coif. Her sweater was a frothy powder blue. In old photos and paintings, young people always seemed older than I was, though they were often much younger. The girl encouraged me to remember.

I'd never seen her before.

This was serious. Straight out of the trauma unit, I'd known my name, my age, the year. I'd known as much history as any American could be expected to remember, could count by tens and fives and threes. I could recall who was in the White House and whether or not I'd helped him get elected. To end the tests, I'd bored the neurologist with a little Sociology 101, plus a dash of social deviance theory, which probably hadn't bought me any new friends. But the point remained: I could recall almost anything I wanted to. Couldn't I?

I reached into my memory, pushed past the white room, the warm hand resting on me, the ambulance, the red carpet rushing toward my face, the dark outline of the student, the gun rising out of the shadow—past that, past that. Past the stuff I couldn't quite remember into the stuff I didn't want to. And then I had it. Doyle. The fight I had with Doyle when we'd broken up, and the sad way he'd flipped his keys in his hand as we said good-bye. That ridiculous little question-mark curl that wouldn't lie flat on his head that day—

A different kind of pain.

OK, then. I could remember that day. That day was pre-bullet. Pre-bullet and deep in the locked files. If I could remember that curl, the swing of the keys, then surely I could remember this woman, this yellow, this Persian rug under my feet.

I glanced down at the rug, at the gleaming wooden floorboards visible at its edges, and then around at all the frames and the bright walls behind them. Of course.

It was all new. The lemonade walls, the frames dredged up from some dusty special collection in the library. The bright, patterned rug without a stitch of red replacing the worn, red wall-to-wall carpet. It would have been ruined by blood or, if not ruined, then a cruel reminder.

And now that I thought about it, those electric sconces on the wall hadn't been here before, either. The whole place had been gutted, rewired, redrawn in a well-timed renovation to wipe our collective memories. Except that I had come back, and now no one could be fooled by a coat of paint and the likeness of Miss Whatsherfanny smiling into the office in question. A public relations plan was underway, and I was ruining it.

I checked for the spot anyway. It wasn't there. The floors had been refinished.

"Did I miss the ribbon-cutting?" I said to the chick in the frame.

"They skipped the grand opening," a voice said.

I jumped. I couldn't help it. For just a tick of the clock the voice had belonged to the kid in the shadows. But the man standing at the top of the stairs was—

"Woo," I said, relieved that my memory could be counted on after all. I could remember the competition, at any rate.

"What are you doing here?" he said.

Jesus, no one had told my department I'd be back. Why did they think I'd gone through all that recovery and therapy? To take up someone else's life? All I wanted was the one I'd almost lost. "Teaching, Ben. Our job, remember?"

"I meant—" His mouth clamped shut. "I'm sorry."

"Sorry I got shot?"

He looked sorry now, his narrow shoulders folding in on themselves. He wore a tweed jacket with elbow patches, his black hair slicked back in a way I couldn't approve of. "Sorry. I mean. I don't know what to say," he said. "Never know what to say at weddings and funerals—"

"No funerals here," I said.

We looked at one another, then away. There had been a funeral, I remembered too late. No one had ever mentioned it, but it must have happened. Here or in the kid's hometown, wherever that was. Who would have gone? Doyle? I would ask Corrine.

"So," he said finally. "So, you're doing great."

I was glad he hadn't seen me when I thought my meds were at home. "Sure. Have you met my new friend here?" I thumped the cane on the new carpet. It was metal, silver. There were fancier styles, but I'd refused them. I didn't plan to use it for long.

Woo's eyes flicked down and back behind his glasses. "You're looking really well."

"The intestinal surgery diet is highly effective." I was pleased to see him flush pink again, and a little angry at myself. Woo needled me, but he didn't deserve this. He was here to welcome me back, when Corrine, Doyle—none of them had made the effort.

"How's the semester looking?" I said.

He gave up a half-smile of relief. "Better than any semester we've ever had, if you believe President Wolitzer. Really busy, if you listen to the chatter."

The chatter. This was what I needed. At Rothbert, there was a low-level buzz of speculation among the competitive. Who would get tenure? Who was up for which association award? Whose project would the dean anoint with his discretionary funding? Only among colleagues could you hear the truth. Who was headed for divorce? Who drank too much? Who slept with his students?

The answer to this last one was always Trotter, from Anthropology. We called it his field research.

"Ben," I said. "What's the chatter on me?"

His face took on the faux cheerfulness of the girl in the portrait on the wall. "Oh, everyone's just glad you pulled through."

"Is no one in this place capable of a good lie?" I said.

He deflated, the fake smile replaced by authentic chagrin. "Glad to see you're still you."

I twisted the cane to see the light run up and down the shaft. I wasn't sure I was still me, but at least one person here could pull off a lie, if it came to it. "What did they say?"

"Truth?" he said. "There was so much of it, it was hard to sort out."

"Lots of theories?"

"Should you even worry yourself with this?"

"They all think I must have done *something*."

He checked the hallway behind him. Right. He probably thought I'd done something, too.

"They're all sorry it happened," he said. "They just . . ." He glanced up at the girl in the frame as though she might jump into the conversation and save him.

"What?"

"They want to understand it."

I could see them. Clustering up around the coffee pots in the kitchenette. Pausing in front of their departmental mailboxes to compare junk mail. The ten minutes before faculty meetings, lingering over the dry dining service cookies. Exchanging glances, checking to see if someone among them had the story. What had I done? What did they have to do, or not do?

Woo would have been in the thick of it.

"Some of them," Woo said to the girl in the frame. "They're shitting their pants."

"Trotter," I said.

He smiled. "Yeah."

"Doyle?"

His mouth dropped open. "But I thought—does Doyle date the students?"

"So that's the going theory? That I was screwing that kid?"

Poor Woo. A fine researcher but a weak subject. He'd told me what I needed to know.

"Maybe it's better to let it go," he said. "Get back to normal."

He looked so uncomfortable I turned to the girl in the painting. The problem with normal was that normal had been shot through. Normal wasn't possible. Normal hadn't even been that great. None of this would I admit, least of all to him.

"Sure," I said. "Normal."

CHAPTER 4

Woo made his excuses and slinked away.

I was armed. My nerves steeled with pain-fighting medication, I knew now what I had only guessed before. Nothing had changed, but I felt more daring. More—to borrow a concept from Woo—myself. I fetched my bag from where Nathaniel had stowed it, wrestled my door closed, and took the elevator to the lobby. The front desk receptionist had arrived. She looked pointedly away.

There were security cameras in the building now. I wondered how much of my triumphant return she'd seen. I punched the button for the automatic door with my cane. I needed coffee.

Normal. I didn't think they'd let me get back to it, and by *they*, I meant the faculty, the dean, the press. But I also meant the students. I meant the faces that turned to follow my progress as I tapped down the walkway and through the courtyard to the next building. I meant everyone.

Outside it was so hot that I reconsidered my need for coffee. But once I stepped into the cool lobby of Smith Hall, up to the coffee hutch outside the dining room doors, and through the coffee server's surveillance, once I felt the paper cup in my hand, I was steadier. Excited, actually. I was back. On campus, having coffee in Smith Hall, listening to the thunderous voices inside the dining hall where students talked around their cereal spoons and gained strength from their own cups. The first day of a new semester, everyone nattering and hopeful. I felt almost normal, almost like nothing had changed. Coffee in Smith before prepping for classes—that was something familiar, something the old Professor Amelia Emmet would have done. Corrine and I had come here three days a week for most of last fall. The two months I'd been here, anyway. I'd been here that last morning, as a matter of fact.

Except you never knew when you faced the last of anything. That was a universal truth I wished I didn't understand. That ridiculous curl on Doyle's forehead came back to me.

I chose a spot on a lobby bench by a sunlit window and sipped, wishing Corrine were here. I had a million questions for her. And I wanted to walk back into Dale Hall with someone by my side. Someone by my side who was on my side.

There were so few options. Lying in a hospital bed for a few months was a precision tool for counting true friends. Cor visited all the time, kept me in contraband chocolate and gossip. But she was the only one. Even Doyle had only come by once.

I could definitely remember things I didn't want to, or I would have blocked out Doyle's visit.

That day, I hadn't been able to figure out if he'd come in an official capacity—he was the chair of the department—or on a real visit, remorseful and concerned. He kept passing along regrets from people we both knew, until I imagined that he'd been elected to come so that everyone else could stay away.

Corrine had reported the colleagues who'd come to the hospital in the early days but hadn't been allowed to see me. Some of them left cards and flowers. Very few came back. Cor, of course. Joss, the only other woman in our department. One of the lecturers from creative writing had come by to ask what it was like to get shot. He was writing a crime novel.

Woo showed up to make a lot of sympathetic noises about how I should take my time getting well. He'd come to my apartment during spring semester, too, long after I needed visitors or wanted them. He'd won a Rothbert Medal, a teaching award from the university, and wanted to make sure I knew it. He knew what to say that day. I wondered that he hadn't had the medal pinned to his chest this morning.

Doyle's visit had come too late for an official visit and even later for a friendly one. He sat with his elbows on his bouncing knees. His graying hair curled around his ears. "Well, you're coming around, aren't you?" he'd said, shooting for cheerful.

"You can go," I said. I'd come through the emergency surgery, the freezing-cold recovery room, the intensive care unit, another surgery, and having all my bodily fluids on an input/output system hanging from the side of my bed for the world to see. I'd ascended to one of the bright rooms on an upper floor, with a window facing downtown Chicago and a ledge on which to display all the get-wells that came in. My ledge made a respectable showing because one of the student groups at Rothbert had adopted me and sent me a series of handmade cards signed by people I didn't know. The feminists. I wasn't their faculty sponsor or anything. Apparently they didn't like to see a sister get shot through her center of feminine power.

On the day Doyle finally showed up, I was sitting up for the first time. I must have seemed like some talking-doll version of myself. Sitting up, blinking my eyes. Since he'd left my place the last time—it would have been a good five months at that point—we'd barely spoken at all, and then just about work. A problem student, a conference we were both considering, something from a journal article. In the hospital, hooked up to every wire in the place, I must have looked like the ghost of someone he'd forgotten he'd known.

I'm the one just coming out of shock, I wanted to say. Ask me something. Tell me something.

When he left that day, it was because I asked him to. When he'd left my apartment the spring day we broke up, I'd asked him to. He'd almost always done what I asked.

Now I wished I'd asked him for more.

My coffee was gone. I wasn't supposed to be taking in that much caffeine, but a second cup couldn't kill me. A bullet hadn't.

I tapped across the room to the barista-boy.

The kid, blushing, waved my money off. I dropped it into the tip jar. He'd have a story to tell.

"Dr. Emmet," a man's voice said. "Welcome back."

As I turned, I hoped my memory would hold up again. But it didn't. This guy—burnished to a high gleam, wearing a collared Rothbert-red golf shirt and khakis ironed to a ruler's-edge sharpness—didn't seem familiar at all. University staff. Nobody would wear that shirt if they weren't paid to. "Thanks," I said and sipped my coffee for time.

"You don't know me," he said. "Phillip Carrington-Wells, from the Office of Psychological Services."

"I know who you are." Not really. I remembered the name from the business card I'd found outside my office. Though we might have crossed paths before now, too. The year before, a student in my intro class—I couldn't remember the girl's name, either—had displayed some troubling behavior. Erratic, isolating behavior in the classroom, strange calls. I'd turned her over to the campus services, Phillip here, and that was the last I'd heard of her. A blip in a semester that grew much more complicated shortly afterward. "Whatever happened to—"

"Can't really talk about it," Phillip said.

"Ah. Thank you. For that. I mean, I know it's what you do—"

"It's what we do. How are *you* doing?"

He had the gentle, probing voice of the ICU. The doctors, the nurses, everyone down to the woman who collected the hospital room trash used that same deferential tone. "I'm fine. Really, I'm fine."

"Good for you, sincerely," he said. "You had us all worried there for a while."

"Yeah, me too."

"If you ever need someone to talk to," he said. "Someone impartial, you know, let me know."

He dug for his wallet and produced another card stamped with the regal Rothbert seal, slipping the card under my fingers on the coffee-holding hand. He had never once glanced down at the cane or my bad leg.

"Thank you." I had no intention of calling, of needing to call, but found myself feeling grateful for the offer. Grateful, at least, that he wasn't staring. "Thank you, Phil."

"Phillip," he said, smiling. "I was never cool enough for a nickname."

"Melly!"

I turned. Corrine stood in the doorway to the dining hall, a paper cup held high and her hand over her mouth. For the blink of an eye, I saw her standing in our office door, her hand just like that. Laughing.

Now she came at me at full speed. When she collided with me, I grabbed her and held on. Together, we managed to keep our coffees and selves upright.

"Holy shit, you're back." She let me go slowly so I could regain my footing.

"I was hoping to see you," I said. I looked around, but Phillip had gone. "Before I completely *lost* it."

Relief washed over me. She looked just right, standing there with her loose skirt and blousy shirt to hide what she called her spare doughnut. Her cheeks were pink and freckled from the sun, her hair pulled back into a flip of a ponytail. Just right, and she looked as pleased as I felt. "This place has been hell, just hell without you," she said, taking in the cane, the high heels. "You look great."

"Having the whole office to yourself—"

"Shut up," she said. "You know how I hate that haunted house."

"Looks like it's been haunted by an interior decorator."

She scoffed and glanced back at the dining hall doors. "You wouldn't believe how long that took. They wouldn't let me use my office for three weeks this summer."

I nodded. Three whole weeks?

Her hand shot to touch my arm. "I'm so sorry. I didn't mean—"

"It's fine. I know."

She let her hand drop, looking suitably sorry for herself. We sipped our drinks. The card Phillip had given me dropped to the floor. Corrine picked it up, glancing at the name. "That guy," she said. She looked at my skirt and my hands full of coffee and cane, then tucked the card into her own pocket.

"Or maybe Dale Hall is haunted by that co-ed," I said. "The one in the painting? Kind of creepy in a Doris Day kind of way."

"She's . . ." Corrine's mouth twisted.

"What?"

"A historical figure or something." A group of students emerged from the dining hall. Corrine watched after them, tucking a loose strand of hair behind her ear. "I think she's pretty."

"Won't argue it," I said.

"Does it feel weird? To be here?"

"So weird," I said. "I thought I'd lost my mind when I saw the hall. The paint."

"The lighting," she said, rolling her eyes. "The rug."

"My DNA sanded out of the floors."

"And his."

We looked away from each other. The barista stood too close. I leaned on the cane and orchestrated a turn toward the door. "I should get back. The mail is four feet high. I'm not quite up to hurdles."

"What about the meeting?"

"Which? Haven't even been into my e-mail yet."

"Faculty meeting in Crane." She glanced at the clock behind us. "In about fifteen."

"But . . . we've never had a faculty meeting on the first day." I was staring at the clock, too, and then I realized what she'd said. Located halfway across campus and up an incline, Crane Student Center was more than fifteen minutes away for the likes of me. "Do you even have your classes planned yet? And your copies made?" I suddenly realized how little prep work I'd done for this return. "Why would Jim call a faculty meeting for the first day?" He hadn't even mentioned it during his retirement campaigning.

"Not a school-wide." Corrine glanced down at the cane. "We'd better get going."

"Doyle? He called a faculty meeting for the first day?" It didn't make sense.

Corrine led us through the lobby and outside, the heat like a door slamming in my face.

"Can you cut across, like, the grass?" she said over her shoulder.

Even with shortcuts, we were going to be late. "Go on without me."

"Don't be stupid," she said.

Without me.

Doyle had called a faculty meeting for the first day of the semester. At nine in the morning of the day I returned. I was lamed and riding pain meds and hadn't taught in almost a year. I was out of practice, and even though we hadn't talked since his aborted visit to the hospital, he knew me. Knew me well. He would have known I hadn't sorted through my mail, my e-mail, my voice mail.

He didn't expect me. I wasn't invited.

CHAPTER 5

I followed after Corrine like a stray dog.

"Does it hurt?" she asked.

I stopped to catch my breath. We had come to the shore of the man-made lagoon, a stagnant little pond populated by ugly fish. I turned my face toward the wide blue expanse of Lake Michigan beyond for the bare breeze it offered. We were close. I could see the rise to Crane's front doors. Steeper, of course, than I remembered.

Hurt? I wished I had the words to explain it to her, but I didn't even have the lung capacity to try. I nodded, leaning heavily on the cane to pivot the broken half of my body around for another few inches of progress.

"I could go see if they have a—"

"Don't say wheelchair."

"—golf cart?"

"That is not the entrance I want to make, Cor." I had offered her the chance to go on without me, but now I was gratified that she hadn't. Embarrassed to walk my Frankenstein's monster lurch in front of her, it was still better than making the trip alone. Also, she couldn't blow my cover. We'd walk into the room of our colleagues together, and I could catch them before anyone gained command over their surprise. They didn't want me or expect me, but I wouldn't allow them the pleasure of pretending otherwise. "Let's just go slow."

There was no other way to go, but she nodded and matched my pace. "Are you sure you want to go over there?"

I pictured them. Doyle, his hair too shaggy for a man of his age, looking as though he'd just stepped off his boat. Baz and his big theories and big hand gestures, Caldwell meek and trying to sit as far as he could from other humans. Caldwell took the social out of sociology,

Doyle liked to say. Joss, bangles on her wrists rattling with every movement. She'd be promoting yet another book. A seriously boring book,
if her last four served as models. And then the three wise men of methodology, tenured before I was born, who never bothered to show up at
staff meetings anyway. And Woo. Woo and his elbow patches.

And Corrine. And me. That was our department, our merry little
band, each drumming our own tune.

"Of course I don't want to go there," I said. "But what else can I
do?"

"Not go?" she said.

"That would be giving him what he wants. He's clearly making a
point."

"Doyle?" she said. "I didn't think he was the clearly-making-a-
point kind."

Why did that stupid curl smashed into his hair come back to me
again? Doyle was just Doyle. Brilliant but oblivious. Slow to anger, slow
to judgment, slow to decisions. Handsome but rumpled. A right mess
that I had stepped into, but not the sort to plan intrigues or even put up
with them. How understanding, how supportive had he been when my
research project had fallen apart? That day when I'd decided two years'
work was derivative and too similar to another book just published by
a colleague at another university, and Doyle trying to tell me to give it
time, give it air.

Before I could stop it, the image came to me from deep memory: a
barbecue grill grate, my manuscript, fire. I sucked in a breath.

Corrine looked over. "You OK?"

I nodded. I'd almost forgotten what I'd done, how the pages curled,
turned black. My name was the last bit of text I'd read before the flames
found purchase. My career, up in smoke. I had far more to recover than
my mobility.

The student center rose steeply before us. Students poured in and
out of the front doors, oblivious to the precarious angle of the hill. Not
a thought, but then I doubted I'd ever noticed the hill before, either.
We watched, while I tried to gather myself.

"I'm not sure I can do it," I said finally. There was pride, and there was stupidity. I wanted to beat the odds but not take up mountain climbing.

"There has to be a door at ground level. What about fires?—Look."

Corrine had found the building's other entrance, a basement-level entry to the dining center where students got their pizza slices and smoothies. The door was unlocked. It seemed a miracle to me, but it had probably always been there, probably always been unlocked. I hadn't needed a miracle until now.

The dining center stood empty at this hour. Another miracle. We passed through the grab-and-go grocery for a bottle of water. Corrine negotiated the sale with the cashier and looked away while I guzzled it. I grabbed a fistful of paper napkins to wipe the sweat off my face and neck. I continued to pat at myself in the elevator, letting Cor guide me completely. I had begun to reconsider the golf cart.

At a closed door, Doyle's muffled voice. We were late.

I mopped my brow a last time. Corrine gave me a bucking-up smile, which I appreciated.

"Do you—I'm not sure what you need," she said.

"A seat, Cor."

She took a deep breath. As though she were the one about to return from somewhere far and long ago. As though this had much to do with her at all. For a fleeting moment, I wished I'd not run into her, that I'd had the chance to miss the meeting. And then I was back from where I'd gone, and it didn't matter that the situation made Corrine nervous, too. Of course it did. How many conversations had she had about the shooting? About me? While I was on my couch, she'd spent a lot of time serving as the buffer between my recuperation and general curiosity, listening to my office phone ring and ring as the reporters and lawyers and cranks tried to find a way in. All the help she'd given me without my having to ask. Life had changed for her, too.

She pulled back the door and held it for me.

Doyle, first. He stopped speaking and turned his head. He didn't look surprised to see me at all. "There you are," he said.

And then the table of them rose to their feet, applauding.

I stood in the doorway. They looked like people I knew, but also like strangers. Baz's hands boomed together; Joss clasped her hands together under her chin, a strange maternal expression on her face. Even the three wise men had deigned to attend, and now I'd have to try to remember their names. Behind me, I heard Corrine joining in.

I didn't move, but they came to me. I was hugged and patted on the shoulder, petted on the back. I couldn't keep up with all the platitudes. A banner of computer-printed pages taped together hung on one wall: *Welcome Back!* Under it, a table laden with doughnuts, a coffee urn, a bowl of cut fruit. Cut fruit was evidence of advanced planning. I glanced over my shoulder at Corrine, who shrugged. Ambushed.

"We were beginning to think you weren't going to make it to your own party," Woo said. The tweed, the hair gel. He was undergoing some sort of prescribed physical transition to senior faculty member. I hoped I hadn't missed all of it.

"I found her in Smith getting coffee," Corrine said. "Like normal."

They laughed and jollied carefully against me until Doyle cleared a path with his voice. "Why don't we let Amelia sit down?"

I grabbed the nearest empty chair while they settled back to their positions. Cor sat next to me. Woo brought an extra chair to my left side. "In case you want to put your leg up," he said.

"No," I said, glancing at the paper plate of pastries and fruit sliding across the table toward me. "That would hurt."

Woo finally set the chair down and circled the table to his own spot. They settled in around me, satisfied with themselves and the doughnuts.

"I didn't get shot in the leg."

They went quiet. One of the wise men—he looked crusty and presidential, so the name that came to mind was Van Buren—paused, cheeks stuffed like a chipmunk, a dusting of powdered sugar ringing his mouth.

It was the cane. A cane was a simple thing. I was up and walking, talking, shrinking uncomfortably from human contact—Amelia

Emmet, PhD, pretty much as they remembered me. Like normal, Corrine said. Except for the cane, and a cane could be ignored. It could also be misread.

I'd predicted I'd be forced to talk about it, but now I could see why I wanted to. They didn't understand. I needed one of those Zapruder film diagrams.

"The bullet—"

"We know, Amelia." This from Doyle. There was something uncomfortable about him. He seemed stiff. Reserved. Not the Doyle who'd slept in my bed for two years, the Doyle who captained a 45-foot sailboat up and down the lake coast like he'd been born at sea, but also not the Doyle I'd worked for after we'd broken up. If it had been anyone else giving me the shut-up, I would have talked right over him. But if Doyle didn't want me to ruin the surprise party by supplying any surprises, I would keep quiet. Maybe they did know everything there was to know. The *Rothbert Reader* had probably published info-graphic illustrations.

"That's what I did with my summer vacation. How about you guys?" I shoved an outsized chunk of pineapple into my mouth.

There were exchanged looks down the table. All I cared about was Doyle. We regarded each other.

"Van Meter and I gave invited talks in Slovakia in May," one of the wise men said.

Van Meter. Not Van Buren. I didn't care.

Van Meter managed to swallow the lump of doughnut packed into his jaw. "It was really quite a good time."

"Slovakia's probably never seen the like," I said. "What about the rest of you? I didn't see anyone else on the intensive care unit, so you must have something to share."

"Amelia," Corrine whispered.

"Correction," I said. "Dr. Talbot *was* there. She could work as a registered nurse at this point."

Woo leaned forward on his stately elbow patches. "I had the good fortune—"

"Next. What about you, Doyle?"

"Joss had a book out in July," he said, gesturing down the table. "I'm sorry, Joss, I don't remember the title."

I laughed. Corrine poked me in the side, and everyone turned to stare.

"Are you OK?" said Caldwell or Baz; I couldn't tell.

"Am I crying?" I wiped at my face. It was dry.

Corrine put her hand on my arm. "Are you in pain?"

I was, but not yet the way I'd been in my office. This was worse in a way, because I wasn't sure there was a pill I could take. What did insanity feel like?

"Do you need some water?" Joss said. She hopped to her feet. I already had a full glass in front of me. Caldwell jumped to help her. Baz or someone else came to stand behind me in case some chore could be assigned. I waved away the glass that was placed in front of me, then changed my mind and gulped it down.

Over the glass's rim, I stared at Doyle. He sat back in his chair, watching the room as though he'd never met a single one of us. I wasn't crazy. I'd been gone for ten months, and in that time, something had shifted. Around the table, the others leaned in, awaiting instructions.

"I'm fine," I said. I could feel a tiny pinprick of white hurt deep in my belly. I'd have to get out of there before my entire department got a show they hadn't paid for. But first, I looked back at Doyle. "You were saying, Nicholas?"

Near my ear, Corrine coughed. She tugged on my sleeve.

Doyle didn't blink. "Since I have the floor," he said and stood.

When he finally turned to face the group, I knew. How did I know? Because it was exactly what I'd told him to do.

"This summer," he said, raising his coffee mug in a toast to himself. "I got married."

CHAPTER 6

"Why didn't you tell me?" I said.

Joss had offered us a ride back to our end of campus. In the side mirror, I could see Corrine in the backseat staring out the window, idly tapping her finger on the glass. Outside: a steady parade of students against a background of scenic matriculation. The campus flourished, lush and green, almost hurtful in its hopefulness, the colors of the flowers bright and aggressive.

"It's not like I'm the one he married," Corrine said.

"You didn't even mention there was someone."

"I saw him with a woman at the organic grocery store buying broccoli crowns. How was I supposed to know rings were next?"

Joss said, "I thought you broke it off between you, Amelia."

We had tried to keep the relationship out of the office, but that was impossible. Everyone knew when he moved in, and then everyone knew when he moved out. And yet I couldn't help but want to keep what was mine—what had been mine—out of Joss's mouth.

"Never mind," I said.

"She did," Corrine said. "She broke up with him, but she still loves him."

"Hey."

"Not that she would admit it," Joss said. She drove peering over the wheel like an octogenarian who had forgotten her glasses.

"Can we not discuss this like I'm not here?"

"You were discussing it as though Joss wasn't here," Corrine said.

"As though I didn't know what you were talking about," Joss said, nodding at the windshield.

I felt like opening the door and rolling out, but that seemed a bad idea for someone so recently patched together. We were also several blocks from our building. If I survived the pavement, it was still a long walk. "Forget it."

"There's not much you can do anyway," Corrine said. "Married is married."

"Tell that to his first wife."

Joss grimaced at me. "Don't get yourself mixed up in that."

"In what?"

"In keeping score. First wife, second wife."

"You weren't his wife," Corrine said.

"Thank you, Cor. I know."

"You didn't want to be, if I remember it right."

"It wasn't just him." I wasn't sure they'd know what I meant. Doyle wasn't the only thing I couldn't commit to. My research, gone up in that unfortunate barbecue. But the thing about an academic career was that, every year, I got to start over. And teaching had always been my passion. I could always teach. "I couldn't—"

"I know," Cor said. Confirming in my head that she was the only person for whom I'd leap into the void. I smiled at her over my shoulder.

Joss stopped for a light. We all watched the students scramble from one side of the street to the other. Corrine leaned forward on my seat and stared with me.

"They seem so young," she said.

"They are so young," I said.

Joss said, "You two talk as though you're both a foot in the grave."

I didn't remind her how close I'd come to the grave, or what it felt like to be teetering on the edge, arms wheeling. I watched one student, a girl wearing a short skirt and kitten heels, flouncing across the road. A lot more stood between that girl and me than fifteen years. After a quick calculation, I had to amend: Twenty years.

But Joss was probably twenty years older again. I glanced at her out of the corner of my eye. Her silver hair was perfectly bobbed around her ears, stylish. Her bangles, her careful manicure. Sometimes she came back from a long break with intricate henna designs flowering from her smooth brown fingers up to her wrists. I didn't know much about Joss, but now I wondered what her life was like and who I could hope to be in a few, rushing years. Did she have anyone at home, or did her publishing record keep her warm? I wanted both. What was wrong with both? And now I had neither.

The light finally changed. We rolled through the crossing as the last of the students jogged out of the way.

"It just would have been nice to know," I said. "That one of my options was closing up."

Corrine let it slide. I knew as well as anyone that one of my options had ceased being an option a long time ago, and it had nothing to do with the woman buying broccoli crowns.

"Who's joining me for a drink?"

"Amelia, for God's sake," Corrine said. "What time is it?"

"I'm not teaching today." Joss shot me a sly smile.

"Last call, Cor."

"I have prep to do for tomorrow. And so do you."

"I'm as prepped as I plan to be. Come on. You don't teach until tomorrow either, right? You have all evening."

"I have—I can't." She sank back and stared out the window.

"Well, I feel like celebrating," I said. The pain in my pelvis was creeping forward, demure but insistent, reminding me of something. I found the bottle of water Corrine had bought me earlier and dug into my bag for my pill bottle.

"You do?" Joss glanced over her shoulder at Corrine.

"I'm alive, aren't I? That deserves more than a couple of jelly-filled." I threw back the pill and the last of the water and sat with my eyes closed until I felt the car swing into the circle drive at the back of Dale Hall.

Corrine got out and slammed her door and, when I still hadn't opened my eyes, rapped on my window. Joss used her controls to roll it down. "Drinking on top of those pain pills could kill you," Corrine said.

"Your concern is heartening." I opened my eyes, the pinpoint of hurt that had been growing wide inside me already receding. "Cor, it's

OK. I went into serious, foreclosure-level debt to save my own life. No plans to do myself in."

"No need to call the hope hotline on you?"

"I'll have a virgin daiquiri," I said. "What's the hope hotline?"

Corrine laughed, but I hadn't said anything I considered funny. Maybe my voice didn't sound the way I thought it did. Or maybe the pills were kicking in, and I hadn't said what I thought I had. "I was joking," she said. "But take it easy, OK? I just got you back."

"I'm not going anywhere," I said. "Except to the Mill. I'll see you tomorrow. Early."

She nodded, but the expression on her face said what she wouldn't—that it might be time to call the hope hotline. Whatever that was.

The daiquiri wasn't virgin. The daiquiri wasn't a daiquiri. I ordered a beer and waited for Joss to say something. When she didn't, I began to wonder if I weren't providing field research for the next Alberta Joss, PhD, sociological study. Women and prescription dependence. Society and social lubricants. Pharmaceutical crutches of victims of violent crime. The pills had kicked in, so this made sense to me. I might have jotted down notes if I'd had a pen.

"What's your next book about, Jossie?"

She sipped her daiquiri. Which was a daiquiri but not virgin. It was barely eleven in the morning, so I had to give her some credit for being with me at all.

We sat in a booth at the back of the Mill, which was a dive in the best kind of way. Cheap beer, dark corners, nothing cute or ornamental about any of it. At this time of day we had the place almost to ourselves. The bartender, Joe, greeted us without a bit of surprise—we went way back—and didn't give us any guff about the daiquiri.

Joss looked up from her drink, made a face, and pushed the glass away. "I have no idea. I always think each book is my last."

"If anyone gets to be morbid here, it's me," I said.

"Not that I've run out of time, Amelia, but thank you for the reminder. I'm old, but I'm not that sort of old." She smoothed her hair. I saw what she meant. She was someone's cool great-aunt who danced the Hokey Pokey at family weddings and sent mildly raunchy birthday cards. "I just meant that whenever I finish a big project, I feel—empty, in a way. I don't know where the next beginning is. Not yet. I've learned not to panic. Something always starts up."

I took a deep pull on my beer and thought about the manuscript I'd put on the cooker. What had I been thinking? Years of research soaked in lighter fluid and set aflame. I'd been making a point to Doyle, but now I couldn't remember which point. That I was wasting my time? That I'd been wasting it with him? A memory came to me: Doyle, pulling me into the tiny berth in his boat.

There's not room for this, Doyle.

Couple smart people like us? We'll figure it out.

In any case, I hadn't had another idea since. What I did have: a secret draft of that book that Doyle didn't know about, stuffed in a box at the back of my closet. But I considered that book truly burned. Once, I'd had a vision of my future. I would publish, travel, research. I would conquer. That book—it would have been my second—should have been making the conference award rounds right now. If I'd lived the way I'd dreamed I would, Woo's teaching award might have seemed like a cereal box trinket.

But I hadn't lived that way. Not really. Not before the bullet, and not since.

I finished my beer in a long drink. I couldn't remember the last time I'd gotten excited about an idea, the last time I'd thought of something worth chasing down and hog-tying. I was between projects, too, except the last one had been a project of survival. A project successfully completed, but no one would give me a MacArthur genius fellowship for making it back from the light.

"Remember that grave you were sliding into earlier?" Joss said. "You look like someone walked over it. As they say."

"Thinking," I said.

"About?"

"Getting shot."

"What about it?"

I signaled for Joe to bring us two beers. "That it's like a project I just finished. Not sure what the next one is."

She waited until Joe had brought the beers and uncapped them for us. I had a history with Joe, but no one would have known it from the silence as he swept the empties off the table and hurried away. Joss watched his hands and then, as he walked away, his ass. Joe, dark-skinned, dark-eyed, and built as though to represent human perfection, was worth watching. What had Corrine said once? *You came all this way, just to hook up with the bartender?*

"I'd have thought that you had a backlog of projects, now that this one's over," Joss said.

"It doesn't—"

"What?"

I remembered the feel of the *Rothbert Reader* clipping Corrine had brought to me in the hospital. A nearly whole page of the cheapest of newsprint, for what was normally the thinnest of news, featuring my seven-year-old faculty photo and a headline as wide as the world: *Professor critical, gunman dead.* Next to the headline, a small, dark thumbprint of a face I didn't recognize. This was the young man who had lain in wait, who'd hidden in the shadows until I'd arrived at an unlikely time, who might have made a sound at the last minute so that I faced him and took the shot head-on, wondering then the same thing I still wondered now. Why me?

The hand like a flower. The hand that wasn't mine. But—

"It doesn't feel over," I said.

Joss threw back her beer like a pro and thumped the bottle down on the table. "He won't hurt you again. I think everyone's pretty much in agreement there."

I saw the dean's face, quietly outraged that I would return, and Corrine's, relieved that I had. And Doyle—he already lived somewhere else, and I was no concern of his.

"From everyone else's perspective, I'm back, so it's over," I said. "But that's not how it feels."

She nodded long and slow, and reached for my beer. "I'll drink this, so you can keep your promise to Corrine."

"I feel like I did die, like I was dead and you all forgot to tell me. And when I came back today, you clapped and smiled, but you looked like—like you'd seen a ghost." I grabbed the beer out of her hand and sat back in the booth. The pain meds had begun to ebb a bit. I felt sharp, poised. Ready. I wasn't quite sure what I was ready for. I raised the bottle in a toast. "Ten months lost, Joss. I have a few questions."

"Like?"

"Like who was that kid?"

"Leonard Lehane."

I blinked at the sound of it. I'd read it, and I'd heard it from the mouths of police officers and lawyers. But not from someone I knew, not so casually. "No, I know."

"He wasn't a sociology major," she said. "He'd never taken the intro class, not from any of us."

"Exactly."

"Doyle checked every record he could think of," she said. "As far as he could tell, this Lehane chap never had a class with you or near you."

"That's what I've been trying to tell people." I flung my hands into the air, beseeching the ceiling. Joe looked up from the bar, ready to deliver another round. I waved him off.

"So the big question you have is—why you?"

"Why me, Joss?" My voice was louder than I realized. The only other customers turned to take a look. I found myself wishing there were more people here. Witnesses. My heart pounded in my throat so that I could barely talk around it. "That's precisely what I need to know."

"Well." She held her wrist to her mouth to cover a ladylike burp. "Sounds to me like you've already identified your next project."

CHAPTER 7
NATHANIEL

"**N**athaniel," my roommate said. "What's up with the horror show?"

I looked up. He meant the photo I'd pinned to my side of our bulletin board, a black and white of the St. Valentine's Day Massacre. I craned my neck to see it again. If it had been in color, it would have been too much for the human mind to comprehend. Six dead, sprawled where the bullets left them, and one guy's head opened up like a can of tuna. Another guy had lived long enough to get out of the photo and to a hospital. I felt a little sorry for that guy. He died anyway, and he didn't get to be immortalized.

In black and white, it had a certain nobility. Horrible, sure, you could argue, but it hadn't been a show. The massacre had really happened, had happened *here*. Well, not in our apartment or at Rothbert, but not too many miles away from where we were having this tedious argument, the real acts of history had played out.

My first day in town, I couldn't wait to be a part of it. Back when I was a kid, my mom and I had watched all the gangster movies. On the way to school, she'd pretend we were on the lam, like Bonnie and Clyde. "Don't tell your dad we drove this fast," she'd said, laughing. Finally in Chicago, I wished she could have come with me, and that we were raging through town in her crappy old car. But two trains and something like sixteen panhandlers later, I stood at a wrought iron fence looking at a patch of grass where the St. Valentine's Massacre had happened, alone. The garage was gone. The whole place had been scrubbed clean of blood, of history. People hurried past, and I could tell they didn't know. They didn't want to know. One day off the bus from Indiana, my things dumped into my new room, my schedule sorted out, and my first encounter with Al Capone's Chicago already under my belt, I felt alive for first time in a while.

"Seriously," Kendall said. "Even if we ever get a girl in here, she's not going to stay."

"We'd have to get two girls for me to care," I said. I pictured the scenario until it broke wide open. "Or about twelve for one of them to look my way. A visit from twelve girls seems unlikely."

"That's your problem. You don't know how to dream big. Or small."

In the two days Kendall and I had lived together, he'd discovered at least six problems of mine. I didn't have a sense of humor. I didn't know enough girls. I didn't have any cool T-shirts he could borrow. For a guy with a legitimate drinking-age ID, I was really lame. And now I didn't know how to dream big. Or small. There had been other problems with me, but I couldn't hold them all in my head at the same time. I had a lot to think about already, and my classes hadn't even started.

"I have dreams," I said, waving at the photo. As an artifact, the photo was a thing of beauty. Behind that shadow here or under this dead man's hand there lay something I wanted to say about violence. A dissertation, hidden among the wreckage. But all I had to say about violence at the moment was that I wanted to understand it. I wanted to crawl into it and fight my way back out. I wanted—something that didn't make any sense. "I have plenty of dreams, big ones."

"That," Kendall said, looking at the photo with disgust, "is a nightmare."

Kendall studied business. He was a sophomore, lean and floppy-limbed like a marionette in too-big pants, full of energy and plans. From New York, he'd already rooted out the deficiencies of Rothbert University and its surroundings. As a roommate, he was fine. I hadn't had much choice. By the time I enrolled, the only housing available were sublets and room-shares. With my lean budget, I'd been lucky to find anything within walking distance of campus. But now I was surrounded by undergrads. The guys upstairs drowned out each other's music with louder music and raced their desk chairs down the hallway.

They'd already broken one of the toilets in the house *skateboarding*. I shared a poorly outfitted kitchen with nine other guys.

Having dreams was not my problem. Being left behind so soon was. I hadn't chosen the right place to live. I hadn't brought the right things to wear. And now, living with Kendall and understanding all the ways I disappointed him, it was clear: I might not be the right kind of person. I looked back at the photo. "I guess I could put it somewhere less visible."

I got up and pulled the print down carefully, then turned to my side of our room. I had a single bed that was too short for me, a wooden desk and chair shoved into a corner, and about three feet of clearance in which to live my life. I could have tacked the picture to the inside of my closet, but in the end, I dropped it into my desk drawer.

"That's a start," Kendall said, and by this we both understood that I was a project. We would cover a lot of ground before I was deemed satisfactory. He leaned close to the mirror over our side-by-side dressers and checked his face. "Did you get that job?"

"The teaching assistant thing, you mean." I thought about Professor Emmet banging past me on her cane, her hair swinging into my chest. The weird interview that hadn't been much of an interview, the brush-off she'd been giving me. And then the crying and the pills in her purse. I'd been giving the assistantship some thought. Did I want to follow Dr. Emmet around, handing her tissues and shaking pills into her hand? "Sort of," I said.

"You sort of got a job?" He gave up on his pores and started fussing with the architectural rise of the front of his hair. "Or you got a sort-of job? That sounds like the kind of job you'd get."

"It's a real job," I said but then remembered how Dr. Emmet had given me something to do only after she'd gone pale and teary. "I think."

"She's hot, right? Your professor?"

"She's—" In my desk drawer, under the photo I wasn't allowed to put up, I also stored the beginnings of another project, a secret one: a file on Dr. Emmet's shooting. I knew all the facts by rote, but sometimes the articles I'd collected seemed to call me from their folder, like they had more to tell me or something to ask. I lived in the city of Capone, of Dillinger, of Richard Speck's eight nurses, of John Wayne Gacy's murdering men and boys and second life as a professional clown—of Nathan Leopold and Richard Loeb's murder of a little boy, just to see what murder felt like. If I wanted to know what violence was made of, I'd come to the right place.

Dr. Emmet's hair, when she walked past me into her office, smelled like the beach. Coconut, maybe, and some kind of flower that didn't grow anywhere near here. It was probably just her shampoo, but I wondered how much of it was her skin.

"She's hot, or your face wouldn't be Rothbert red. You going to get an A-plus in socializing with the teacher?"

"Sociology, not socializing," I said. Kendall got a lot of things half-right, but he got my program completely wrong.

My dad always got my program wrong, too. He got me wrong. He worked as a factory mechanic and couldn't understand why I needed another degree. Why couldn't I stop studying and get a job, he asked. How was I supposed to explain to him that even after this degree, all I would ever do was study? That any job I'd get would be a job *studying*?

"Calm down, egghead," Kendall said. "It was a joke. I meant, do you think she'll want to tutor you? You know, on the side?"

I ignored the nudge-nudge in his voice. "Dr. Emmet is a truly fascinating scholar in my field. I'd be lucky—"

"Emmet?" He gaped at me in the mirror. "Are you serious?" He jumped for the backpack on his bed and pulled out a balled-up newspaper. "Do you mean her?"

He flattened the newspaper against himself and turned the front page toward me. Amelia Emmet, PhD, had made it back on the front pages, and this time simply for showing up to work. I took the paper from Kendall and studied the photo. Dr. Emmet, her weight shifted onto her cane, coming up the walk to Dale Hall. By the look on her face, the paparazzo—if you could call a photojournalism student shooting for the *Rothbert Reader* that—had surprised her. She looked fierce. She looked good.

"That's her, right? Sheesh, what are you *thinking*? People get shot around her, dude."

"She's the one who got shot."

"And that student," he said. "Do you want to be next?"

"Did you even read the story?" But I knew how wrong and biased some of the stories had been. When Kendall reached for the paper, I held it away from him.

"He's dead. What else do you need to know? You dig that kind of stuff," Kendall said, waving his hand at my now-empty half of the bulletin board. "But you don't want to be the guy leaking brains from your ears, am I right?"

"Violence is a really interesting sociological—"

"Forget what I said about after-hours tutoring, kid," he said. "Do not park in the handicapped zone, if you know what I'm saying."

And this was what my problem really was. I opened my mouth to tell Kendall how offended I was by his ableist joke, how wrong he was about the facts of the case, and what an absolute shit he was to call me a kid when I was three years older. Except all the thoughts pinged around my brain without anything falling into the right slot. Kendall shook his head and, taking a last look at himself in the mirror, left me gaping like a fish on land.

I waited for a while to make sure he was gone, then opened my desk drawer and returned the photo to the wall. It was my half of the bulletin board, and I didn't really expect too many girls to be trooping through. Not for me. Not for him, either, since he was kind of a dick.

Of course that was the kind of guy girls liked. Better than they liked me, at least.

I reached deeper into the drawer, took out the file I'd kept for the last year on Dr. Emmet's attack. Below it lay another photo I'd have liked to hang up: my girlfriend, Bryn. My ex-girlfriend, actually, in her bikini on the beach in Gulf Shores, Alabama. She didn't fill out the bikini all that well, and sunglasses hid her eyes, probably her best feature. She'd sent the snapshot to me while we were separated by a half-dozen states, and it had set me on fire. She lived down south, starting her first job, while I was in Indiana, in my dad's house, waiting to hear from Rothbert while I printed stories from the web and trimmed articles out of newspapers mail-ordered from all over Illinois, giving myself the creeps, to be honest. I should have left it that way. The surprise trip down to see her turned out to be a mistake. The message Bryn had left out of her letter was that she'd already met someone else but hadn't broken up with me, because of my mom.

I liked to think of myself as a thoughtful guy. On the drive home that very same night, I'd had plenty of time to think about what I had learned. About her, about me, about life. You can't help who you love, wasn't that right? She couldn't help loving the other guy, and I couldn't help loving her. I couldn't help how angry I felt about my mom and how her death was mucking up my life. While she was sick, we'd watched a thousand hours of old black-and-white detective movies under an old green knit blanket with frilly edges. She was sick at home for a long time. Without her, I took to watching the news and developed a fondness for all the bad news going on in the real world. After the funeral, I'd pulled the old blanket toward me to watch TV. The yarn had taken on all my mom's smells—her perfume, her medicine, her decay, her death. On the back of the couch it would stay. We could never move it. All of this was forever.

I couldn't help how much I hated being inside my own skin, how desperately I wanted to cut myself open and let whatever was inside free.

I replaced Bryn's photo in the drawer and took up the folder of clippings on Dr. Emmet. By now I'd wrung all the information from them I was likely to get, but still I sorted the pile. By timeline. By depth. By publication. Looking for the connections, making notes.

Sliding the clips around on my desk, I wondered what Dr. Emmet would say if she knew how much interest I took in her situation. If she knew that I had applied to Rothbert only after I'd heard about the shooting. That I had turned down a better financial aid package at another university to come here and study with her. To come here and study *her*.

I was sure she'd tell me to find another assistantship.

I was sure she'd tell me to go to hell.

I reached for my scissors and, taking my time, trimmed the article from Kendall's paper to add to my file.

Someday, I hoped, I'd figure out what all of this meant and, maybe, what it meant to me.

CHAPTER 8

My first class session as a graduate student was methodology—study methods, use of statistics, field research strategies. I sort of got a hard-on just thinking about it all.

But the professor turned out to be a thousand years old and kept dropping his chin to his chest as though we'd just witnessed his last breath. And then the chin would pop up again, half of what he had been saying lost in a mumble, and we were stuck there for at least a few more minutes.

A couple of cute girls sat next to me. I could already tell they weren't my type.

My type—as though my type didn't eventually take up with someone who was more her type.

These girls propped their laptops open, but instead of taking any notes, they typed instant messages to their friends and moved things around on some social networking site. Before class, I'd heard a few of the other students strike up a conversation about how much they'd drunk the night prior. In graduate school. I couldn't believe it. I liked a good microbrew as much as anyone, but I couldn't help thinking that these people didn't understand something fundamental about graduate degrees. You didn't go get one because you didn't want the party to end. You pursued one because you found yourself lacking in some area of knowledge that was important to you.

Some of these people were likely here because they hadn't found a job with their first degrees. Some of them might want to save themselves the trouble and go turn in an application at Macy's.

But then I had to turn that thought inward and wonder if I wasn't the one wasting my time. Hadn't my dad as much as said so? Hadn't I already been wrong about so much, including the moral character of at least one girl my age?

"In short," said the professor, and we all snapped to attention because his voice rang of dismissal. "In short, methodology is the hook on which you should hang your cap."

Whatever he said next, he said to his belly and shoes. The class sank back into their seats.

I'd been giving some thought to methodology in regards to my study of Dr. Emmet—although my problem at this point wasn't how to conduct a study. I thought I could probably figure out how to study her if I knew what result I hoped to find. But that didn't sound very scientific.

I raised my hand.

The professor stopped in mid-mumble and looked up from his gut. He seemed surprised that any of us were still in the room. "Yes, uh?"

"Nathaniel Barber, sir."

"Professor Van Meter, Mr. Barber. Fine to meet your acquaintance." His head nodded down but buoyed back up in time so that I also heard the next bit. "Do you in fact come from a long line of hair-trimming professionals?"

The class shuffled in their seats. The two girls glanced over, took a look at my hair. "No, sir. I don't believe I do."

"From a long line of sociologists, perhaps?"

My dad's dad had been a farmer, but that hardly seemed the sort of thing I wanted to say to my entire class of cohorts on the first night of class. We had to study side by side for the next several years and compete with one another in ways I didn't understand yet. "I suppose you could say that I have some field researchers in my family tree, sir."

"A leg up, then, Mr. Barber. Now what could be troubling you so early in the semester?"

"I wondered, Professor, how you choose your method of study if you don't know what you're looking for."

To my surprise, the rest of the class turned from me to Professor Van Meter to hear what he'd say.

He shook his head. "Dear Mr. Barber. The point isn't necessarily to choose what you're looking for, but to choose to *look*. If you choose to look in a way that is serious, consistent, *methodical*, and scientific, you will find. If you look with open eyes and open mind, Mr. *Barber*, you will find a line of questioning that you can *expand* and *explore*."

This seemed wise and impassioned enough to applaud, but then I wasn't quite sure what I'd learned. Except that it seemed I could start my study of Dr. Emmet at any place and time that made sense, even if I didn't know what I hoped to discover.

"Thank you, sir," I said.

"Of course, of course." The professor tucked his chin into his chest and was silent. When his head rose again, he said, as clearly as anything he'd said so far, "Class dismissed."

As we gathered our materials, the professor stood, put his chin down, and left the room.

"Whatever you did and however you did it, do it again next week," said one of the girls.

"What?"

The guy on the other side of me clapped me on the shoulder. "We're done a half hour early, buddy. You can ask a question any time you like."

"It's quarter draft night at Nick's," one girl said to the other. They both had bronze-y blonde hair in ponytails. They looked like they'd been called in to audition for the same role. "You coming?"

She was looking at me. I had time to think about all the times I'd ever wished for a girl to look in my direction, all the times since Bryn had told me to drive back home that I'd wanted someone, too, so I could send a photo to Bryn of a different girl in a different bikini. I couldn't think of what to say. Yes, as an answer, didn't occur to me.

"I have to study," I said.

"Classes just started," the other girl said, and in her voice I heard the judgment that would stick. I'd missed my chance to be the guy who finagled a break for all of us by asking a question. That ship had sailed. Now I was the guy who read the book before it was assigned. These two qualities were mutually exclusive. In my head, I heard what Kendall would have said. *Your problem is you're a shithead.*

"I have—a special project," I said.

The three of them all turned toward me. I hadn't won the first girl back. She was the prettier of the two, shorter and curvier, and her eyes were wide and blue.

The other girl sneered. "I bet," she said, her voice suggesting that my special project might involve nudie magazines and a box of tissues.

"Didn't you just start the program, too?" the cuter girl asked.

I wished I hadn't mentioned the project. I really was a shithead.

"Then how are you doing research already?" the guy said. He was tall, lean, and liquid in the joints, the kind of guy Kendall wanted to be but wasn't. A surfer or a skateboarder in body, and a sociology major at heart? I wasn't buying it. I wondered how many med schools he didn't get into before ending up here.

"Did you get an assistantship?" said the girl with the blue eyes. I wanted her to keep looking at me, to try one more time to ask me to come with them.

"Yeah," I said, gulping hard. "Yes. I'm assisting Dr. Amelia Emmet."

She gasped. "That poor woman."

"The one on the front page of the *Reader* today," the guy said, nodding at me with something like approval.

"Didn't her last boyfriend try to kill her or something?" the other girl said.

"It was her student," the guy said.

"No," I said. My voice a strange croak that shut them all up. "It was—I mean, he was a student, but not her student. That's the really interesting part."

But I had lost the cute girl again. She stared at me in horror. "What are you doing for your—project?"

Nothing I could say would rescue me. Everyone else in the class had gone, and the hallway beyond rang silent in the absence of their retreating steps. Maybe a lie would have sounded better, but I decided, without the thought I usually liked to put into things, on the truth.

"I don't know what I'll be doing yet."

The girls exchanged glances and hurried to gather their purses and books.

The guy looked me up and down. "You might want to ask," he said, slinging his backpack over his shoulder. "Before it turns out to be something you're going to want to kill her for."

CHAPTER 9

My second class of the semester would be Dr. Emmet's. I wanted to be prepared. I was her assistant, wasn't I? Well, I still thought I might be, even though I had no idea what that meant and hadn't seen or talked to her since that day in her office.

I lay in my bed with my feet hanging off the end and reread the *Rothbert Reader* clipping from the day before. The story wasn't much of a story. She was alive, which everyone knew, and she was back on campus. From the photo, if you were paying attention, you could tell that she hoped the photographer and perhaps everyone else in the world would drop dead. That was the only news—she was on campus, and, implied, maybe you don't want to mess with her.

"Are you beating off to that?" Kendall called from his bunk.

"You're such a juvenile."

"Let me have it, then."

"I need it for reference."

"For reference, my dick," he said. "I mean, *your* dick."

"Stop discussing my dick, Kendall, or people will get ideas."

The good thing about sophomores: they still cared what people thought. He shut up, flopped around in his bed for a while and, after a few minutes, began to snore.

He was still asleep when I came back from the communal bathroom down the hall. I dressed silently, then slipped out. Inside my backpack, the file on Dr. Emmet. Time to start my study.

I hadn't seen the lake yet, but the path I chose through campus afforded a glimpse of the sparkling surface in the breaks between buildings and trees. I had selected Rothbert based on the faculty—*one* faculty member—and hadn't even realized the campus bumped against Lake Michigan. But now the water seemed like a benefit directly from a brochure I hadn't read. Kendall had already been to the beach to scout for girls. This was a good university—I hoped girls here hung out at the library.

The library. I stopped and searched around for a landmark, only to find that I'd walked all the way to the south entrance to campus. A larger-than-life statue of someone I didn't recognize stood at the edge of the walk, his bronze hand gesturing benevolently. Somehow I'd already passed the library. I unhitched my backpack to find my map.

"Anything we can help you with?"

On the other side of the statue sat a table and three students. Behind them, a long bulletin board displayed the work of the student groups' postering crews. The Christian group, the feminists, the ultimate Frisbee kids. I remembered this part of the experience, when students herded themselves into smaller and smaller groups. Frats, honor societies, film clubs, dance and improv troupes, mock UNs and student government.

One of the guys waved his hand. "Over here. Tough week?"

"No," I said. "My week has been fine."

"Look, take a magnet, will you? Stick it on your fridge." The guy had a wide grin and slick hair like someone selling unwieldy kitchen appliances on late-night TV.

"I don't have a fridge." Anything I put in the shared kitchen would be fair game, I'd learned that much.

"Take a card then, at least. And a pen."

"We have to pass this stuff out before we can stop sitting here," another student said. This one had a bored face, a bored voice. He was slumped behind the table as though he'd been handcuffed there.

"Shut up," the girl said.

"I have class at eleven-fifteen," the unhappy guy said. "I have a deadline."

I felt a little sorry for them and definitely a bit superior. I could skip it this time—the forced camaraderie, the buttons, the posters, the trying to make friends. I'd met Bryn by joining a writing group. She was a poet. Sort of. But that was a mistake I didn't have to make this time. This time, I wasn't a student. I was a scholar.

"Give me a card or whatever," I said.

The salesman hopped up and gathered a handful of things from the table. "A button. Two pens. I'll give you a magnet, too. Give it away to a troubled friend."

I should have been flattered that he thought I had friends. In my imagination, a crew of friends grew up around me, and I was offended for them.

He dumped the loot into a baggie and held it out to me. "We're from Psychological Services. You ever have a really bad day, you can call the number on the pen. And the card. And the button."

Psychological services. The suicide watch, he meant. I hardly knew what that meant as a student organization, but I knew what it meant to need watching.

That night, after a twenty-four-hour round trip to have my heart broken, after Bryn—I hated myself for even remembering that night, but now I couldn't stop it. How I'd searched the medicine cabinet of our house to see what options I had. How the steak knives we never sharpened had glinted in their drawer. How'd I'd wanted to tear myself to pieces, leap from the top of the house, anything to make the rush of fear and loneliness stop.

The guy tilted his head a millimeter. "You OK?"

He didn't really think we'd share a moment here under this statue. This was a show for the others, who were starting to exchange glances.

"Sure. Do you know where the library is?"

"You a freshman?"

"*No.* I'm a graduate student in sociology."

"Oh. Trudie's majoring in psychology." He waved for the girl.

"It's not the same thing," I said.

"I'm Phillip."

"Great," I said. Trudie arrived. She had pigtails. "Great."

"Trudie, this is—"

"Nathaniel." I wish I were the kind of guy who thought on his feet. Bram Stoker. Amadeus Mozart. Charlie Brown. Anything. Instead—"Nathaniel Barber."

"Good to meet you," Trudie said.

"I'm fine," I said.

They both stared at me.

"I was just thinking about—maybe volunteering or something," I said.

"That is such a *great idea*," Phillip said. Trudie nodded like a trained monkey at his side.

"*Great* idea," she said.

"I lead all the volunteer training," Phillip said. "Just stop by or—"

"I'll call." By now I just wanted to get away from them.

"Great," he said. "You have our number."

"I do?"

His smile diminished a watt. The guy left alone at the table threw back his head and laughed.

Trudie turned on him. "Shut up, Win." She flicked her hand at the statue. "You're letting down the founding father." He flipped her off.

"Oh, right," I said. "I do. On the—magnet." I raised the baggie, like a tip of a hat. "The library?"

The library stank of modernity, a large, sharp concrete ordeal that looked like a prison. I had passed it once already, but the only signs on campus were small and understated to the point of invisibility. Inside, all of the study carrels stood empty, all today's newspapers hung neatly in place. I had the feeling that I was the only person in the building, that someone had mistakenly left the doors open and the lights on the night before. Or like I was the first person to wander into a crime scene.

Some kids played cowboys and Indians. I'd played crime scene. Sometimes I still did.

I found the periodicals department, the files, a row of microfilm viewers. Still no people, but I could hear someone in the room behind the information desk. I waited for a while, then started making incidental noises—fingernail tapping, throat clearing, paper shuffling.

Nothing. At last I raised my backpack above my head and let it drop to the ground. A woman appeared in the doorway. She looked a lot like one of the women my dad had taken to dinner since my mom died, cushiony and comfortable as a piece of furniture.

She looked at her watch. "Early bird, eh? Can I help you with something?"

"I'd like to see microfilm for October 11 of last year."

"Which paper?"

All of them, but I couldn't say that. "The major Chicago papers and then—what's the Willetson paper called?"

"The *Courier*."

"And the *Rothbert Reader*, too."

She disappeared through the door again. I picked up my backpack. Someone else had come into the area, a girl with sleek black hair and glasses, who sifted through the day's newspaper editions. This girl and I were the only students out of something like seven thousand who had come to the library this early in the morning, this early in the semester. I felt a sort of kinship rise up—was it enough to start a conversation? The girl picked up a Chinese-language paper and studied the headlines.

The postcard I would write to Bryn: *My girlfriend speaks three languages and did her Fulbright in Beijing. What's new with you?*

The librarian came back with a set of long, thin boxes under her arm. "Here's the first installment. Go get settled and I'll bring you the rest. You know how to use the system?"

"Of course." I turned my head a little toward the other student and adjusted my volume. "I'm a grad student. In sociology."

"Congratulations," the woman said. She stacked the boxes in front of me and tapped them one at a time, doing some sort of calculation. "OK, I still owe you the *Reader* and the *Willetson Courier*."

The girl hadn't even looked up. I took my things and went to the film readers. In actuality, it had been a while since I'd used one of these hulking dinosaurs. But if you wanted to do newspaper research, it remained the closest thing to looking at the old papers. Newsprint being thin and cheap, it disintegrated quickly. There was no such thing as a complete newspaper archive, but when I pictured myself digging in the stacks, that's what I saw: me, rising up from a leaning tower of newsprint with the evidence I'd been looking for in my hand. Eureka!

Or no. Nobody said that.

I pondered the right phrasing, fumbling to thread the film reel through the machine and onto the empty spool on the other side. I started with the *Tribune*, the city's largest circulation paper. A blue button progressed or reversed the reel. After a few minutes, I had the system working and had wound through the dates leading up to October 11, the day Dr. Amelia Emmet's assailant shot her. Except there was nothing. No notice, not even a brief paragraph.

The librarian walked up with more boxes. "The *Reader*, and then here's the *Courier*. What's wrong? Is it jammed?"

"No. I just—" I wasn't sure what to say. A secret project was supposed to be secret. "I was searching for a news item, and it's not here."

"Maybe the *Tribune* didn't report it. Did it happen in Willetson?"

"The *Tribune* reported it," I said. I had the marked-up clip in my backpack already. I'd been hoping for a fresh copy.

"Well, that's not even a year ago," she said, looking over the top of her glasses at my screen. "What's the story you're looking for?"

"Never mind. I'll find it."

"Why waste your time? If it's that big a deal, I'd remember—"

She did. She remembered October 11 precisely.

"Did you say you studied sociology?" She didn't wait for me to answer but reached for the blue button and sped through a line of pages until the *Chicago Tribune* nameplate showed itself again, and we were reading the headlines on October 12 instead. "The *Tribune* is a morning paper, hon. Professor Emmet was shot in the evening. The news—" She gave me an uncertain look. "The news didn't get printed until the next day."

"Of course. Thank you." I hoped to put a dismissive tone into my words, but the librarian only reached in and framed the image better. There it was: the scene outside Dale Hall and the small square photos, side by side, of Dr. Emmet and the student, whose face I knew almost as well as my own.

"That poor dear," the librarian said.

"She's fine," I said. And then felt my cheeks go hot when the woman turned to me. "I mean, she's as good as can be expected, considering. She's back to teaching—"

"I didn't mean her."

"But—"

"The Chicago papers didn't spend much time on this," she said. "Certainly not enough to get it right."

Her anger made me think maybe I was getting things wrong, too. I had most of the facts already. Maybe instead of library research, I should be out among the people, interviewing and watching. Out among the chimps, Jane Goodall-like, talking to people like this woman, who had clearly lived through the ordeal and had opinions. I would have to rethink my methodology.

I couldn't think fast enough to switch the conversation with the librarian around to information gathering. She stood up and started back toward the desk.

"Wait," I said. She didn't. "Wait. Who got it right then?"

I saw the student with the Chinese paper look up and notice me at last, just as my voice turned pleading.

The librarian reached her desk, pausing on the patron side. "In my experience, no one ever gets it completely right," she said. "Probably no one ever will." She didn't turn around but kept walking until she'd disappeared through the doorway, hidden once again.

CHAPTER 10

The first task of the Sociology of Deviance and Crime course was to negotiate the sociology of the room. First to arrive, I had this one chance to decide how I would view Dr. Emmet and the rest of the class for the semester. The sociology of proximity and space—someone else could do that dissertation, but it was still interesting.

I studied the setup of the room. Long table, ten chairs. Not a lot of elbow room. Dr. Emmet would probably sit at the head of the table near the door.

I'd just chosen the perfect chair—three away from the head of the table for scientific distance—when another student walked in, glanced around, and dropped his bag at the very seat I'd allocated to Dr. Emmet.

"Hey," he said, reaching over with a confident handshake.

"Hey." I could hear more people coming down the hall and maybe, underneath their voices and footsteps, the tap of Dr. Emmet's cane. "I guess I thought Dr. Emmet would sit there," I said.

"Oh, we don't have to go in for that nonsense, do we?"

"Which nonsense?"

"I'm just practicing. Deviance, get it?" He sat down and promptly put his feet up on the table. He wore beat-up motorcycle boots, the kind of thing I would never be able to wear without looking as though I'd just stepped off a community theater stage. He leaned back, settled in.

He only had to wait a minute. The group walked in and behind them, Dr. Emmet. She looked a lot better than the last time I'd seen her. She looked really good, actually. Her eyes went straight to the boots. She used her cane to scoot them off the table. "Handicapped parking only," she said.

Do not park in the handicapped zone, if you know what I'm saying.

I swallowed hard and glanced around. Among the other students: the two nearly indistinguishable girls and the guy from my methods class, exchanging looks as they sat across from me. Motorcycle Boots found another seat.

Dr. Emmet lowered herself into her chair and set her cane on the floor. A flash of something passed over her face, but she sat up and took out a pen, a sheaf of papers. We were all trying not to watch, but of course she must have known that. She tapped the stack of papers on its edge for a second too long.

"All right, it's time," she said. "I'm expecting six of you and here you are—five, six. I like it when the math is easy. We're going to spend most of our time tonight setting out the course for the semester and getting started with a little deviance. Theory, that is."

I could see what kind of teacher she must have been—the kind who could be playful even in complex conversations, the kind who could make a joke at her own expense to make the greater point. Now, the smile she managed was tight.

"We're going to talk about the distinction between formal deviance and informal deviance a bit, get you started on some theory to see how you think." She shot a lidded look down the table at the guy in the boots. "If you think wrong, then I'll just have to remold you until you think right."

I laughed. No one else did. Everyone turned to stare, but Dr. Emmet found me and gave me a small smile, a real one. "Nathaniel. Thank you. Good to see you again. Now before we get to the formalities, let's lay waste to the elephant in the room."

The room went still.

"I study and teach the sociology of crime," she said. "Recently I had the chance to do some detailed field research. I almost can't imagine a scenario in which you haven't already heard this—I was shot last year. That's why I have the cane. That's why I need the seat near the door. That's why about halfway through class tonight, I will have to get up and go take pain medication."

No one said anything. Dr. Emmet gave every one of us a chance to look her in the eye.

"Some of you will know about this, and I expect the rest of you will be looking it up on the Internet before we meet again. Let's cut to the proverbial chase. I haven't taught this class since—in a while. You're all graduate students. You're all adults. I hope that you act that way, that I'm not placing undue respect on you that you will not earn. I hope that you're all here for the right reasons."

Her eyes landed on me.

"But let me be honest with you: I'm no longer sure what I think about violent crime as a social construct. I'm no longer sure what I think of criminal deviance. In the past, I've started this course letting the students pick apart terms like 'senseless violence.'" She gestured into the air, then hid her hand away. It might have been shaking. "I've come to understand that most violence is senseless, or at least it should seem that way."

I wished I'd brought a recording device. No one took notes. No one breathed.

"I can tell you one thing about the topic I didn't know last year," she said, glancing around the table. "Getting shot *sucks*."

This time everybody laughed.

At the break, Dr. Emmet got up with some obvious effort. "Twenty minutes," she said. "Or as much time as I need."

The guy in the boots immediately took up the nearest girl's attention. I stood, stretched, and headed for the vending machine. I was deciding between an orange soda and a candy bar when I heard someone behind me. The cute girl from my other class. Cara.

"Hey," she said.

"Hey." I decided on the candy, ripped it open, and shoved half the bar into my mouth.

"How's your special project going?"

I chewed and chewed, realizing how idiotic I must look. She smiled and reached past me to drop some quarters into the machine. A sleek can of diet soda rolled out.

"Good," I said finally. "I mean. I don't know." I considered the rest of my candy while Cara sipped her drink. "Where's that other girl?" This was the problem with conversation. I didn't have time to think things through.

Cara glanced down the hall. "Julia?"

"Yeah, I mean, I thought you two were twins or something."

"We don't look a thing alike," she said, tucking her hair behind her ear. Bryn did that, but I still didn't know what it meant. That she needed a haircut? Or regretted not wearing a ponytail? "She's prettier than me."

"I don't think so," I said, and then realized how I sounded. Cara smiled. "I mean. I thought—"

The rest of the class crowded around us. I had no idea what I was saying anyway. Better to stop talking.

The other girl, Julia, and the guy from our other class, who I'd learned was named Ryan, walked up to us. Julia helped herself to a sip of Cara's drink while Ryan stared into the snack machine. "Got any money?"

I got out my wallet. If the assistantship didn't come through, I'd need to find a job. Maybe two. I gave him a dollar.

"You're awesome." But he meant the bag of chips he had his eye on. "How's your project?"

I shrugged. The library visit had been fruitful in a way. I had some new sources for my files, but hardly any new information. But then the librarian. *No one would get it right.* What did that mean? What did it feel like to go through life believing something so—ambivalent? What about science and truth? There were ways to get things right. There had to be. "I'm in the research phase," I said.

"Did I tell you that kid is in my class?" Ryan said around a mouthful of chips. "Well, his roommate."

The girls talked quietly to each other. Ryan was looking at me.

"I'm sorry—what?"

"In the class I'm the TA for," Ryan said. "I met the students this morning. Bunch of business and chemistry majors. They are *devastated* to be there. There's like a vibe? In the room? I think they might stage a revolution. Man, Sociology 101. Like I wanted to take that again."

Cara and Julia pulled away. I shoved the rest of the candy in my mouth and talked around it. "But you're not taking it again. You're teaching it."

"Yeah, that's cool, I guess."

About ten, I guessed. About ten medical schools he hadn't gotten into. "So which student is in your class?"

"That kid. His roommate, I mean." Ryan made a gun out of his hand and shot it at the side of his head. "Shooter McDude, I don't remember his name."

"Leonard Lehane? Er—his roommate?" I searched my memory for the roommate, but I was pretty sure I'd never read anything about him. "What's his name?"

"I so don't remember. At all. There were twenty of them at least. Heard someone talking about it after class. Hey, we're thinking about hitting the Mill after this—"

The elevator doors opened and Dr. Emmet emerged. "Race you," she said.

We slipped down the hall, the tap of her cane urging us forward.

Dr. Emmet let us out a little early, too. It wasn't because of anything I said this time. Except that just after she dismissed us, she leaned toward her cane and shot backward as though it were hot. "Nathaniel, will you stay for a minute?"

Ryan and the girls looked at one another and hurried.

"Hey, meet you at the Mill in a few, Nathaniel?" Ryan said.

In the second half of class I'd learned that Ryan came from California, that Cara got nervous when asked to speak in front of people, and that the guy in the boots probably didn't have a motorcycle but really was a douchebag. "I'm hoping to wrap this up in under four years," he'd said, flicking with nonchalance at the closed cover of his notebook. Dr. Emmet kept it together pretty well. "This?" she'd said. "You mean the study of complex human interactions? If you want, *you* can wrap it up tonight, and we'll get on with our lives."

During my introduction, I'd kept pretty close to the facts. Name, undergraduate university, hometown. "What's something interesting about yourself, Nathaniel?" Dr. Emmet had said. I drew a blank. For a moment, the only thing I could think of was the St. Valentine's Day Massacre photo on my wall. "I'm not that interesting," I said, and then felt like an idiot when the others laughed. The worst thing to say, because it was the truth.

"The Mill?" I said to Ryan now. "Maybe. Sure."

They started to file out. At the last minute, Ryan came around to my side of the table and left a folded piece of paper on my books. "I remembered," he said. "Because—well, if you meet him—" I opened the note and saw a name I didn't know. *James Baker.* I nodded to him as he slipped out the door.

Dr. Emmet waited until the last of the footsteps had faded down the hall before she opened her eyes.

"I'm really sorry," she said. "About the other day. That was no way to get off on the right—foot." She sighed. "The right foot. I have to start thinking about what comes out of my mouth."

"That's OK. I mean, I was happy to help."

"Are you?" She gave me a strange, solid look, sizing me up. My mind jumped ahead, and I didn't like where it went. "*Happy* to help?"

"You said maybe a—an assistantship or something?"

"Absolutely. Yes. That's for real. I just—I could use some help in ways that wouldn't *technically*—officially—"

I tried to keep what Kendall would say out of my head. "That's no problem."

"It might be something really stupid."

I thought about that. "Did you need something right now?"

Her eyes slid away from me. "Will you pick up my cane for me?"

"Sure," I said.

"And help me stand?"

"OK."

"I took my pill," she said.

"OK."

"But sitting here. Three hours almost."

"That must hurt."

"A f—great deal." She gripped my arm and raised herself to standing. "Seriously, starting tomorrow, let's set aside an hour to get you started. Can you make it to my 101 class tomorrow? You can be my TA for that class, two days a week, plus some things on the side."

On the side. I felt that one deep down. I would never repeat a single word of this conversation.

We were making our way to the door. She still held my arm. She was thin, too thin and, maybe I was imagining this? Shaking, as though her entire body hummed. "Do you want to teach? Research?"

"Research. Write. And teach."

"I can help you with all that. Really. I just need—I could use some specialized help until I get back on my feet." She shook her head. "Dammit. Why are so many clichés based on feet and legs? I have to stop relying on clichés, that's all."

"It's no problem."

"I'll help you, is what I'm trying to say. What do you need help with?"

I thought of the photo of Bryn in my drawer, of that dark night when my dad had left me alone in the house and I searched attic to basement for something I couldn't name. Then: the girl, studying the Chinese newspaper with her head tilted to one side. Cara, her eyes round with horror. "Nothing. I mean *plenty*, but right now—"

"What?"

"Do you know where the Mill is?" I said.

She laughed, at first low and then loudly, until I joined her, not really sure why.

CHAPTER 11
AMELIA

Finally I stopped laughing. Did I know where the Mill was? I certainly did. At one point, my mail could have been forwarded there.

"Did you want to go, Dr. Emmet?" Nathaniel said. He'd walked me down the hall to my office and then, without me asking, waited for me and escorted me to the elevator, through the Dale Hall lobby and to the parking lot. "To the Mill, I mean," he said now. "With us." He grinned in a way that made me think the kid hadn't had an *us* to speak of in a while.

I did want to go. I wanted the beer. I wanted the Mill. I wanted to sit in a high-backed, cracked, red faux-leather booth and have a drink with my students. Laugh with them, get to know them. A thing I had done all the time, before. Before. I was beginning to hate that word, which cleaved my life into two spheres, the second one a lot less promising. The second one, in which I was stuck forever.

"Not this time," I said. "But keep asking."

His grin twitched a bit.

"I used to go to the Mill with my classes the first night. Every semester. It's just been—a long day."

"No problem. I mean—some other time."

He was a cute kid. "I'll see you tomorrow then," I said.

He loped off in the direction of the Mill, and I was left to my own devices. I eased into my car as slowly as I could. Getting in and out of the car was the hardest part. Finally folded into the shape of the seat, I tested my ability on the pedals before navigating out of the space, then the faculty lot and campus to city streets. The commute, on foot—at least on sturdier feet than mine—took less than fifteen minutes. By car, it was ridiculous. Five minutes, tops, and I was pulling into my apartment lot, trying not to nick my neighbor's Subaru.

A cute kid. Not that long ago someone Nathaniel's age would have been a viable option for me. I couldn't think of them as men, but that's what they were. Live wires, every muscle in their bodies tensed toward a fantasy they'd already imagined in full detail. Of course, I'd gone the other way—Doyle was fifteen years older, had an ex-wife, a mortgage on a beautiful home he didn't like, a boat and slip in the harbor. A fine pedigree in family, education, in everything. And two kids. And now a current-wife, too. Not viable.

The students weren't, either. Rothbert's strict ethical code—and really, my own—outlawed relationships between students and faculty. It wasn't about age. It was about power, and the abuse of power that always seemed to follow. I'd seen ugly scenes played out, heard terrible stories. He said, she said. Grades inflated. Letters of recommendation and other prizes given out to the sexual favorites. As a student, as a faculty member, I'd had my share of inappropriate offers. The trick was: never allow for gray areas.

I hadn't aged many calendar years since the last time a student had hit on me, actually. But the timeline had jarred loose. In one short year, I'd gone from young professor, not bad-looking, better-looking when I smiled, straight down the scale to crone. The male students had once looked at me in a way that I understood—I'd been absolutely viable for them. Wish fulfillment.

Now the cane.

I couldn't imagine that any of the students in tonight's class would want me at the Mill. They didn't want to talk to me. They wanted to talk *about* me.

Except Nathaniel. Nathaniel seemed serious, focused. I hoped I wasn't reading him wrong.

I launched myself out of my car. My building's locks operated by punch-button codes, thankfully, no keys to juggle along with my cane, my bag, the books in my arm. I'd had a ground-floor apartment all along. "Lucky you," Cor had said when she'd helped me move back in from the hospital, and then shut up when she saw the look I gave her.

Inside, the tidiness of my apartment surprised me anew. The cleanliness was a phenomenon of the After part of my life. A nice Lithuanian woman came twice a week to keep my mess out from under my own feet. The neatness was nice, but it felt false. Was false. My apartment was small, bare, folded, and put away. Without Doyle and Doyle's stuff, it had seemed cavernous, and now this antibacterial way of living turned the place surgical. I lived in a museum.

Of course, the order masked how chaotic everything really was. The books were lined up on the shelf by color, since Ausra's English was selective. Things were in their place, but I couldn't find anything. The dishes were clean, the counters clear, but I wasn't hungry. The bed sheets got changed, but I'd forgotten how to sleep. When I did sleep, the dark dreams came. The manuscript I'd worked on for the last two years was burned, as far as anyone knew, and my head was empty. I'd announced to my class that my feelings on crime might have changed. But I didn't know if they had. I couldn't know—I couldn't think.

Sounds to me like you've already identified your next project. Not as easy as Joss made the enterprise sound. I had to be able to think, didn't I?

But if I never pursued answers to the questions I still had, would I ever be able to concentrate on anything else? If I couldn't work, what would I do with myself? Who would I be?

I threw my bag down, and then picked it back up and hung it on the back of a chair. I set the books in a neat stack on the table. Who was I now? Not myself, no matter what Woo said. If no one treated me the same as they used to, was it even their fault?

I sat on the edge of my couch and eased back into the cushions. In less than twenty minutes, I'd have to move to a straight-backed chair or to bed, or I'd be stuck here until someone found me. Twenty minutes spent staring at the TV? Flipping through an academic journal? Or a celebrity magazine Cor had left? Calling my ex-boyfriend to ask him about his wedding? I wished I had a book. A page-turner. A trashy mystery.

Except—did I really need more lurid whodunit in my life?

Leonard Lehane. His name came to me like the image of his hand rising out of the dark hallway. All I knew was that name, the spare bits they'd published in the few articles I'd been allowed to read, sitting up in the hospital bed with a series of titanium rods holding me together. A chemistry major or engineer or something. Not a religious zealot, not an activist, not a peep out of the kid as far as any hatred toward me or women or academics or anyone else.

And yet he'd been willing to wait. He'd been willing to kill, and willing to die instead of facing the consequences. What had his mother said in one article I'd read? A quiet boy, shy, troubled. I didn't care about any of that—what else could she say? Why had he wasted his trouble on *me*?

My mind drifted to Doyle. What was he doing now, nine-thirty on a school night, first week of the semester? New wife, new beginning. I imagined her a blonde and tall because I was neither. What did Doyle's kids call her? Were they at the wedding? The family photo presented itself: Doyle and his bride and Sarah, eleven, the maid of honor, and Ty, eight, holding the rings on a pillow at his dad's side. The best man. I was nobody's mom, but I missed the sound of my name coming from their mouths. I'd never see them again, unless Doyle brought the family to campus.

Oh, God. What if he brought her to campus?

What if she worked at the university?

What if I knew her?

What if she started hanging around Dale Hall all the time? Dropping in between classes, bringing over little boxed lunches from the gourmet grocery to share with him, laughing with her mouth wide.

I could see her head thrown back, hear her bawdy laugh, and I had no idea who she was.

Would they have more kids together? The blonde, sitting in Doyle's cozy office with her feet in his lap, caressing her own swelling stomach.

And what did she think of me? The poor ex-girlfriend, hobbled and alone.

Barren. Ruined.

I couldn't stop. I had two trains of thought—gunshot, Doyle, Doyle, gunshot. They were wires, crossed, tangled—spliced. Gunshot, Doyle. That was all there was.

If I didn't figure this out, I didn't know if there'd ever be anything else.

I leveraged myself out of the couch with my cane, my leg and hip already stiff, and staggered to my office. This space wasn't tidy. It didn't have to be. I hadn't done any work since—*the accident*, my mind supplied. Ausra was under orders to leave it alone, but the room embarrassed me. My life embarrassed me. I couldn't believe I'd let Cor hire a housekeeper. Every time she came, I let myself spiral into guilt and self-loathing, wracked by the social class implications of a woman who'd grown up poor having a cleaning service—no, a cleaning *woman*, another human who had to deal with the details of my day-to-day mess.

The desk had grown a layer of debris: the few news clippings that had been Corrine-approved and delivered on her visits, sympathy cards, and the other strange but inoffensive correspondence I'd received.

One of the things I'd so carefully filed away in the pile was a note left on my car a few weeks ago. I hadn't even been driving my car at the time, but, left sitting alone with its sad blue wheelchair hangtag in my building's parking lot after everyone else had gone to work, my car provided an easy mark.

That was the day Corrine had come with more magazines and found the kitchen trash heaping. When she came back from taking it out, her cheeks were pink from two minutes in the sun.

"Do you know someone named—Rory?" She handed me the note and dropped into the couch next to me. "It was on your windshield."

"No. What do you think? Man or woman?"

"Does that really say Rory?"

"Rory McDaniel," I read. The name and a number, that was all. "Lawyer. Or reporter. They're the ones who leave cryptic notes."

"Have you—would you talk to one of them?"

"And say what?"

"Don't you want—" She'd grown pinker. "It's infuriating. Someone can just—attack, and there's nothing you can do to get your life back."

I hadn't quite given up my life yet, but I didn't say so. "I think I've had all the publicity I'll ever need in one lifetime."

"If you're sure." She hadn't pushed me, which I always appreciated about Cor. She saw my side.

Publicity I didn't need. But a reporter, someone connected, someone out there gathering information, might be useful. I didn't have much to give in return—but the reporters didn't believe that.

The article Corrine had clipped for me from the *Willetson Courier* lay near the top of the desk debris. In the center of the clipping was a large cut-out for what must have been an alarming photo. I was grateful not to know what I was missing. Then my faculty photo, looking pretty good. Leonard Lehane's blurry student ID photo. I studied his face again. He looked into the camera, fierce, determined. He could have been anyone, and yet he wasn't anyone I thought I'd ever met. I skimmed over the article, an even-keeled write-up, just the early facts and nothing sensational. Cor wouldn't have let me keep it otherwise.

Byline: Rory McDaniel.

I hesitated for another moment, and then picked up the phone and dialed the number on the note. An automated voice-mail system picked up, a robot voice inviting me to leave my information. "This is a message for Rory McDaniel," I said. "Amelia Emmet." I added my office phone number and hung up. There. We had shared the same information with each other. If that didn't entice him, her, whoever Rory McDaniel was, I didn't know what would.

I stared at the phone until the object itself grew strange and the regret kicked in. What door had I just opened?

CHAPTER 12

Corrine had a coffee waiting for me when I arrived at the office the next morning. She sat behind her desk with her phone to her ear and hung up when I came in.

"You are an angel," I said, slinging myself into place behind my desk and taking a sip. "And I don't even believe in celestial winged beings."

"None of them came to visit you in the hospital?"

"Only you."

"Thought I'd save you the trip over to Smith."

I hit the power button on my computer, nibbling at the cup's plastic lid. The trip to Smith wasn't that difficult, now that I'd given up on the stairs. "My doctors do want me to walk around," I said.

"The same cranks who told you not to drink with your pain meds? Are we listening to them?" Corrine's phone began to ring. She tapped at her keyboard, shaking her head so that her ponytail swung side to side.

"I'm just saying. You don't have to save the trip—we could walk over together."

"I was over there early."

Cor was no more a morning person than I was. I started to say so, but then I saw the two of us inching our way across the knoll between the two buildings, and everyone pretending not to watch. Being stared at wasn't my favorite pastime, but how did Corrine feel, dragging her feet along after me?

"Thanks. Early bird catches the beans for us both," I said. Cor's cheek turned red. Her phone rang and rang. "Are you going to get that?"

"Students," she said.

"Trying to get into your classes."

"Or out of them." The phone finally stopped. "You had a call earlier. And your student stopped by already."

79

"Which one?"

"Collar buttoned up past the point of being able to breathe?"

"Nathaniel," I said. "My graduate assistant."

"How'd you get a grad assistant?"

"I believe I'm being pitied."

She looked away. At least she hadn't called me lucky again. Sometimes, when she said things without thinking, Corrine seemed younger to me than she was. We were nearly the same age, but she really could pass for one of the students. She had long, messy hair, baby-faced pink cheeks and freckles. We'd been friends the minute she'd joined the faculty. A true friend like I hadn't enjoyed since childhood, she knew my doubts, knew where I'd grown up and how. I could be myself with Cor—my real self, not the face I put on when I walked into the rarified air of Rothbert's country club training ground. The real Amelia Emmet, who wondered if I belonged, who wondered if I would ever feel as though I did.

Sometimes, though, she got things incredibly wrong. Like with Doyle.

When Doyle and I were together, there'd be small slights, little digs and jokes that didn't need to be made. I'd started wondering if Corrine had designs on Doyle, but she didn't seem to see him that way. "Your boyfriend," she'd say, her voice contemptuous. Worried that I'd get some form of nepotism within the department? None of the other faculty showed signs of concern, and, as Joss had pointed out, they'd all known.

"Maybe she's jealous of me, not you," Doyle said once, and I had to think about that long and hard—she hadn't liked Joe much, either— before I dismissed it. I decided the jealousy stemmed from my being in a relationship at all, when she wasn't and, as far as I could tell, hadn't ever been. Cor had grown up in an ivy-covered house far up the lakeshore, a place I'd visited once over winter holidays when I couldn't argue that Christmas Eve alone sounded more fun than hot cider with her family. The opulence astounded me. I spent the evening sneaking away to count bathrooms and trying to justify that Cor, my dearest friend, turned into a petulant teenager in the presence of her parents. And in the presence of my boyfriend. I'd learned to take it in stride. And now it didn't matter.

Her phone started ringing again. She pulled her ponytail tighter and ripped the phone off its cradle. "Hello," she said, her voice flat.

I tried to direct all my attention to my computer. In an office as tight as ours, we had to try not to hear each other's conversations. If my phone rang and it was Doyle calling from off campus, Corrine might choose that minute to walk down the hall to the bathroom or to take a trip to check our mailboxes downstairs. Sometimes her mother called—she always rolled her eyes in the exact same way—and I took my turn giving privacy.

This sounded like a student call, so I stayed put and fired up my e-mail. What with the party and the impromptu happy hour, and then last-minute prep for my classes, I hadn't cracked it yet this semester. I had a plan: Delete everything sent to me prior to a week before this semester started. Anyone who had tried to contact me over the last ten months probably knew by now why I hadn't gotten back to them. Or they were trying to get in touch with me for reasons I didn't care about.

Pages and pages of e-mails disappeared at the click-click of my mouse, but then I reached the files from last fall, then October, then October 11. Messages I should have received along with the rest of the campus—reports of gunshots, emergency alerts to stay inside, high-priority alerts to the inhabitants of Dale Hall to close and lock their doors, not to emerge from their offices no matter what they heard. Bulletins to keep students away from this corner of campus. Alert. Alert.

One e-mail from Doyle, my name in the subject line.

I couldn't read it. I deleted it with the others.

That left me with a manageable amount of correspondence to ignore. I picked up my phone. I had managed to clear out the voice mail in a similar slash-and-burn fashion the day before, but I already had another message. A man's voice.

"—stop—" I heard Corrine say, her voice throwing me for a second. I missed part of my message but caught the name. So Rory

McDaniel was a man. The things you learned in college. Mr. McDaniel seemed to be giving his phone number again, along with information to meet him. Today, the Mill, at a time I might be able to make if I left the moment my class ended. He didn't seem to be asking but telling.

I hung up my phone and thought about that. I wasn't even on the fence: I wanted to stand him up.

"I'll talk to you later," Corrine said under her breath but didn't hang up.

I grabbed my files and textbook, my coffee, my cane. "Class," I said, and ducked out, closing the door behind me, although I was dying to know about Corrine's call. It hadn't sounded like a call from a student after all but sounded, in fact, like a lover's spat. Doyle was married, and Cor had a boyfriend? What else had happened while I was gone?

Outside in the hall, I was met by the pale-lipped co-ed from the past. If these walls could talk—

I didn't finish the thought. I didn't want to hear what these particular walls could say.

CHAPTER 13

I was early to class, but someone else was earlier. Nathaniel paced the hall outside our classroom, his hair flopping into his eyes and his lips moving as though he was rehearsing lines for a play. He looked up, caught me watching. "Did you need something?" I asked. "Dr. Talbot said you came to see me."

He shook his head slowly. "I just—"

"You just came to see if I needed my armed escort to class?" I handed off the stack of papers I'd brought and the key to the door. "You don't need to promenade me from place to place, Nath." I glanced to see what he thought of that. As a nickname *Nay-th* probably belonged to a different name, a different boy, but it saved me syllables and therefore time. Plus, the kid could use a little lightening up. "I'll give you some actual work to do."

He managed the door, flicked the lights.

"Start with those." I nodded to the papers in his hands. "Put one on each desk in the first four rows, and if you see any of the students pick one up to take to the back rows, break their hands."

He laughed. And he hadn't blinked on the nickname. Good boy.

The teacher's desk was a skinny-legged table at the front of the room, cold on the elbows and no bulk to hide nervous hands or jumping knees. I'd have to pull it together. I'd managed a rousing discussion with my grad students the night before, but these were the true customers of Rothbert's wares. These were freshmen mostly, ripe but still attached to the vine, or sophomores shopping around. Some would be sociology majors, but some would be picking up a social science requirement and counting the minutes until they could get back to their theater or marketing majors. Most of them would be too immature for such a rigorous university. But this was the first day, and first days held promise.

For one thing, freshmen were the only people who hadn't lived through last year's gunfire. They didn't know anything about me. I didn't have to start with violence. I didn't have to explain myself.

I sat behind the table and let my cane lie at my feet.

"We'll get back to normal, Nath. I promise."

"It's no problem. Working with you is—interesting."

That was the truth, poor kid. "Let's hope these students think the same thing, without knowing how interesting I am."

They started to filter in, their hulking backpacks over their shoulders. Nath took a seat at the back and shot unwelcoming looks to anyone who edged away from the designated area. Within a minute or so of the official start time, the front four rows were filled with beautiful youth, young people all studiously ignoring me. The promise of a new year.

"I'll call roll in a minute," I said, drawing the languid attention of the room away from their phones and laptops. "For now, let's get to know one another a bit."

I saw Nath look up, his face wide and concerned. I shook my head at him. We weren't going to get to know *me*. "In the back is my esteemed colleague, Nathaniel Barber. Mr. Barber is your teaching assistant for the semester."

Nath brushed the hair out of his eyes and tried to withstand the weight of the entire room's attention.

"I'm Amelia Emmet. How many of you are sociology majors?"

Two students raised their hands, hesitating when they saw that no one else did.

I looked them over. Why so few majors? This was going to be a tough room. "You two, as peers, may well someday call me by my first name, but for now let's all go with Dr. Emmet, and I will extend you the same courtesy." They all stared at me until I began to think I had something smeared on my forehead, something green between my teeth. What had I been thinking? The first day wasn't full of promise. It was full of dread, always the worst, and I was out of practice. "Mr. Barber, will you call roll for us?"

Nath rose and came to the front of the room. I slid the roll sheet toward him, hoping he wouldn't see that my hand shook. "Let's also hear your major and hometown."

"Debra Anderson," Nath said.

One of the sociology majors raised her hand again. "Sociology, and I'm from—here?"

I would never get used to the inflection the young women used—everything was a question. They were certain of nothing. If I did my job right, I might train that uncertainty out of them, but it was only the first week. I wasn't sure I could do my job right. I watched the students shift in their seats, already bored. This was the only thing I could do. What if I couldn't do it?

The sight of my manuscript on the barbecue came back to me. That hollow feeling I remembered from early adventures in shame. Discount lunch hollow, cheap shoes hollow.

"From Chicago?" I said.

The girl nodded. End of conversation.

Nath was staring hard at the list of names.

"Mr. Barber?"

"James Baker," he said. Nath raised his eyes to study the class, zeroing in on the boy who put his hand in the air.

The boy wasn't the baker, but the dough. He was pudgy, with small eyes behind glasses too big for his face. As soon as everyone turned to look at him, he blushed a deep and alarming red. "H-here. I mean. Undeclared." He swallowed hugely and stared at his desktop. He looked like a lab rat. "Pittsburgh."

I'd have to train the girls to speak in the declarative and the boys to speak in sentences—maybe I was in the wrong room, and this was supposed to be an English course. For foreign speakers.

No one here wanted to be a scholar. They'd chosen the class for reasons their parents handed them, or they hoped someday for a job and a paycheck. None of them loved the topic, not even the majors. They had no sense of the scale of the world and how it worked. Or the dangers in it. I saw—

—*the dark hallway, the hand and gun rising out of the blackness*—

Stop.

The walls flying away and the red carpet rushing at my face.

Stop now.

My eyes darted from student to student. I'd hoped the younger students would be my blank slate, but what did we know about any of them? Their backpacks were huge, lurking. They could have carried anything into my classroom.

The next name didn't come. I glanced at Nath and found him watching the previous student like a specimen in a jar. Nath's mouth hung open, as though he were counting his teeth with his tongue.

"Nath?"

His attention snapped back to the list. He studied it for another moment and then went on with the names until we'd learned that the rest of the class studied a varied list of topics and hailed from all over the country. I couldn't concentrate. Criminal justice, one said. I looked up but couldn't even separate the kid from the crowd. Where had these kids been last fall? Had they arrived for a campus tour, eager to choose Rothbert, and been turned away? *Sorry, folks, but for your safety . . .* Had they seen the news online while they researched their college choices? What did they think when they got their Rothbert acceptances in the mail? Why had they chosen to be here? Why had they chosen to be in this room with—of all the professors who taught the intro course—me?

Nath returned to his seat. I'd led this course every semester I'd ever taught, including the years when I was in a position like Nath's. Introductions, outline of the class, the expectations I had for the semester, early dismissal if I needed it. I could do this.

"Sociology is the systematic study of our human society," I started. The words unlocked some deep layer of memory. I spoke from knowledge I'd taken in years and years ago, hoping, for once, that the students weren't paying serious attention. "To study society means that we adopt the sociological perspective. That means we pay close, detailed attention to particular behaviors in particular people in order to find larger truths."

I didn't normally sit during a lecture. Something possessed me to grab my cane and stand before the class. They all looked up from their laptops and phones and watched me excavate myself out of my seat.

They'd know. They either knew already, or by the end of the day they'd find a way.

I imagined the room spilling out and the students returning to their own orbits, the questions they'd ask someone in their dorms or their next classes, the rumors they'd hear, the jokes. Some of them were probably sophomores. They would know. They would tell the others.

The next time I walked into this room, they would all turn to stare.

"We have to dig beyond the easy answer, beyond the assumptions that get categorized as common sense or worse—"

Autopilot failed. I stopped mid-sentence.

I walked the perimeter of the class, buying myself a little time. What had I been saying? Nath's head swiveled to watch me.

"Or worse, stereotype," I said. "We have to look at the ways that society, not individual decisions, determines our lives. Take your situation here at Rothbert. If I asked you how you'd chosen to study here, you might say that one of your parents went here, or that you didn't get into Harvard and this was your second choice." Had I begun to sweat? "But when we look at things from the sociological perspective, we'd have to admit that you're here, first and foremost, because you're a particular age—you're at the age at which people go to college in America."

The room wasn't particularly useful for pacing. I reached one side of the room and turned around to start back. The cane squeaked on the floor.

"Another reason many of you are at Rothbert is that your family can afford to send you here. If they couldn't, you might have chosen from a pool of different schools, based on financial aid considerations. Or you might be looking for a job right now in a terrible economy."

I looked out at the sea of boredom. "But you get a four-year reprieve from that," I said, noticing that none of them as much as blinked. These kids. They really did think the world would be fixed by the time they graduated. Or that it didn't matter if it were still broken. It wouldn't matter to them, because they'd had years of privilege behind them and decades more ahead. I fanned myself and continued, "Someday you'll want a profession of some sort, and the good news is that sociological study is good for lots of careers out in the private sector. Advertising, journalism, law. Any type of work in which it's helpful to understand your fellow man." No reaction, no interest. Nothing. Only Nath in the back nodded. I was definitely sweating. "In other words," I said, "all types of work."

Had I not taken my medication? At the thought of the pills, I believed I could hear them rattling in their bottle. Like Pavlov's dogs, I could feel their texture on my tongue, could taste the bitter orange oval before I swallowed. They were upstairs in my bag. Safe and close, and I didn't even need one now. My pain, already buried under their influence. I ached for them anyway, and for a day when I wouldn't have to know their precise satellite coordinates.

Sweating. Sweating and maybe breathing too hard.

"The study of society can encompass almost any aspect of our daily lives." The room seemed wider now. "What are some of the things you're interested in? Hobbies, habits."

No one spoke. Had they all gone? No, they were all here, staring up at me. I felt as though I were seven feet tall, Alice in Wonderland with the brackish taste of cake in my mouth. Had they always been this far away? Hadn't Nath made them sit in the front rows? "Things you're passionate about," I said. I felt really hot. "Nothing? Nothing interests you?"

One of the students cleared his throat.

"Yes? Did you want to say something?"

He shook his head. They'd all shrunken in their seats, unwilling to share the spotlight. I saw two students exchange confused looks and, sticking out from an open backpack, a *Rothbert Reader*, and my face, glaring.

They knew. They knew, and they were unwilling to associate with me.

I saw them spilling out the door and going straight to the registrar to find another social science course. My classes, diminishing by twos and threes until only Nath and I—

"No one—" Burning hot and then, suddenly, cold. Had someone opened the door?

The hand rising out of the dark, a gun.

I whipped around to see the door, the cane catching on the tile and then free. Something flew at me from the corner of my eye. The cane rattled to the floor, then nothing. Nothing but black and silence.

CHAPTER 14

I woke up in the white room, a hand heavy on my stomach.

I heard moaning. Me. Me, moaning. I blinked into the light until I knew I wasn't in the ICU.

"Dr. Emmet, are you OK?"

"No ambulance," I said. Tried to say.

"Be still now, Amelia."

"Nath."

"Yes." Far above me.

"Nath, dismiss the class."

"They're gone, Amelia. Stay down—"

Doyle?

I sat up, holding my head onto my shoulders with my hands. "What happened?"

"You fell," Nath said.

"Mr. Barber." Doyle knelt next to me. "Could you run down and meet the EMTs?"

"Sure."

"No ambulance."

Nath stopped and looked between us.

"No choice, Amelia. Go on, Mr. Barber."

The door shut behind him. Doyle reached up and took my hand away from my temple. "Is that where it hurts?"

All over, I wanted to say. I hurt all over. The back of my head, the front, my left shoulder. My leg, of course, and pelvis, outside and inside, and deep, deep down.

I could finally open my eyes and see him. I hated his look of concern.

"You have to stop toppling over," he said. "The first time, a bullet, sure. But today? People are going to start to talk."

"Not funny."

"You used to think I was funny."

I hadn't been this close to him in a long time. His nose was pink with sunburn. In good weather, he nearly lived on his boat. "I used to think you were a lot of things."

He wouldn't ask me. Before, he would have asked me for the sake of the conversation and full disclosure and argumentative rhetoric, but I wasn't the before Amelia anymore, and he wasn't the same man, either.

"How did you meet her?"

"Do you want to try to stand?"

"Please tell me I don't know her."

"You don't. Here, let me help."

He steadied and delivered me into a nearby chair.

"Does she have kids?"

"Does the back of your head hurt? Jesus, you took a spill, didn't you?"

"How many?"

He sighed. "None."

That was something. "What do Sarah and Ty call her?"

"By her name."

"Which is?"

"I thought you were hurt."

"I am." So hurt. And like a child, poking at the sore spot. I couldn't tell him how often I wondered if I shouldn't have died on the wine-colored carpet of Dale Hall, if, by living, I had cheated fate or some vengeful god I didn't pray to. That whatever happened after the shooting was my fault, for surviving. When I couldn't sleep, this is what happened. Wound tight in self-pity's clutch, I couldn't separate Doyle's leaving and the gunshot. Had he left me before, or had he walked into my hospital room to say good-bye? Doyle's hand, a gun, rising out of the dark. "I'm hurt. But I'll live."

"Counting on it." He smiled, but I could see how flimsy the offering was.

"How did you meet her?"

"Amelia." He looked tired. Old. Not just older than I was, but a man who'd lived a long time, had maybe given some thought to his own mortality. "Are you getting some help? With all this, I mean, not with—"

"I'm fine."

"It would be normal to falter a bit."

"I don't falter."

The door opened, and Nath came in. He wore a grave face, like a mask he'd put on. "They're coming up the stairs."

"I'm not going to the hospital."

"Insurance purposes," Doyle said.

"I think I've hit the cap on my insurance."

"Not yours. The university's."

"I don't care—"

"Melly." Doyle put his hand on mine. "You don't have to care. I will do the caring."

As always. As ever. He didn't say these things. I heard them in the hollow way he spoke to me now. He'd cared too much for too long, so little in return.

The ambulance crew walked in like frat boys who'd heard rumors of a good party. "Somebody have a fall?" one of them said.

Doyle stood, his hand sliding off mine. "Get checked out. Let me know how you are."

"I'm fine," I said, and wished it were true.

The EMTs let me walk to the elevator, because the gurney didn't fit inside. They seemed to know that already, which made me wonder if one of them had carried me down the Dale Hall stairs last year.

Outside, I threw Nath my car keys. "Come meet me after I'm sprung."

"When will that be?"

"Give them an hour to figure out that my major injuries are preexisting, and then throw a fit in the emergency room until they let you see me. Do you know how to fake a seizure?"

He looked at the keys. "I have something to tell you."

Of course. The kid hadn't signed up for this, had he? "You don't want to be my grad assistant anymore."

"No, I do. It's just—"

"Ma'am." My rescuers held the back doors of the ambulance open. One of them bowed and swept his arm toward the cart inside.

"A minute. What's wrong, Nath?"

"James Baker is in our class."

"I think I recall you reading off that name."

"He was in a different 101 class earlier this week," he said.

"Maybe he liked our schedule better."

"Maybe he liked you better."

"I'm very likeable." One of the EMTs made a sound in his throat. "As a teacher."

"So you don't know him? I mean—I didn't, either, but I'm not the one—"

A chill went up my spine. I knew where we were. "Who is he?"

Nath glanced at the EMTs and back. "Last year, he was Leonard Lehane's roommate."

"Ma'am."

I held out my hand to them. "If I'm holding you up, why don't we just agree to meet there? Nath, are you sure?"

"That's what I heard. I guess if I had to say was I *sure*—"

"But someone told you that's who he was. Could there be another James Baker?"

He shrugged. "Another James Baker in the intro soc course this semester? I guess it's possible."

There were only a few thousand students at Rothbert. I could calculate the actual likelihood, but it was hardly worth the math. Lehane's roommate wanted to get a look at me. Like so many others, he wanted to stare.

Or tell me something.

Or finish what his friend had started.

Now I remembered the kid's pink neck, his rabbit eyes behind thick glasses. He'd sat four feet away and hardly looked in my direction.

"Why?" I said.

"I don't know."

"He sat there for an *hour*," I said. "Was he trying to make some kind of point? Was it—oh, God. Was it a protest?"

"I can find out."

"You can?"

"I can—I can try," Nath said.

"*Professor.*"

I glanced at the EMTs, nodded to them, and then transferred the nod to Nath. "Got a date with a waiting room. Nath, if you can—do you really want to do this?"

He hesitated, but only for a blink. "I do."

"OK, but be discreet. Don't get into any trouble. Don't—Nath. Be cool, all right?"

He thought about it for a second before nodding back, solemn.

I was the one in trouble.

CHAPTER 15

Hours later Nath tracked me down at the hospital, true to his word, and drove me home, quiet and thoughtful when he handed over my keys.

"Do you—" I'd almost asked him in, and for what? "Thanks for picking me up."

"Sure." He looked uncomfortable and eager to get away. "I have— homework." He hitched his backpack over his shoulder and started off toward campus. The poor kid had saddled onto quite a Derby champ, but he seemed to be holding up.

Holding up better than I was. I tapped slowly toward the door to my building, feeling all the places on my body that had been introduced to freefall. Reintroduced.

Plans started to form: hot shower, tumbler of wine, and an extra dose from the pill bottle. How much did I need to take to make sure I slept through the night? I looked at my watch: it wasn't yet five, but I felt as though I'd lived a week in this single, jarring day.

I stopped, glanced at my watch again. I was supposed to be somewhere, and in a rush I remembered that I'd missed my appointment with Rory McDaniel. I would have made it if I'd left straight from class, but I hadn't counted on an ambulance ride or a three-hour wait in the emergency room.

"In all the excitement," said a man's voice. "You probably just misplaced me."

He stood under the awning of my building's back door, flipping a set of keys around his finger.

In this gesture, I saw Doyle, his sheepish good-bye, and was annoyed. I didn't know this guy, but I knew whom he would turn out to be. He was tall, fuller-bodied than Doyle, and wearing a jacket that looked as though it had been handed down from an even taller, bigger brother. Or a Dumpster. He had dark hair, but when he stepped out from the shadow of the building, the scruff on his face caught the sun and glowed a secret red.

"If it makes you feel any better, I also misplaced about twenty-five students," I said. "Did you literally chase the ambulance?"

"You're thinking of lawyers. Reporters sit with their feet up playing computer solitaire until something comes across the scanner."

"Sorry to interrupt your game."

"I never win anyway. Why do we play games against ourselves that we hardly ever win?"

"Did you really want an answer to that?"

He blinked at me. "Am I getting near your research, Dr. Emmet?"

"I imagine you already know about my research."

"I've been looking for a copy of your book—"

"My dissertation is out of print. Why would you want to read about post-traumatic stress disorder? Tough times at the paper?"

"Not that one," he said. "The new one. Maybe you can spot me an advance copy until it's published."

"I don't have another book."

His veneer dropped, showing his confusion. He'd done his own research.

A long time ago, I'd been confident enough to put the working title of my manuscript-in-progress on my faculty web page and in a bio for an industry association site. I'd pulled both of these references since my little patio barbecue, but even without the book, the title lived a life separate from mine. As far as I could tell, that was the purpose of the Internet: to capture everything ever said or done and never let it go.

McDaniel regained his steady, lie-breaking gaze. "So you are not the author of *Silent Witness: The Sociology of Violence in the American Midwest*? That's all just irony?"

I took a few exaggerated, limping steps past him toward my door, letting him get a good look at my cane. "Nice title. I do teach sociology and the social aspects of violence. But you must be misinformed."

"I'm hardly ever misinformed."

"Why did you leave your number on my car?"

"Why did you call me?"

This was all a mistake. I should have never called, and now that he was here—uninvited, now that I thought about it, stalking my apartment for the second time—I wanted no part of this conversation. "I'm the one misinformed. I thought you did car detailing."

"You don't want to tell your side of the story?"

"If I knew my side of the story I wouldn't have called you."

"What's that mean?"

He was handsome, I noticed. Maybe that was part of the problem. I wasn't in the mood for handsome. "There's no story."

"See, that's what people say when there's a story bigger than they know."

"If I don't know—look, Anderson Cooper, I'm sorry I wasted your time—"

"What do you remember about that day?"

"Nothing. That's the truth. I was out cold."

"I wasn't."

The article I'd saved, the photo cropped out to save me from knowing too much, had been published with his byline. "You were there."

He shrugged. "You came over the scanner."

"Lucky you."

"Well, I'm not counting on the Pulitzer or anything. You're not that big a story."

"Then why are you leaving sad notes on a handicapped lady's car?"

"I believe the term you're looking for is *disabled*." He had a crooked smile. Probably got him all kinds of interviews and favors. "And I didn't know my name and phone number could convey such deeply held feelings."

"Why are you here?"

"I'd like to know why you were shot."

I helped myself to the pause in our conversation to punch in my keycode and open the door. McDaniel could be a sociological study all his own. The big-boy clothes, the calculated facial hair. That smile. I tapped inside and turned, my arm holding the door ajar but blocking his entrance. I released the door.

"We want the same things," McDaniel said, moving so that we could see each other through the slowly closing door. "I wasn't misinformed about that, was I?"

I caught the door with my cane. The day I'd had—I couldn't keep living like this. I didn't have time for handsome, but I had all the time in the world for utility. He'd been interviewing people, taking notes. The whole time I'd been in the ICU, he'd been hitting the pavements.

"The Mill at eight," I said, and was gratified to see McDaniel's eyes narrow. Someone else had taken control. I moved my cane, leaving him on the outside.

CHAPTER 16

NATH

She'd skipped right past Nathan to Nath.

I felt like a different person, the kind of guy people would call Nath. Nath—now that I'd heard it coming out of Dr. Emmet's mouth, that's exactly who I was. I practiced being Nath. Nath Barber, walking across campus. Nath Barber, holding the door of the student center for a couple of cute girls coming out, a backward look to see the flip side. Nath Barber, checking the lobby scene of one of the dorms like I belonged. Only a few guys sat watching something loud on the lounge TV. A girl leaned on her elbows at the front desk, thumbing furiously at her phone.

"Excuse me," I said.

The girl looked up against her will.

"Hi."

Her expression stayed blank. Be cool, Dr. Emmet had said. Probably she hadn't realized how tall an order this would be. Nath Barber, playing it cool. "Hi, I'm wondering if you know how to—"

And then I realized I couldn't ask what I was about to ask.

How did I find out which student had been roommates with the kid who'd unloaded a gun on a professor last year? The question alone would put me outside the reach of discreet and way on the other side of cool.

The girl glared. Her black hair grew in careful spikes against her forehead and cheeks. She looked like she was emerging from a mouthful of black teeth.

"Is there a campus directory? For students, I mean?"

The girl sighed. "They put one out every year. But it takes a while?" she said. "We only have the one from last year."

"That's it," I said. I must have sounded too happy. She kept her phone close as she scrounged through a couple of drawers, never turning her back on me. At last she brought a slim booklet to the desk.

"Not supposed to let it leave the desk," she said.

Be cool. I reached over and slid the booklet away from her. "I'll just borrow it *here*, then."

I pulled a stool over to sit across from her and opened the book between us. She dragged her own stool back from the desk and resumed tapping the phone, but with more muscle. Her friends would hear about me.

The directory navigated easily. Within a minute I'd located Leonard Lehane's name, mailbox number in Quinton Hall, and the phone number he had used last year. Under the surveillance of the desk clerk, I took a notebook and pen out of my backpack and copied down the information. Then I turned to the B's and found James Baker. Sure enough, he'd lived in Quinton Hall, too. He had a different mailbox number—I took this down in my notebook—but the same phone number.

I closed the directory and looked at my notes. Nothing to do but call. The desk phone sat inches from my hand. "Can I use the phone?"

I didn't wait to be told the rules.

Someone answered on the first ring. "Yo."

"Can I speak to James, please?"

"Who?"

"James Baker?"

"He doesn't—oh." His voice dropped. "I know who you mean. He's third-floor. Got a single this year."

A single room, as opposed to the troublesome doubles that most underclassmen lived in. A student who'd lived through his roommate's suicide could probably count on some privacy the next year.

I thanked the kid and hung up.

I reached for the directory again and flipped through it until I found a campus map. The little buildings were color-coded and labeled; Quinton Hall was two candy-colored squares away from where I sat.

The girl didn't look up when I slid the directory back across the desk. It occurred to me that she must have lived through Dr. Emmet's shooting—well, not lived through it, since she'd probably been across campus or behind this very desk. Or under it, texting her last words.

I didn't have the nerve to ask what it had been like. How would I ever be able to do field research?

I picked up my pack, thanked her, and struck out through the lobby to the front doors and back outside.

Campus was quiet, but not yet dark. Night classes were in session, but it was still too early for the revelers to be out. I hadn't been at Rothbert long enough to know what the drinking week looked like. Maybe Wednesday was too early to start. I thought longingly of the tight booths at the Mill, where Cara's thigh had brushed up against mine the night before. Cara, Julia, Ryan, even the guy with motorcycle boots— we'd piled into the horseshoe-shaped bench around a single table.

"Do you think she really needs that cane? I heard—"

"She got shot through the gut, man. That's got to hurt."

I'd said as little as possible, thinking of Dr. Van Meter's advice. I only had to decide to pay attention. I studied each peer's face as best I could. Ryan seemed bored. Cara tapped her foot under the table. Julia leaned forward on her elbows, fueling the fire. "Don't you think she must have been banging that kid?"

She must have scored near-perfect on her graduate exams to get into Rothbert, but this was the best she could do.

But then Ryan turned to me. "Hey, what did she want from you?"

The conversation had turned from sleeping with the professor to my relationship with Dr. Emmet much too quickly. The rest of them went silent.

"I'm her grad assistant," I said. They waited. "I picked up her cane for her."

"That is so sad," Cara said. "That poor woman."

Dr. Emmet would've kicked her ass for saying so, but I liked Cara even more. They left me alone for the rest of the night. Somehow, I'd managed to pass some test I hadn't signed up for. A different kind of entrance exam.

Or maybe they were all there right now, this time talking about me.

I found Quinton Hall with no trouble and went inside. When I couldn't locate the stairs, I pressed the elevator button. A couple of students came to wait with me. I let them get into the car first, and one of them obliged by pulling out a key card. All I had to do was pretend to reach for my wallet, let the kid wave me off. "What floor?" he said.

"Three, thanks."

I crossed my arms to keep from fidgeting, but the other students didn't give me another second of attention. When the elevator stopped on the third floor, I stepped out as though I knew where I was going. When the doors closed behind me, I stopped and looked around.

If I belonged here, I would walk with purpose. Would I glance into rooms where the doors hung open? I started off, trying for casual, authoritative. Friendly. Trying for cool.

The hall was long and empty, most of the doors pulled shut. I could hear a few voices, a loud TV. The rooms I could see into were messy, unsettled. Still the first week of classes. These kids didn't seem to know how to be so near one another yet. I started to feel nostalgic about dorm living. Until I remembered that, essentially, I still lived in one.

In one open door, a student sprawled across his skinny bed with a tiny TV propped between his feet. In another room, a guy leaned into his computer screen, his face lit blue. In another open door, a kid dangled from his loft bed, his phone to his ear.

No one stopped me or asked who I was. How easy was this? I thought of Leonard Lehane, hanging around the second floor of Dale Hall, no one asking him what he needed. What if I was someone with a grudge and gun? Bang, that kid loses his game. Bang, the guy hanging out of his bed falls to the floor.

I'd never even held a gun. That night, lost without Bryn, I'd been looking for a way out, but I'd had few options. The glint of metal in the cutlery drawer. Old cold remedies in the bathroom. I'd chickened out. Hands shaking so hard that the medicine cabinet door still didn't hang right. Finding myself in the shaving mirror. *How could I disappear? I want to disappear.*

I stopped. I hadn't been sad, exactly. I'd been—mad. So mad that I couldn't find the end of it.

If my dad was the kind of guy who owned guns, I might not be here. A gun would have worked.

The television voices led me to the end of the corridor, a room with its door open. As I got closer, I could see that the room wasn't a bedroom but a lounge. A group of students played cards at a table in front of the far window. Their voices dropped when I came in. The air seemed electric, but it could have been my nerves. I'd pinned my hopes on flopping down in front of the TV to eavesdrop for a while, but the loud action sequences came from next door. This room had no TV.

Turning to leave, I noticed one of the students had a bright pink neck.

I plucked a magazine off a wall rack. The kid had his back to me, his head down, but I was convinced. It was James. I dropped into the least stained of the lounge chairs and turned a few pages.

"I'm not," one of them said. I glanced over. James's neck had gone violet. "I'm really not," he said.

"We never said you were." I couldn't see the speaker past James, but he had a talk show voice, a soothing coo that made me edgy.

"That's why you're here, then, letting me win dollar poker?"

"We just dig you, James," another student said. He didn't seem to mean it. I peeked at them again. This kid seemed familiar: the way he slumped in his chair, his bored face. Another student from the 101 class, maybe. The guy on the other side of James leaned back and caught me watching. I turned back to the magazine but couldn't focus. He seemed familiar, too. I'd only been in town a week. How many people had I even met, that they were all looking like someone I knew?

"Deal me out," said the talk show host. He stood and stretched at the window.

"Come on," one of the others said. "I'm down twenty bucks."

"I'll pay you twenty bucks to leave," James said. "Each of you."

"You heard the man," the bored one said. "He knows his own mind."

The guy at the window made a noise. The others stood and collected their things. James scraped the cards together. "I'll go get some money."

The bored one snickered.

"Let's just call it even," said the one at the window.

What was I doing? I flipped to the cover. A car magazine, of all things. I hadn't learned anything, and I was trespassing. If I stayed much longer, I'd probably lose what little cool I had.

James said, "You guys can stop coming over—"

"Weren't you going to give us a call?" the one at the window said, loud.

There was a pause in the televised violence next door. I glanced behind me, but they'd all gone. Only the talk show host, James, and me.

"You. Nathan."

I turned. They were both looking at me.

"Nathaniel," I said.

CHAPTER 17

James's face flowered red while I struggled with my memory until at last I placed the smooth-talking guy under the bronze statue with the genuflecting hand, handing me a baggie of magnets and pens. "Oh, right," I said. "You're the—"

James flinched. *Suicide watch.*

"I'm sorry," I said. "I don't remember your name." The other one, the droll one—he'd been under the statue that day, too, begging me to clear the table so he could go. I still had one of their pens in my backpack.

"Phillip," the talk show host said. "And you're in social work."

"Sociology," I said. James's eyes shifted to the side uneasily. "Oh, hey. James, right? I just realized—aren't you in my class?"

"I'm dropping."

Phillip pulled his chair back out and sat. "Did you take on too much?"

"I have a shrink if I need to talk about my *feelings*," James said.

"Are you dropping both sections of the class or only Dr. Emmet's?" I asked.

James's head whipped in my direction. I realized that I'd given away something I hadn't needed to.

Phillip frowned. "Amelia Emmet?"

"The whole class," James said. "It's boring."

"Seemed pretty exciting to me," I said. "What with the teacher passing out."

"You really shouldn't be in that class," Phillip said.

"No shit." The kid's face flared to magenta. "I'm dropping, I said."

Phillip had been watching James, but now he turned to me, his hands clasped on the table. "Now what's this about—fainting?"

"I just wanted to see her." James spoke into his chest. "I won't go back."

"We really need to talk about your decision-making—"

"Shut the hell up, Phillip," James said, lifting his chin so that he was loud and clear. He certainly did know his own mind. "I said I already have a five-hundred-dollar-an-hour friend. An *actual* psychologist."

James apparently knew something of Phillip's own delicate spots. Phillip's mouth twitched with advice withheld. "Well. I'm here if you need me."

"If I ever need you," James said. "I might actually think about killing myself."

"That's the exact thing I'm supposed to report. But I won't. I know you're just saying it to—"

Hurt me. I heard the words as though he'd actually said them. James snorted.

Phillip picked up his book bag. He seemed to want a parting shot. He took a deep breath.

"Good to run into you again," I said.

"I don't think it's a good idea—"

"See you around," I said.

"Fine. James, I'm here if you ever need me. Sincerely." He stalked through the lounge, stopped to shove a handful of brochures into the magazine rack, and was gone.

James and I sat in the silence for a minute or two. I could still hear the TV and, past that, a couple of guys shouting and horsing around in the hall.

"Jesus," I said. "What a jackass."

"Me or him?"

I hadn't won James over. "Him. What did you do?"

"You know." He shuffled the cards into a Vegas dealer's bridge.

"I don't."

"Dr. Emmet." He set the cards back on the table. "I didn't know she would freak out."

"About you?" Now I saw it as James had. The poor kid. Was there any reason to keep him in the dark? But he seemed so glum and pink. "She didn't freak out about you."

"Why else?"

Actually, I wasn't sure. We hadn't talked about it. I wondered now if we ever would. In some ways, Dr. Emmet had pulled me closer, letting me see behind the curtain—but I didn't know what I was seeing or understand it.

"I guess she was—overwhelmed or something. She got hurt last year, you know."

James blinked at me. "I heard."

"Sorry. I know—I mean, I guess it's no secret that your friend—"

"He was no friend of mine." James stood up. "Those dipshits made me miss dinner."

He seemed so young, forlorn. Chubby. I hated to assume that food was important to him, but the evidence was strong. "Do you want to order a pizza?" I said. "I'll treat."

He looked me up and down, until I realized he was calculating his own assumptions. I must not have added up to much. "I'll pay," he said. "You probably need what money you have."

James's room turned out to be the room next to the lounge. When he opened the door, a giant flat-screen TV mounted to the wall exploded in sound: gunshots, screeching tires. James stopped in front of the screen, sniffed at the mayhem, and walked to a desk in the corner where a laptop glowed to life as soon as he touched it. The room was big for student living. Two beds were pushed together in front of the screen. A pile of clothes spilled out of the open closet door. A corner suite, the room had its own bathroom and a double helping of wide windows. The curtains had been pulled back to reveal the dark branches of a tree outside.

"Nice place," I said.

"You know it's a myth, right? That students whose roommates kill themselves get a single the next year? For free? Total lie. My dad had to back up the truck on this one."

The trash was topped with an empty pizza box. I gestured toward it. "It's OK if you'd rather have something else."

"I get pizza all the time. The food here is awful."

I'd only eaten a couple of meals in the dining halls—I ate ramen noodles most of the time—and I hadn't found the food bad. James had different standards. Higher—except he'd seemed sad to miss food he'd written off as bad.

"Did you and Leonard order pizza a lot?"

"That was sloppy."

"What?" But I knew what he meant. I was no—I couldn't even think of a detective. Sherlock Holmes. Was that a real person? I was no Sherlock Holmes.

He held up a single finger, his cell phone to his ear. "Hey, Quinton three hundred-thirty. The usual." He glanced at me. "Make that two usuals."

I went to the window. The tree blocked most of the view James's father had paid piles of money for. He couldn't see the lake or the skyline of Chicago, any of the stuff from the brochure. Down below, a walking path led away from Quinton Hall and toward my apartment. Dale Hall peeked out of the trees, a light on in one second-floor window. If I hadn't dropped Dr. Emmet at home myself, I might have wondered.

"At my old school," I said. "The rumor was that you got a four-point-oh. Automatically."

"For a roommate?"

"Yeah. My roommate was a dick. He never would have killed himself. He didn't want to hold me back, though. If I had the inclination." I felt as though I were doing lines from a script, but this was actually true. My freshman roommate was the one who told me the rumor. *If you kill yourself, I get on the dean's list.* He hadn't started a campaign or anything, but when he went on academic probation that winter, I knew what he was thinking.

"I already had a four-oh, and I'd have a single this year anyway," James said. "I hated Leo. He could have saved himself the trouble."

"You hated him?"

"Don't get excited, Matlock." James sat back in his chair and turned his eyes to the TV. "He shot himself. But yeah. He was a loser."

James Baker had some nerve calling someone else a loser. What qualities would make Leonard—Leo?—unworthy of James's friendship? "Was he poor?"

"I have no idea. Probably not—RB's not for charity cases, is it?" He glanced at me, looked me up and down, shrugged. "Not usually, anyway. He cried."

"He—cried? When?"

"All the time, I mean. He cried all the time."

I'd assumed that Leo had emotional problems—you didn't raise a gun to your own head without a certain level of anxiety—but this was news I hadn't heard anywhere else. "About what?"

James finally glanced from the screen, surprised. "How well do you think I knew him? Jesus."

"You lived with him—"

"For less than two months, man. Random freshman roommate assignment, I pull the short straw, and ten weeks of listening to him cry later, I'm that guy. Forever. I didn't know him, and I didn't want to."

"Why did you switch to Dr. Emmet's class?" I said.

He'd been pumping himself up, gaining against what little leverage I'd come in with. Now he faltered. "Coincidence."

"Nope. Different class on Monday, but then your name shows up—"

"Fine. I wanted to see what she was about. Leo killed himself over her, right? I wanted to catch a glimpse before I dropped the class. Dropped both the classes. Man, it's so *boring*—"

"Why do you think Leo killed himself over her?"

"That's what everyone says."

"Did he ever mention her?"

Something ka-boomed on TV. We both turned to watch a bus crash into a building. "That's filmed in Chicago," James said. "See that high-rise? Downtown on the river."

"I haven't been downtown yet."

"You should go," he said. I had a vision of James's life just then. Things were both incredibly easy and incredibly difficult for him, but he didn't care how anyone else lived. He didn't like people enough to live with a roommate or to take a single class on how they lived and interacted. Leo, me, any other human. No one else was worth his notice.

"Did Leo ever mention Dr. Emmet?"

"Not to me. But I wasn't his best friend."

My pulse quickened. "Who was his best friend?"

"He didn't have one." James didn't even glance up from the flaming bus. "As far as I could tell, he didn't have any friends at all."

CHAPTER 18

I didn't stay for the pizza. James hardly noticed I was going. No one stopped me on the way out to see who I was or what I was doing there, which was lucky since I'd lost track of the answers. Dr. Emmet would be relieved to hear that James had no ulterior motives. I had done the thing I'd offered to do.

But still, I felt as though I'd left something unfinished.

I found the stairs down to the lobby and my way outside. The path back to my apartment took me under James's window, lit by the shaking white light of bus explosions.

After only a couple of steps toward home, I stopped. The last thing I wanted was to go up to my room and find Kendall there. To hear all the ways in which I failed his esteem today.

A breeze blew in from the lake. I turned that way, pulling up the collar on my fleece. The shore was mostly deserted, except for some girls walking in close formation, then a couple holding hands. The guy blinked at me, ready if I turned out to be a challenge. I hadn't known how suspicious wandering in the dark could be. Were my clothes really that bad?

Rothbert's land grant came to an abrupt stop at the lake's edge, a twenty-foot cliff over a meager beach below. There was a dock somewhere, I'd heard. I peered over the edge. Darkness, a weak tide. One tiny slip, and how long would it take for someone to notice I hadn't made it back?

The hairs on the back of my neck rose. What if? There was something attractive about it. Student missing. The police called. Prayer vigils and search parties.

I toed the edge of the grass, easing my weight over until I felt the ground give. My foot slid a few inches down the embankment, and I landed on my ass, fists full of long grass.

"Hey," someone said. A jogger, strips of reflective material up his arms and legs. In the near dark, he looked like a stick figure. "Are you OK?"

"Me? I'm fine."

He didn't believe me, but why would he? I stood, dusted my hands off, and started back toward town, my pace picking up.

I cut through the neighborhood of old houses west of campus. The houses here seemed built out of the bedrock, tall and watching. Some of them were built luxurious, others severe and frowning toward the sprawling mess of the college. Windows glowed behind thin curtains. I caught a movement inside one house and wondered what it would be like to live there, to be in Willetson under another, permanent arrangement. To know that you had finally landed where you would stay.

A sudden memory came to me. My dad coming back from somewhere, opening the front door dressed in stiff clothes I'd never seen before. My mother waited to hear what he said, but I only wanted him to go away again. We'd been having a good time, my mother crawling with me under the fort we'd made with blankets and the cushions from the couch. My lips stung from a Popsicle. I hadn't cared what my dad had to say. Now that I cared, I couldn't recall what the verdict had been, what words my mother waited to hear.

When was this? When had my dad ever owned a suit? The longer I tried to pry the memory out, the deeper it dug in. I turned to look at another twilit house, imagining the welcome mats just inside, other families waiting for arrivals, other dads coming home with disappointment on their faces—

Not in the cards. That's what he'd said. Whatever that meant.

The Mill was busy. Wednesday was not too soon to start the weekend. Most of the people crowding the bar and the tables at the front looked younger than I was, too young to be carrying legitimate IDs. A few of them even wore Rothbert-red shirts. No one cared. They had found themselves a boisterous, fun time here at the Mill, as dark and local as it had seemed to me yesterday.

I worked myself toward the bar in increments, rewarded at last when two girls sitting at the bar stood and left. I grabbed one of the stools and put my back between me and everyone else. The tremendous noise made me wonder if I'd stumbled into a different bar altogether, if I shouldn't squeeze back outside and go home. Kendall would be there, but here I was crushed into a narrow room full of Kendalls.

Someone nudged into the slim space between me and the next seat. The bartender, a bald black guy with muscles that made me wonder if he dead-lifted full kegs, took that moment to ask me what I wanted, and the other guy, bumping into me, reached in. "The weiss ale," he said.

"Hey," I said.

It was Phillip from the suicide watch.

"And whatever he wants," Phillip said.

"The same," I said.

The bartender stepped away, and I shot Phillip a look. "Leave a little room, will you?"

"Could tell you the same thing." Here, among the fake IDs, Phillip seemed tired, more weathered, older than I'd thought. A wizened grad student who never left? Maybe he was a professor. His arms were thin and roped, like the guys from my high school who took advanced shop classes. His voice was easy and confident, but he couldn't seem to sit still. He tapped the bar, bounced his knee. I wondered how a guy like Phillip got involved in the campus suicide brigade. That couldn't be a good story. "He's at risk, you know," he said. "I'm just trying to ensure he makes it."

"He doesn't seem like the kind to off himself."

"They never do." Our beers came, and Phillip waved me off. "You can get next."

The implication being that Phillip and I would be having another beer together, either tonight or at some future event. I took a regretful drink. As much as I needed to meet new people, I couldn't imagine hanging out with a suicide counselor. That, I didn't need.

"What about Leo Lehane?"

Phillip cut his eyes at me over the rim of his beer, taking his time. At last he thumped his glass down. "What business is it of yours?"

"Not my business. Except that you were trying to educate me, and I need an example. Did Leo Lehane seem like the kind of—"

"Leo was a troubled guy."

"You're the expert," I said. "What kind of trouble?"

"Are you one of those guys who stops at accidents to gawp and get in the way?"

I had to think about what to say, because I was. Not car accidents or if a kid ran his motorbike into someone's grandma, but if blood and guts had spilled, I was interested. But only if the guts had long been cleaned up, the players gone to hell and infamy. In my desk drawer, along with my dossier on Dr. Emmet, I also kept a list of locations to visit while I lived so near Chicago. Capone's grave, a speakeasy that had been turned into a neighborhood sports bar, the places where the bad guys had gotten theirs from other bad guys. Dark alleys and bright courtyards and little unassuming bungalows in the suburbs, places that had been swept of their history and spots that had sunk only lower since they'd made their way into the books.

"Violence is a social construct."

Phillip wiped his face with his hand. "Have you ever been in a violent situation?"

Somehow I didn't think being shaken down for lunch money back in junior high counted. "James said that Leo used to cry," I said.

"James might be a liar. Did you think of that?"

"He says he's fine. Truly, he seems like a dude who thinks too highly of himself to deprive the rest of us of his company."

Phillip shot me a look. "You seem like that to me, too. Have you ever had suicidal thoughts?"

I concentrated on my glass. "Hasn't everyone?"

"Not real thoughts. Not serious ones. If you'd had serious thoughts—"

"I'd know?"

"You'd know how lucky you are to be sitting here."

Sitting with Phillip didn't make me feel lucky at all. Less than a week into the best years of my life, and all I did was dangle off precipices and hang out with the teacher. Or whatever Phillip was. But I knew what he meant. *I want to disappear. How do I disappear?* Lucky to have come to Rothbert, lucky to have met Dr. Emmet and people like Cara and Kendall, lucky to take a deep breath and be able to notice things like being able to take a deep breath, being able to make decisions as simple as whether or not to shave. To get out of bed. And then to progress so far as to move to a new city, to step out of the dark place and find something that interested me. I'd been down the rabbit hole, but I didn't want to tell this nut about it. Besides, that was behind me. "Have you had suicidal thoughts? Real ones?"

"Yes."

He waited for me to ask. Great effort went into not asking.

"These students," he said. "Sometimes they're a mess. Sometimes they fool you. Sometimes they convince you. I had to let myself into a student's room once because he'd convinced everyone else that he was fine. He wasn't fine."

So Phillip wasn't a student. I didn't think he was a professor either. I was beginning to understand that the suicide watch wasn't his activity or his hobby but his life. Somehow this was worse than hanging out with the teacher. "Is he fine now?"

"I believe he's an investment banker now." He nodded at my empty glass. "Next time?"

"Yeah."

Phillip slid off his stool and hitched his bag over his shoulder. "No matter how healthy you think James is, he shouldn't be in that class."

"He said he'd drop it."

"If he doesn't," Phillip said. "Could you please let me know? As a friend?"

Friend of mine, friend of James. I wasn't sure I wanted to be either. "He'll drop."

"You seem pretty sure of how well you know James."

Maybe that was what I meant, that I knew the kid already. Or I recognized him. James liked his comforts, and being near Dr. Emmet hadn't given him anything but a rash.

"I'll let you know."

Phillip thanked me and left. I stared at my empty pint glass until the bartender came back. I either had to order another or head out, and my head was too full to shut myself into my claustrophobic corner of my room. I held up a finger for another and reached for my wallet.

Over the bartender's shoulder, I saw someone else gesturing toward the bar.

Dr. Emmet.

She hadn't caught the bartender's eye, but she caught mine, and blinked at me as though she were sending semaphore messages.

Dr. Emmet, and some guy.

CHAPTER 19
AMELIA

Rory McDaniel proved to be sharper than I'd hoped.

We'd slid into the booth at the back of the Mill and settled what we wanted with Joe, who gave me an inscrutable look, and then the reporter turned on me, on the record from the word go. "I figure you've got very little to bring to the table."

"I am the table, pal." That didn't sound exactly how I'd wanted it to. "This is my life. I own this."

"I would have said that Leonard Lehane owned this."

"I'm his heir, and this is my legacy." I reached for my cane and tapped it on the underside of the table.

"What do you remember?"

"Not a thing."

He shrugged. "Not very useful. I could do this without you."

"Drink both the beers, then. I'll go home." I started my retreat from the booth. He didn't stop me. "Are you going to call me back just as I get to the door? Because you could help a handi—a disabled lady out and not make her get up if she doesn't have to."

"Fine." He tented his hands at me. "Tell me what you remember —*really*."

I sat back. I'd spent the last ten months trying not to remember anything from that high back shelf of memory. Now I'd sit here with a stranger and let myself relive the trauma? After the day I'd had?

But the highlight reel engaged anyway. Black hallway, gun rising. A face above me as I lay on the floor—just beyond memory's reach.

Joe came with our beers. I watched the muscles in his arms. When he left, I steadied my hand and reached for my bottle. "What are you bringing to this endeavor, then?"

"Mobility?"

"Screw you," I said.

"Checking for a sense of humor. That's a no, then." He picked at his beer wrapper with a thumbnail, his jaw set. "I've been working this story since the first siren, read every word written about it—wrote the rest—and I have to tell you: Something stinks."

"Did you seriously just say, 'Something—'"

He flicked a hand at me. "You know what I mean. What does your gut tell you?"

My gut had a hole in it, an affliction never more than a few seconds from the top of my mind. If I'd ever had any intuition to speak of, it had probably leaked out along with ninety percent of my original blood supply, most of my reproductive organs, and six inches of my intestines.

"I'm feeling pretty literal these days," I said. "You don't want to talk guts with me. Why don't we stop asking each other questions and start talking?"

"That was a question." He took a long draw on his beer, his mouth twisted into a smirk on the bottle, and then put it down with what looked like resolve. "Leonard Lehane didn't have any friends to speak of, didn't do too well in school, probably died a virgin. He kills himself. I can believe that. I can willingly believe that. But he didn't seem like the kind of guy to take anyone with him. And if for some reason he thought the afterlife would be lonely, why did he decide to march over to a corner of campus he didn't visit often, if ever, and take along someone he'd never met?"

"That's also a question." This was the exact doubt on my mind, but I felt pressured to take the other side. This reminded me of Sunday mornings with Doyle, the paper spread out between us. We hadn't been one of those lovey-dovey couples. When we talked, we locked horns, even if one of us had to slip into devil's advocate to hold up the banter.

I missed him. What would he tell me to do about all this? I didn't want to know. "Maybe Leo didn't want to kill someone he knew," I said. "Too difficult. Too messy."

"Why did he want to kill anyone at all?"

Virginia Tech. Northern Illinois. The shooting from the bell tower at that university in Texas back in the '60s that had forever marred the concept of having a bell tower around. Campuses like Rothbert attracted lots of high-strung people unaccustomed to concepts like failure. They wanted to stand out and found themselves in a crowd of people just like themselves or worse—smarter, more driven, more connected, more successful. "If he kills himself, who cares? If he takes someone with him, people notice. Kilroy was here?"

"That's the typical theory, but I'm not sure it fits."

Typical. At first I thought Rory had zeroed in on my train of thought. Everyone wanted to fit in, but no one wanted to be average.

But he didn't mean Leo was typical. He meant I was.

I taught at one of the preeminent higher education institutions in the country. I had a doctorate. I had theories that were far beyond *typical*. This McDaniel person, this reporter? I was supposed to take him seriously, with his messy haircut and his big brother's suit jacket? He didn't know how thin the ice under his feet had become. I couldn't make a smooth exit, but I could still leave.

"Typical theories are typical not because they're pedestrian," I said, "but because the simplest theory is often the right one. It's not bad science to think about the general by looking at the particular. It's sociology. Are you buying?"

Rory, for the first time, looked as though he'd lost his script. He blinked at me, fumbling for his wallet. "Sure, OK. I didn't mean to—"

"Let me get his attention." I watched Joe's profile, waiting for him to look my way. He was a profile sort of guy, chiseled, aloof. He'd never needed to hire a bouncer for the bar. But he'd always looked my way. My first years at Rothbert, before dating Doyle, I'd been a more *regular* regular of the Mill. Joe and I'd had lots of time to build up to, execute, and recover from a raging, no-strings-attached affair. He harbored a sixth sense for when I sat on the other side of an empty bottle.

The bar was busy, everyone standing shoulder to shoulder. That's when I saw Nath. He looked miserable, wedged in between strangers at the bar.

"I didn't mean to offend you," Rory said.

"You could never offend me."

"I'm not sure you mean that in the good-natured way of friendship. Let me start over—"

"Don't bother," I said. "I've had the typical response, but you— you're special."

"At last she notices." He sank the rest of his beer and sat his empty bottle next to mine. I couldn't help thinking he'd turned the bottles into symbols, aligning us. I resisted the urge to move mine away. "I think the kid had a reason for shooting you. I just can't figure out what it was. And I don't know how to."

"Besides asking me. Which you haven't done." I glanced back at the bar, but Joe was busy. Nath was talking to someone I couldn't see, looking squeezed and put-upon.

"Did you have a relationship with Leonard Lehane?"

"Nope."

"You'd never met him before?"

"Not that I know of."

"Never had him as a student?"

"Surely you checked that out." Joe was turned steadfastly away. We didn't have our understanding any longer.

The cane. The cane changed everything.

"Am I not asking the magic question?" Rory said.

He had my attention. "What does that mean?"

"The unasked. The one question no one has asked you that you would answer yes to. Instead of nope, no, no way."

Doyle, our bed, my head lying on his arm, asking me again. *Will you never say yes to me?*

I struggled to fold that memory, put it away. That one could go to the back of the shelf, no problem.

"If there's a magic question, I don't know it." One more try at Joe. I held up my hand, ready to wave, as I watched him scan the room. And then, beyond him, Nath's eyebrows shot behind his floppy hair. He'd seen me.

My hand hung in the air. Did I want Nath to come back here or did I want him to stay where he was? It didn't matter. Nath had Joe's attention. He pointed back to us and began making his way through the crowd.

"My student," I said.

"That's what I asked," Rory said.

"No—this student."

Nath stepped up to the table, Joe just behind with three beers.

"I thought you'd be in bed," Nath said to me.

Everyone froze. Finally Joe set the beers down. "I'll put these on your tab."

Nath's face glowed neon.

"Your students are very attentive, Dr. Emmet," Rory said, his voice as greasy as a butter knife. "Is that—typical?"

CHAPTER 20

Nath, eyes shifting all around, struggled for his footing. "I meant—you should take care of yourself. Dr. Emmet."

"Nathaniel is my teaching assistant," I said. "He had to witness my—accident." The word didn't come easily. "Today."

"Indeed." Rory slid deeper into the booth, making room. "Won't you join us? Nathan, was it?"

This was too much. "Wait—"

"Nath." The kid swung his backpack under the table and plopped down across from me.

"Rory McDaniel."

They shook hands, McDaniel amused. Nath's jaw squared. If he hadn't wanted to join us, he could have stayed at the bar. I wished he'd stayed at the bar. How had I let this get away from me? "OK, look—"

"So what happened today, Nath?" Rory took one of the beers and held it out. Nath took one of the bottles still on the table and handed it to me, then grabbed the last for himself and drank. Rory was left holding his own beer.

"Dr. Emmet led a terrific lecture on beginning sociologic theory."

"And then?"

"McDaniel," I said.

Nath didn't look in my direction. "Her cane got caught up and she fell and hit her head."

I liked the way Nath told the story. I tried to retrieve the memory, but all I came up with was the red carpet of Dale Hall rushing at me. I had no highlight reel from today. I'd been unconscious before I hit the ground.

"That must have hurt." Rory turned to me now. The smirk was invisible, tucked away in his voice.

My hand shot to the back of my head. I hadn't needed stitches, but, yes, it hurt. "Is that funny to you?"

He shot a sideways look at Nath. "Some things are funny."

I put my beer down.

"Dr. Emmet," Nath said. "Are you OK?"

Not OK.

Nath leaned across the table. "Do you need to go home?"

I did. I needed to go home, before I'd agreed to come here, before I'd had a single word with Rory McDaniel. And come to think of it, if we were choosing moments to return to in order to choose another way, how far back would I go? To the evening I'd gone into the office for a late errand and stumbled into Leonard Lehane's troubled life? To the day I'd sent Doyle on his way, his key ring one key lighter? To a moment so far behind me I couldn't remember, when I'd chosen this left instead of that right, and had ended up being this Amelia Emmet instead of another? I'd always thought myself lucky to have found the right path, the right version of myself, but now I wasn't sure. I was no longer the person I was lucky to be.

"Yeah, Dr. Emmet, maybe Nath here should take you home."

"I can get home on my own. Nath, I'm sorry to take you away from your friend."

Nath blinked. "He's—no friend of mine."

"That's good to hear," Rory said. He grinned at us, tipped his beer back and emptied it, watching to make sure he had our attention.

"What?" Nath said.

"Good to know you're not hanging out with that crowd, is all," he said. "A guy hangs out with that group too much, sometimes he takes them up on it."

Nath's mouth opened and closed, opened again. "Leo."

"Leo, is it," Rory said.

I was lost. "Someone?"

Both men turned to me, but Rory had the advantage. He wanted to tell me. Nath clearly didn't.

"Nath's drinking buddy runs the suicide watch on campus. He had a rather big setback last year."

I looked at Nath. So did Rory, and in the split second I had with

Nath over the table, I shook my head. One, two almost imperceptible shakes, but he saw me, understood enough to close his mouth and tuck his surprise away. He sat back in the booth. "Is that his deal?" Nath said, his voice gone smooth. "The guy kept trying to give me a pamphlet."

If sociology didn't work out, he had a future on the stage. Or as a con man.

Rory checked us both. "I'm a reporter, kid. I pay attention. You weren't talking to that guy? For a half hour?"

"He was really persistent."

I hardly heard what Nath said. My mind raced ahead. If Leonard Lehane had been under the suicide watch, what did that mean? What did that group know? And how could I get them to tell me?

Nath shot me a confused look from under his hair. He gave me an idea. "We shouldn't make light of it. Depression. It's a—serious issue. Nath. You should maybe—maybe you should take the pamphlet."

"I should?"

"Next time you get a chance. Get some help with your—situation."

Nath swept at his hair and glanced uncertainly at Rory.

"Nath. Friend. Are you having sad times?" Rory waved his hand in the air to fetch Joe's attention. "Will a brewski cure it?"

"Brewski," I said. "And you work with words?"

"And you work with people?"

"I study people."

Across from me, Nath leaned over the table.

"Through a long-range scope?" Rory said.

"Clearly, you have more people skills."

Joe came to the table with bottles hanging from between his fingers. "Another round?"

"I think I've had enough," I said.

"I think," Nath said. He swallowed hard, raised his eyes to me. "I think I'm going to kill myself."

My car was outside. For the second time in one day, I handed Nath the keys. McDaniel sauntered past us to his own car, the imp's grin still playing at his lips. I watched him open the door to a bright yellow Jeep. A Peter Pan complex, on top of everything else.

I waited until he was gone. "You were playing the game in there, right?"

Nath walked to the driver's side, holding the keys up to the streetlight.

"Nath," I said. "You don't really—"

"Of course not." A bit snappish. He had the car open, the lock undone for me. I held my breath to slide in. My apartment lot was hardly a quarter mile away, but I'd driven and was grateful I had. The concierge service I'd come to expect from Nath embarrassed me. I couldn't walk a quarter mile? A thousand nights like this, I'd taken the long way home, on foot, trying to find a spot between the bar and my apartment where the light pollution didn't block out the stars. The rocks. The rocks at the lakeshore were best, and if I'd had enough beer or a little too much, I often walked past my neighborhood and around campus to the lake. The water, black, whispered upon the shore.

The dark water had been the companion of my recovery, from my hospital room, late at night when I should have been resting. But I rested all day. At night, I lay awake. On hard days, I found myself charting out an academic article on suicide practices. Self-immolation, seppuku, the new-fangled assisted sort. So many hard days.

Luckily I'd already passed my own darkest hour.

I'd never told anyone about it. I didn't have the right words to explain what I'd come to think of as the black room. The white room was where I finally woke up, but before that—the black. No windows, no doors, no visitors, no cards from emerging feminists. It wasn't even a room, but a box, a sack, a skin. No light, no air, and the only thoughts I had were sharp. Could I even call them thoughts? I wore them, breathed them. They clawed their way out of my mouth in the form of a scream and wrapped around me, until that was all there was. It wasn't hell. And when I woke up in the white room, that wasn't heaven. Both seemed to me now like real places I'd visited, although I only had proof of one. The hand, in the white room. The heavy hand on my chest that held me to the earth. A real hand, a real room. The other place—I hated to admit it, but I thought I knew where I'd been. If I had even been *I*— the soul of Amelia Emmet, the anima that separated me from the pro- verbial clay. Given the chance to sink into itself, the piece of me that made me myself had gone to ground. Minutes? Hours? Days? I don't know how long I stayed there, locked inside the black room, where the worst pieces of myself lived.

That room had been death itself, and I'd made it out. I'd never choose to go back. As hard as my recovery since the black room had been, I'd never had an authentic suicidal thought.

"Did you know that guy at the bar or not?" I said.

"James Baker is dropping your class."

I glanced at his profile, lit from the dashboard. He looked tired for someone so young. "How many new friends did you make today?"

"Like, eight. But they won't be calling."

"James is in with the watch, as well?"

"It's like they're trying to recruit him. To kill himself."

I think I'm going to kill myself. Nath and I had understood each other in the bar, but did we really? I wasn't sure I understood what we were doing myself. I had no idea what happened to a Rothbert student who voiced suicidal thoughts. What had I imagined? That we'd go undercover in the suicide watch, he and I? Who did the watching, and what did they watch for?

"How far are we taking this?" I said.

We had come to my lot. Nath, the chauffer, already knew where to park. He killed the engine, pulled the keys, and handed them to me. "I'd like to stop before the trigger pull, if that's OK with you."

"Not funny." I thought of my mother, my father, beloved people who had died real and complicated deaths too early. What was I courting? I'd faced death once, and once was enough. I said, "Let's just forget it—"

"He never said anything about working with Leonard Lehane,"

Nath said. "That's weird, right?" He tapped his hand on the wheel. "Or is that, like, professional courtesy? Don't bring up your failure rates while talking to a new customer?"

How had we even come this far? "Listen. Let's stop this. James Baker is out of the class. That's all I needed. The rest of it—I might have to live with a certain amount of ambiguity."

Nath shook his head.

"You have better things to do, for one thing," I said.

He got out of the car, so I followed. My body creaked, stiff and complaining. I should have been in a hot shower, in bed. Instead: a late night, a bar, and nothing had come from it but the end of the line.

"Better things, sure," he said.

"Right, Nath? We have a class to run, and you have enough to do. Classes, research. I could put together a reading list for you."

For a moment, Nath seemed not to know where he was. "Reading list."

"And friends, Nath. Girls. Or—it's not all about reading and study. You didn't come here for this. You're a young man, smart and attractive." He blinked away. One or both of us might have been blushing. "And young. Your life is wide open. God, you don't even know it. That's how young you are."

"Sometimes," he said. "I wish I could skip over this part."

"Which part?"

"Nothing," he said. "Never mind."

Youth was wasted, et cetera. "You should be having the time of your life."

"I'm not, though," he said. "That's—that's the part. All the parts where I'm almost, not quite, not—"

He shoved his hands into the pockets of his jeans and scuffed a tennis shoe back and forth on the concrete. The noise satisfied an itch, brought us back to this moment. Here we were: alive. The kid didn't even know how tenuous a grasp we had on all this, all the parts he wanted to leapfrog over.

But I had to admit—I'd been where he was. Life being so short, if you knew where you wanted to be, who wouldn't want to skim a bit for the action scenes?

"It's been the weirdest day," I said. "I just need to sleep."

He stared at the ground.

"Promise me, OK, Nath? Let's forget about the suiciders and get back to our healthy, normal, pedestrian bleak thoughts."

He looked up, surprised. And laughed.

Good boy.

PART II

CHAPTER 21
NATH

I t was October before I realized I'd never made it back to downtown Chicago. One Saturday morning I slipped out of my room before Kendall was up and took the train to the city.

After a few hours of the wind whipping at my jacket, I ducked into a dirty theater playing old slasher flicks and tried not to pay attention to the company I was keeping. A flier in the lobby led me to a downtown spot where a company ushered tourists onto a bus tour of old crime scenes. I knew it would be embarrassing, but I wanted to see as much as I could. Two guys dressed in striped, double-breasted suits ran the show. They gave the ladies fake red roses and played a recording of machine gun rat-a-tat to signal everyone in the bus to duck. I couldn't bring myself to play along.

We made a circuit, scooping up bus window views of the old shops in Little Sicily where the big names had smoked cigars and ordered hits. One of them was now a restaurant with a two-hour wait list. We slowed down for a look at the empty lot where the St. Valentine's Day Massacre happened, and the woman next to me clucked her tongue. "There's nothing there," she said. I could have explained to her. Nothing stays the same. But she had other evidence. We'd already passed the Biograph Theater, where John Dillinger bled out. They still put on shows at the Biograph.

After the bus dropped us where we'd started, I walked the eight blocks or so back up Michigan Avenue to get a closer look at one of the stops, a church that had been shot up in a mob confrontation. New stone steps covered most of the old damage, but one hole, high in the façade, couldn't be disguised.

I reached up and stuck my finger into the hole.

I expected to—feel something. Some momentous connection to history and infamy. Some sense of danger.

Hayseed, come to the city to stick his finger in a Capone bullet hole.

I felt only disappointment, but I'd started to get used to that. Things at school had settled into a pattern. Class. Class with Dr. Emmet. Study. Class with the undergrads. More class. Writing papers. Grading papers. Taking questions on assignments from 101 kids who really didn't care about sociology or want to do their own work. I'd gone for a beer at a bar across town with Cara and the others from our research course and managed not to embarrass myself or bring up Dr. Emmet. My days took on a plodding simplicity. Everything dropped into schedule. Everything settled. Everything except me.

I'd overslept twice the week before, late enough that I'd missed a study group for the introductory class and had to reschedule six pissed-off freshmen. I'd locked myself out of my room more times than I liked to think about.

That night at the Mill with Dr. Emmet, I'd seen my opportunity. If I could get in with Phillip's group, I'd know everything I ever wanted to know about what happened to Leo, what happened to her. I'd pretend to need their help. I wasn't sure how much I needed to pretend at this point.

"What gauge did they use, Professor?"

I yanked my finger out of the bullet hole. Of course it was the reporter from that night—Dr. Emmet's friend, though she didn't seem to like him. I'd seen him three times since then. Just now, I realized those sightings weren't a coincidence.

Professor. Soon enough, and he'd still be doing the obituaries. "Tommy gun. What are you doing here?"

"The *Trib* offices are just down Michigan."

"Yeah? But don't you work for the *Willetson Weekly Thrifty Pages*?"

"Ouch, kid. Yeah, I work for the *Courier*. I had a meeting in the city today."

"Did you also have a meeting in two other places where I would be this week?" I said.

He nodded. "You're pretty keen, then. That's good. Can I be honest with you?"

"My guess is no."

He shook his head and broke into a grin. "You sociologists are of a cloth, aren't you?"

I didn't trust the smile. I knew there were guys who smiled for anything, because their lives had given them nothing but good news. Good-looking guys who let their hair grow a little long, shaved half as often as they should, showed up everywhere expecting to be let in. Rothbert crawled with them.

"I got the feeling you and the good doctor Emmet had some mighty plans," he said. "I like mighty plans." He walked to the cathedral stairs and dropped onto a low step. "But Jesus—no offense, Hail Mary—was I wrong. The two of you mope around like all the air's been sucked out of the atmosphere. What are you doing?"

I glanced back at the hole. He'd seen me doing it. "Seeing the sights?"

"No, I mean what are you doing about this Leonard Lehane thing?"

"Nothing. She told me not to."

"What is she doing?"

I glanced at my watch. "She's probably grading quizzes—"

"Dipshit. Keep up here. What is she doing about the Leonard Lehane thing?"

"Why should I tell you?"

"So she's doing something," he said.

"No. But if she were, I still wouldn't tell you." Who was the dipshit here? Not me.

McDaniel eyed me. "You're awful protective of your teacher."

I shrugged. She was my research subject, not his.

He shook his head and gazed across the street. "You hear about the flower shop used to be there?"

"The mob one." I sat on the top step. "They come to get the flowers for their buddy's funeral, and the guns open up."

"Chicago used to be one of those places where you could be in the wrong place at the wrong time. You know what? It still is. Anybody wanted to kill me, and they were looking for a chance, they could roll by right now, reach out with a gun, take me down. You'd be toast, too, a casualty. Still happens."

"Who'd want to kill you?"

McDaniel leaned back on his elbows. "My ex-wife has some ideas."

"What'd you do?"

He leaned toward me. "Trade you. Fact for fact."

"I don't care that much." I stood to leave. My next stop was a sports bar that used to be a speakeasy. Burgers, fries, and a secret passageway in the basement for rum running.

"You're a hard case."

On the bottom step, I paused. My dad said the same thing. "What do you mean by that?"

"I don't know what makes you tick. Not sure I want to know." He yanked his head toward the bullet hole. "But I was sure about one thing, and now I'm not sure."

I waited. He let me. "What?"

"I thought you wanted to help Dr. Emmet." He stood and dusted himself off. "But I must be wrong."

"You can't possibly believe that's going to work. Just because I don't study psychology—"

"Then why are you sitting on your pockets here, looking glum as hell?"

He had a point. Classes, studying, the list of articles and books Dr. Emmet had given me to find and read—none of it made any difference. I was miserable. In class, in the library, even the other night, having beers with the other students. All I wanted was to be somewhere else. Not back at my room, not back home. I was itchy, inside and out. When I tried to think of somewhere to go, I imagined standing in the dark under the glowing windows of James Baker's dorm room.

"What am I supposed to do?"

"You tell me. You and Amelia seemed to be hatching something."

I didn't like the familiar sound of her name from his mouth. That night I'd interrupted them at the Mill—was that a date? Last week I'd had a weird dream about Dr. Emmet. The kind of dream I couldn't tell her about or get out of my mind. Now when I saw her—let's say I got itchy then, too. Sweaty, itchy, and shamed. "That suicide watch—"

"Yeah?" he said.

"They were working with Leo before—you know."

"They also offered psychological services to anyone on campus who was aggrieved," he said. "After."

"Really? Phillip?"

"Your friend Phillip is a trained staff psychiatric professional."

"I thought he was a student when I first met him."

"He'd like that. He brings in help when tough news hits, but he runs things. The watch students would have been in the thick of things last year, taking calls like they do. Pixie. Surly. The other one."

"Pixie? Do you mean Trudie?"

"Trudie." McDaniel took a notebook out of his jacket pocket and slapped at himself until he found a pen. "Last name?"

"Don't know. Who's Surly?"

"My affectionate nickname for one of them."

"I know which one you mean," I said. "I wanted to call Phillip the talk show host."

"Good one. Why didn't you?"

"He told me his name."

"See, Nath, I like you. You deal in facts. You've got a good memory, too. You might be a born investigator. We could really get some traction here."

"Traction." The big back tires of a John Deere tractor came to mind, and I remembered trying to climb the giant treads of one in my grandpa's barn. Just a kid, feeling like I was climbing a mountainside. The thrilling moment when I slipped and started to fall, someone's hand at my back. I could imagine my mom letting me take the risk, saying, "Don't let your dad know we did this." That trill up the spine returned now. I pushed it down.

"If we could work together," he said.

"You're trying to make me your sidekick."

I had to give him credit. He worked hard to keep his patience. He swallowed a mouthful of what he wanted to say and tried again. "I want to help Dr. Emmet."

"You want a big headline with your name under it."

"Nothing wrong with getting what I want at the same time. Helping her and helping myself—those aren't mutually exclusive. Surely there's something you want." His eyes drifted back to the bullet hole. "Is there a way to get what you want and help your teacher at the same time?"

What did I want? I hadn't been into the drawer with my file in a few days. When I thought of my clippings and notes now, I felt like an idiot. There had been a time when I first arrived at Rothbert that I was sure I stood on the verge of something big. I'd located the epicenter on a map and found a way to get there. I'd launched myself out of my small town, out of Indiana, out of my dad's judgment and into the confidences of the very person I'd come here to meet. Here I was. What did I want? Only everything, and it had slipped away.

"I can't do anything." My voice sounded like someone else's. McDaniel had the decency to look concerned. "Sorry," I said.

I turned to catch the train home. *I couldn't do anything.* How many times had that come to me, loud and clear as if from God. And this was my religion, the one thing I believed: I couldn't do anything. That was my problem.

CHAPTER 22

When I got back to campus, it was late and I was starving. I'd been living on fistfuls of sugared cereal and my supply of microwave noodles, but I didn't feel like subsistence living tonight. Smith Hall had late dining hours, I remembered.

Red sauce pasta, chicken breasts that had been under the heat lamp far too long. I wasn't choosy. Some vegetables for a change. The garlic bread looked good. I piled my plate high with little buttery rounds, grabbed a glass of milk, and turned to choose a place to sit. The tables had long ago emptied. I pulled out a chair and tucked in. Mediocre food, but at least Kendall wasn't here to tell me that only men living in homeless shelters ate ramen.

I hadn't brought anything to read except the handout from the mob bus tour, the text of which I'd already studied while everyone else ducked to recorded machine gun fire. They'd included the same photo from the St. Valentine's Day Massacre I had on my wall. Poor-quality printing. And they'd cropped out the spilled brains.

"You're the guy who broke up my poker game."

"Sorry?" I recognized the student immediately this time. My mouth full of garlic bread, the word came out *surly*. That's exactly who he was: the bored, impatient kid from the suicide brigade.

"You broke up my poker game last month," he said.

"I guess. Were you down much?"

"I'm never down. I enjoy the sport." He had a glass of milk with ice, swirling it as though we'd run into each other at the Playboy Mansion.

"I never thought of poker as a sport."

"You have to lose in order to break a sweat."

This guy looked like he'd never produced a drop of perspiration in his life. A walking catalog ad: striped oxford, creased khaki pants. Before I came to Rothbert, I hadn't known that real people dressed like this. Blond hair that flipped just so. I hadn't known that people like this really existed. "Natha—Nath Barber."

"Winston R. Harlan. The second."

The way he said it, I felt as though I should have heard of him. "What's your major?"

"That's a pick-up line if I ever heard one."

"What?" I realized my mouth, still full, was hanging open. "I mean, sorry—"

"Relax, Nath. It's a joke. I think the what's-your-major question is the what's-your-sign of our generation. We've all crammed into the nation's higher education institutions to get the pedigrees." He waved his free hand toward the door in a sweeping gesture. The campus outside, his empire. "The master's is the new bachelor's. We're all in competition for jobs that don't exist. You're simply trying to triangulate me in the universe of the university, see where I stand."

I swallowed but couldn't think of a thing to say. "Sociology," I said.

"Political science. Call me Win." He swirled his drink again. The ice clinked against the glass. "You friends with that Baker guy?"

"No."

"Weirdo, right?"

"I was his teacher. Sort of."

Win took a sip of his drink. "Huh. That's cool. You're a—"

"I'm a PhD candidate. A teaching assistant." I didn't feel like getting into the whole thing about Dr. Emmet right now. "Anyway, James dropped the class, so I guess I'm not anything to him now."

"Lost cause."

He sounded like Kendall, talking about me. "Maybe it's too early to write him off."

"He's not going anywhere. Phillip's wrong. He can't stand being wrong, but James? That dude couldn't be bothered to kill himself. He'd have to order someone to come do it for him."

I couldn't help it. I laughed. I'd gotten the picture in my head: James dialing for the suicide delivery service. Ordering the usual.

Win sat down. "So what does your father do?"

What's your sign? What's your father do? Had I time traveled? "He's—he manages a manufacturing outfit." That was fairly close to the truth—he managed two other greasy-fisted men on the factory maintenance crew.

"Mine, too. Ways and Means Committee. How's the spaghetti?"

"You mean—in Congress?"

"I can't believe you're eating that."

I'd heard that the next generation of power went to Rothbert, but I hadn't met them until now. Of course I hadn't interviewed any of them the way Win grilled me now. Maybe Kendall's parents served with the United Nations. Or Ryan's parents had stars on the Hollywood Walk of Fame. I hadn't taken an interest. Or maybe I was trying to avoid *triangulating* myself too well. "What does your mom do?"

"Spends money. That's what my dad says when the microphones are off. Yours?"

For a moment I imagined Rory McDaniel meeting this kid, the polished pennies in his shoes, the swirling cup of milk. McDaniel had the wrong idea about who I was, but he'd be able to see right through this guy. "Tragically deceased. Having your nightcap?"

"I wanted a White Russian, but we didn't have any milk."

Over Win's shoulder, a security guard had his feet up on an extra chair. Even students who could legally drink weren't allowed to do it on campus. I didn't know the punishment but imagined it severe.

Win jerked his head toward the guard. "Don't worry about him. We pay their salaries, and our dads pay for their welfare state."

How exactly a working man benefited from welfare, I didn't ask. Win probably had conservative sound bites for all the rules he wanted to break. I watched the drink swirl. I'm pretty sure I'd never tasted a White Russian. "Are you in Smith?"

"I eat in the dining hall here a lot, but I live at the Castle. Bought it at recession rock-bottom prices. Three bed, two bath, hot tub. The only way to live."

"You bought a castle?"

"Not Her Majesty's Service or anything. Rothbert Manor. That stone tower downtown. Our grocery service is usually spot-on, but I guess I need to yank up the order on milk if Dutch is going to eat that much Cap'n Crunch."

I couldn't help it. I liked him. He had absolutely no clue what he sounded like. A douchebag, born and bred. But he and the others like him—weren't they the true heirs to Rothbert? I was an interloper, but they—they were the DNA of the university. Their forebears got the land grant, put up the capital, sent their sons and their sons' sons. Sometimes, standing on the front porch back at home, I got a little misty over land, tradition. But who was I kidding? I wasn't a farmer. I had no mechanical or electrical or anything-ical talents. My legacy, if you could call it that, would die with me; I couldn't carry it and probably wouldn't carry it on. "That's your roommate? What's Dutch short for?"

"Ver Hoegen," he said. "We throw good parties."

"Throw down the moat," I said.

"You should come by."

"—let the peasants come pay duty," I said.

"People usually just bring a bag of chips or something, sure."

We grinned at each other.

"Seriously," he said. "Stop by sometime and have a beer. Dutch and I play a lot of video games and watch a lot of porn. Just not Thursday nights."

Porn. With another guy? What happened when—I had to leave that train of thought. "What's Thursday night?"

"That's my night on the hotline."

"The—oh."

"Night shift, once a week. I get a lot of homework done."

"Nobody calls?"

"Wouldn't say that. People call. Slimeballs hoping to talk to college chicks. Girls calling to complain to someone when their friends go on dates."

The overhead lights dimmed and rose quickly. "Finish up, there," the security guard called. Win downed his drink.

"Does anyone ever call—upset?"

He shrugged. "Sometimes one of them will be a crier. When there's real trouble, we're supposed to keep the person talking until the pros take over. Want to know the truth?"

That trill raced up my spine again. I didn't care what he told me or that his truth might be different from my own. For the first time in a while, I felt honest curiosity. "What?"

"Some people call and pretend it's a wrong number. I've taken a lot of pizza orders."

I waited for the punch line. "I don't get it."

"To hear another person's voice," he said. "One girl called and pretended she was talking to her sister. For an hour."

I got it. "How do you handle that? Like, all the time?"

"One night a week. It's strict, or else you'd end up talking to the same people every night, getting to be somebody's security blanket. That's tricky. Even if they're not calling to kill themselves, they're tedious. I'm not stocked for boring, you know?"

My mind went back to the morning under the bronze statue when Win had laughed at me. When I'd said I would call, and Phillip and Trudie had agreed: such a good idea. But hadn't Phillip already seen through me? Had they meant I should come in to volunteer, or that I should come in to get help? Which idea, exactly, was such a good idea? I stood to deposit my tray, Win trailing along after me. He left his glass on the table. I grabbed it and put it through the chute with my dirty plate.

"The other thing," he said.

"There's more."

"They only call between three and four in the morning."

"You sit on shift all night and the phone only rings between three and four?"

"Three is when the bars close. Remarkable, right?" He slapped the shoulder of the security guard on the way past. "Phillip won't let us call it rush hour."

"I can see why."

"It's a rush, though."

Outside, the air was cool. Kids passed us wearing Rothbert-red sweatshirts, their hoods pulled up and their hands in their pockets. "What do you call it, then?"

"Nothing around Phillip. He doesn't have much of a sense of humor."

"About suicide."

"About anything."

I'd seen this, and now I owed that humorless dick a beer. I hated owing anyone anything.

Win pointed out to the lake. "Been out there yet?"

"On the lake path?"

"No, on the *lake*. Take the skiff out, turn off all the lights, let the skyline light the way back. Bottles of tequila in the hold, of course."

I shook my head. "You have a boat."

"Out there, you can't believe how dark it is. You can actually see a few stars. But it'll freak you out, that kind of dark."

"Yeah?" Stargazing was one thing home had over this place. You could see every star from my dad's porch. His *skiff*, all the lights out.

That dark night after Bryn sent me home, that's what had saved me. I hadn't called anyone, hadn't ordered a fake pizza to hear another human's voice, but I also hadn't found a sharp knife or anything in the medicine cabinet that would have done any work for me. I found the front door, the porch. I felt like climbing the giant oak in our yard to the smallest branches until something snapped beneath my weight. I wanted to tear my clothes off and run down the gravel road until I met a set of headlights. Just for a moment, I considered climbing into the attic crawl space and hiding myself where no one would ever find me.

Instead I found the sky and stars and lay down on the boards to keep an eye on them as they spun overhead.

My dad had been on overtime that night, a big muck-up at the plant, he'd said later, home the next morning. That's where he found me: curled into a ball on the porch, the stars hidden by the dawn. Always a dawn. I'd made it, and something inside me that had seemed broken was—not fixed, but not quite as ragged.

If Win wanted to know what could freak someone out, I knew a few things.

"Always darkest before the dawn," I said. My dad, with the same words, knowing or not knowing what he'd been saying to me that morning.

"That's it," Win said.

"What?"

"It's always darkest before it's light. That's why we call it the black hour."

That—

—I remembered the feel of the porch planks under my back and the effort it took to press myself there, just there, until the tide pulled back again—

That was the best name for it I'd ever heard.

CHAPTER 23
AMELIA

I'd planned to skip the president's reception, but Corrine started her buddy system campaign an hour earlier than I expected.

"Not all of us have tenure, Melly," she said. "Come kiss some ass with me." She'd worn a nice outfit, left her hair out of the ponytail. I recognized effort.

My chair squealed as I turned to face her. "If we go, I'm having wine."

"At least I'll know what to tell the emergency room."

"I'm going to need wine. Or bourbon. Is Joss coming?"

She chewed on her lip, ruining the gloss she'd gone to the trouble to put on. "How is it that you and Joss are best friends now?"

"You're still my one true love. Have you seen her drink? I want her at my elbow to say all the things I want to say."

"And when did you start to censor yourself?"

"Today," I said. "Or if Joss isn't there, tomorrow."

"What's the big deal?"

"What do you think?"

"So? He'll be there."

"And so will she."

I'd given the matter some thought. Sooner or later, Doyle would introduce the little lady around. Tonight's reception, hosted by the university president and his wife and attended by our colleagues from across the campus, seemed a likely debutante ball. I had responded to the invitation with a resounding *no* a week ago. But I'd taken a little care with myself today, too. Just in case.

144

"An even better reason to go," Corrine said.

"How do you figure?"

"You don't want her to think she's won, do you?"

"Cor. He married her. She's won." But Corrine knew how to get me thinking. If I didn't show up, I'd go down as the housebound invalid Doyle used to live with. If I showed, looking good, best foot—ha—forward, and let the campus take a look at me, I was the brave survivor Doyle used to live with. The courageous fighter with great breasts and shiny hair that Doyle used to live with.

If I were her, I guess I'd be hoping I didn't show up.

Which made my decision for me. I couldn't win, but I could prevail.

"I'll go. I heard they hired four new tenure-track profs in the film department. At least one of them has to be Hollywood cute. And straight. Maybe we can give some campus tours."

Corrine turned back to her computer without comment, reminding me of that weird phone call she'd had. A boyfriend? Maybe we weren't searching for good-looking tenure-tracks anymore. For her, anyway. High time I considered myself single. I just wished I were off the tripod already. The cane gleamed at me from the floor.

"Cor, tell me the truth. The cane. I mean, you notice it, right?"

"It's hard to miss. Especially—"

"What?"

"Well, it's not like anyone's going to ask you what happened, are they? They know."

"People see me differently with the cane."

"People?" she said.

"*Men.* Joe."

She cut her eyes at me. "Mel, you're on *medication*. What are you doing at the Mill?"

"Met a—student."

She nodded, but I had the feeling she stared through me. She probably could tell I was lying, but she'd never guess the truth. Even I couldn't believe I'd gone to meet that McDaniel guy. I'd been thinking about that night ever since. What a waste of time. I didn't need him and his mobility. I was mobile and, more than that, I could work smart. Who was handicapped in that department? Not me. "Cor, I've been thinking about that kid. Did you go to the service?"

Her eyes focused. "Which—oh, Mel, leave that kid alone."

"Well. He's dead. I'm simply curious. I think I'm allowed to be. Did you go?"

She shifted her attention back to her computer and clicked through her e-mail. "They had a little thing out by the lake. The funeral was somewhere else. Somewhere downstate."

"Who else went to the lake thing?"

"Mostly students, but—it was small. Administration types. Jim went. Doyle."

Of course. Doyle would have gone to show that, even if the kid had shot one of his people—the woman he'd loved—he held that all people were good at heart. He believed in second chances. Third. Fourth.

I tried to imagine a clutch of people standing at the rocks overlooking the lake, the wind roaring. Jim Perry and his round belly hanging out of his good suit, Doyle listening with his head tilted. I was wrong about the debutante ball—apparently I'd already missed the party of the year.

"Was she there? With Doyle?"

"It wasn't really the sort of thing you bring a date to. The whole thing was a waste, start to finish. His parents made a mess."

Parents. I hadn't really given the parents any thought. Chastened, I turned back to my own computer screen. Nothing there seemed worth the time. I called up an e-mail from a student in my introductory course but couldn't understand what she wanted. Leo Lehane had parents. I'd already encountered his mother, quoted in a news story, but I hadn't really thought it through. Sociologically speaking, people who were alone, or felt alone, committed suicide more often. But Leo had people. Someone out there mourned him.

And not just his parents—who else missed him? Students in the hallway who watched me pass and said nothing? Or the faculty and staff I didn't know who suddenly seemed to know me enough to bounce a curt nod in my direction. Of course they knew me, now that the *Rothbert Reader* had resumed coverage.

Cor had never let me near most of what had been printed last year. I'd missed some critical knowledge about Lehane. McDaniel said he didn't have many friends, not much of a life. But he'd come from somewhere. Now, no matter who he'd been before, he couldn't be anybody but the shooter.

"What did they do? The parents."

"Amelia." Corrine sounded tired. Exhausted, really, and she was the one who wanted to go to a party instead of grabbing some student center pizza before night class. "What do you think they did?"

They must have cried and wailed and fallen to their knees. The things people did when there's nothing to do. I'd done them. Everyone had. "Did they blame the school?"

"No."

I sat with that. But the lawsuit and the subpoenas I'd been able to deflect—having a hole in your gut offered exactly one benefit, and that was getting out of stuff you didn't want to do.

And then I knew. They hadn't blamed the school. They'd blamed me.

When would I cease to be surprised? And while we were on the topic of time healing nothing at all, when would other people stop rearing back when they saw me? Nearly six weeks into the semester: I taught, attended meetings, sat on committees, held office hours. I adjusted. It was the only thing I could do. I wasn't supposed to wallow anymore, and good thing—I didn't want to. But other people were allowed to feel how they wanted for as long as they wanted. The gossips, the bug-eyed starers, the mouth-breathing photo hounds from the *Reader*. They got to make the rules, and I had to live by them.

"You and Joss should go without me," I said.

"What?"

"I'll just slow you down."

"That's self-pity. You should be ashamed."

"I can't keep up with all the things I'm supposed to feel bad about."

"Screw them. Who cares?" She lifted her chin, her tough gesture, but she still looked like someone's kid sister, brought to the party but left on the porch. She'd given up swearing at some point, which didn't help.

"I do," I said. "I mean. I don't. But you don't know how hard this is."

"You're not the only one this has been hard for."

"I know, I know." Except—who else had come back from it with a limp, I wanted to ask. Who else kept a bottle of orange pills near to hand in order to keep her body from disintegrating into white, nuclear pain? I sighed. "I feel like everyone's staring at me all the time."

She looked away, down, found a spot of dust on her shoe to brush away.

"Is that the truth, Cor, or is that just how it feels?"

"Maybe—maybe it's a little of both."

"Then how the hell am I supposed to stand around a punch bowl with half the campus faculty and let them stare?"

"No way," she said. "They'll be lucky to get ten percent of the faculty."

"Funny. Tell the ten percent I said hello."

"Come on, Mel. I'll make it worth the trip."

"You just want to park with me in the close spots. You've been eyeing that wheelchair parking pass all semester."

"I hadn't considered that. Now you have to take me. I swear we'll have a good time."

"How?"

She rolled her eyes toward the windows and chewed on her lip gloss. "OK. When I meet Doyle's wife, no matter what she looks like, I'll ask her if she taught second grade in Winnetka 1978. What a coincidence, I was a *student*—"

"Even if she's younger than we are."

"Especially if she's younger."

"Get Joss. The bar lines will be long."

CHAPTER 24

There were no disabled parking spots. We parked three blocks away and inched through the neighborhood to join the line of people waiting to be seen through the front door. From the back of the pack, I heard the president greeting his guests. "So glad," he said.

The Wolitzers were a tidy couple with tidy, college-aged children, trim, small people who ran marathons and stalked across campus with the flush of health upon them. Mrs. Wolitzer, an academic with her own pedigree, taught journalism and listened to everyone who spoke to her as though she might be asked to follow up with an investigation. President Wolitzer owned at least seven sweater vests in Rothbert red and jangled with energy.

I had hoped to slip in unnoticed. As if slipping in unnoticed was something I could still do.

"A receiving line," I said to Corrine. "Like it's a wedding."

"Sort of an anniversary party," she said. "Another year, zis boom bah."

"Don't get me wrong. I'm glad to have another year."

"Put on the happy face." She already had hers, and it hardly looked fake.

The line lurched forward on the flagstone walk as another group found their way past the pleasantries. "Cor, what am I going to say?"

"He'll probably ask you one of the questions you get all the time."

"I only have rude answers for those," I whispered. The line moved forward. Corrine shot me a here-we-go look and turned to greet our hosts.

"Thank you so much for coming," Mrs. Wolitzer said, pulling Corrine through the door and propelling her forward. "I'm sure you're having a busy semester."

Before her sentence had even finished, the hostess had dropped

149

Corrine's hand and reached for mine. My hand rested on my cane. I fumbled to rearrange, but the damage was done. Her rhythm broken, Mrs. Wolitzer's face opened in surprise before she could help it. And then that expression dissolved and she mustered a new one. "Hello, *dear*," she said, grabbing my left hand but letting me make my own momentum forward. "How *are* you?"

This was one of the questions for which I had only rude answers. I nodded my head, hoping that the slight inclination of my chin suggested humility and perseverance and good-natured getting-on. I was as stalwart as a Roosevelt. Corrine passed through the handshake with President Wolitzer and spun out from the line as though released from a do-si-do. He turned, his hand already out, to find my slot in the works empty. The Mrs. still had me. "We're so pleased you could make it," she said. "Shall we find you a seat? Malcolm."

The president broke out of formation to reach for the hand his wife finally released. He stood half a foot shorter than I and had the softest hands I'd ever encountered. "Dr. Emmet. How are you faring?"

No nod would save me now. "Holding up, sir. Glad to be back in the classroom."

The gentle handshake slowed. "I hadn't realized—Excellent to hear, Dr. Emmet. We're thrilled to have you here this afternoon. May I—" He gestured into the party. Past Corrine's crossed-arm impatience, the rooms roared with sunlight and voices.

"Oh, no," I said, hearing my horror too late. "I mean, I can find my way. You should greet your guests. But thank you. Thank you"— another nod toward Mrs. Wolitzer, the line of people backed up behind me—"for having us."

I tapped past Corrine at a clip. "What was that?" she hissed at my back.

"My new life."

One half of the first floor of the presidential home was a long ballroom set with elbow-height tables and low seats along the outside walls. The two bars, stocked but backed up, lay across a sea of people I couldn't begin to ford.

"I can't go in there," I said.

"What do you want to drink?"

"I need to go." I could feel the pinprick of sweat at my temples and the back of my neck. I'd taken my pill, but so had I the day I'd fallen in class. If I had a repeat performance here, in front of all these colleagues, I'd never be able to set foot on campus again. Any campus. "I need to get out of here."

"How am I supposed to get back?"

"Joss is coming later."

"Look, you made it past the guards at the gate," she said. "Let's get a drink and find a less crowded spot outside."

The people who'd been in line behind us poured around the island we'd formed. No one bumped or jostled me—there was my leprosy to consider, after all—but I could feel the room tighten, the oxygen thin. I looked longingly at the sets of French doors opened to the covered patio and, beyond that, an expanse of carefully trimmed lawn. "I'll take a—a water," I said, and launched myself toward daylight.

All the faces outside were unfamiliar. One set of eyes after another glanced up and away. The tent ended, the patio. My cane found the soft grass, but I kept going until I'd reached the high brick wall that enclosed the estate. Above, the leaves of an imposing oak stirred. I forced myself to feel the breeze, to take in the air. Ivy hung off the wall, and I concentrated on one perfect, nodding leaf. Corrine would be back soon with my water, and I'd make her understand how delicate I was. The back gate? Would it be open?

I turned to find Doyle coming across the lawn, his arm around a woman.

He was right. I didn't know her.

When they reached me, he hesitated, a blink of pleading eyes that I would behave myself. "Nancy, this is Dr. Emmet. Nancy Chambers, uh, Doyle."

Mrs. Nicholas Doyle looked soft. Chubby through the waist, dark hair that fell in fat, dark curls, a gray cardigan from which an aura of angora threads floated. I had an itch to reach out and poke her with my cane. She was thick, but had skinny legs and wore high heels she didn't seem used to. She'd already noted the cane and didn't offer her hand. "Nice to meet you, Dr. Emmet."

"Call me Amelia."

"Amelia." She smiled. Nothing. My name meant nothing to her.

"Or Melly. My closest friends do."

Doyle shot me a look, but Mrs. Doyle didn't blink. "Melly, then. You teach in Nick's department?"

Nick. In the second of shadow that played across his face, I could see the new persona Doyle had adopted to lasso and land this tottering lamb of his. Doyle wasn't Doyle. Not the man I'd loved or refused to marry, but a revised edition. God, what had he worn to the singles mixer where they'd met? Or was she a teacher at the kids' school? She might be a few years older than I was, but she was still much younger than Doyle. I found myself suddenly incurious, except in regards to where Corrine had gone and when my drink would come. I already regretted the drink being only water. "I do. Teach there. In Nick's department."

"You'll be able to tell me all the dish."

"Dish?"

"All his deep, dark secrets." She laughed and reached for him. Doyle tried to smile. He managed to bare his teeth.

"We don't tend to have—secrets in the department," I said. "On the contrary."

"Exactly what I mean," she said. "We're still getting around to all that back story couples have to get through. Such a whirlwind." When she giggled, she gained a little extra chin. I concentrated on that, because otherwise she was adorable.

"Oh? How long have you known—"

"Amelia teaches the sociology of violence," Doyle said.

"Baby," his wife said. "I'm going to turn to violence if I don't have a drink in my hand soon. Melly, how about you?"

"I have one coming." I looked toward the doors and then at Doyle. He couldn't possibly leave me alone with her. He didn't trust me. He shouldn't trust me.

Nancy raised Doyle's hand to her cheek and kissed his knuckles. "A white wine. Champagne if they've got it."

"At your service." He glanced at me. "Anything at all, Amelia?"

"I'll go in with you."

"Don't be silly," Nancy said. "Let's find a—right there, that bench has our names on it."

"I really need to find my friend. I'm her ride."

"You weren't leaving already, were you?"

"Back soon," Doyle said, and was off across the yard.

We both watched until he was inside.

"Well," Nancy said. "Let's relax."

"I—uh—"

"I mean you can relax," she said. "Don't hurt yourself trying to tell me. I know who you are."

"So. How long—"

"And we don't have to chitchat," the new Mrs. Doyle said. She held out her hand and straightened the ring on her finger. Doyle's mother's. "We're not going to be swapping recipes over the back fence."

"Good." Suddenly I felt more certain than I'd felt in a while. What could she take from me? She already had Doyle. Everything else, off-limits. "I hate to cook."

"I heard that about you."

This was the game. She'd heard things about me, but I didn't know which things or how true. "I'm legendary," I said. "I don't know anything about you."

"I'm a private person."

"Excellent," I said. "That's easily accommodated."

We stood in silence, me grinning at her like a fool until she realized I wouldn't ask a single thing. She glanced up at the house.

"Nick will want us to get along," she said.

"*Nick* wants no such thing."

She pulled on the front of her sweater, twisted the hem. "What will we say we've been talking about?"

In another world, I would have liked her for this. I had Corrine, but the truth was that I hardly had any friends left from other parts of my life. I had colleagues. I had ex-boyfriends. I had distant family members who shared the polite disregard I had for them. Women were at their best when they kept close women friends or had sisters they could turn to. Study after study had proven it, and yet a sociological study of women's pairing habits couldn't bring me to join a book club. I'd rather shoot *myself*.

Too bad Nancy and I had met the way we had. We might have been able to drink and tell lies together.

"He'll assume that I've been regaling you with stories of our sexual past," I said. "That's what he expects of me. You couldn't possibly help but come out on top. So to speak."

She paled. "I don't want to hear about that."

"Not going to tell you."

"Why not?"

I couldn't win with her. "I'm a private person, too."

"I thought you were *legendary*."

"Oh, I am."

Now she flushed pink and turned on her heel toward the bench. She had me there. I had to follow. Doyle had left us together, and he'd expect us together when he returned.

Damn Corrine and that glass of water.

Nancy minced to the bench and sat on the far end. She eyed my halting approach. I didn't want to sit. I'd have to get back up. If I could help it, this woman would never see me scraping to my feet like a tortoise rolled onto its back.

"I work in a charter school," she said.

I didn't care.

"I'm forty-five, never married before."

More than that—I didn't want to care.

"Used to ride horses when I was a girl, but now I want to raise Shetland sheepdogs, breed them. Live on a farm somewhere." She gazed out at the lawn. I recognized some of the faculty and administration, mostly men. The faculty wives I could pick out stood at their brilliant husbands' elbows as if providing some sort of physical evidence. They didn't have much to say to one another. Their haircuts were severe, bobbed. None of them wore soft sweaters.

I didn't care. I couldn't. I hadn't sat on the bench, but I'd been forced to see this party, this party and all those to come just like it, from where she sat. Bleak. Or at least, you could see it that way—if you weren't happy as shit about everything else you'd gotten in the bargain.

"You'll be fine."

She glared at me. "I don't need your reassurances."

"That was the only one I had."

"I'm going to tell Nick we talked about Willetson and the lake. And the weather, before we ran out of topics, got uncomfortable, and decided not to try to be friends."

"No one calls him Nick," I said.

"That way he won't expect us to be chummy the next time we run into you."

"I can't see him expecting that."

"I hope not to run into you all that often," she said.

"Your concept of him is really interesting."

"Amelia—I can still call you Amelia, can't I? Amelia, it's time for us to understand each other. Nick and I are married—"

"No one calls—"

"I *do*." She gave me a look of such pity that I felt something important and fragile inside me strain against cracking. "I call him Nick. And I'm the only one who matters."

Joss grabbed my arm as I hobbled through the Wolitzers' foyer.

"Is there no booze?" She brushed impatiently at her skirt. "Should've known to bring my own."

"Can you take Corrine home for me?"

"So there's booze? She's had too much?"

"I mean back to campus. I have to go, OK?" I'd left Nancy on the bench, alone. Damn her and her pity, her Shirley Temple hair. Ridiculous creature.

Joss tilted her head and looked at me over the top of her hipster glasses. "I can take her. Is everything all right?"

Nothing was, but I couldn't talk to Joss here, and I couldn't wait for Corrine to come back from wherever she'd gone. "I'm just—exhausted. I don't have the nerve for this anymore."

She nodded, her eyes sliding away and past me. "There's Corrine. I'll go make sure she knows she's got shotgun. Take *care*, Amelia. Get some rest."

Joss patted my cane hand on her way past. On the far end of the ballroom I saw Corrine next to one of the bars. No drink in her hand, and she didn't even seem to be in line. She stood next to a bookcase hanging at the edge of a group admiring the Wolitzers' artwork. The group included a professor or a trustee and his entire family, from the looks of it. What idiot would bring his mother and adult children to this? A bow-tied bartender approached the group with a tray of drinks. Corrine was included in the offer. The elderly lady, stately as a queen, turned and checked Corrine top to bottom. One of the young men, prim and attentive to the lady as a concierge in his Rothbert-red tie, caught me staring.

Phillip Carrington-Something. He smiled and waved. I looked to see if I also knew anyone else in the group. The other young man was the real thing: this kid's suit probably cost half my annual salary. He turned and seemed to note me. For a moment, the shelf of memory wobbled. I knew him from one of my intro classes last year, I supposed. Maybe he hadn't liked the grade he'd gotten. As I turned away, the elegant lady brushed Phillip away from her.

Corrine had ditched me for easy drinks? Not that she'd bothered with my water. I could have waited for next year's reception with as much likelihood of getting a drink brought to me. She'd adopted a serious sucking-up policy.

A crash. I shrank away from it, stumbling over the cane. My heart raced. Nothing, it was nothing. Someone had dropped a glass. I sensed those around me watching and hoped the Wolitzers weren't among them.

Doyle emerged from the crowd with a trio of wine glasses and paused in the wide doors. He'd see his wife, a stranger in a strange land in an out-of-season sweater, left alone on the lawn. He'd wonder at my lack of social skills, the depths to which I would sink to hurt him. He'd wonder what he ever saw in me. He'd have to think for a long time. This time, he wouldn't bother.

I waited until the Wolitzers were directing the cleanup of the broken glass, then slipped out.

CHAPTER 25
NATH

When class broke up, the rest of them headed to the Mill while I hung back to help Dr. Emmet. She'd shown up to class a few minutes late looking peeved and distracted but pretty. Dressed up, her hair loose. When one of the girls complimented her, she blushed. "Stuffy faculty reception," she said.

Class discussion had stumbled and halted, but she didn't seem to notice or care. Finally she looked at her watch and asked if we minded cutting class short. No one minded. I walked her to her office and then out to the parking lot.

"I've got it," she said, jingling her keys.

"You sure?"

"See you tomorrow."

I shoved my hands into my front pockets and started off.

"The Mill's the other way, young scholar," she said.

I turned and walked backward a couple of steps, shrugged.

"You OK?" she said.

"Just—yeah, OK."

She didn't believe me, but it was the truth. School was OK, the teaching gig was OK, campus food when I got tired of cheap noodles, going to the Mill once a week. All of it fine. The problem—I'd figured on more than that. I'd staked everything on it.

When I opened my door, Kendall, stretched out in his loft bed, said, "Somebody called for you."

"Bryn?" I hadn't known I'd been waiting for her call.

"Who's Bryn?" He sat up on an elbow. "Dude, do you have a *chick* back home?"

"She's—no. Who called?"

"Number's over there." He gave an ambiguous nod toward my side of the room. "A guy."

Which only left my dad. When I dialed, the phone rang and rang. I held on. He had no answering machine and usually had to come from outside where the latest fixer-upper waited in the drive with its hood propped open. At twelve rings: "Hello?" He didn't sound out of breath, had walked in for the phone like a man with all the time in the world.

"Hey, Dad."

"I told that young man you didn't have to call me right back."

"I wanted to."

"Well, then." That was his embarrassment. Affection had been Mom's business. He didn't know how to give it or to take it. Maybe it was the only thing we had in common, other than how much we missed her. "Well, then, you're OK up there?"

"Fine," I said. Was there any other answer I could give? "How about you?"

"Keeping busy enough. Someone asked me about you the other day. Can't think of who it was, now."

I couldn't think who it could be, either. And if anyone had asked, it would have been polite chit-chat. *How's your son?* they might've asked when the line at the A&P took longer than normal. *He's just fine. Up at college*, my dad would say. *Still?* He wouldn't have a good answer for that. Still.

"Busy at work?" I asked.

"Yep, I fixed every dab thing in the place this week."

That's what he said every week. I tried to laugh. We'd run out of things to say already.

"Spent a little time at the old barn this week. Cleaning it out."

"Grandpa's barn?"

"Needed done, sooner or later."

My grandfather had been gone for years, his house down the road sold, his land fallow until the lean economy passed and someone could afford to buy and farm it again. The old barn, sturdy but locked up since the funeral. Six years—this was definitely later. "Cleaning for what?"

"Auction," he said. "About time to get it back to use."

"You're selling it? All—" My voice twisted unexpectedly. Out of the corner of my eye, I saw Kendall turn his head toward me. "All of it?"

"Not sure it'll all go. But better to offer it up before the rust wins."

"What's—what's in there?" I hadn't been inside since long before he'd died, but I remembered the smell. Oil, sawdust, sweat. Hot Indiana summers, my grandpa had a six-foot-square industrial fan to keep the air moving. Even with the breeze, the place grew sweltering.

"The usual. Tools, parts. A tractor he bought to fix. Not sure anybody here will want it broken. They would've taken it—" He took a deep breath.

To him. To my grandpa. Anybody with a broken machine would have brought it to my grandpa's barn. And now they sometimes brought it to my dad, though he didn't take in tractors except to tinker for a friend. On the side, for a six-pack and gratitude.

Dad cleared his throat. "Now they got to take it into town and leave it for a month and a half. Half the season gone."

Not for the first time, I wished I'd ever wanted something this simple, to fix things that no one else could fix and fast enough that everyone got their crops in on time. To be useful, to be practical and handy to have around. My grandpa had wanted something he could have. My dad didn't have the same skills, but he worked well with his hands and could make a living doing what he liked to do. When you could work with your hands, you had options.

If I couldn't hack it at Rothbert, my options—

I had none.

"But at a good price," my dad was saying, "maybe somebody will take the tractor off our hands. Better than leaving it to sit there."

A tractor always sat in there. The huge tire, the feel of the giant tread under my small fingers and a hand on my back as I teetered. I couldn't remember reaching the top, only the urge to climb. Even knowing I could fall, reaching. I had never wanted anything within my grasp.

"When's the sale?" I said.

"Next weekend. The town festival, so lots of folks will be in for it."

"I could come help you."

"You—you want to?"

"Is there something I could do?"

"Son, there's plenty of work to go around." He sounded pleased. Proud. I could imagine him telling the lady behind him at the A&P about this. "How will you get down?"

"A bus. I'll figure it out."

"Good, good. Nathaniel—well, then."

"I'll see you next weekend, Dad."

"Have a safe trip down."

I set the phone back in its cradle and looked at it. A long bus ride, the effort of lugging grimy tools and bits and pieces out of the barn, the whole day spent in the sun among strangers or, worse, at the town's annual fall festival, where everyone I'd ever known would want to hear what I was doing with my life. A tedious, hot day spent explaining myself, the town crowded, and then another bus, another five hours back to Rothbert.

The phone rang.

"Aren't you popular," Kendall said.

I hoped for a moment it was my dad, calling back to talk me out of coming. The expense, the time away from my studies. But that's not how my dad would think. It rang again. "Maybe it's for you."

"I only give out my cell." He waved his phone in the air. "Since I only talk to people who live in this century."

I picked up the phone. "Hello."

"Who's this?" a male voice said.

I hated people who did that. As though they'd called from the center of the universe. "This is the person you called. Who's this?"

"Is that Nath? Nath, are you getting pissy with me? Dutch, watch the bottles—"

"Win?"

"We're going out on the boat," he said. "Do you have any booze?"

"Uh, no." I found myself flattered he'd remembered me at all and wished I'd kept a bottle somewhere for the occasion.

"Come anyway. It's a great sky night, and we have plenty."

"I've never sailed before."

"Dutch'll do all the heavy lifting—"

I heard a protest rise up in the background, and Win laughed.

"He has to work off his indentured servitude to me. All you have to do is drink and hold up your end of the conversation."

To be cool, in other words. Why did everyone expect me to be capable? A sailboat, on Lake Michigan, at night. My pulsed kicked. Was that even safe? But that was my small town, my small life talking. The true inheritance I'd received was a provincial mentality that did me no good anywhere else, that didn't let me be anywhere else, and even when I clawed my way out, kept me begging to come back.

No, I have to study. No, I have to work on a special project. What a moron I was. "Where's the dock?"

"That's my man," Win said.

CHAPTER 26

There was no dock. I'd seen a beach on the south end of campus, but Win's directions sent me down the dark lake path and an overlook, dark boulders below. The tide was low and quiet. Out a few hundred feet or more, a white light shone.

"Win?" I tried to see a way through the rocks. Was he crazy? "Are you there?"

"Ahoy," Win cried from the dark. The white light bobbed. "Find the no swimming sign, and then climb out."

He was crazy. The white light seemed impossibly far away. I felt my way out onto the rocks, slipping and almost twisting my ankle. Gentle waves lapped too close to my feet.

"Over here," said a voice, below.

I peered into the shadows. A single piling stuck out of the water, an inflatable dinghy bumping against it. Inside, a big guy with a cigarette hanging from his mouth. The oars dangled in the water. "How—"

I looked out into the blackness. Second thoughts, third.

"Come on," Dutch said around his cigarette. "The beer's getting warm."

My foot found a flat expanse. I sat and stretched my legs for another hold. "Is there room—"

"Drop your foot down, you pussy. Worst thing, you get a little wet."

"I can't swim."

"It's a puddle right here," he said. "My ass is scraping the sand."

At the last second, I was sure I would drop into the lake, but I found the inside of the dinghy with first one foot then the other and let myself fall blind into the tight opening Dutch's girth left for me.

"Are there any life jackets?"

He took up the oars and shoved us off toward the light. "How can you not know how to swim?"

163

"Not a lot of lakeside property where I'm from."

"You never had a pool?"

I'd forgotten whose company I kept. Dutch was a resident of the Castle and had probably swallowed the silver spoon by now, along with a super-sized portion of entitlement, by the look of him.

"I grew up in the country."

"Which country doesn't have swimming pools?"

I gave up, concentrating instead on how far from the shore we were. It wasn't just a foot deep here. Over my shoulder, Win's boat grew. It had a white—body. I didn't know the words for any of it, but I couldn't help being impressed. For one thing, the boat was huge. A kid my age, younger than me, owned this. He could operate this at night. Two guys and beer, and they could still send themselves out to sea. And, I hoped, safely back.

I heard singing and listened for the tune.

What do you do with a drunken sailor? Er-lie in the morning.

We lurched in our little tub toward the white light until we were nearly under it, the boat looming. Dutch rammed us into its side. There was another piling here, a buoy bobbing next to it. He tied us to the piling and pulled us up to the boat. There, in large script letters: *Ladykiller.*

Win appeared, hanging from a rope on the deck. He spun around it as though on a playground, out over open water, his feet dangling, and back onto the boat before I hardly knew what he'd done.

"Ahoy, me Hearties!"

"Ahoy," I said weakly.

"Prisoner for the brig, Captain," Dutch said.

"He's just joking," Win said. "Come on up."

My legs had gone loose. I hauled myself into the craft and fell to my knees.

"Jesus, Nath," Win said. "What'll you have?"

"Whatever."

Dutch climbed over me and reached for a bottle. "He can't swim."

"I didn't plan on swimming." Win handed me a beer. I gulped at it to keep the bottle from shaking in my hand. "Unless you want to," he said. "I'm up for anything."

"No, thanks," Dutch said. He sat on the bank of seats and started to kick back. "Do we even have to hoist the anchor?"

"It's not sailing if you're hanging out next to the dinghy," Win said.

"There's hardly any wind," I said. If we stayed here, the most diffi-cult task would be getting back into the dinghy. No—those rocks. But we were still within a few hundred feet of the shore. The blank of the lake felt heavy at my back.

Win took the empty bottle from my hand and shoved another beer at me. "Just a pleasure cruise down to the lighthouse and back. We don't need much."

"Lighthouse?"

"See, Nath? You haven't seen the sights."

Dutch heaved a sigh. "Weigh anchor," he said and climbed back over me to crank at something. I dragged myself off my knees and up to the seat he'd left. It was a padded bench with only a thin silver rail sepa-rating me from the water. People did this for relaxation? I sat forward, my elbows on my knees.

Dutch hurried by again. Behind me, an engine began to purr. We glided slowly away from the dinghy and out onto the lake. A breeze kicked up. Dutch dropped the engine and scurried around, tugging at knots and pulling at ropes and talking to himself.

"You worried?" Win said.

"Is there something I should be—doing?" I didn't see any life vests, but I couldn't ask now, not again.

"Watch out for this," Win said, patting a wide horizontal beam.

"Avast," Dutch said without enthusiasm. Win ducked out of the beam's reach as it swung around. A large white sail overhead flapped and filled.

"The boom," Win said. "Easiest way for a landlubber to see the bottom of the lake."

He seemed a little flippant on the topic, and for the first time I wondered how much he and Dutch had been drinking. A light at the front of the boat and behind—there were words for these things, I knew—did little to cut the dark. "How far is the lighthouse?"

"Be there before I have to piss," Dutch said.

"South of campus, what, a few miles," Win said. "You haven't been outside since you got here, have you? 'Do you know where the library is?'" His Midwestern twang was spot-on. "'Has anyone seen the library?'"

Dutch laughed.

We were slowly moving south along the coast, Rothbert's buildings lit up like jewels on a strand. The campus seemed small, like a doll's house version of itself. Only an hour ago I'd made plans to get out of there, but now I couldn't wait to get back. Dry land. Dry, steady land.

"Where do you keep the boat?"

"Marina down the lakeshore. We'll put her in dry dock after the Night Sail."

"Isn't this a night sail?"

"*The* Night Sail," Win said. "Rothbert tradition. The sailing club, faculty, anyone with a boat. We take them up the shore and back one last time before the season ends. An excuse for a party."

An excuse for rich people to be rich people. "When is that?"

"Saturday. You could be on our crew, if you want."

Dutch made a noise.

Win shot him a look. "You were no good to me last year, remember? Drunk by nine in the morning, you don't get to be captain."

I knew as well as anyone that no one but Win got to be captain. "What's the occasion tonight?"

"Haven't been out for a while. Classes get in the way."

"Political science, right?"

"The father-approved major," Win said. "Psychology?"

"Sociology."

I could see Win nodding thoughtfully in the dark. "Do you know all the professors in the department?"

"Just Van Meter and, uh, Emmet this semester. I met another one, but I can't remember his—Woo, maybe?"

More nodding, and then he stopped. "Emmet? The one who—"

"Yeah."

"Have you been to, like, her office?"

I knew where this was going. Undergrads were so immature. First Kendall and now Win, who I would've given more credit. "Of course I have. I'm her graduate assistant."

The disdain I'd tried to put into my voice must have gotten through. He let it go.

"What do you study, Dutch?" I said.

"Popular culture." He belched.

"TV," Win said. "Video games. Chinese takeout menus." He hustled up more beers and passed them around. We'd switched brands. Change in taste or proof of progress?

"Emmet," Dutch said. "That the one who took a gut shot last year?"

Win didn't seem interested anymore. He hopped up and went to the back of the boat to stare into the dark, the lights of Rothbert getting small as we sailed toward the distant Chicago skyline.

I didn't want to talk about Dr. Emmet, didn't want to hear the half-truth version and try to convince the other side they had the story wrong again. To hear the story and care too much. Again. "Yeah," I said.

"That dude was a dick," Dutch said.

"Yeah."

"A hot prof takes you downtown, and you blow her away—"

"Shut up, Dutch," Win said.

Dutch wasn't done. "That's, like, shortsighted."

"Shut the hell up, Dutch," Win hissed. He pitched his beer bottle out into the lake. In the silence, the splash seemed large.

I was glad to hear someone else shut down the common tale, and then I realized: Win worked the phone bank for the suicide watch. He might have taken some calls from Leo, before the guy had gone ahead and done whatever he wanted to do. A setback, that reporter had called it.

"It's no one's fault," I said.

Win pushed past me to the cooler and fished for something deep in the ice. "What are you talking about?" He came up with a tall bottle, clear, and unscrewed the top.

"He was messed up, right? Nobody could've stopped him."

Win threw the bottle back and drank. He wiped his mouth with the back of his hand and stood silent and still, as though we waited for something, together. In the dark, I couldn't see his face.

"Lighthouse to starboard," Dutch said.

A thin beam of light spun over us into the lake and away. I turned. A white shaft of a lighthouse rose over the shore, its body lit from the ground. How ridiculous and fantastic that the light still spun, even now that so few boats must run the lake. No more freight down from Detroit; roads were faster. The Outfit, Capone and all of them, would have run rum into Willetson back in the day this way. I was probably seeing the same sight they had, sailing now over a dropped cask or an enemy's old bones. That was the thing I'd come to understand about this place. I'd only scratched at the surface of what there was to know, but even a superficial nick revealed both the dark past below and how thin the patina covering it was.

I knelt on the bench and leaned onto the railing, imagining the silent, black nights those men had endured.

"Ready to jibe, Dutch," Win said, taking his bottle to the back.

"Yeah?" Dutch said. He let his empty bottle fall to the deck and kicked it aside. "Jibe-ho, bitch."

I glanced back. Win faced away, taking in the skyline.

"Hard-a-lee," Dutch called.

"What's that mean?"

The boat swung under my feet, throwing me forward into the rail. Something slammed into my shoulder, and I was caught off-balance, too high on the bench, and then over.

Time slowed. I heard Dutch shout before I realized I was the one. I was the one. *Man overboard*—and then I crashed into the water: head shoulders body feet, all the way down and into the cold water.

Under. I clawed for the surface, but it didn't come.

Everything was dark. My lungs grew tight. How long? I fought against sinking. Where was the boat?

I thought of my dad in the line at A&P, the only story he'd ever have to tell. The guy who drowned. Water dripping into the coffin, rot. I couldn't find the surface.

My head hurt, my shoulder. I fought for the surface, the water cold, cold. I couldn't find the—

I put my hand through the lake to the other side. The sky.

Under the water, I could see. I could see everything. Everything was right. Everything made sense. Everything would work itself out. The stars were bright.

A hand grabbed mine.

Then I was flying, banging against the boat with my body, hurt, and nothing made sense.

I lay on the deck among their legs, coughing and gagging. I'd forgotten the boat, Win and Dutch, forgotten everything but water and the feeling, just before taking flight out of the lake and back into my body, of hands. Many hands, and the water. Hands and water, as though I'd been the most adored at a riverside baptism.

I crawled to my hands and knees, the last thing I'd eaten finding daylight again. Their top-siders jumped back. "Jesus, dude," Dutch said.

Hands, I remembered. Hands, under my arm, hauling me out. One hand holding mine. I retched long after my stomach was empty. I gagged and gasped, still feeling the press of the other hand on my shoulder, holding me under.

CHAPTER 27
AMELIA

By the time Nath had walked me to my office and then out to my car, the campus parking lot was almost empty. "The Mill's the other way, young scholar," I called as he walked away. He shrugged, claimed to be OK. Something nagged at him. Me, I figured. The kid hadn't planned on becoming my valet, had he? Hadn't plunked down the next few years of his life at Rothbert only to play my Boy Friday every day of the week. He acted like someone who wanted to be anywhere else but here.

I felt the same way.

Although, really, I didn't mind being here, standing in a gentle breeze coming off the lake. At another time of my life I might have walked down to the shore before heading home or convinced Doyle to take the boat for an evening sail. Or, at *another* other time of my life, I might have gone to the Mill myself and waited for Joe to close up and walk me home.

I let myself imagine that all these lives still carried on. All these Amelia Emmets, walking to the lake without assistance, resting her hand on Doyle's leg on the drive to the marina, playing with the paper coasters on the Mill's bar and watching TV to pass the time. And don't forget the Amelia who focused on her research, who spent hours poring over her notes and tapping at her laptop. Don't forget the Amelia Emmets I had killed myself.

Or the Amelia Emmets that I'd never let see the light of day. The one who might have practiced clarinet harder and might still know how to play. The one who could have gotten pregnant that first rela-

tionship and be divorced with a twenty-plus-year-old kid by now. The
one who stayed near home and took watch over her parents until they
died. The one who had no regrets about how she was raised: how little
money, how little opportunity. That Amelia might be in her bed now,
doing a crossword, listening to *Letterman* on TV and the dog snore.
That Amelia might be wondering what could have happened if only
she'd gone to college.

I caught the tiniest movement in my peripheral vision. A car, one
of the few vehicles left, was parked across two spots, askew. Someone
sat inside, watching.

I hurried toward my car, fumbled with the keys, located the blue
light of the emergency phone at the edge of the parking lot, calculated
my odds, took another look—

A Jeep. A yellow one.

Inside sat Peter Pan himself.

"Are you kidding?"

McDaniel leaned out his window as I approached. "Nice night,
isn't it, Professor?"

"What do you want?"

"Nothing at all. Enjoying the splendors of a fall evening."

"Stalking, you mean, or do you hang out on campus hoping for
gunfire?" I stood back from the Jeep and took a look. I'd seen a similar
vehicle the day before, parked across the street from my apartment.
"Have you been following me?"

"I drive around quite a lot for the job, you know. It's a small town."

"Three million people live in Chicago."

"I meant Willetson, Professor, our beloved suburban village. But,
yes, even out there in the greater municipal area, you can run into
people you know. More than you think." He grazed me with a loaded
look. "Bumped into young master Nath the other day. He didn't tell
you?"

He hadn't. Should it bother me that he hadn't? "You must have
slipped his mind."

"I must have slipped yours. You never call, you never write."

"We don't have anything to say to one another," I said. "In fact, I'll let you get back to your splendors." I turned and started away.

"I thought we had some shared intentions here."

I walked on, hearing his door open and the sound of his footsteps galloping to catch up. "I won't be chased," I said. "By the way, you're parked illegally. Not to mention badly."

"What about Leonard Lehane?" he said.

"If you're going to be following me a great deal, I'd recommend purchasing a pass for the lot."

"What about the suiciders?"

"The spaces across from my apartment are metered, as you know. Bring lots of quarters."

"What about Nath?"

I stopped. "What about him?"

"He seems more hangdog than usual. Do you think the pamphlets are getting to him?"

"A lot of graduate students experience a letdown once the semester gets underway," I said, watching McDaniel's smirk slide into place. "Why am I bothering to explain it to you?"

"I've long considered getting my PhD." He raised himself ramrod straight and looked into the middle distance, a commemorative statue of himself. If he'd raised his hand just so, he might have mirrored the statue of the founding Rothbert on the other side of campus. His voluminous tweed jacket nearly fit him. "Dr. Rory McDaniel. PhD," he said. "Esquire. Limited Liability Corporation. But really, what I want is to be knighted." He relaxed into his slump. "I'm working on it. It seems they want you to be a good person for that sort of thing."

"Work harder." I started toward my car again.

"You brought this on yourself." He didn't follow me. For a moment, I thought he might let me go, and then his voice came again, sharper, purposeful. "Who was the lanky fellow at the reception today? The one with the curly-haired lady friend?"

I'd reached my car, and good thing. I stumbled the last step, catching myself on the hood with the flat of my palm. I pictured myself, flushed and wild-eyed, pushing past the line of colleagues waiting in the Wolitzers' doorway. "I believe those receptions are by invitation only."

"I had one—"

"From the *president*—"

"—from Rothbert's first lady," he said.

"Why would Mrs. Wolitzer invite you?"

"She's a colleague." He pantomimed a what-could-I-do shrug. "Misses the days of deadlines, I guess. She's been chatting me up on a few ideas she has to raise the profile of the university. Stories on faculty research, big donations to the university, that sort of thing. She wanted me to mingle, sniff out some possibilities."

"Sniff out the free booze."

"The best way to raise the profile of the university, I say, is to solve its most outrageous crime."

"As far as she's concerned, it's solved."

"You and I don't believe that."

I remembered President Wolitzer's arched eyebrows when I said I'd returned to teaching. *I hadn't realized.* "She'll be against it, as a matter of fact," I said. "They've put it to rest, and anything you'd write now would be exhuming the dead."

"You know who I don't care about? The dead. I care about the living."

"Should I start calling you Sir McDaniel?"

"I'm serious. You, Nath, Lehane's mother. If one of you wanted me to drop it, that would be one thing—"

"I've asked you to drop it three times."

"But you don't mean it."

"You don't know a thing about me."

He squinted at me. "The lanky guy, nice pressed pants, messy hair—"

"My boss."

"You don't mean that, either. When you lie, you get a certain look. Like you might have to take a piss."

"Charming."

"It is, actually. You lie a lot. Look, if you're satisfied with the way things stand, that's fine. The university seems to be. Lehane's mother isn't."

What outcome would be satisfying to the Lehanes? "How do you know that?"

"I've interviewed her," he said, looking toward the lake. "And she's been to town a few times since—well, since. He's buried in their town, but she still comes here."

I looked out at the lake, too, and saw a lone white sail coasting past in the dark. "Why?"

McDaniel shook his head. "You've never had the rug ripped out from under you? A grave is a grave. Rothbert is the last place her son was *alive*. I wouldn't be surprised if she's been to your office."

I turned away, chilled.

"In short," he said. "I don't think Mrs. Lehane would mind if I exhumed some facts. And if she doesn't mind, why should you?"

I minded that I'd ever called the number left on my car, that I'd started something I couldn't seem to stop. What I minded more was that the mere mention of Doyle still dug at my gut in a way even a bullet hadn't. When I turned back to McDaniel, Dale Hall loomed over his shoulder. From here, I could see the dark windows of Doyle's corner office.

"You can do whatever you want," I said.

"Fine," he said, but I could see it wasn't the answer he wanted. I could read some of his twitches, too.

I opened the car door, threw in my bag, relocked the door, and started back toward Dale Hall.

"Where are you going?"

"If you follow me, I'll get a restraining order."

"That's ridiculous—"

"And I'll have a chat with the Wolitzers about your plans for raising the university's profile. I'm pretty sure this isn't the story Mrs. Wolitzer's asking for. And—on my way past, I'll smack that blue panic button over there. Have you ever seen the university police hustle? They're a bit touchy lately."

"I've witnessed them hustle when the fireworks go off." He yielded to let me pass. "I was the one awake that day, remember?"

At the edge of the parking lot, I paused at the emergency box for a glance back. He stayed put.

How had everything gotten so messy? A kid I didn't know had chosen me and then ducked out so that all the fallout was mine. For a moment, I hoped that if there was a hell, Leo Lehane burned there. Then I thought of his mother, standing outside the door to my office. Searching the floor for bloodstains.

On the walk back up to Dale Hall, something picked at me. I went back over the conversation until I found it.

I've witnessed them hustle when the fireworks go off.

McDaniel had been on the scene. He'd said as much. But if he'd seen university police racing across campus that day—if he'd actually seen the scurrying—that put him on campus prior to the alarm. Not back at his office listening to his scanner, not out roaming his Willetson beat.

Already on campus. Already a part of the story.

At the doors, I checked to see. He leaned against his Jeep, still watching.

CHAPTER 28

Inside, Dale Hall glowed like a church. Somewhere down the corridor I could hear the quiet noises of someone giving the copy machine a lesson it wouldn't soon forget.

I stood inside the door, watching for McDaniel to follow me. After a while I stepped back outside and searched the parking lot. He'd gone.

I didn't want to be here, but I also didn't want to go home. Take my pill, take my glass of wine. Home, which was a mess despite the cleaning lady and my own weak efforts. And in so many ways, far emptier than Dale Hall.

I let myself take the elevator—only the surveillance camera left to judge me—and pressed the button. In my pocket, I felt for my keys.

On the third floor, the elevator opened up to a foyer more like the one the second floor used to have. I paused, checking the darkest corners. Joss's posh, senior faculty office and the trio of adjoining offices the nodding wise men kept were all deserted. Doyle's door stood at the end near the stairs, tucked behind the landing and facing toward town and trees. He couldn't see downtown Chicago or the lake, but in the winter, his office kept the heat.

I'd arrive at his doorway, wrapped in two sweaters and a scarf, still frozen through from my drafty space.

Come here, he'd say. I loved him best when he didn't ask, when he seemed absolutely sure of himself. He'd find a few spare minutes to wave me in, he'd close the door, and we'd sit together in the sagging chair in the corner.

I was cold now, too. I hadn't used the key to his office since we'd broken up, hadn't thought to use it. Maybe it was a security blanket. Maybe it was a souvenir. Maybe it was that I'd always assumed that some things hadn't changed, some things couldn't change. But he had, or I had. Or—I wasn't sure.

There was nothing for me in here, and yet I wanted to open the door. Because I could.

Don't hurt yourself trying to tell me. I know who you are.

But did she? I didn't think so. Nancy knew the tiny pieces Doyle allowed her to know, and he only knew what I'd offered, and none of it was everything. I still had the key. I still had everything I came in with.

"Except my dignity," I said to the door. Did I really look like I had to pee when I pretended he meant nothing to me? I turned the key.

The last time I'd been inside had been the week before the shooting. We'd called it quits the spring before, his things extricated from my place one afternoon while I taught. He hadn't even left a book or a tie I could return later. To be able to see him, to make seeing him at school regular again, I'd had to walk in and ask him something that belonged here, to Rothbert and not to anywhere else. The memory of that conversation fled back out of reach. Maybe I'd asked him advice on a student issue or we'd talked about publishing or about my fall teaching load or an internal department grant to write another book. I would have kept to the subject. Standing in his doorway that day, I would have made myself clear.

And he would have listened and answered and done all the right things, because that's how Doyle was. We had several more conversations here and in the hall before he came to see me in the hospital, but that first conversation, after the move, here, over his desk—that was the clinical end of our relationship. Surgical. I should have left the key, but I hadn't.

So? It was a souvenir.

I went to his side of his desk and pulled back his chair. A manila folder sat in his seat. I moved it to his desktop and sat down. I didn't know what I was doing, but that didn't stop me from wanting to do it. Could sitting here allow me to see things as clearly from his point of view as easily as I'd seen them from Nancy's, in the Wolitzers' backyard?

Nothing came to me, except the obvious. Nicholas Doyle wanted to share his life, and I had refused him. More than once. I loved him best when he was sure of himself, but I made him unsure of himself.

My belly and hip throbbed. Standing on the president's lawn, teaching, the extra trip up here. I'd pay for it tomorrow. Or pay with a hangover from the extra pain meds I'd take. I wanted to stay a little longer behind Doyle's oversized desk, in the cup of his well-worn leather chair. Listening to the hum of the campus and the town beyond his windows felt like nostalgia, but nostalgia for a moment I'd never lived. A photo of his kids watched from a shelf.

I stood slowly, my hip giving a sharp reprimand.

And then I saw it. *Lehane.*

The manila folder I'd moved from Doyle's chair wasn't labeled, but a sheet of paper inside stuck out enough for the name to rise and strike me. I flicked open the folder to a sheaf of legalese. Near the back of the stack, I found the page that had drawn my attention.

Lehane, Richard and Pamela. Such throwaway names. I couldn't imagine them. I could barely imagine their son a real person. His photo, often published near mine, had become an image out of history, a commemorative postage stamp.

The document read far over my head. It mentioned an address, a town in Illinois I'd never heard of. Doxley? My hands itched to take the document down to the photocopier for a quick duplicate. I would have done it if the copier hadn't been two floors away, if the left half of my body hadn't begun its drumbeat for the pill bottle.

In the end, I swiped a sticky note from Doyle's notepad, hand-copied out the address, and folded it into my pants pocket. I shuffled the pages back together and left the folder where I'd found it. The key, after a hesitation, I dropped into his desk drawer. And then I limped to the door and out.

In the elevator, I began to wonder at myself. The boy shooter's address in my pocket, as though I planned to do something with it. As though I had a plan at all.

The door opened to the second floor. I had meant to go straight to the lobby and home. Whatever impulse had brought me here was gone. Home, home, the edges of myself sanded off by a well-timed medical intervention. I hit the lobby button and the door-close. Rumor had it that the door-close buttons in elevators the world round were for sociological studies only. How often would the rat pound at the button to close the doors a second earlier?

Six times.

The doors started to close, but then—the barest flicker of light.

I threw myself between the doors and out into the renovated hallway.

There it was again, just a pinprick of light. This time I caught the movement, located it high on the wall opposite my office. The elevator doors closed behind me. I took a step, and the light danced.

Fire.

"Who's there?" I called.

Dread settled like a stone in my stomach.

"Anyone?"

I found myself planning my counterattack. How high to lift my cane, the right angle to strike at a face or a groin. I would need momentum. I'd be nothing against a gun. If a gun rose from the dark—there was no dark, but I shook anyway. My hip pinched when I took a step.

Standing in the center of the hall, the light became clear. A reflection. The flame sputtered in the glass of the framed co-ed. I stumbled forward, at last released from my stupor. A *fire*?

A candle had been propped up on the lip of the bin outside my office door. It had tipped, the wick burning a spot into the wall and blistering the plastic panel above it. My name was singed and warped.

I blew out the flame and peered into the landing and down the stairs. "Hello?"

The shuffling sounds of someone else at work downstairs were gone. I heard a group of voices passing by outside. Students, loud, pleased to be where and who they were.

The thick, yellow candle smelled of a flower I couldn't name. The wick was long, new. It hadn't been burning for long. I peered again into the corners behind the stairs and down the way I'd come. Leo Lehane, once, had stood just here. I couldn't keep from checking again.

The hallway smelled of bouquet and barbecue, of hot plastic.

I reached for the candle and recoiled. There was something tucked behind the candle at its base.

I knew at once: I had been waiting for this, whatever it was.

I checked the hall again, listened down the stairs, and reached again for the candle.

A piece of notepaper, folded into a tight accordion. Time had been taken to get the folds crisp. I pulled the paper open like a window shade. What had I expected? That the note was for Corrine? That a mistake had been made? That someone had not deliberately left a fire to burn my name off the wall of Dale Hall while the pink-cheeked co-ed across the hall bore witness?

The note was not for me.

Leonard Lehane, it said. *Rest in peace.*

OK. That was fine. Unattended fire was always a bad idea, but the message: indeed, Leonard. Rest up, buddy. I didn't mean what I said about sending you to hell. My nameplate was ruined, but no real damage had been done.

But—somehow, I knew.

I swept my hand inside the bin, coming up with a crumpled piece of paper. So unlike the careful origami of the other message, but I knew this was the true quarry of the night. I smoothed the paper against the wall and considered it.

Professor, it read. *It should have been you.*

I panicked.

The candle and message to Leo Lehane I dropped into the garbage, and the secret note, into a pocket. I hopped down the stairs, clinging to the handrail and ignoring the pangs ringing up my leg and through my gut. Out of Dale Hall, down to the parking lot—my car the last one this time—and off campus. I surprised myself by passing my apartment and doing a loop around the small downtown, too fast.

Who had done this? Who would bother?

One circuit, two.

Lehane was dead, but whatever he'd started hadn't burned out. He didn't have friends, but had he not acted alone?

I forced myself to let up on the gas, to find the people in other cars and along the street, to find faces. Young people in clutches, laughing their way back toward campus. A family with a child asleep on his father's shoulder.

I pulled up each person I knew in my mind, checking them against my fear. Woo? He disdained my education and probably didn't like me personally. Doyle. He'd wanted more of me than I'd been able to offer. I ran out of candidates fast. I'd met people at conferences I didn't like, certainly, but at what point of my life had I picked up an enemy?

Three circuits, four, until at last I nearly idled. A parking space opened in front of the Mill.

Inside, the weeknight clientele was sparse. Joe looked away from the TV, his face dropping the ten-minutes-'til-close scowl and contorting into something else I didn't recognize.

"I could use one, if you're still serving," I said.

"If you can drink fast." He pulled a beer from the cooler at his knees and waggled it at me. "Bad day, Teach?"

"Bad." We met at the bar. I slid onto a stool and made short work of my promise. When I put the bottle down, it was half gone.

"That bad." Joe hadn't gone to college, and sometimes he didn't seem to believe me about bad days. Had a keg blown up in the basement? No? Then I hadn't had a bad day.

"Longest day of my life," I said. "Second. No, third, but those have all been recent, you understand."

"Heard you fell the other day. That sucks."

"No argument here. My—" I'd been about to tell him Nath's story, that my cane had gotten caught up, but why bring Joe's notice to my third leg? My skin began to hum with the thought that the day might not be over. A long day might be turned around by a long night. Maybe I'd been coming here all along. "It was nothing." I took up my beer again, glanced into the empty corners. "Lonely in here tonight. Surprised you're not already locked."

"I must have known you needed one." Joe took up a rag and swiped at the bar without commitment. I watched his hands, the twist of his neck as he turned to catch a score on the TV. A familiar moment, here. I'd come to pick him up from work and take him back to my place so many times, and after that period of my life, sat here with Doyle and argued in low voices that Joe wasn't all the things that Doyle needed to worry about. Younger, sexier, a mindless fling. It hadn't mattered in a long time, but Joe turned me on.

In my pocket, the note burned its words against my hip. *It should have been you.*

But it hadn't been. What was it the students said, when they wanted to justify going out on weeknights, staying out late when they had tests and essays? A song lyric or a bumper sticker—

You can sleep when you're dead.

My thoughts rushed ahead: my hand on Joe's arm, the short drive home, stumbling into bed and not worrying for the first time in a while about looking like a fool.

"Look—"

His eyes found mine and slid away. He turned to wipe the back counter, but I'd already seen the bright flicker of panic—of horror— that I might ask him the question we both knew I wanted to ask.

I hadn't always had to be the one to ask.

I never would again.

"Thanks for staying open." My breath was short, my voice rasping. I reached for my wallet.

Joe waved me off. "On me."

The pain in my hip had nothing on this. For a moment, I forgot about the note in my pocket, the fall, the bullet that had put this all in motion. It was a gift, really, that Joe had given me. I'd forgotten about the pills in my bag and what would happen if I didn't take them on time.

I'd forgotten everything but the black room, where I'd been robbed of everything but my own raw materials. And the person I was hadn't been enough. I had never been enough and now I understood.

I lived in the black room now. Always. Always I would remain here.

CHAPTER 29
NATH

The phone rang. In my dream I dove from the sailboat into the water. That's where the phone was, and I had to call for help. I swam down, down into the dark, reaching. I'd call Dr. Emmet, the President of the United States, that reporter—

"Asshole," Kendall moaned. "Get the phone."

I pulled the phone into my neck. "What?"

"Ahoy, matey."

I sat up. The dream flew away. I was left with the muck of dread on my skin, and my throat scratched from coughing lake water from my lungs. My shoulder and back ached.

The sail back last night had been silent. I'd crawled into and out of the dinghy and back onto the rocks with shaking legs, clawing my way up the shore and away from Win and Dutch without a word.

"What do you want?" My voice hardly sounded like mine.

"To apologize," Win said. "That—shouldn't have happened."

"You made it happen. Do you think I'm stupid?"

"I'm the stupid one. It was a shitty thing to do. You could have been hurt."

I felt hurt. "Fine. You're sorry. Thanks for calling."

"Let me make it up to you."

The pressure on my shoulder of a hand holding me under. "That's not necessary."

"Don't be a dick."

"I'm never getting on a boat again, actually."

"You're on my crew for Night Sail, dude—"

"When was the last time someone drowned during Night Sail? Not interested."

"You can think about it," he said, as smooth as a politician to the last. "Do you want to come by the hotline sometime?"

I tasted the green lake in the back of my throat. "What's that supposed to mean?"

"You are one touchy guy," Win said. "I meant you could stop in, see what it's all about. You seemed interested."

My blood thudded in my ears. This was what I'd been waiting for. Why I'd come to Rothbert. Why I'd gone on the boat.

Had one of them really held me under the water? I couldn't convince myself. I remembered struggling to find the surface and, at the last, giving into a feeling of elation. That moment when everything went clear, everything I'd ever done or been or said turning bright and good. Flying. And the moment after, out of the water, gagging for breath and heavy with my own body, wet clothes, and real life. Painful reality, when I'd just figured it out.

Euphoria. That was the word. I didn't want the boat, or the hotline, or a sociology degree several years away. I wanted to try that feeling out again. I wanted to swim in it. Maybe Leo Lehane knew something none of us wanted to admit. Maybe a little brush with death was good for the soul.

Sure. All I had to do was call the number on the pen or magnet some early morning and tell them that, and I'd certainly find out everything I'd ever wanted to know about the Hope Hotline. From the inside, and then from a padded room. There had to be an easier way.

"I'm interested," I said.

"You know where it is?"

"I'll find it."

"My shift starts at ten."

"At night?"

"The graveyard."

"What?"

"The overnight shift. I start at ten and get out at five. Unless I've got someone on the line. Up for it?"

Like the lake had never happened. I'd looked up sailing terms since my swim. Jibe. That's what he'd said, and Dutch had wasted no time. Jibe was the order that turned the boat around and sent the boom swinging. The boom—that's what it was called and also what it did to you if you stood in its way. They'd known exactly what they were doing. Dutch would have done it for sport, but what game was Win playing? Invite the dork out for a joy ride and then dump him in the drink? And now another invitation. If this turned into another mousetrap, then I wasn't a very bright rodent.

"I really am sorry," Win said.

"I'm up for it," I said. And even though I didn't forgive him, I found that I meant it. I was up for it, whatever it was.

When Win hung up, I held onto the phone. I couldn't face a minute of the intro class, not today. Luck was on my side at last: the steel wool in my throat made for a convincing sick call. Dr. Emmet's office voice mail picked up. Even better.

"Dr. Emmet, I hate to do this—"

"You're not sick," Kendall said. I cupped a hand around the receiver and hurried through my excuses.

I hung up and lay back in bed. But he was right. I wasn't sick. I was mad. I jangled with it until I couldn't stand to lie there any longer. I got up and grabbed some jeans from the closet floor.

"Told you. You couldn't take a day off even if you were dead."

"Shut up, Kendall."

I shoved a few books into my backpack and hurried out of the apartment. I was halfway down the block before I faced the fact that I had nowhere to go. I walked toward the lake until the image of my foot sliding off the embankment came to me. I stopped and considered my options. The library couldn't contain me. Dale Hall. The student center? I couldn't picture myself anyplace I knew, except—

I looked at my watch.

When the Mill's door opened, I reached and held it. The bartender, same guy as always, gave me a side-eye look. "A little early, isn't it?"

"You wouldn't be opening this early if people didn't sometimes need a drink."

"I meant—how old are you?"

"Old enough to worry about my own liver," I said. "Do I have a usual yet?"

He remembered me now. I took the back booth and laid out my books. Within a few minutes, he dropped a coaster on top of my textbook, then the bottle.

I moved them off the book. "Start a tab."

"I guess she's teaching you something," he said, walking away.

I opened the text and flipped to the chapter I needed to read for Dr. Emmet's class. Stared at it, parsed out the first sentence, the second. The words didn't seem to connect. I could have been reading about quantum physics or pet fashion for as much as I could concentrate.

Had one of them really held me under the water? I rubbed my shoulder until the pain flared. Proof, at least, that I hadn't imagined the whole thing.

The door opened. Dr. Emmet stopped when she saw me. Then she turned to the bartender.

"Breakfast, with a lot of booze."

"Melly—"

"Like a screwdriver, but with a *lot* of screw."

"I wanted to—"

"Joe, I'm working on a couple hours of sleep. Whatever it is, I'm not—you know?"

He nodded and pulled a glass from above his head. "I just—"

"Joe, *really*."

She headed my way.

"Dr. Emmet, I can explain."

She waved a hand at me. "I don't care how early you drink if you don't care how early I do. What's wrong with your voice? Are you sick?"

She hadn't heard my message. "Sort of."

"You should be home."

"Home isn't—my roommate's there." Somehow this conveyed what I meant. She nodded. The bartender brought her drink. Something clear with a splash of orange juice.

"Start a tab."

He rolled his eyes and left. Dr. Emmet reached for my textbook and stroked the cover. "I always thought I'd write a better book than this."

"Why don't you?"

"It's complicated. Big project, years of research and analysis." Her eyes slid past me until I was sure she was thinking of something else, then snapped back. "Maybe I will yet. And then there's whatever work you'll do. Your dissertation. Have you given it any thought?"

The dissertation I wanted to do on the crime that had left her so miserable? Suddenly I saw what a creepy idea this was. The incident was far too recent. She had no distance, and I had no right.

"A little. I—I'm not sure what I want to do yet." I pulled the book out from under her hand and tucked my materials away.

"Well. You have time. Actually, the worst part is that I did write a book better than that. You'd be hard-pressed to find a copy of it."

"You never published it?"

"I burned it. On a barbecue grill."

"Why?"

I must have looked horrified. She laughed. "I'm not sure," she said. "I think it had something to do with feeling—out of control. You know?"

I knew. Otherwise, I wouldn't also know what dull steak knives looked like in moonlight.

Dr. Emmet threw back the last of her drink and looked toward the bar for a long moment.

"Do you want me to get you something?"

She shook her head. "The other night, do you remember when you said you wanted to skip certain parts? Of your life?"

The bartender finally looked our way. I raised two fingers and pointed toward her glass. "Yeah." Maybe I shouldn't say things like that. Even if they were true.

"I think I've felt that way my entire life. Except—my entire life, Nath. I've never wished for the moment I was in." She shrugged. "And now, of course—well. That's a hell of a way to live."

The drinks came, two tumblers of anonymous liquor covered with a thin layer of juice. She made short work of hers, then reached for mine.

"It would have been a hell of a way to die, too," she said.

"You didn't."

"I will. Someday. Maybe violence won't have anything to do with it. I hope. I'd like to go out quietly. In the night, eighty-nine years old. Somebody, somewhere, sad about it. That's all anyone ever wants, isn't it? Thanks, Joe."

He'd brought two more drinks. Bigger tumblers, less juice.

"My mom died," I said. My screeching voice rendered the statement hideous. Dr. Emmet looked up from lining up both drinks on her side of the table. "Cancer. Just, uh, last year."

"That's awful."

"Yeah."

"In her bed?" she said.

"In a hospital bed, after being sick at home for a long time. There's something to be said for dying in a hospital, though. I mean—old age, in your sleep, sure. But. But we—were able to leave it there afterward. Mostly. There's this afghan on the couch—"

I couldn't tell her about that. Couldn't tell her about the forest-green squares, the frilled edges. How it smelled of sickness and her shampoo and something else, pungent and ripe.

"I'm so sorry." Her words slurred at the edges.

I shrugged and tried to smile a little. Grief unnerved people. Something I'd learned a long time ago.

"That's the part you want to jump past," she said. She had the last of the drinks in her hand. I waved off the bartender as he tried to bring us another round. "That's the real stuff, there. As usual, I'm selfish. I want to leap past the—the *humiliation*." She raised her voice for this last. The barman paused, then poured the rejected drinks into the sink.

"Maybe we should get you home, Dr. Emmet."

"Here's what I've been thinking. Just because I didn't know him, that doesn't mean he didn't know me."

"Leo."

"Think about it. Say you want to make some point about violence. Say you want to make that point at Rah-rah-Rothbert." She flicked her fingers like pom-poms. "Say you manage to get a gun. What a cute trick it would be to track down the professor who thinks she's got this vio-lence thing strapped down to the examining table and give her a sur-prise. Huh? That's what I've been thinking."

Her empty glass hit the table, heavy. She looked toward the bar. "Is he bringing us another?"

"Don't you have to teach today, Dr. Emmet?"

"Does that make sense? Or am I foo—" She hiccupped. "Fooling myself? Maybe he looked me up in the faculty directory. I've been known to turn a few heads. *Right, Joe?* Used to. Used to turn—"

She looked over the row of empty glasses, then brought her elbows to the table and let her head fall into her fists.

"What?" I said.

"This is the part I want to skip. Right now."

I reached across the table, then recoiled when I saw the bartender watching. "This we can skip," I said. "Give me your keys."

CHAPTER 30

The drive took only a few minutes, but Dr. Emmet fell asleep before we reached her building. I sat for a while, giving her a chance to wake up on her own, thinking about Leo. Had the kid had some point to make? Or thought he did, only to have the meaning lost, like Dr. Emmet's book, on fire in the barbecue? A big gesture, and nothing to show for it.

"Dr. Emmet."

She cozied against the door.

"Dr.—*Amelia*."

"What?"

I got out and went to her door. A few heavy knocks on the window got her to sit up so that I could open it, unbuckle her, and pull her out. I remembered the cane at the last minute.

I was her cane now, half-carrying her toward the door. "Which key?"

"'s code." She managed a few buttons, sagging in my arms with the effort. If she hadn't been recovering from a bullet wound, I might have thrown her over my shoulder. Instead, I hauled her inside as carefully as I could, tried the code I'd seen her use on one door for the next, and hustled us both into her apartment before any nosy neighbors gathered around.

Dr. Emmet sat heavily on the couch. She winced. "Pills."

I took her bag from across her chest and rummaged until I found the bottle, the same one I'd retrieved for her at our first meeting. This time, I checked the label. The name of the drug was familiar, one of the pain meds my mom had taken at the last. "These? The orange ones?"

"Two."

I filled a glass half-full at the kitchen sink, thinking about the heavy pours we'd had at the bar. Back at the couch, she'd slumped to one side. I handed her the glass and shook a single pill into her hand.

"*Two.*"

"That's your second."

She peered at the pill, then accepted the water and tossed it back.

I took the bottle back to the kitchen to find a hiding place. We'd done this for my mom, too, before the hospice nurse had taken over. The freezer would work. I'd leave a note, and when she could read and understand what it said, maybe she'd be ready for more pills.

"I know what you're doing," she said.

"You do?" For a second I thought she might tell me something useful. I didn't know what I was doing. Then I realized she might mean my secret project. I stared at her, waiting for the pronouncement.

Nothing came. Her head lay against her chest in an awkward angle. "Dr. Emmet?"

Nothing.

Ohgod.

I rushed to her side and nudged her. "Dr. Emmet, please wake up." Had even one pill been too much with all the alcohol? My mind leapt ahead to how much trouble I'd be in. Killing my research subject? So goddamned stupid.

I shook her shoulder until her teeth clattered together.

"Sssstop," she moaned. "What?"

"OK, OK. You're not—oh, Jesus. OK. How do you feel?" I leaned in to see her fluttering eyelids.

And then she threw up all over me. Herself, the couch, the floor.

She fell off the couch onto her hands and knees and retched until I was sure I'd join her.

When she'd finally stopped, the place was a crime scene, her clothes a total loss, and some of mine.

"Nathaniel," she said. "I'm so—"

And then she started to cry. Not the silent tears of pain from our first meeting. The real kind, wretched and endless, like someone from a movie. Like someone at a funeral.

I patted her shoulder.

After a while, she quieted, sniffled. Her breath evened out. She wiped her mouth with the back of her hand. "So sorry," she whispered.

Dr. Emmet sat on the floor, wrapped in a blanket, while I tackled the floors and couch.

"I should probably say that I never saw my life coming to this," she said. "But that's a lie. I've been headed here for quite some time."

I didn't say anything. I'd thrown away the sweater I'd been wearing and located some cleaning supplies under the kitchen sink. In a way I couldn't have explained to her, it felt good to have something to do. My dad and the nurse had taken most of the heavy work for my mom at the end, but I'd done my share during the first rounds of chemo. Scrubbing Dr. Emmet's carpet seemed like I'd found a portal into another afternoon, another soiled floor. A slip through time to when I'd had more hope. When I looked up, the sight of Dr. Emmet rather than my mom jarred me back.

"No, really," she said, though I hadn't put up any argument. "The whole time. I've been in over my head all along. Wait 'til I tell you how long shoes had to last in my family. The hand-me-downs from people I'd never met. Didn't want to meet. Hoped I'd never meet while I wore one of their shirts." She looked around as though she'd just walked into the room for the first time. "This is all someone else. The person I was supposed to be. The person I promised I'd become."

I'd stopped scrubbing and leaned back on my heels.

"They tell us all we have to do is work," she said, smiling in a strange way at her hands. "Work hard. Work harder than anyone else, and you'll rise. You'll—find a way out. But it's lonely once you do. They don't tell you that. The ones you leave behind don't understand." She gave a strange, wheezy laugh. "But then the people you meet along the way aren't yours, not the way—not the way the others were, or like you need them to be. You know how they got me?"

I'd lost track of which *they* we meant. "How?"

"They gave me a scholarship. They gave the poor little smart girl a scholarship so that she could go make something of herself."

"And you did, didn't you?"

She gazed over the room again. In a corner, I saw some framed cer-
tificates and diplomas, stacked on the floor in a careless pile. "Yes. I
certainly made *something* of myself."

"All clean," I said.

"You didn't have to do that. The—Ausra would have gotten to it."

"Ausra?"

She glanced away. "Cleaning service."

The rag went into the trash, the supplies back where I found them.
"When? And then you'd have to find a new housekeeper. She'd definitely never want to see this place again."

"You have every right to be pissed at me." Her voice was hoarse,
her eyes puffy.

"Your turn to get cleaned up."

"I can do it."

"Really?" I said. "Go ahead and stand up, then."

We both knew she couldn't. Cane or no cane, she'd be on the floor
until someone pulled her up. She wouldn't look at me.

"If you could get me to the bathroom, I'm sure I could take it from
there."

I didn't think that was likely either. "We'll see."

"I could call someone. My—" She thought for a second. "Friend."

She didn't sound certain that such a person existed. "I'm your
friend," I said.

"But you're—"

"It's OK."

"It is?"

How to explain to her the last year of my mom's life. How everything fell away, how everything real became a symbol of itself. How my
mother's body became a talisman, a prayer, a wish. A moment of silence
we all shared.

In the bathroom, I held Dr. Emmet upright while she brushed her
teeth at the sink, then unwrapped her from the sodden blanket. She
slid off her shoes, revealing strangely pale and naked feet.

This was—fine.

I helped her remove her sweater, her arms skinny in the T-shirt underneath. Then the T-shirt, my eyes averted. It was not OK in the least. She was who she was. She was not a specimen. She was not a whisper or a prayer. She was flesh and blood, the warmth of her body radiating toward me.

She paused, her hand at the button of her jeans. "Is it OK?"

I nodded, still not looking. She was not the memory or the shadow of herself. It shouldn't be OK. It wasn't. And it was.

I steadied her, her arm around my neck, as she pulled the pants down and stepped out of them. Bra and underwear, and long, pale legs.

I wasn't looking, but then I was. The mirror. I could see the raw pink splotch in her abdomen, an explosion of new skin and scar tissue.

She found my eyes in the mirror.

Is it OK? I knew what she really wanted to know, but I didn't know the words.

"You're—"

She hung from me as though I were a life raft, watching my lips for what I would say.

"You're beautiful," I said.

The space between us disappeared. Her lips were on mine, soft at first, then hard and hungry. For a moment I was gone, my body not my own.

I held on like a man drowning.

CHAPTER 31
AMELIA

I t wasn't a kiss.

Was it?

I had started this. Or had he?

I couldn't decide. I didn't want to decide. I pressed into Nath, checking myself against him.

Was I alive?

Yes.

Was I desirable?

Yes.

My body hadn't forgotten anything. Damaged, but not broken. Not wasted. I felt myself rise into Nath's grasp, placing myself at his mercy. His hands were clumsy, but he was learning.

Learning.

I faltered. Nath dropped to his knees and kissed the tender flesh next to my scar. Everything else faded beyond my attention. His mouth—

I opened my eyes. In the mirror, I watched as Nath ran his hands up the backs of my legs, hooked his thumbs under my panties, and tugged.

"No."

He held on, flicking his tongue at my navel in a way that made the floor fall out from under me. My knees shook. I reached for the edge of the sink.

"No—Nath. Stop." I grabbed the back of his hair and pulled. He looked up, eyes still somewhere else, his lips swollen.

"Why?"

He thought he knew why. He thought it had something to do with me being his teacher. But that was not the truth.

The truth was that I didn't want to kiss him. I wanted to consume him. I wanted to take everything he was and had and make it mine.

What kind of teacher was that? What kind of human?

"I—can't."

"You want to." One hand traced the curve of my lower back and brushed over my ass. I wasn't teaching this kid a thing he didn't already know.

Part of me did want to. I stepped backward.

He dropped his hands, adjusted his khakis. "Right."

"Nath, I'm so—"

"Please." He cleared the pleading note out of his throat. "Please don't apologize."

He'd be burning with rejection. I knew it well, better than he'd probably guess. Joe's look of panic the night before shamed me. How long would Nath glow with embarrassment when he saw me or thought of me? It was too late to do the right thing.

Nath pulled himself off his knees to sit on the side of the tub. He reached for handle of the tub faucet to start the water.

"I can do it," I said.

"People can drown in two inches of water." He sounded like he knew what he was talking about. "Don't take any more pills tonight."

I clutched the sink's edge until the water was deep enough, then waited until Nath had turned his back to drop the last of my clothes and step into the bath. The water was scalding, and I was glad. Of all the grime that I needed to sear off my skin, this last layer seemed the least likely to come off. He'd added some shampoo to the water for bubbles. I gathered them to cover myself. "Forget what I said about Leo Lehane. I don't care anymore. I mean—it's fine if I never understand it. I'm dropping it. Promise me—Nath, promise me you'll drop it."

In his efforts not to look at me in the tub, he stared at an empty spot on the wall.

"Nath?"

"I hate that."

"What?"

"The—the not knowing," he said.

I did, too. Could I live with it? I thought I could, since it looked as though I'd have to. "Not much we can do about gray areas. Besides, this is my burden, not yours. I should never have dragged you into it."

He looked at me, then away. We sat for another minute or so, listening to the tiny sound of bubbles popping. At last, he said, "You'll be—uh, OK?"

Not allowed to apologize, I couldn't think of the right words. "You can go."

When he left, he pulled the door delicately, as though closing in a sleeping child. I listened for his steps and then the front door. Then my own breathing, until I despised the sound.

I woke in the cold bath, my chin dipped under the water line. I sat up, startled.

The sound came again.

Footsteps.

I stretched for a towel and dragged myself out of the tub, dripping, shaking, looking around for any kind of weapon.

"Mel?"

Doyle?

I cracked the door, a heavy bottle of shampoo raised. "Nicholas, for the love—"

His shoulders slumped. "Jesus, change your door codes once in a while. And you might try getting a cell phone." He flicked the hall light on and took in the towel, my dripping hair.

"I've been home all night." My teeth chattered. I searched for a clock. "What time is it?"

"Then answer your home phone when it rings. I've been calling for an hour."

I hadn't heard the phone. Maybe Nath was right to worry about those two inches of water. "What's going on?"

"What happened in the living room? You need to declare a federal disaster in there."

"Why were you calling?" I said.

"I—I don't remember."

That was a lie. I put down the shampoo and tightened the towel. What would Mrs. Nick think of him helping himself to my apartment while I was half-naked? I'd already had one near miss with bad decisions today. I didn't need another. "Why don't you try to remember while I get dressed? Is Nancy in the car?"

"She's at home."

"What did you tell her?"

He blinked at me for a moment too long. "I'm not sure why I bothered."

The visit began to unnerve me. Late-night visit, unannounced. The wife left at home. I found myself checking Doyle's hands to make sure they were empty.

They were. I wiped my hand over my face. It had come to this. "You were just—worried?"

"Should I be? Passing out in the classroom? Hanging out at the Mill all hours, a student trailing after you wherever you go?"

Now I understood. "Are you following me, too?"

"*Too?*" he said. "I'm not even going to—tell me that I don't need to worry about you, about our students. After last year, I can't write off your bad behavior and let something happen again."

I couldn't even argue the bad behavior. "You didn't let anything happen the first time. Dammit, Doyle, it had nothing to do with you. Or me."

"Are you sure?" He shoved his hands deep into his pockets. "No one else is sure. They all want to be on your side, but they're not sure."

Wolitzer's surprise that I'd returned. Jim's retirement offer. They weren't on my side. They were on the safe side.

"I'm sure," I said.

"Because if it happened again—"

"I have no more control over that than I did the first time."

"Control is actually what I'm asking of you," he said.

We stared at one another. Doyle didn't even know the half of it: Nath, and all the sad ways I'd leaned on him. "I've got control. You're going to have to trust me."

"I hope so, Amelia."

"If you leave now, I'll change the codes behind you."

He turned on his heel and stalked to the door. At the last moment, he paused. "You know what I told Nancy tonight? I told her I needed to check on a friend. I think—I think I have to stop thinking of you that way."

Again: the soft door close. The way men said good-bye.

CHAPTER 32
NATH

Stupid.

The door to Dr. Emmet's building slammed open, then closed with a slow and silent click behind me. It was still light out, hardly evening.

I'd ruined everything. Or maybe she'd—no, I was so stupid.

I shouldn't have looked when I said I wouldn't. Had I said that? Wasn't that what I meant when I said it was OK?

Or did I mean—

My fault. I'd wanted to see the scar. I wanted to touch it. I wanted it to be mine, for her to be—mine.

Not romantically.

Not *necessarily* romantically. But—any way I could.

I wiped my hand across my face, smelling the cleaner I'd used on the carpet. Had that all just happened? I felt as though I'd crossed an invisible border into a different country or across the dateline into another day with no sleep. The rest of Willetson went on working, but I lived somewhere else, somewhere in-between. It was not a real place. I wasn't real. None of this—

Down the street, I saw a yellow Jeep, parked but with someone inside, watching. That seemed pretty real. I skirted the street and took to the alleys toward home.

A breeze kicked up as I passed campus. By the time I reached my building, the wind cut at me. I could feel the lake in the air; it had something to say.

My room, Kendall-free. I flopped onto my bed, but that sent me back to Dr. Emmet. The way her mouth opened, let me in—

I was charged, a race horse strapped into a carousel.

I shouldn't have left her.

I couldn't have stayed.

Ruined. I'd ruined it.

I reached for the phone and dialed. Changed my mind, changed it back.

"Hello?"

"Bryn," I said. "It's me. Nath."

"Nathaniel?"

"Yeah, how are you?"

"I'm—fine. How are you? You sound—uh, how are things going?"

"Great, great." Did we know each other well enough that she could tell I was lying? We'd known each other, once. I remembered those nights, a woman in my bed. Me, not believing my luck. "I'm good. Getting lots of work done. I got a TA job with the professor I wanted to work with."

"The one from the newspaper? Nathaniel—"

"I go by Nath now." I sounded ridiculous, even to myself. "Just a nickname a friend gave me."

"That's—that teacher. You're being careful, right?"

"Are you still with that guy?" I said. "What's his name?"

"Nathaniel, are you sure you're OK?"

I wasn't. I felt feverish and raw. "Yeah, yeah. Just really busy." Just eviscerated, I wanted to say. And not because of her—strange and wonderful and terrible that after what I'd almost done to myself over Bryn, she wasn't the best or the worst thing that had ever happened to me. My luck hadn't been that good.

So then. Nothing much had changed.

"I'll let you get back," I said. "To whatever."

"Nathaniel—"

"Nice talking to you."

Nothing much had changed. Except everything.

The next day I shuffled between my bed, the kitchen for a microwaved bowl of noodles, and back to my bed. I felt shredded. I hadn't heard anything from Dr. Emmet, and I waffled between being mad I hadn't and being mad at myself for expecting to.

"What's wrong with you?" Kendall said, watching me in the mirror. I sorted my clippings on Dr. Emmet's shooting. Again and again, her photo: the same hesitant smile, the same tilt to her head. Some of the clippings showed their age and use. I should laminate them, take them to the copy shop and have them preserved. I let the scene play out in my head: The copy shop guys give me the uh-oh look. Someone calls the police.

Bad idea.

"What?" Kendall said.

Had I said something? "Nothing. Never mind."

Kendall launched himself into his loft and peered at me from above. "Are you OK?" He cleared his throat. "If you ever need to, you know, talk to someone—"

"Got it covered." This he could take however he wanted. That I was speaking with someone already, that I had plans to, that I didn't need anyone at all. I had it covered, and he could feel good about asking. "Got it under control," I said.

The truth was that I'd be seeing the people he meant in only a few hours. I thought back to the night I'd announced plans to kill myself at the bar. I'd seen it so clearly. If I pretended to need help, if I dug deep to resurrect the helplessness I'd already known, I could fool them. I could walk right into the hotline and ask for that hope they promised on the refrigerator magnet. And the pen.

But now. Now I didn't need a way in. I didn't need an excuse. I felt bad enough; the only thing I needed to pretend was that I was fine.

I sorted the clippings again. The only thing I needed to pretend was that I was cool.

The hotline operated from a bunker crouched in the basement of the student center. The place had low ceilings, flickering fluorescent lights, pillaged vending machines. Good thing you could order hope by phone.

A frosted-glass door announced I'd arrived at the right place. *Hope Found Here*, it said in script. A rack crammed with pamphlets hung nearby. I stopped and took one. On the cover, a girl sat at a window, her chin on her hand. *The blues—are they something serious?* the headline read. *Talk to someone you can trust.* The same sort of business inside, and on the back, a photo of Phillip listening to a student, his hands clasped as though he were holding himself back from hugging someone. Something about his expression cut through the fog until I had the first coherent thought I'd had in a while.

Truly, the guy could benefit from dialing it down a notch or two.

I tucked the brochure into my bag and went to the door. It was locked.

I gave the door a few good tugs, rattling it in its frame. A clock over the door said it was ten on the dot. I gave one more yank, and then the door swung open and a student wearing a Rothbert ball cap stuck his head out.

"Can I help you?"

"Here to see Win Harlan."

"He's not here yet, but I can talk to you."

The playbook lay open before us. Offer to help at every stage. Don't let the troubled person walk away from you. "I'm—sitting in," I said. "To volunteer. Maybe."

The guy gave me a long look. "We took bets on who was out here." He gestured toward a small sign I hadn't paid any attention to. *Locked 24 hours. Ring doorbell.* The sign hung over a doorbell. "Can't really let you go for long, though, can we? Considering."

"I didn't see the bell."

"Yeah. That's when we worry most." He glanced over his shoulder, shrugged. "You can come in and wait, I guess."

I hadn't expected much, but inside the Hope Hotline glowed yellow and cheerful, a large room with plenty of empty space, mats on the floor, and beanbag chairs grouped in a circle, like at a preschool. The corners of the room held pairs of puffy chairs. One area had been marked off by hip-height cubicle walls, each cube outfitted with a phone. Against one wall, a coffee station to rival any café.

The girl with pigtails—after a moment, I recalled that her name was Trudie, not Pixie—twirled a stir in a mug and watched us approach. She checked her watch and gave the other student a raised-eyebrow look.

"He's here for a ride-along with Win."

"Really? Phillip's going to love that." She looked me up and down. "I know you—"

"So what's the deal with Phillip?" I said.

"Narrow it down," the kid groaned, throwing himself into a beanbag. "Everything's a deal with Phillip."

Trudie shushed him. "We figure, you know, he's got serious baggage—"

The kid jumped back in, "Like he knew someone who killed themselves or, like, his mom—"

"Let's not talk about it," Trudie said. "He could come through any minute."

The last person I wanted to see, especially if he didn't allow outsiders hanging around. "This is a pretty good setup you guys have."

"It's only fair," Trudie said. "We're here forever, and hardly anyone ever calls. You kinda do start to consider suicide after a while."

"What about the black hour?"

They both squinted at me. "How do you know about that?" the guy said.

"Win has such a big mouth," Trudie said. "We could get into trouble, so keep anything he told you to yourself."

"In trouble with who?"

"Phillip hates it when we—well, it's not like we make fun of the callers. But sometimes—we're here all hours, OK? You have to talk about something."

"I do my homework," the guy said, throwing up his hands. "I'm innocent."

"You do homework and flirt with the new recruits."

"Only the female ones," he said to me.

"What do you say about the callers?" I said. "When you're here late and Phillip's gone?"

They exchanged a quick look. "Phillip's here every night," Trudie said. "He's dedicated."

"He sleeps here sometimes."

I nudged a beanbag chair with my foot.

"In his office," she said, nodding her head toward the far corner of the room. A built-out portion of the wall nearly hid the door there, but once I'd seen it, I couldn't believe I'd missed it. Phillip's secret office in the deeply buried basement hideout of the suicide watch. Where he could do-good or maybe hang out on whatever the university might pay him, medical and dental, in a plush room to meet young girls. I had to hand it to him. He was the one with a nice setup.

Behind me something beeped. We all turned to watch the door open.

"Ahoy, ahoy," Win said, sliding in like a returned hero. "The captain is back at the helm."

CHAPTER 33

He stopped short when he saw me. "Too soon?"

I didn't think I liked Win as much as I'd hoped to. But that wasn't important. I hadn't come for any hope. I hadn't come for any friendship, either.

The other guy said, "Wait. Are you the kid who jumped off Win's boat?"

"I didn't jump." Win did have a big mouth.

Trudie eyed me, revising.

"He's right," Win said. "He was bucked. *Ladykiller* didn't like the look of him."

They laughed while I struggled over "ladykiller." And then I remembered: in script, on the back of the boat, my lungs on fire. "I guess you don't need me for your Night Sail crew, then," I said.

"Serious as a gunshot, this one," Win said. "Fine. Let's get this party started. Only—this is pretty much what we do for the first four hours of the shift. I believe I warned you."

My eyes shot to Phillip's office. He was due any minute, and nothing happened for hours. I needed another dose of *be cool*, and fast.

"How about a tour?"

Win swung his arms wide. "This is it. Let's tour the coffee bar."

Someone had made a fresh pot. Win poured, and I doctored mine with cream—real cream from the small fridge under the table—and sugar. This was luxury. The Hope Hotline seemed better funded than I would have guessed, but then what university wanted to be caught slighting the psychological services of its students? Especially after a student had offed himself.

"So how often do you get a call from someone who's really serious?" I said.

"They're never serious," the other kid said.

206

"Aren't you off-shift now, Zach?" Trudie turned to me. "Once in a while."

"Never," Zach said. "Phillip says they—"

"Phillip says, Phillip says," Win said, staring into his mug. "I guess Phillip won double prizes when he recruited you. Counselor *and* number-one fan."

"Fine." Zach grabbed the backpack at his feet and stood, slinging it over his shoulder. "Have a good night *working*."

"Like you have any better offers," Win said. He saluted the kid out the door and plopped into a beanbag, holding his mug high and steady. "The fewer encounters with that one, the better. That kid bothers me."

"They all bother me," Trudie said.

"Except me, of course," Win said.

"Especially you."

"I'm special," he said. "At last."

"What does Phillip say? About the students who call?" I said.

Win looked my way. "You're very *interested*, aren't you?"

"Well." I dropped into a beanbag, all knees and elbows, a drop of hot coffee splashing my wrist. I dug deep for Kendall-like remove. "I thought I might volunteer, but you're not doing much to convince me."

"First of all, it's not up to you," Win said. "If you volunteer, then you get run through with process and paperwork and training until they know you better than you know yourself. It's hardly something you can be ambivalent about. And then it's up to Phillip if you get to join, which hours you get, how many calls you can take. If Phillip doesn't like you, then you're better off buying a couch and hanging a doctor-is-in sign over it."

I glanced at the clock over the entrance, calculating my options. "That settles it, then. Because Phillip doesn't think much of me."

They both sat up. "What's his reasoning?" Win said. "I'm still undecided."

"Maybe I threw him into the lake."

Win looked toward the clock and sighed. He was a half hour into his all-night shift and, I could tell, regretting he'd asked me along.

"What Phillip says about the callers is: the ones who call are the ones who won't do it. The ones who really want to kill themselves don't want to be talked out of it. They go for it."

"How inspiring," I said. Trudie laughed. "Has anyone gone for the gold recently?"

"An electrical engineering student ran his car into a tree in the quad my freshman year," Win said. "He meant it. And a kid on the football team OD'd on steroids over winter break two years ago."

"What about that girl who took all her roommate's Ritalin?" Trudie said. "Homecoming princess or whatever."

"Was that last year? Forgot about her." Win ticked them off on his fingers. "Pills. Pills. Tree. I feel like there's one missing."

"Gun," I said, my voice cutting through the room in a way that made them both stare.

Pills, pills, tree, gun. Listed out that way, I couldn't decide if one suicide a year was more than Rothbert's fair share or not as many as we might expect. "One problem with Phillip's theory, though. I heard Leonard Lehane called here before he shot himself."

"But he was different," Trudie said.

I turned to Win. He shrugged, sipped his coffee. "He was more like—a mascot."

"Do you often adopt callers?"

Trudie smiled. "He was a nice guy. Weird. But nice."

"It passed the time, talking to him," Win said.

"You both talked to him?"

"I think we all took a call at one point or another." Win turned his mug in his hands. "He called—not just a lot. Every night."

"You don't know that," Trudie said.

"Yes, I do."

Trudie narrowed her eyes.

"Phillip would kill you," she hissed.

I put my cup aside and fought the beanbag chair to sit up. "What?"

"The call log. Phillip keeps it," Trudie said. "Nobody gets to see it."

"How'd you see it, Win?" I said. "Is it here?"

"I had the opportunity once. I took it."

"What were you looking for?"

"Nothing specific."

I remembered him swirling his cocktail, Hefner-style. Maybe he was the kind of guy who went after the forbidden for bragging rights alone. But I didn't think so. "Bullshit."

He threw back the dregs of his coffee, but we waited. The clock made time audible. "I was curious if faculty ever called, OK?"

"And?" Trudie crouched, ready to pounce.

"I didn't see any names I knew," he said, glaring at me until I wasn't sure if we were still having the same conversation.

A beep, and then the door swung open. Phillip did the smoothest double-take I'd ever seen. "Nathaniel Barber. You stopped by to pay off that beer you owe me."

Trudie and Win glanced at me and then one another. We all heard it. Phillip didn't sound like a guy who disliked anyone in present company, and especially not me.

"Win offered to show me around," I said. "In case I could be of any assistance."

"You're recruiting, Win? That's fantastic. Gunning for student counselor of the month."

Win shot me another inscrutable look. If I'd been on *Ladykiller*, I would have reached for the railing and held tight.

"We have a training session coming up," Phillip said. "I'll put you on the list."

None of this sounded like the rings of fire Win had suggested I'd have to negotiate. Where was the background check? The knowing me better than I knew myself? "Sounds great."

"This Saturday."

"Oh—"

"Something wrong?"

I thought of my dad's voice when I'd offered to help with the auction. "I'll work it out."

"Great," Phillip said, beaming.

Win stared at his feet, his ears a strange shade of pink, like a bunny. Like James Baker.

"I don't usually allow ride-alongs," Phillip said. "But—"

"Why don't I go then?" I struggled out of the beanbag and to my feet. "I'll get trained up, and then come back and dig in where I'm needed." I sounded like an asshole, but Phillip nodded thoughtfully and walked me to the door. "You understand," he said. "Confidentiality is a big deal for the students who call."

"Sure," I said. I'd arrived in the depressing basement hallway again, stuffed full of information. "When they don't call—"

"That's the worst."

I nodded back toward the hotline headquarters. "This all goes to waste."

Phillip studied me. "That's not exactly how we see it. When they don't call, we don't get a chance to help them. Once you've been through that, well—you want to do whatever you can. See you Saturday."

I took the stairs. Not until I'd reached the top and had turned the landing corner did I hear the beep of a key card and the door open, Phillip going back inside.

The thing I found myself wondering, outside and away from the oppressive dullness of the basement and its polar twin, the over-bright playroom, was Leo, always Leo. It bothered me until I had worked the thought to the surface and turned it into a thesis.

If the people who called didn't really want to die, then people who made repeated calls wanted to live even more. Leo. Leo hadn't wanted to kill himself. But he had. He was special, Trudie had said. In the parlance of science, that made Leo an outlier, mucking up the experiment.

Or—

I stopped at the front door of the student center to let the thought collect itself. It had started to rain. Dr. Emmet and the night before felt far away. A pair of girls bustled by outside with umbrellas held against the wind.

Or maybe Leo wasn't an outlier. Maybe he'd been exposed to another, unseen variable.

My mind raced. Most people who called didn't want to die, but this kid had, and did. What had happened to Leo Lehane? He was special. He was special *to them*. And he'd done the one thing they tried to prevent.

What did it mean when your pet turned and bit you, precisely and for the kill?

CHAPTER 34
AMELIA

Friday morning, with the entire weekend wide before me, I lay in bed and let myself wander back to the hall, the candle, the scrawled insult, rest in peace. The warped, browned nameplate outside my door, which I would never be able to explain. Was that the damage they'd meant to do?

It should have been you.

They'd done more damage than a little singed plastic, whether they meant to or not. How could I go back to my classrooms now, knowing that any one of my students could have been in the candlelight vigil outside my office for Leonard Lehane?

And then Nath. Nath.

I'd been in bed since Doyle left. The phone had rung a few times. I imagined Doyle calling, letting it ring, hanging up. Each time, the fantasy grew brighter, and less likely.

It might have been Nath.

What was the protocol here? Should I call? Apologize?

He didn't want apologies. Which didn't leave me with much.

The phone began to ring again.

Corrine. If I were lucky.

I wasn't lucky, so it would be Nath. Or Doyle, really, but to dress me down for more rumors. Some of which had sailed past rumor into truth.

I'd canceled class that day, of course, but if I was honest with myself, I didn't need a day. Or a weekend. I needed—something. A new start. A new identity. A new country?

I'd only had eight credit hours of a foreign language, but people learned, right? Or maybe that woman from Toronto I'd met at the conference a few years ago might pass along my resume. Maybe I could get a tenured spot. It would have been easier with a book, but I could still teach—

My gut flipped.

I'd managed to stand in front of my students after the fainting episode, to explain and apologize. But every time I'd thought of facing the students after that note, after Nath, my stomach had taken a top-of-the-roller-coaster plummet. If I was being honest with myself, I wasn't certain I'd ever be a good teacher again.

I had decided not to be honest with myself. I flipped onto my back and threw my arm over my eyes to keep out the day.

Maybe the calls were from Dean Jim Perry, calling with a pink slip after a talking-to from the president for letting me teach again.

Or a student who'd talked my home number out of the dean's office.

Or the student who'd left the note, making sure the message had come through.

Or—the problem with not getting up to answer the phone was that I could spin every ring into the end of the world.

The phone went silent. A group of people walked by outside, their voices as near as if they stood in my room. Students, probably. I pulled my elbow off my eyes and found the clock. Or office workers on their way to lunch. Another pair hurried by, laughing. I trailed them by their mirth all the way to the corner and out of range. When was the last time I laughed with a friend? Had fun? The last time I'd felt like my life belonged to me, that I didn't fill it out like a hand-me-down suit jacket. I sat up and peered through the blinds, checking for the yellow Jeep. Even McDaniel had given up on me.

Two days off my hip had proved restful. I left the cane against my bedside table and stood, putting weight on my left side. For a moment I saw myself walking to campus, getting a jump on midterms while I had some energy.

A twinge through my gut sat me back down. Joe's horrified eyes flitted through my memory, then Nath's profile as he tested the tub's water temperature. I forced them to keep me company. Imagining again and again the moment when Joe's pity turned into something even more sour. In Joe, at last, I'd seen myself. In the way Nath wouldn't look at me, I'd seen the life that would be my punishment. Stares, surreptitious or not, the whispers that followed in my wake from students in the halls, strangers. With people I knew, I could count on careful conversations, sharp glances away when I said something that didn't fit, somehow, this new person I'd become.

That new person—I hated her. I hated that I was expected to be her. This wasn't my choice, and yet I was supposed to be changed. Better.

I wasn't better. I was worse.

Much worse. The new Amelia Emmet was someone I'd never hoped to be, and it felt itchy and insufferable. I could see everyone's point, actually. Leo, troubled but young, his life ahead of him. He might have recovered. He might have come through the other side better.

Me. Her. Why was she still here, if this was all she'd ever be?

It should have been her. It should have been me.

But it hadn't been, and for that I would be punished.

For that, I would punish myself.

Doxley, Illinois, lay more than two hours to the west of Chicago. A burgh, if that term still signified, far enough off the interstate that I realized too late a stranger pulling into town might draw attention. That I might be making a mistake.

I hadn't meant to go.

In the mess of my clothes on the bathroom floor, I'd found a shred of paper in the pants pocket. The note. I threw it away, then reached in and took it back, tore it up, and flushed it down the toilet.

The other pocket crinkled, too. The sticky note from Doyle's desk with the address I had no reason to know. I stared at it. *I wouldn't be surprised if she's been to your office.* I waffled between anger and something fluttering against the inside of my ribs. I picked up my cane and walked the length of my apartment. Twice. Three times. Time stretched out ahead of me. I couldn't go to my office. I couldn't go to the Mill.

And now, as I rolled into the tiny town, I had a bottle of water, my pain pills, and the address for the kid who'd tried to kill me. Going into enemy territory, unarmed in every sense.

Doxley sat under a heavy sky. A grocery, a family-name pharmacy, a bank. Each building was a box of bricks unto itself, unneighborly, broad faces frowning toward the line of cars and trucks parked at angles into their sidewalks. A gas station with full service, an auto-parts store. The town seemed like a movie set, where something horrific could rip through the calm façade any second. I saw a single person walking along the sidewalk, human tumbleweed. I tried to look purposeful behind the wheel.

Somewhere there would be a school where Leo learned his way into Rothbert. Somewhere among the quiet streets, a house where his mother had marked the progress of his height against a door jamb.

I swung down a side street. The town seemed ridiculously small, a narrow channel hulled out of farmland, but big enough that I had to drive up and down the streets looking for the right name, then the right number. I found the school, the library, and a hundred perfectly normal homes before, finally, the perfectly normal home that had housed Leo Lehane's childhood.

I passed the house and parked, watching it in the rearview through the swaying branches of an elm in the front yard. It could have been any house on the block. The color, the shape, the neat yard—none of it told me a thing about Leonard Lehane or his family. Maybe only that he'd come from a respectable town, from a family who took pride of ownership in their honest and, considering what Rothbert cost a year, modest surroundings. An American flag flapped from a post mounted to the front porch. I checked the rest of the street; each house flew one.

I knew places like this. My own was hundreds of miles away. No one I loved lived there anymore, which left no reason to visit, though

I hadn't done that enough when they'd been alive, either. No time. School, more school, then the academic treadmill I couldn't step from for a moment. Or—maybe there was more to it than that. My house had never been the one on the flag-flying street, never the one with a tidy lawn and a front porch swing. Not the kind of place you brought friends to, not after you'd been to their homes.

Small towns caught and trapped regret and disgrace like corners gathered dust. They gave me the hives.

A curtain in the nearest house flicked. My cue.

I lifted my foot off the brakes and continued up the street and to the corner.

Straight into the path of a yellow Jeep.

Shitohshit. The odds were bad, but I turned my face away. The Jeep stopped, blocking me.

"I knew it," the familiar voice yelled at my rolled-up window. "Grading quizzes, my ass."

No use. I'd been good and caught, and I couldn't go anywhere unless I gunned my sedan over the curb and into some nice Doxley family's box hedge. I rolled down the window and peered up into McDaniel's open-sided Jeep. For once he wasn't wearing the big brother jacket but a blue dress shirt open at the throat. The shirt appeared to be his own. He slapped his steering wheel with the flat of his hand and grinned at me. I hated him nearly as much as I hated myself. "What's this about quizzes?"

"Don't even try. Nath said you weren't up to anything, but the two of you didn't fool me for a second."

"Nice day for a drive." My face burned. The day was turning gray, the horizon roiling. The flags all along the street behind me would be blown flat by the wind. If he'd pull forward two inches, I could get away from him and ahead of the storm. "I was curious, all right? You can't blame me for that."

"I encouraged your curiosity, Professor. I just wanted in on it, but you and the wonder boy had to have your fun."

It hadn't been fun. I felt the dark edges of my own sorrow too keenly now to believe I'd ever once thought we might send Nath into a fake suicide spin to get inside that group. Nath. I'd let him down so hard. I wondered what the call center students would do if a faculty member called in.

Maybe Doyle was right. Maybe it was time to see a shrink.

"I'm not really operating under any plan," I said. "Can you move your car?"

McDaniel glanced down the street. "I could. Or you could back up and go see the Lehanes with me."

A wave of revulsion washed over me. "What would that accomplish?"

"Well, she wants to get a look at you, and you're—curious, was it? I wouldn't mind a front-row seat. Take a few notes, got my camera right here—"

"No way," I said. "I've been in the news enough. And I'm not going to sit for forgiveness portraits."

"She's not forgiving you anytime soon."

"I didn't *do* anything."

"Then you have nothing to fear, right?"

I feared everything. That was what I couldn't tell him. Or Doyle, a psychiatrist, or even some anonymous hotline operator. I would never be able to explain how brittle my bones felt, how the lightning bolt of ache through my gut served as a constant reminder not just of the attack but of every failure of my own before and since. I'd come here for punishment, but I didn't need the help. I wore the only punishment I needed on the inside of my body. My body, which had always been hollow, always felt broken.

"I can't go into their house."

McDaniel looked queasy. "Good point. I don't think she'd want to go to Main Street with you, either."

The grid of the town played itself in my head. "The library."

"Maybe. This is up to her, you know."

"It's up to me, too."

"Will you be at the library, if I let you go?"

"Are you prepared to keep me stuck here? All I have to do is back up—" I threw my car into reverse and rolled back.

He pulled forward to keep our windows close. "Fine. You're free. It's all up to you. Please be at the library."

"Does she really want to see me?"

"She says, but—" He shrugged.

It couldn't be mere curiosity. It could only be that her anger needed to find its focus.

"I'll give you twenty minutes to get her there," I said. "Then I'm going, and all offers are off the table."

McDaniel hesitated, but what choice did he have? He looked at his watch, and I looked at mine.

CHAPTER 35

I had to drive the tree- and president-named streets again, up and down the grid, before I discovered the library a second time. The wine stone building was less stoic than those on Main Street, more welcoming even as I stared at the door and wished I could turn and run. McDaniel wouldn't waste the time I'd given him, but was she home? Would she change her mind? Would he have to convince her? I checked my watch again, hoping for all manner of scenarios.

A woman with an armful of books came out of the glass door and held it for me.

"Thanks," I said. Thinking: meddler.

The library was one vast room with a staircase in the corner leading to a lower floor. Just inside stood a swiveling rack of worn paperbacks. I chose one and watched the door.

"We have a much bigger romance section downstairs," someone said.

"I'm fine." The street outside stayed empty.

"That book isn't any good. I feel compelled." The woman came to my side to aid me.

"Really, it's OK."

I felt the paperback slip from my fingers and finally looked at her, my head full of impolite ways of deflecting her attention.

She was smaller than I'd expected. Younger. She had large brown eyes behind outdated glasses, like his. Shape of the face, square of the jaw. I'd only seen one photo of him, the student ID photo with his dark, intense eyes gleaming, his mouth held tight and militant.

"These are better." She held two books in her hands, glancing between them and me until she'd taken me in, before she could place me and deal with facts that must have seemed irreconcilable. Her chin pointed away, and she found something over my shoulder to study.

"You're the librarian," I said.

She put one of the books back, smoothed the cover of the other. I could see how she didn't want to lose the only prop she'd been given for this two-woman show. "I'm a—volunteer."

"That's—" I could hear my voice begin to rise toward patronizing. That's what? Great? Healing? Who was I to think my benediction was the one she waited for?

She nodded, petted the cover again. She put the book back on the rack, the whole contraption rattling under her shaking hands.

"I'm not sure why I came," I said. "I'm sorry."

"They said—you don't know anything?"

"Nothing helpful," I said. In the silence afterward, I felt the true weight of this admission. In the face of what this woman had lost, I had nothing, was nothing, and had never been anything else. "I wish I did."

"You really didn't know him?"

I looked down at my shoes. Why had they not walked me out of here already? I tried to recall the grainy photo from the paper, his glasses thick, his hair too long and hanging into his hard and accusing stare. Sometimes I could almost trick myself into recognizing him. Somewhere, high on that back shelf of memory, must live the moment when I'd seen his cold eyes above the gun. For her sake, I tried.

Nothing.

She patted at the neckline of her sweater, smoothing herself now that she had given up the book. Mrs. Lehane—I remembered that her given name was a throwaway but not what it was—was a smoother, a fixer. A curtain straightener, the one who always tugged the towel on the bathroom rack into plumb. I imagined her going from one normal room in her normal house to another, fussing and arranging, folding and tucking, waiting for her life to hang true.

"He was," she whispered, "a very special boy."

Well, what else could she say?

Thoughts crawled up from my wretched gut to simmer at the base of my brain, resisting. If Leonard had been so special, why didn't he have any friends? Someone to tell him it would be OK if he just gave it another day? If he'd been such a unique little butterfly, where did he get the gun? If he'd been a little more special, could he have succeeded and killed me?

I'd spent a lot of time on the receiving end of the scrutiny he and I should have shared. The words—*very special boy*—had struck a secret well of rage. I didn't want to believe it was there, but my gut burned with bile.

I grabbed at a nearby chair to steady myself. Mrs. Lehane's attention darted from that hand to the other, resting on my cane. She'd rather not have seen the cane, I could tell. *Special* boys did not cause such problems. Just as she was pissing on my version of the story, my cane posed hearty evidence against hers.

What was I supposed to say, though? "I'm sure—" I'm sure you thought so. There was nothing more I could say. "I'm sure he was."

She searched my face for the lie.

"He's my only child," she said. "He's—my only. Here." She went to the desk and reached behind.

I stiffened. Her purse. Unlikely scenarios rushed at me.

She pulled out her wallet. I took a deep breath. What was taking McDaniel so long?

"He was such a darling little boy."

How many times did I have to say it? I'm sure he was.

She came to me and held out an old, yellowed snapshot, trimmed into a tight square. A young boy's face filled the image. Five or six years old, maybe, but I wasn't a skilled guesser. The kid mugged at the camera, his eyes squeezed shut.

"Cute," I said. I had no experience with this. Was he cute? I couldn't tell. He made me think of Doyle's kids, but maybe only because they were all small, a different species. I held the photo in my hands a respectable amount of time, then handed it back.

She took it, studied it, returned it to its slot, dug out another. In this one, he was older, wearing some sort of camping uniform with unfortunate knee socks. Less chance of being cute, less comfort with the camera. Ten, eleven. I was bad at this. Bad at being interested, at spending the time. What did I owe her, anyway?

Mrs. Lehane returned the scout photo to her wallet with precise and careful movements. I thought maybe I'd never treasured something the way she did this photo, but then there were a finite number of them now. The last photo of her son had been taken. All the lasts, actually. The last word to him spoken. The last time the phone would ring and she could rush to it, hoping it was him. For the first time I thought I might see the life she faced. To raise a child, to protect him, to fight for him, to make sure he was ready for the world, wipe his face, wipe his ass, pick him up from every tantrum and every scrape, to reach the part where the kid's all grown up, a fully formed being, a sigh of relief—and then to have that door slammed shut. The last everything.

Which was just the sort of punishment I'd had in mind for myself. I felt worse. I hadn't known I could feel worse.

She used the tips of her fingers to pry out another photo, took a long look, and then held the image out for me on the palm of her hand. This one, too precious even for me to touch.

I reached for it anyway, ignoring the little snap of electricity when our skin connected. The kid, as grown up as he'd ever be, turned in profile, unaware. A sharp nose, but everything else soft: eyes, cheeks. Only a kid, not the haunted guy from the newspaper. I thought—

"What?" she said. She held out her hand for the photo.

"He was a handsome young man," I said.

"Yes."

"They—the newspapers should have used this one."

And meant it.

Because if this photo had been in the paper, we could have saved ourselves some trouble.

I knew this kid.

"What do you mean, *now* you know him?"

McDaniel had arrived in time to catch me scuttling from the library. He'd hurried to catch up, plucking at my sleeve as I brushed

past. He saw Mrs. Lehane at the door and marshaled me to the lee side
of his Jeep.

"I don't *know* him. I've seen—that face. *That* face. Not the one in
the newspaper—" I turned my profile to McDaniel. "From the side? A
glance, I mean, real quick. I've seen him." Not just the profile, though.
In his student ID photo, the soft-focused image I'd folded into my
nightmares, the kid had looked ready to hate. In the photo his mother
kept in her wallet, he'd been caught unposed, his eyes open and wide.
That very special boy, a real person.

McDaniel sighed. "It's a small campus."

But the photo hadn't merely captured some aspect of Leo's face that
the newspaper photo hadn't. The snapshot came with sense memory, so
that I felt the moment I'd seen him, felt it on my skin and in my bones.
Unease. The itch that I should jump up, move. I willed myself back to
that moment, let the wariness chase me. I was in a hurry. I was—leaving
my office.

"He was standing outside my door. Before that day, I mean. He
was—he came to Dale Hall for some reason."

McDaniel watched a car pass and turn out of sight, then the empty
street. "This isn't going to make the front page."

"This is my life, OK? Not some story."

"If it were a story, it would mean something," he said.

"You don't think it means something? That I've interacted with
this kid after all?"

"Interaction." His look was heavy. "Did he say something to you?"

I tried to put the moment back on, but it seemed far away now.
"He was in my way."

"If anyone asks for a recounting, I'd leave that part out. When was
this?"

"I think we can narrow it down to the two months Lehane and I
were on the same map point," I said. "Sorry. That's all I have."

"He came to see you in your office, and you brushed him off. Is that
what we've decided?"

"No, he was—waiting. He never came into the office, but he—"

Unease. I'd had to rush out. The image was so clear now. Leo Lehane, standing, one foot tucked up behind him against the wall across from my office. Just where the co-ed's portrait hung now, his head turned away, and then I was past and had only the shadow of awkwardness, receding.

"He was waiting," I said. McDaniel made a disinterested noise while I tried to reel the memory backward to the moment I'd hopped up from my desk to leave. Back to my desk, and the urge to make myself scarce. It hadn't had anything to do with him; I hadn't known he'd be out there.

"He was waiting for—"

Another student. Another student who'd come to see not me but Corrine. My mind rushed forward to Cor, standing in our doorway, her hand over her mouth. Not laughing. "Oh, shit."

"What?"

I didn't know. I couldn't see anything but Corrine's face, stretched in horror. "Nothing. You can't print any of this."

"You're right. I haven't heard anything worth the ink it would take."

"Good."

He frowned. "Tell me."

"You said it. Nothing worth the ink."

McDaniel wiped his face with his palm. "The two of you, I can't believe it."

I tried to calm myself. I couldn't jump to crazy ideas. I couldn't even separate the crazy ideas from one another. The two of us—Mrs. Lehane? I couldn't work out how the two of us had aligned. I glanced back at the library doors, but she'd gone.

"You and your boy scout," McDaniel said. "You're up to your necks, but you won't admit it and you won't ask for help."

A spatter of rain hit my neck. I felt for the drop. The black sky had caught up with me. I imagined the slow going back through Chicago, the hypnotizing wiper blades. "I don't know why I'd ask you for help."

"I'm the only one paying any attention. I'm the only one who—who. Who *cares*." He looked away. "I mean—"

Adrenaline rushed through me. I felt it, too—that charged atmosphere when two orbits collide. I knew it well—I knew what it was like for looks over drinks to go long and suggestive, for the air to thicken. I remembered it, but from another lifetime, as though it had happened to someone else. Another dead Amelia Emmet.

Or maybe it wasn't me he cared too much for, or the Lehanes, but this—all of this. I remembered the way McDaniel had watched me all the way to Dale Hall's doors, the shadow of another idea that wouldn't go away. How far would he go for a front-page story?

Or it was nothing, my imagination, another thing I'd gotten wrong. I remembered Nath's hands on me. I could get things very wrong.

"What I mean is," he said, recovering. "I'm the casual observer. An uninvolved third party."

"You've climbed over too many backyard fences for casual."

"I can see the things you can't." A drop of water hit his shoulder, plopping a dark blue circle onto his sleeve. He glanced at the sky, surprised. Another drop. He brushed at himself. "For instance, you and the kid aren't working together very efficiently."

I had to call Cor. Maybe she'd remember what I couldn't—but it was such a long time ago. She hadn't been in a bed for the ten intervening months with nothing to occupy her. She'd gone on with the year; she'd covered for my absence, taught an extra course, advised my handful of thesis students and all of my undergrads. Not to mention that she'd visited me, taken out my trash, brought me Thai noodles and celebrity mags. She probably wouldn't remember, and I already knew what she'd say.

Leave it alone, Melly.

But now I wondered: For my benefit or, somehow, for her own?

I let out a deep breath. "The kid and I aren't working together at all, unless you mean our section of Sociology 101. We—well, we had an idea." I waved it away. "We decided against it."

He scraped me with his eyes. "You don't even know."

The tension had flattened, his embarrassment gone. The pitying tone in his voice made me want to cower for what he would say. All the power belonged to him, and I didn't remember handing it over. "What?"

"You decided against it, but here you stand in Leonard Lehane's hometown. Curious enough to hunt down his town, his mother," he said. "But I know one little Indiana farm boy who's out-Miss Marpleing you at least two to one."

"I don't believe you."

"So he's really out on his own? Didn't know the scamp had it in him."

Corrine, everything. It all fell away. Nath? He couldn't be. Everything he'd seen, everything I'd let him see. That night—

"No." I sounded strangled. "No, we talked about it, and—it wouldn't have worked, and it was too much to ask."

"Do you really believe that? That anything is too much to ask of him? For you to ask, that is, Professor Emmet?"

I burned. "He's just a kid."

"A kid with more than a passing interest. Who would do anything—"

"No." All the weakness I'd let him see. All the mistakes. All the— oh, God. The tears, the pills, the bathroom scene. He'd seen me drink myself into a stupor. He'd seen my scar. I'd nearly devoured him whole in some ridiculous—

Psychotic break. That's what the student paper would call it. A *student*, after all this business with Lehane, after all the denials of wrongdoing. No one would believe me now. Nath had everything he needed to ruin my life. I'd given my power away, but I hadn't given it to Rory McDaniel.

McDaniel watched me. I could feel the fireworks display going off on my face. "What's he doing?" I said.

"Not sure, but I was right that *you* were up to something, wasn't I?"

I would never admit it. But if I never talked to him again, I wouldn't have to.

"I'm going to try to beat this rain," I said. Though I knew that the road would lead me into the rain, and the storm would blow down on me the entire way. More punishment. More and more. I still didn't know why this had all happened, what Corrine hadn't mentioned or maybe didn't even realize, or why Nath had gone against my wishes.

The sky opened. I dodged past McDaniel. From the safety of my car I saw him jump into his Jeep and jerk the flimsy zippered windows into place. Taking his time on purpose? I wasn't sure. I started the car, cranked the washers to full speed, backed up, and began the slow crawl out of McDaniel's sight and back through the town toward the highway and home. I watched for the yellow Jeep for a long time before I relaxed.

I knew he'd let me get away, and for a moment I felt such a rush of gratitude that it surprised me.

CHAPTER 36
NATH

The phone rang, late. Or early.

"Gottabekidding," Kendall moaned from his loft.

I fumbled for the phone. "Hello."

"What was all that shit?"

"What?" I sat up. The clock said 5:00 a.m. I rubbed my eyes clear. Still 5:00 a.m. I only knew one person who'd be on that schedule. "What do you want, Win?"

"That 'Phillip doesn't think much of me' crap. You on some kind of undercover mission? Feeding us lines so we'll tell you all our secrets? Did Phillip tell you to talk to us? Are you with the *Reader*?"

I remembered that Dr. Emmet had asked me that once, and I'd not understood the question until her photo appeared on the front page of the student newspaper. "I'm not a reporter, but even if I were, you didn't tell me anything—"

"The thing about the call log could get me strung up in front of the university ethics board. Suspended. And then the press, and then my dad, and then I'm dead, OK? So don't pretend you don't know what I'm talking about."

The press? I finally caught up. "Your dad, the senator."

A long groan from Kendall's direction. He'd come home early from a party, so drunk I'd had to leave my desk to help him into his loft. I'd given him some pain reliever from a bottle he left on my side of the dresser, a glass of water, and an empty trashcan to tuck into the covers up there, just in case.

"US representative, dumbass, but in the Beltway they like to hear about badly behaved Rep kids as much as they do badly behaved Senate kids. I'd make CNN if it was a week my dad's trying to get something passed."

Forget the boat incident, forget all the ways he'd made me feel bad. He was a guy who cared what his dad thought of him. That I could understand. Yesterday I'd had to call my dad and let him know that I wasn't coming home to help with the auction. I'd had less comfortable conversations, but only with Bryn when she broke up with me. He'd taken it well. Too well, saying that he understood and, no, he could manage. He wouldn't be disappointed in me, but I could be disappointed in myself. I felt tender and bruised from it, as bad as I'd felt freshly dragged from the lake.

"I won't tell anyone about the call log," I said. "I'm not there to get you into trouble."

"Why *are* you there?"

"It's—" From where I sat, I noticed my St. Valentine's Day Massacre photo missing from the bulletin board. "Complicated."

"Please, no sad stories of friends you couldn't save. I'll puke."

"I'll spare you if you let me get back to sleep. I've got a lot to do before I sit through hotline training."

"Yeah, I noticed you passed the first hurdle pretty quick. But there's no shortcut on the training. It's like a job interview with a bonus rectal exam."

"Don't ruin the surprise," I said. "Good night."

I hung up but knew I wouldn't be able to sleep. A gray light poked at my eyes through the blinds.

The phone rang.

Kendall moaned.

I swung my legs out of bed and pulled the telephone line out of its jack.

Enough.

I'd grabbed my robe and towel from my closet when I remembered the photo, fallen from the wall. But when I looked under the desk, it wasn't there. A thumbtack still stuck in the board. I glanced over in the half-light at Kendall. He lay on his back, snoring in long, wet swipes at the ceiling. I'd have to ask him about it later. Or—I pulled my drawer open. It lay there, face up, on top of the file on Dr. Emmet. I didn't remember losing the last argument about the photo.

I left it there but closed the drawer a little louder than I needed to and slipped out for the shower.

I wasted all the time I could, sitting down to an early breakfast in Smith Hall's empty cafeteria and ambling across campus with my eyes on the sky, a gray blanket overhead. I paused at a bulletin board and noted some roommates needed, a band looking for a drummer, a flier for Night Sail festivities. I checked the date on my watch. Night Sail was tonight.

All that time wasted, and still I arrived at the hotline door early and fidgeting. After a few minutes waiting in the dank lobby, I pressed the button. It was a 24-hour hotline, wasn't it? Somebody would be in.

Phillip came to the door. "Eager. We like that."

"Am I the first one here?"

"You, my friend," he said. "Are the only one."

"Oh?" Somehow I hadn't seen that possibility. "Did you have some cancellations?"

"More like we attract interest in dribs and drabs."

"I'm a drab."

"I wouldn't say that." Phillip held the door for me. "OK if we use the natural light? Budget reasons."

The overheads were off. The natural light came from a couple of ceiling-level slot windows on the far wall, but they lent the room an unnatural grayness, turning the Hope Hotline headquarters into a black-and-white version of itself.

He went to the coffee station and started two mugs. "Sugar and creamer, right? We're down to nondairy, I'm afraid. You didn't have any trouble getting the morning free, did you?"

"Yeah," I said. "I mean, yes, cream and sugar. No trouble."

The door to his office had been left open. While he took his time with the drinks, I tried to get a better look inside.

"You're sure? You seem a little distracted." Phillip turned the handle of one of the mugs toward me. "We can do this some other time, if you want."

Of course I was distracted. I imagined where the call log might be, how it might be any help to me at all. I had pinned all my hopes on this meeting, and now there weren't any other volunteers to distract Phillip. And some other time? I'd already let my dad down and still suffered from a low-gut feeling from it. I didn't want to talk about it, but what else did I have to offer at this point? A story about Dr. Emmet that would get her fired? "I was supposed to go home this weekend."

I understand, Dad had said. But he didn't, because I hadn't given him a good reason or a truthful one. But he'd said he did, which made me feel worse.

"Where's home?"

"Indiana."

"Big family over there?"

I stirred the grit of nondairy creamer off the rim of my mug, missing the fancy cream from my last visit. The coffee seemed to be a lesser brand this time, too. The whole room seemed ugly and lonely, not at all what I remembered. I wished Win would swipe his pass card and launch through the door. "Just me and my dad."

"You two must be very close."

"Sure."

"Hope you didn't have plans down there you had to cancel?"

"What's—look, should we get started?"

"We've already begun," Phillip said. "When we pick up calls, this is what we do—draw people forward, talk about whatever presents itself to avoid long pauses. We remind them of the relationships that sustain them."

I sipped at my mug to keep from having to say anything. The coffee wasn't just a lesser brand. It was awful.

"So you and your dad were going to hang out this weekend?" He nodded encouragingly.

"I was supposed to help him clean out my grandpa's barn. He—my grandfather, I mean—he was a farmer and a mechanic."

He stood back, giving the answer more space than it required. "He died? That's tough."

"I guess."

"Were you close with your grandfather?"

I tried not to scratch my forearms. I didn't know why, but I really wanted to scratch my forearms. Phillip's voice had dipped into the talk show host murmur. "Not really."

"And your dad is a farmer and mechanic, too?"

"A factory mechanic. He also fixes stuff for fun. Cars, mostly."

"Do you fix stuff? For fun?"

The training already had the feel of that probing exam I'd been promised. No wonder that James Baker hadn't wanted the attention of the Hope Hotline. It was hot, all right, under this spotlight. "So, this is the—training course? The whole thing?"

"This is it." Phillip retreated to a set of the comfy chairs in the corner, adjusted one so that it pointed directly at the other. "All we do is talk. You need to learn patience with the process, whether you're on one side of the conversation or the other. These are often long, tedious conversations. You have to be able to withstand them. Come sit."

I took a last glance at the open office. Inside: a desk, a chair, some inspirational posters, books in a wall shelf. Would I even recognize the call log if I saw it? I joined Phillip in the little circle of trust he'd constructed. "Who's answering the phones right now?"

"I am. The daytime load is always light, so I often cover the less-popular shifts. Early Saturday morning is pretty unpopular."

"They said you sleep here."

His mouth, twitching, settled on a wry grin. "They were joking," he said. "They're high-strung, high-stress. The calls get to them sometimes. I'm aware of the games, the us-versus-him thing. As long as they're here on time and work well with the callers, I can live with it. It bonds them together, and they need each other. Now." He tented his fingers under his chin. "Now what you're doing by bringing up that piece of information is called deflection. The caller needs to talk about himself. That's one of the reasons we encourage the volunteers not to divulge personal information. It diverts the caller away from themselves, right? Keep the focus on the problem, finding a way to turn the conversation—lightly—toward the caller and away from the called."

The called? I barely had time to register my dislike of the term before he was back on me. "So what do you do for fun?" Phillip said. "Since you don't fix things?"

I wanted a chance at pretending to be the called. Pretending to be the caller sucked. "My classes. My assistantship."

"Right. With Dr. Emmet. How's *that* working out?"

"Fine." I felt a layer of sweat on the back of my neck. It was hot in here. Budget concerns on the air-conditioning, too?

"You don't want to talk about her," he said.

"No. I mean—I don't have much to say."

"She's not working with you as directly as you'd like."

That—I couldn't say that. "We work together well. It's just—" What was it *just*? I felt the truth of it, as soon as I'd let the word go. I hadn't even known I felt anything but admiration for Dr. Emmet. Admiration, not to mention desire.

But I did. Frustration? Impatience?

Maybe it was the rejection talking. She'd given up on Leo. And then on me. She didn't care enough about the truth to go looking for it. She wasn't what I expected. She wasn't what I'd hoped. I felt turned inside out. "You must be good at your job," I said.

Phillip tapped the air with a finger. "Deflection."

I'd lost the thread of our conversation. I really wanted to scratch at my forearms, the palms of my hands. They *itched*.

"Do you have a crush on her?" he said.

"What? No." The word *crush* had nothing to do with me, with her. The itch under my skin, however, had everything to do with how I felt. Disgust? Her approach to life disgusted me. Her lukewarm attention to the classroom. She'd just go on with what had been handed to her. She would put up with all their shit. She would let me draw close, and then close me out. Maybe she'd done something just like this to Leo Lehane, after all. I didn't know what to believe anymore. She was broken. I was broken. And I couldn't fix things.

"It's normal if you do," Phillip said. "She's a very attractive woman."

"She's not my type."

"You're gay?"

"She's not that much not my type. I just—I have—"

"You have a girlfriend." His face split into a wide grin. "That's great."

I hated to tell him that he was no good at this. "We—we broke up."

The wattage of the smile dropped to nil. "I'm so sorry."

"It's, well, it's fine." And it was. The call to Bryn had settled that life disappointment for good. I didn't wish for her anymore.

I wished the training would end. I wished that with everything I had left.

Phillip put his mug aside and leaned even closer. "That explains a few things."

"Not really. I'm OK. Maybe there was a time—"

"When Win told me about the boat incident, I really wondered if I shouldn't reach out."

"Wait. The boat—"

"Some people won't ask for help, but I was encouraged when you came by—"

"The boat thing was Win." I tried to remember what Win had said to Pixie and the other guy on the day I'd come to trail after him. Trudie. Dammit, that reporter had gotten into my head. That was another thing I could hang on Dr. Emmet, introducing me to that nosy jerk. *Bucked*. The boat had bucked me off, because it didn't like the look of me. Like the boat was a person, a woman. Like Bryn had *bucked* me off for a new guy. Like Dr. Emmet had—

"It was—a prank," I said. "Win had his friend turn the boat so that I'd fall."

"I didn't mean to upset you."

"I'm not—look, it was a joke."

He nodded sadly. "Win isn't the most mature student I've met. Despite what he thinks or who he spends his time with. Let's talk about something else."

God, what else was left? My dog got run over when I was nine— had we peeled that vein open yet? If he'd got hold of my mother's death, I'd be on the floor by now. I wondered if I could get him to shelve the entire conversation. "Maybe—"

And then all four phones in the room rang.

CHAPTER 37

I jumped. The noise was brilliant, as though God himself were calling.

"Excuse me." Phillip hopped up and jogged across the room to the nearest phone station. He raised his deflection finger at me to signal the minute he'd be. "Sometimes we get wrong numbers. Hello, you've reached the Rothbert University Hope Hotline. How may I help you?"

He listened long enough that I knew it was the real thing. A caller was reaching out to the called. He turned his back on me. "Tell me what's going on." At last the talk show host had turned to his next guest.

Relief. I put down the rest of my coffee and got up. I'd seen most of the room already, but I toured the inspirational posters now to stretch and shake off the funk. I took a deep breath, cracked my neck.

Another phone started to ring. I looked over to see what Phillip would do. Could you put a suicide hotline call on hold?

But it wasn't the hotline. The ringing came from the open office door.

I sidled to the open door, waiting for Phillip to stop me. He murmured into the phone, his back still turned.

With a single step, I was inside, at once scanning the shelves, the desktop, the slightly open desk drawer. Another ring. I grabbed the phone, and gently lifted the edge of some papers on the desk.

"Hello?" someone said on the other side.

"Oh, right. Hello. I mean. You've reached the Rothbert University Help—Hope Helpline. Hotline. What can I help you with?"

"Probably nothing." It was a guy, young. A voice I recognized, but not Win's. "Who are you? Where's Phillip?"

"He's on the other line."

"I thought I called the office."

"He's taking a call. You know. A call."

236

"Nobody kills themselves on Saturday morning. Is this that new guy? What's your name?"

My foot hit something under the desk. A black bag, hanging open. I sat at the desk and rifled inside the bag as silently as I could. "I'm not supposed to give out personal information."

"You can give your name, jerk. Put Phillip on."

"He's on a—" If the kid hung up, I had no reason to be in the office, and now I had every reason to stay. Inside the bag, a thick sheaf of papers clipped together. There were no headings, no clues, but the columns were divided into names, long numbers, short numbers, more information than I could process with this kid yapping in my ear.

"He'll be a minute," I said.

"Why are you in Phillip's office?"

The long numbers were ten digits—phone numbers. In the column of shorter numbers, none of the entries went higher than 2400. Time of day, in military code. I held the pages on my lap and flipped through them. There was a column for date of call, and the log went backward, slowly, week by week, day by day. I hit a page with a small mark in pen. The name of the caller was Jazz Starling. The name repeated several times, but I didn't see another mark.

"I said, why are you in Phillip's office? He doesn't like anyone in there."

"The phone rang," I said.

"Definitely the new guy."

I skimmed page after page, ten pages or more, until another mark, another name. Summer Hightower. And then William Kanowski. Many names repeated a few times, sometimes for a half-page or more. The marks were rare.

"Don't do that," Phillip's voice said.

I dropped the manuscript and looked to the door. He was still in the other room.

"Don't count yourself out so fast," he was saying to the caller. "You have to give yourself a chance to fail."

I spent the next minute picking up the papers and returning them to a tidy pile, listening for the click of a phone in its cradle.

"He's going to kill you," the kid on the phone said. I could picture him now. One of the called, to use Phillip's mythic language. The one Win had chased away the other night.

"I'm, uh. I'm trying to help."

"Look, tell Phillip to call me on my cell—"

"Oh, was that him hanging up? Hold on."

A page near the front of the stack had a crinkle on the edge that wouldn't smooth. I pulled it out and tried to roll the wrinkle flat. And then I didn't care about anything but what I read. The sheet was filled with exactly one name. I put the page back in place, checking the pages on either side. More calls, the same name.

"Well, is he?" said the kid on the phone.

"Is who what?"

The dates changed, the times changed, but there were thirty or forty calls from one caller, one name I hadn't expected.

"Stop wasting my time," the kid said. "Tell Phillip I'm running late, OK? That's all I wanted."

"Wait—"

He hung up. I put down the phone quietly and grabbed a notepad from Phillip's desk. Listening for Phillip's approach, I flipped through the log, copying down the names with marks.

In the other room, Phillip said, "Are they there now?"

I stuffed that note into my pocket and hurried for another sticky note and wrote the quickest thing I could think of. I crumpled that note into my other pocket. I still had the pen in my hand when Phillip came to the door.

"A few ground rules," he said. The talk show host was gone.

"Sorry. The phone rang, and it seemed like you might be a while."

"Had to call campus police for her," he said. "Can't be too safe."

"Totally. The call was that student from the other night—I'm really bad with names."

He sighed. "Another thing to work on. It doesn't help to forget someone's name while they're contemplating suicide."

"Zach, that's it. He's going to be late."

He took in the pen in my hand. I put it down, shoved my hands in my pockets for the note, only to realize I couldn't remember which pocket held which note.

"I already have one pain in the ass on the volunteer staff," he said. "I don't know if we're going to be able to use your help."

"Win," I said.

He rubbed his face. He looked tired. "How'd you guess?"

"You said earlier—"

"Win is a fine person, and I'm sure he'll do Rothbert proud. As his forebears have done for many generations." He managed to catch hold of the soothing voice again to add, "He's distracted by his own agendas. Normal stuff."

"Why do you keep him, then?"

He swiped at the air in a never-mind gesture. "Come out of there, please. Did Zach leave any other information?"

I extracted one crunched note out of my pocket and held it out. Phillip pulled it open and read the large letters: LATE—CELL. He looked up, shook his head. "Today's a loss, I think. Maybe you should— OK, if you want to try this again, we can."

Try again? I wasn't sure I could survive it. I wasn't sure I could avoid it.

"OK," I said, because I had to leave my options open.

The call log, instead of offering answers, had led me to a new question.

How was Win Harlan both a dedicated member of the called and a repeat offender caller, worthy of an entire page?

"Yeah," I said. "I think I need to come back."

It was almost noon by the time I got back to my room. Kendall's arm hung from his bunk, and his alarm rang loudly enough to vibrate the room.

"Serious alcohol abuse, Kendall."

He didn't stir. At least he'd stopped the window-rattling snoring. I hit the snooze button for him, but that only gave him three minutes or so.

I went to my drawer, took out the St. Valentine's Day Massacre photo, and tacked it back in place. There. The room was half-mine, end of story.

On my desk: a stack of quizzes from Sociology 101 awaiting a red pen. Research I needed to start for my methodologies class. An essay I needed to outline, at the very least, before I sat through Dr. Emmet's next class. I was a week behind, everything considered.

I fanned the projects out. Hard to imagine spending time on any of it, feeling as wrung out as I did. I stared at the pages, remembering the way Dr. Emmet's hair slid across my arms. Her naked back under my hand.

I didn't know if I had it in me to finish the semester, let alone the degree. Kendall's alarm sounded again. I waited for him to reach for it. I'd never get anything done if this kept up.

"Aren't you missing class?" I walked over and slapped the snooze button again.

His hand hung outstretched from the bed, palm up.

"Kendall, get up."

I flicked his hand. Nothing.

I flicked it again. Then grabbed it and shook it. His hand was cool and clammy. "Kendall, you're freaking me out—"

I hauled myself up to look at him.

His face—

I fell back from the bed to the floor. His face was white, his eyes wide.

His lips, blue.

CHAPTER 38
AMELIA

The rain beat down all the way from Lehane-ville back through Chicago and up Lake Shore Drive to my apartment. The whole trip, the pain pills sang their luring song, but I resisted, letting the ache keep me at attention on the slippery roads. The lightning bolt inside me burned. My hands, from gripping the steering wheel or in solidarity with the horror of the rest of my body, froze into claws.

In my apartment's lot, I dropped my keys twice before commanding the last of my faculties for entry into the building and my front door, for finding the nearest glass, the tap, the pills in my bag. I heard their lovely rattle, took maybe one too many. I had time to call Nath and give him a piece of my mind, but I didn't have the mind. At some point, I lay down.

I dozed and fumed until I had a speech, equal parts apology and accusation, ready to dispatch. I reached for the phone. The little shit.

My alarm said five something. In the morning? I stared at the clock, making sure. I'd slept through the night, and now it was too early to call. I would call him anyway. It served him right.

But the phone rang into infinity, until the campus operator cut in to tell me to give it a rest. I hung up only to call again. Again. Got up, brushed my teeth, called. Getting dressed, I came across the boot box in the back of my closet. The final resting place of my book manuscript, my career, my self-respect. I should have another barbecue soon.

I called Nath's number again. The time on the clock embarrassed me now. I'd been dialing the same number for hours. Obsessed? Maybe.

I tried Corrine: home, office, cell. Nothing. I hadn't been this angry in a while. I hadn't been this angry since Leo Lehane. Hours passed. I lost count how many phone calls I attempted before I realized I'd have to go roust them out.

I remembered Corrine in the doorway. Her hand over her mouth not from laughing but from alarm. Of course. Of course she'd heard the news and come running. I must have regained consciousness before the EMTs took me away—it made sense now. Maybe I could talk her back to the day with Leo and the other kid. Maybe her memory wasn't kept so far back on a shelf. I'd ask, just as soon as I'd shaken the Mickey Spillane from Nath.

"The little shit," I muttered to myself, huffing out of my apartment, down the sidewalk, and onto campus. Far-off sirens carried in the wind.

I'd never visited a student in his or her room and could imagine what Rory McDaniel would say, how he could spin any move I made next into a story. The wrong story. McDaniel wouldn't be the only person paying attention, much as he liked to think so. I was playing with fire. What was the right story?

I consulted the nearest map kiosk, which didn't tell me what I needed to know, which was where the hell the kid lived. A quick detour into the nearest building for a glance at the student directory, and I was back on my way across the sloping campus lawns and out into the adjoining community and the not-quite-ramshackle houses the students had taken over.

McDaniel thought Nath was working with me. Working *on* me. I imagined Nath's guileless face looking up at me from the back row of our classroom—and then his half-closed eyes as I wrenched our mouths apart—and was newly enraged. What game was he playing?

The noise in my head was enormous, and then the sirens cut through. They'd been going too loud for too long. I turned in time to watch two campus cop cars plow across the sidewalk and skid to a stop in front of an apartment building across the street. The black uniforms I knew so well scrambled out and inside. I looked around, finding the address. Nath's building. Three, four squad cars, and then a fire truck lumbered up to join them, man after man hopping out like clowns from a circus car. In a moment, all the rescue workers had filed inside, leaving the cars to wail the news.

I took a few steps back into the shade of a tree, pulling at a dangling branch. An ambulance, another patrol, more black uniforms racing into the fray. I thought briefly of Nath's safety, brushing the possibility away along with the branch.

I'd have to track him down later. I turned and headed for Dale Hall.

The campus sidewalks didn't go anywhere. Sure, students could use them to get from building to building, from one class to another—but not directly, not quickly. The sidewalks curved, offering languid tours of scenery I didn't care to see. Maybe once I'd been awed by the verdant lawns, the fat tulips every spring, and the tall grasses by fall, by life itself, youthful and bright. I supposed that was the idea. Send the prospective students, their parents, and anyone else who trod upon Rothbert soil the long way round to feed them a true sense of the bountiful land, color and vibrancy kept up with alumni dollars. What a fruitful backdrop for the higher education of tomorrow's leaders.

By the time I reached Dale's doors, I felt as though I'd finished a marathon. I stopped to catch my breath, noting the long sidewalk behind me.

I had. I had done the equivalent of a marathon, for me. I'd completed a full tour of campus, up and back, while my car and its little blue wheelchair hangtag sat back at my apartment building. The last time I'd walked to work, I'd been carried off campus on a stretcher. Today, I'd returned to a place in my head that was pre-attack, pre-Lehane. No—post-attack, post-post-Lehane. A place so angry that I'd had fuel enough for the journey.

And here I was. By the power of my own two feet.

Finally: a foot cliché I didn't mind using.

I took a quick inventory. I was tired, physically used up, but I didn't feel as though I'd fall down. Not as though I couldn't make it back. No taxis needed to be called, no emergency pick-ups—which was lucky, since I'd seduced and then rejected the valet—and no pills since the night before. I felt tired but amazing.

"Dr. Emmet, why, my goodness." Jim Perry emerged from Dale's doors, his hamster-sized eyebrows raised in wonder. Why was it such a surprise that I kept showing up where I worked? "Let me get the door for you."

"I was leaving, actually." I didn't want to go up to my office and grow creaky and sore in my chair. I wanted to take another lap around campus, or take my time getting home and give Corrine a call with the news. I didn't care as much about finding Nath. He'd turn up, and I'd have to ask him some questions. Calmly. Without judgment. Without violence. But later.

"Fine day for a walk," he said, and then blustered and coughed. "I'm sorry, I didn't mean—"

"Not at all. That's what I'm doing. Walking."

"Oh? Excellent, excellent. I was just thinking of you, in fact. Funny running into—" His face dropped into mild dismay. *Running.* Other people could still stumble over feet and legs and all the other words they weren't supposed to say around me. I had walked to campus today. I gave him a benevolent nod.

"Uh," he said, looking all around for a root by which to pull himself back up from the cliff. "Was doing the class schedules—you know how far in advance we have to sort it all out—but that got me thinking. Why couldn't we add a Sociology of Disability course next fall? A study of all the angles, taking on issues of ability and disability—taking apart *normal*ism, if you will."

The word disability pinged me, but I'd heard of courses like this. "Johns Hopkins has an entire program, I think."

His hopeful look grew into a wide smile. "A social, political, economic, and cultural issue. Disability must have its own life. Its own history, its own biography." A little spit had gathered on his bottom lip, he was so excited. "A new field of inquiry, I'm sure, but think of the opportunities."

It wasn't a new field of inquiry. Like I said: Johns Hopkins, to start a list. That quivering saliva on his lip made me stop and think—opportunities for *whom*?

"Who would teach it? Oh, you're kidding me."

"You'd be great. Think of it. The *press*, Amelia." The spittle flung. I took a step back. "At last you could use your—celebrity, however unfortunate it's been—to your advantage. You'd be a shoo-in for grants, fellowships. Doyle and I could kick in travel stipends for your book tour—"

"I'm writing a book?"

"It's time you found the silver lining," he said. "An expert in violence and in disability, who has a disability caused by violence? Forget the academic market and go for the book-of-the-month club. *Good Morning America*. That Letterman fellow."

Jim Perry had never seen a *Letterman* episode in his life, my guess. I imagined my walk across the stage, the silver cane shooting the glare of stage lights back into the audience. "Do you know what people think of me?" I said. "I'm not writing a book. That book, anyway. My manuscript—"

"Your manuscript," he said, the bushy eyebrows dipping forlornly, "is gathering a little dust. I'm sorry to say it, but it's time to move on from the barbecue. Oh, yes, I heard about it. Dr. Doyle was quite concerned about your state of mind, you see. *Quite* concerned, and so was I. Your dissertation was a beautiful piece of work. Your tenure materials—superb. The manuscript, I believe, could have found a publisher. I'm sure many would have been all too happy—but let's begin from where you are. You need to start over, and you have the opportunity. Who do you want to be?"

The manuscript had found a publisher, but I'd missed deadlines, sidelined edits. I'd had it under control once, juggling everything. Teaching, researching, committee work, the life of an academic. Then something had changed and the book wasn't finished—still, yet. Never *deliverable*, as my editor put it, as though my life's work fit into a couple of Chinese food containers.

It would have fit into a single container, after the fire.

But the balance of my life had teetered long before Leo and the gun. Long before my ten months of isolation and physical therapy, the dark room still far in the future. Long before Doyle flipped his keys and left—

Doyle.

I'd lost track of my book about the time Doyle started proposing.

Doyle, whose love was so rich and full and filling, like a dessert I couldn't finish. I saw us now as I never had. Doyle, so generous, so giving. Giving and giving until I couldn't take on everything he had to give and still carry the load I had come in with. Doyle, whose life had begun long before mine, was fully formed. He needed nothing from me and had no room for anything I had or was.

Who did I want to be? Only myself.

I couldn't even blame him for it. When I'd walked onto the campus of Rothbert that first fall, fresh from grad school, I was not young, but still naive. By reaching Rothbert, I'd imagined that I'd made it, that I'd crossed some invisible line in the sand. The folks back home would never know me. And yet that's what I felt about the people I met at Rothbert. They would never know me. I would never let them.

I hadn't been myself for a good, long while. The first Amelia Emmet I'd ever killed was the true one.

"Maybe Joss would want to give the study of disability a try," I said.

Jim sighed. "Yes, she probably would. But think about it."

"I will." I could certainly guarantee that.

I turned toward home, the lightning bolt in my gut promising a storm.

CHAPTER 39

At the crucial turn toward home, I continued toward the Mill. To hell with awkward conversations. I'd already walked to work and headed off an odd overture from my boss. If Joe wanted a piece of this action, let him try and take it.

I leaned into the heavy door, feeling how far I'd walked, how far over my limits I'd gone.

Joe came from the back storeroom. "Hey." He glanced at his watch. Early. He would have just opened the door. The breakfast crowd: me.

He said, "I think we should—"

"I think we don't need to, OK? Bloody Mary, please."

What could I expect if I let him go through with it? An apology at best. At worst, he could find something new and more insulting to say to me. Like: We're going to build a new wheelchair ramp, and hey, you're an expert. I didn't expect or want anything at this point. I'd grow a little more scar tissue, that was all. The psychic kind. Thick skin. High defenses.

A little too late for that. How had I come to let Nathaniel Barber burrow so deep into my life?

I thought of that first day, my office, the excruciating pain up through my hip until I couldn't see or hear or feel anything but panic. The tears, and then his prim little package of tissues. The tissues, probably. They were the product of a boy raised polite and concerned, a young man perhaps far too prepared for the worst to happen to him. All because of my desperation. If I hadn't needed someone, if I hadn't needed rescue that day, none of this would be happening. That little shit. That little Boy Scout and his twee package of hankies.

Joe tossed a napkin onto the table and thumped my drink down. He stood for just a moment too long.

"Start a tab."

247

He left, shaking his head. The front door opened, both of us turning to see with whom we'd spend the rest of the morning.

McDaniel, of course. All my luck was bad.

He leaned over the bar and said something to Joe, then started toward me.

"You can ignore me," I said. "You can do your serious drinking at another table. I don't mind."

He jangled the change in his pockets. "Not going to get anywhere drinking Bloody Marys." He pulled off his big jacket, laid it across the top of a nearby chair, and slid into the booth across from me.

"This is healthy. The vegetable group is covered. Seriously, you don't have to—unless you're still following me?"

"I'm not following you." He cut his eyes away. His thumbs flicked at one another on the table. "Anymore."

Joe brought another napkin, another tall glass filled with tomato juice and a stalk of wilted celery, and left without a word.

"Sometimes I end up in the same place as you," McDaniel said.

"Like, for instance, today. How about the day that will live in infamy? I believe you said you were already on campus that day. Just a coincidence, I suppose?"

"I—cover the university beat."

I watched his thumbs flicking. Nervous tics made me nervous. "Sure, sure. And what *beats* were you covering that day?"

"Some event in the student center. Nothing—hey." He sat back. "I'm getting a vibe here."

Joe looked over at us and then reached for the remote. Sports news, around the clock, always available to drown out noisy drunks and conversations he didn't want to hear.

"You're not getting any vibes from me," I said.

"I am. You think I had some warning? Do you think that someone called in a warning?" He patted at his pocket, then glanced at his jacket with longing. His pen, I realized. We were on the record. "What have you heard?" he said.

"What have *you* heard?"

He hid behind his glass, taking a long drink.

"You do have something," I said.

"Have you heard from your little buddy?"

"What's going on?" I sat forward in the booth and remembered that I hadn't taken my pills. I'd rather pass out again than have McDaniel see me take them. And I'd rather die than have McDaniel see me pass out.

"I can't talk about it yet," he mumbled.

"What were you doing on campus that day?"

His face shifted. There was something there—he had the expression of a student who hadn't done the reading for class. And then he brightened. "Oh, my God. You think I had something to do with the shooting."

When he put it that way, I really didn't. "Well, you have to admit—"

"That's what you think? Jesus, what *do* you think? Was someone else involved? Is this what Nath's digging up? Suicide pact or what? Who's he talking to?" He reached for his jacket.

I had no idea what Nath had dug up—that was the problem. The bigger problem was that I'd started to think about every person I'd ever known as a collaborator. Over at the bar, Joe glowered in our direction. Could he have had something to do with this? Doyle, heartbroken after I'd finally asked him to leave. What if he'd thought he couldn't live without me? Ben Woo, always angling to keep up with me, to pass me by. Well, he'd certainly done that. What if he'd constructed my downfall for his own gain? The problem with not knowing was that I could suspect anything and anyone.

I held my head in my hands and talked to the table. "Drop the pen, Scoop. What were you doing on campus that day?"

"If I tell you, can I get my notebook out?" He waited until I looked up and nodded, then spread his hands out on the table and looked at them a little too seriously. "It was a career fair in the student center—"

"Bullshit."

"No, wait. Really. I went to the career fair that day." He cleared his throat and looked away. "But not to cover it. I just—went."

"You—went. To the career fair." What did that mean? "You're looking for a new job? So what?"

"Journalism is dying, in case you haven't noticed. Not that I was ever Pulitzer material."

The silence could have used a denial. *No way* or *your work is great.* I didn't have it in me. "So you went to the career fair," I said.

"You can't tell anyone."

I stared at him. "Explain it to me. What's so awful?"

"*Public relations.* The guys at the paper would never let me hear the last, and you know I go to Rothbert journo classes sometimes, and I have to tell them, oh, yeah, come on out, the water's fine. But it's not. It's a hard job, long hours and late hours and it pays like crap."

I waved at Joe for two more drinks, gesturing toward the taps. "On me, then."

McDaniel rubbed at his face. "What's wrong with wanting more out of my life than eating dinners out of greasy bags and keeping a shaving kit in my Jeep? The guys talk it up like we're saving the world. My life is—dropping everything because vandals tore a tire track through a rich dude's lawn. Or trailing after Gretchen Wolitzer, hoping she might introduce me to someone doing something half interesting over in that ivory tower of yours. I follow the press releases, Amelia. I might as well be writing them. I—wanted more. I thought I could sustain the—you know?"

I knew. The fire in the belly. I had fire in my belly now, but not the right kind. And when the hell did we become girlfriends? I dug through my bag and found the pills. I popped two as Joe dropped the beers and retreated.

"What's that?" McDaniel said.

"Headache."

He watched me put away the pills. "The day you got shot, I thought I'd finally got my break."

"Really nice," I said.

"Didn't know you, did I? You were just a story. A horrifying story—do you remember hearing about Virginia Tech or Columbine or, God, Newtown? Do you and your colleagues sit around at faculty teas and wonder, 'What if so-and-so came in right now with a rifle?'"

I didn't bother disavowing him of the tea concept. "That shooting at Northern Illinois—that one was close to home. We talked about it then." The year I was up for tenure. Every move I made, I felt as though I were being filmed, and then I looked up from a lecture to see Doyle's face in the slim window of the classroom door. We weren't dating then; he was only my department chair, a charming guy I needed to impress. In the end, I cut class short and huddled in my office. In the early hours, we found out, you don't know how isolated the event might be, if it's one guy in the clock tower, or if it's something larger. That's what the 2001 terror attacks had done to the entire country, but on college campuses we'd been on edge for much longer. Something about the high-stress environment, the competition, the sitting-duck quality of a community within a community. "Ever since that University of Texas tower shooter. The one in the sixties? I don't remember his name."

"Charles Whitman," he said, catching the heavy look I gave him. "Funny what you run up against in the research phase. He had a brain tumor, did you know? They found it in the autopsy."

"How many did he kill?"

"Sixteen. Injured thirty-two more. He headed that column of history for a long time. Then Virginia Tech—"

"You have an interesting level of recall on the topic."

McDaniel grimaced, downed his beer. "I've been—going over old notes."

"No wonder you're looking into another line of work."

"I don't mind hard stories. Hard stories sell papers, win awards, get you noticed."

"Is that what happened?"

"Your story moved through too fast," he said.

"Didn't feel like it to me."

"I tried to get in to see you at the hospital every day for six weeks, until my editor told me to drop it."

"I wasn't dressed to receive." At six weeks out, I still visited the black room, in and out of consciousness.

He looked uncomfortable. "So . . . Nath."

"You know, we don't travel together in a pack. He's just my student."

The thumbs started flicking again. He looked as though he were doing sums in his head.

"Why are you concerned—" I remembered the sirens, the ambulance, firefighters, and stood, banging my thighs against the table. "Is he OK? What happened?"

McDaniel pulled me back down. "He's not hurt."

"Was it a fire? I saw the trucks, but I never thought—"

"How well have you gotten to know him?"

I swallowed the knot in my throat and reached for my beer to stall. "Not very well." The real question: how well had he gotten to know me? "He's been—helpful. While I found my feet—"

"He's new to campus, isn't he?" McDaniel said. "I mean—think about this for a minute before you dismiss it—could Nath have anything to do with what happened to you last year?"

"That's ridiculous."

Joe turned the TV volume higher.

"Give it a minute," McDaniel said. "Where was he last year?"

"He would have been in college in—I can't remember where he's from."

"Indiana. A few hours from here."

Something about his voice made me go still. I took the offered minute. Now I had to wonder if I'd ever met Nathaniel Barber before this year? I'd taken almost a year to find Leo Lehane hiding in my memory. I didn't have the guts to try and locate Nath on that back shelf as well. "What is it?" I said.

"Nath's roommate was found unconscious this morning. Not sure of his chances."

"They think Nath—hurt him?"

McDaniel slumped against the wall. "My friend on the campus police force thinks he hurt himself."

Relief fluttered through me. I mean, poor *kid*, but really—

There had to be more. "What does this have to do with me?"

He reached into his back pocket and pulled out a small square.

Unfolded, it was newsprint, roughly clipped and marked up. Under-
lines, circles, notes scrawled in the tight margins. I saw these notations
first, then the page, the same page I had back in my home office, but
with the photo intact. I could finally see Dale Hall and all the huddled
masses keeping vigil out front. It was touching, really. I wondered why
Corrine hadn't wanted me to have it. Byline Rory McDaniel. Photo
credit by Rory McDaniel, I saw now. "You brought a camera to the
career fair?"

"I have a camera in my pocket right now. This is one of the many—
let's call it dozens—of clippings and prints found when the campus
cops ran up to take care of that kid this morning."

"Who is this roommate?"

"You aren't following. They found this stuff on *Nath's* side of the
room. In his desk."

The handwriting on the clipping came into focus. I'd let Nath
handle some short-answer quizzes in the intro class. He'd done a good
job with them, giving each student a thoughtful response in careful
handwriting just like this. "I don't understand."

"I don't either, but something isn't right. Amelia, it looks like Nath
has been—I don't want to use the word stalking, but the police will.
And he has some rather disturbing images on his side of the room. Not
to do with you, nothing like that. But disturbing enough to warrant a
look around, and especially when you combine it with—with this." He
waved his hand at the article. The article he himself had researched and
written. Information now playing out in a different dimension. I knew
what he must be thinking: Reporting horrible stories was one thing,
but clipping and preserving them, another.

I looked up from the photo. I thought I might know why Corrine
hadn't wanted me to have it.

"We study violence," I said quietly.

"You're OK with this? You didn't see the postcard he had hanging
up, like it was a vacation snap. The St. Valentine's Day Massacre. I mean,
come on. A pile of dead gangsters is not wall art." He was getting red
in the face. "And I didn't even tell you that when I ran into him down-

town—yes, fine, I followed him. I found him standing outside Holy Family with his finger in an old Capone bullet hole like he was the Dutch boy stopping up the dike. There was also a photo of a girl in a bikini in the kid's desk, and you better believe they're checking to see whether that chick's alive."

The front door banged shut. We both looked over.

Nath stood there, his head hanging crookedly. "Sergeant Miller from the Rothbert campus police reports that Bryn is quite well. Engaged to be married, actually," he said, raising his voice over the TV until Joe cut the sound abruptly, and we could hear the last few quiet words. "Good for her."

"Sorry, kid," McDaniel said. "But you have to know what it looks like."

I should have seen what it looked like a month ago. It's OK, he'd said, and it couldn't have been.

I grabbed a fistful of money from my wallet and threw it on the table. I stood, fighting every exhausted cell in my body. No choice but to walk home, though there was no one left in the world to care if I made it. Corrine pushed to the surface of my attention. I needed to find her—now.

"I can explain," Nath said, reaching to stop me as I brushed by. I felt the light touch of his fingers and felt sick for both of us.

"Nath, I don't even know what to say—no. I have one question for you. I told you to drop it. How is this dropping it?" I pointed to the clipping lying on the table in front of McDaniel.

Nath swallowed hard, glanced at McDaniel. "I didn't—"

"Did you drop it, or did you stick your nose where I didn't want it?"

"That's from before—" He couldn't look me in the eyes. "I dropped it."

It was a lie. We both knew it. McDaniel knew it. Joe knew it. We could have polled strangers passing by, and they could have seen the lie on the kid's face. What did he have to gain from it? Or hide, by holding to it?

What had McDaniel asked? Did we sit around and take bets about students and guns? It wasn't a joke, and we didn't treat it that way.

When a student's personal struggles showed themselves, there was protocol, there were people specially trained on campus to help them gain control. That ultra-sincere guy from Psych Services who'd handed me his card seven times over the last year. There were people who handled this stuff, and it wasn't me.

"Rothbert has a very far-reaching ethics policy," I said. "Dishonesty of any kind—" But I couldn't think of what to say. The far-reaching ethics policy was suddenly something I had to worry about myself. "We also have a renowned mental health center—"

I still owed him an apology.

I'm sorry I trusted you. I'm sorry I started this stone down the hill.

The sight of him made me crazy with regret. All the parts of myself I'd let this kid see. Like the title of the book I hadn't published—what he knew would live on forever. What he knew—was everything. Some of it not true, and some of it more true than I could ever explain away. "I'm not going to try to understand," I said. "Do us both a favor. Drop the program. Drop the program and go home, Nathaniel."

I turned and started out, ready to deflect excuses, apologies, tears. But nothing came.

He watched me leave, and had nothing to say.

PART III

CHAPTER 40
NATH

Everything had gone to crap. Dr. Emmet disgusted with me, sending me home. That reporter looking at me like he'd seen the bottom rung for sure. And Kendall in the hospital, and nobody saying whether he'd make it or not.

I didn't know anything about that, but that's not the way the campus cops had acted in our room, especially once they found the postcard on the bulletin board and then the file on Dr. Emmet in my drawer.

"Got a little hobby, do we?" one had said, all of them trading not-so-subtle glances over my head. "Or two?" He'd pulled out Bryn's snap-shot with the tips of his fingers, as though I might have been using the photo for—special projects.

They managed to get Bryn on the phone, confused and concerned, but alive and well. When they'd finally let me go, I'd torn down the stairs past all my gape-mouthed housemates, knowing I had to get to Dr. Emmet before that file got loose, before things spun out of control. I checked her apartment—the code burned into my brain—then her office. Her officemate opened the door an inch or two, looking like she'd just woken up. I thought I heard someone moving on the other side of the door, but she swore Dr. Emmet hadn't been in. It was Saturday, too early for the Mill, but then I went to the Mill anyway only to find that the jerk journalist was all over it like I was the story of the century. If the university police wanted to find a stalker, I knew where to find one.

Now the door shut behind Dr. Emmet, and he and I looked at each other. The bartender shrugged and cranked the TV volume.

McDaniel waved me over with a glass. I should have turned around and gone, and was almost surprised to realize I was making a beeline for his booth.

"It's not at all what it looks like, right?" he said. He gestured at the bartender, who came with two cold bottles before I could think of a thing to say. I saw the clipping from the *Willetson Courier* on the table, my handwriting all over it, and fell into the booth.

"How—where did you get that?"

"I wrote it. The better question is where did you get it? I thought you didn't show up at Rothbert until this fall."

"Back issues online."

He looked impressed. He shouldn't have been. His paper had a pretty elaborate system and reasonable prices. "So you've been looking into this for some time."

I noticed the notebook at his elbow. "Interview over."

He smiled. "No problem. My friend over on the campus police force will be happy to explain to me anything I need to know."

"Will he explain how you got that clipping out of a crime scene?"

His smile slacked. Ah ha. They were such pros on the campus force. Now I had something to work with.

"Crime scene, huh. Their guess is he overdosed." He slid the clipping at me across the table. "Did he party?"

"Shut up." I took a deep gulp of my beer. Free drink, after all, and now I needed one. I had to go home? Drop the program, start over. Start over doing what? Abandon sociology? Abandon everything. Go home, take up a bank job or become a manager of the local discount grocery. A bachelor's degree went far at home. But that wasn't what I wanted. *Go home, Nathaniel.* That's not who I wanted to be. "I don't know Kendall all that well."

"That's what Leo Lehane's roommate said about him. You don't play nice with others, either?"

I sank back in the booth and pretended I was there alone. I hated that anyone would lump me and Leo together. He'd shot someone. I wasn't going to forget that, even if I'd come to feel sorry for him. The guy had become the sad mascot of a team of poorly trained do-gooders. How many times had he called? As many times as Win? More than that Summer Hightower, or—I thought for a minute and couldn't come up with the other name. Jazz. If I'd had more time with the list, would it have yielded more super-users of the Hope Hotline services, more special notations? Whatever it meant, one fact still stood. Leo hadn't gone quietly. He'd shot someone before he shot himself.

Shot himself. That night in my dad's bathroom, and I'd only found out-of-date cold medicine. A gun took courage, in a way. During my own dark night, I didn't even have the guts to go the pill route. I guess Leo had something to him, after all. He'd had the guts to forgo the easy—

"Overdosed on what?" I said.

"What?"

"You said Kendall overdosed. What did he take?"

"Some kind of pills."

Pills, pills. I thought about that for a while. "Do you cover Rothbert all the time? Like, is that all you write about?"

He sniffed at me, took his time. "Rothbert is a very complex organism."

"I'm not dicking around. Are you the only one who writes Rothbert news? Would you have written about—like, misfortunes that have happened on campus? Before Dr. Emmet's shooting, I mean."

"Misfortunes? Rothbert students rarely suffer misfortunes. But yeah, I guess if any had happened in the last six or seven years—God, seven years." He flopped backward and threw his arm over the back of his side of the booth.

"A Rothbert student killed herself last year. She took some pills. I think maybe they belonged to someone else."

"Her roommate. Prescription pills." His attention was mine. "Pretty girl, student government. What about her?"

Pills, pills, car, gun. "And some kid rammed his car into a tree? Did you write about that?"

"You seem strangely conversant with Rothbert's woes for someone so new to the community." He lifted his chin at me. "Two or three years ago, I think, the kid in the car—frat president, honor society, perfect grade point average. You've been hanging out with the death brigade, haven't you? Is this what they talk about? The ones who don't bother to call?"

"And then an athlete. I can't remember—he overdosed on steroids, but he might have died at home—"

"I wrote about him," McDaniel said. "Rothbert doesn't lose students lightly. I mean, I'm sure most universities commemorate, but this is Rothbert we're talking about. I'm surprised there wasn't a parade and twenty-one-gun salute when Jazz died."

I must have jerked in my seat. McDaniel gave me a careful look.

I swallowed. "Jazz?"

"Promising quarterback, real star. He was supposed to be this hardship success case from south LA, but the truth came out not too long after he got red-shirted. Rich kid like the rest." He shook his head. "The NFL already sniffing around. All I'm saying: he never would have been a hardship case."

I reached into my pocket, pulled out the crushed note, and spread it open on the table. *Jazz Starling.*

McDaniel ripped the note away and gave it and then me a series of hard looks. "Jazz. Kanowski, Hightower. These are—these are the kids. What kind of research are you doing? Who's Win Harlan?"

I grabbed it back. "Nobody." I needed to go somewhere and think. Not my room—Kendall's side torn up and mine raked through—but somewhere quiet.

"You know him, don't you?" McDaniel said. "Is he in trouble? This is not a good list to be on."

I put my hand on the marked-up newspaper clipping to take it with me. "I don't know." I'd noticed something about the clipping I'd never noticed before, something I couldn't have noticed until recently. A couple, close to the camera, arms around one another. What a touching scene, love in a time of terror.

"What?"

I shook my head, downed the last of my beer.

McDaniel followed me out of the booth, grabbing at his coat. The bartender nabbed him. He hadn't paid his tab. I saw the golden opportunity and took it, letting the door slam and taking an alley to hurry out of sight. I knew where to go, a place that would be quiet as long as I didn't bring the loudest mouth I knew.

CHAPTER 41

In the library, the periodical section looked as empty as ever. I passed the desk, the same plushy woman on duty who'd helped me with my research on Dr. Emmet. Only weeks ago, but it felt like years. In some ways, I wished the woman had simply let me fail. Wouldn't my life be a lot simpler right now if my project on Dr. Emmet had come to an unceremonious halt the second I'd arrived on campus? I'd be in the same place—square one—and maybe not so tangled up in whatever this turned out to be.

There was an empty table off on its own, a painting of a stern matriarch guarding it from the wall. I sat with my back to the portrait and watched the doors until I was sure I'd lost McDaniel. The crumpled note, moist from my fist, fell to the table. I laid the clipping in front of me and looked between them.

Starling, steroids. Kanowski, car. Hightower, Ritalin. The callers.

And Harlan, Win Harlan of the Capitol Hill Harlans, still walking among us. And in the clipping, with my handwriting all over it, there Win stood among the crowd, his arm thrown around a girl as she hid her face from the horror they could only imagine inside. He was only one small player in a broad field, but I'd come to know his specific all-American profile. Rothbert was a small campus, but it seemed to me that the politico's son managed to pop up in unlikely places. What did I know about him, really, except that he'd decided to throw me off his boat in the middle of the lake, knowing I couldn't swim? He'd eventually pulled me out. Saved me. I didn't understand his motives then, and I didn't understand his motives now. Was it possible, though, that he was cruel enough—

My mind bucked. I was spiraling toward something I couldn't believe.

A guy who didn't mind a dirty trick or two. A son who needed his dad to believe a version of him that might not be the real one. A caller, someone who showed up on Phillip's call list time after time, who had turned around his life to become one of the called.

Maybe former callers who made it through the black hour were the ones best equipped to help others? I couldn't see it. The training exposed every crack, whatever good that did. I'd barely made it through a two-hour session. How did someone who showed up on the call log fifty, sixty times make it through?

This list didn't make sense. Why had they had to call in the first place? Football star, fraternity president, student leader, McDaniel had said. Future politician? Good-looking kids, wealthy. Rothbert's finest—and the ones who'd meant it.

If the call logs from Phillip's bag were accurate, the ones who meant it did call. They called a lot.

Phillip kept track of the failures. That's what it was. He kept track of how many calls, when and who and after a certain number of interactions, you made the list that no one wanted to be on? Weeks and weeks of calls, and then a small pencil mark to note an entire life lost.

I imagined Phillip in his little kingdom, the office no one was supposed to enter, hauling out the logs to find the name, hesitating to place the tiny mark. All that work put in, all that sincerity expended. That shiny, colorful room built in honor of the work the group did—and then to lose a student anyway. No wonder he prickled when I joked about James Baker. Losing even a single life must feel like you're losing the battle as well as the war.

Win Harlan's name on the list dug at me.

"Your nasty little project isn't done, then?"

The librarian had recognized me, too. She stood with her fists buried into her sides, fairly twitching from the effort to engage filth like me in conversation.

"Sort of."

"I'd hoped you'd find enough real work to keep you from borrowing trouble."

I shuffled the list and clipping together and held them under the flat of my hand.

"This university is a good place," she huffed. "Bad things happen, but so do the good. But no, you don't come in looking for our list of Nobel winners, do you? The leaders, the teachers, the humanitarians. A lot of good people have passed this way." She jutted her chin behind me. I escaped her raw disgust by taking a look. And then another. The stern matriarch in the painting over my shoulder was a serious-faced woman, not as old as I'd assumed, ramrod straight but pretty, golden. She could have been anyone.

She couldn't have been anyone else.

"A lot of good people. This is a good place—"

The hair on the back of my neck stood up.

"—it's not for everyone, and I know sometimes the kids just don't fit in, bless them—"

The portrait outside Dr. Emmet's office. That girl appeared much younger, but she had the same flushed-with-health face, the same steady, coy mouth. The same family? A small plaque was set in the wall underneath. I stood to read it.

Dale R. Harlan.

I read it twice, three times.

"—sometimes," the woman blathered on, "I want to hug them and let them know that it doesn't have to be this—"

"Who is this?" I said.

The librarian blinked at the portrait. "Dale Jane Rothbert, of course."

"But who is she? Rothbert? As in—*Rothbert* Rothbert?"

"The Rothberts are the founding family of this university. It is a sad state of affairs when the students take no interest—"

"It says Harlan. Did she marry a sen—a congressman?"

"You're thinking of someone else," she said.

I stared at the face on the wall. It wasn't only that she had to be the same woman in the other hallway. I felt as though I'd met her, could picture her standing at a cocktail party, swirling a drink. Throwing back her blonde head to laugh as though the world was a pearl onion at the bottom of her martini—or the ice cube in the bottom of her White Russian, made with dining hall milk.

I was definitely thinking of someone else.

"That would be her daughter-in-law, I guess," the librarian said. "Dale Rothbert's *son* became a politician."

And her grandson had become a kid on the Hope Hotline list. What did it mean? I held my head in my hands and waited for some magic idea to strike.

"I didn't mean to upset you," she said more quietly. "Another student this week. What gets into your heads, I don't know. You lot—sometimes you break my heart."

"Leo," I said, lifting my head.

Her face softened. "Sad boy."

"You said—you said they got it wrong. What did they get wrong?"

She turned away, her rounded cheeks creating a Hitchcockian silhouette. "Only everything. That boy was lonely, don't get me wrong. You don't spend so much time in the library if not. Weekends, early, late. You don't spend all your time getting to be friends with the periodicals clerk if you—but there was something to him, something that wanted to rise above. I can't get over the feeling that he never would have—"

She swallowed hard.

I remembered Kendall's pale face, his lips turned blue. He never would have tried to kill himself. Never.

The problem with you, Kendall would have said, is that you believe what other people tell you.

"He never would have killed himself," I said.

She shook her head, the barest movement. "Something bad got in."

They got it wrong. I reached for the list and clipping and crumpled them both into my pocket. I thought I knew what she meant. Something bad had gotten in years ago.

In the hospital lobby, I realized I'd come empty-handed. No flowers. No get-well card. The magazines in the gift shop were too tame for

Kendall's tastes. The tastes I thought he might have. It occurred to me again how little I knew him. I understood James Baker a little better. An odd spot to be in, to be the person standing to the side of something as large as death.

I felt a weird quiver up my back. The creeps. It had been a long time since anything had given me the shivers. Not that I hadn't gone looking for them.

Negotiating the white halls, my shoes squeaking against the floor, I couldn't help glancing into open doors. I expected my mother in each bed.

At the door to his room, I peered in. Kendall reclined in the far bed, chopping the air with a remote control. A TV in the corner of the room skipped from image to image.

"Hey," I said.

He glanced over, took a double, and threw down the remote. "Finally. Someone I actually know."

I stepped inside to see he already had visitors. Two of them, sitting on the other bed. Win, his legs swinging, and Phillip.

I stopped short. "What are you doing here?"

Win winked. "We're bringing the good news of the Lord—"

"Just visiting," Phillip said. "Like you."

"Except he's my roommate," Kendall said. "My friend. You guys are strangers cutting into my cartoon time."

I hadn't known Kendall and I were friends. For some reason, I thought he might be mad at me. Mad at being saved, if he'd really meant to take pills. Or if someone had—my mind bucked again. Bucked, like *Ladykiller* throwing me.

"Taking the hope to your door," Win said. "This is something we do. Apparently."

Kendall looked like he might throw the remote at Win's head. "I didn't try to kill myself, douchebag."

"Technically," Phillip said. "You did. Mixing alcohol and pills is a fatal error. You got lucky—"

"I didn't take any pills. I told them already."

"They found a trace of some serious painkillers," Phillip said. "Can't remember the name, but they're orange. The big guns—"

Orange. "How do you know that?" I saw an orange pill drop into Dr. Emmet's palm, her certainty that she should have another.

"Kendall was referred to us through the official channels," Phillip said. He had that brochure-photo look about him. He was here to *care*. "The university takes this sort of thing seriously and calls on us to make sure—"

"Get out," Kendall said. I had never liked him more. "I'm not suicidal. I'm awesome, OK? Lesser beings go that route, but not me." He glanced at me meaningfully.

"Kendall probably needs to rest," I said, clearing a path to the door.

Win hopped up and threw the patient a jaunty salute. Phillip slid off the bed with a long look at me, then Kendall. "I hope you know that you can give us a call anytime—"

"I have my own friends," Kendall said. "Real ones."

Phillip must get this reaction everywhere he went. I gave him a what-can-you-do smile and walked them out.

In the hall, Win spun on me. "Look, Night Sail is in just a few—"

"No."

"You said you'd help." He turned his back on Phillip. In a lower voice, he said, "Was hoping to talk to you, clear some things up."

"I'm not all that interested in maritime travel these days. I'd be no help, anyway. All I remember about my sailing lesson is how to drown."

He grimaced. "You don't have to do anything. Dutch and I will handle the vessel. We could use the bodies. The rules say we have to have a full crew. For my boat, that's at least three—"

"I'll help," Phillip said.

Win stepped back and took in Phillip, licking his lips. "You will? Yeah, OK."

"Rules? Is it a race?" I said.

"Not officially," Win said.

Phillip snorted. "Another fine Rothbert tradition—"

"Not everyone has boats," Win said.

"Very few people have boats, actually," Phillip said. "The rest of us crawl into steerage and try not to take up too much air."

"Ballast," I said.

Phillip shot me a smile. Win scowled between us.

"Everyone goes," Phillip said to me. "This is Rothbert at its best. This year, I'd like to see it from the water."

"Be my guest," I said.

"You should come along." This from Phillip, who made the invitation sound as though it was his boat. Win watched him from the corner of his eye.

"You weren't there the first time. When I was on *Ladykiller*—" I saw the word as though for the first time. How had I never really heard the word?

"*Ladykiller*," Phillip said. "Someone thinks highly of himself. Or has some explaining to do."

"Maybe both," Win said. "Do you know where the tie-up is?"

Phillip did. They settled terms to meet and parted. I turned for Kendall's room, but before I'd gone too far, Phillip called to me. Win had gone.

"What now?"

"Please come tonight. I could use—the company. I don't know what I mean, but Win—"

"He's acting weird?"

He studied me long enough that I almost said the thing I couldn't say. I found that the words wouldn't quite form. *Win*. It didn't make sense. And now the orange pills. Was that a coincidence? Was someone trying to tell me something? Or was it more than that? Maybe those pills hadn't been meant for Kendall to begin with.

What made sense to me now was how tired Phillip seemed, how weary. I didn't know how he did what he did. I'd only lost a few hours of sleep and had bad things happen near me. How did someone do that every day?

The image of two orange pills falling into my own palm came to me. My mom, near the end, had required bigger doses than that. And then I knew. I had given Kendall the pills. But how had the bottle gotten into our room in the first place?

Go home, Nathaniel.

Well, I would. We were all in this stew together: me, Leo, Kendall, Phillip, Win. Dr. Emmet seemed peripheral, as though this had never touched her. She could kick me out of the program, but she couldn't kick me out of town. Until my assistantship money ran out. Until I knew what I wanted to know.

I had to know. I'd lost everything else. She could live with her gray areas, but I couldn't.

I thought again of home, of standing on my dad's porch with no clue what to do next. This might be the last time I was certain about anything.

"I'll meet you at the rocks," I said. "Dutch is probably drunk already, right? You'll need a third."

CHAPTER 42
AMELIA

By the time the door of the Mill slammed behind me, I knew walking to campus that day had been a mistake. My gut had passed through the threshold of pain into numbness, taking my bad leg with it. Lack of sensation I could handle, but the leg wouldn't lift. My heel scraped the sidewalk monstrously. I kept my head down. Everyone must be staring.

I hated that everyone-must voice in my head. The same one I'd struck out of my life over and over. I'd expected adulthood to be different, but in some ways nothing had changed. Everyone else had a private school degree. Everyone else drove a better car. Everyone else had already written another book, had a better office, took their boat out on the lake. Everyone else had already found the right person to start a life, a family. Everyone, everyone.

Corrine knew what I meant. We'd spent hours turning the issue over. Philosophizing. Scheming. What did we want? How could we get it? What if we had to settle?

I'd have settled right then for being home. I wanted a bath. I might get into the tub, but I'd never get out. I'd have to settle for a shower, another pain pill or two. I wanted to talk to Corrine, but I could be talked down to an early bedtime and waiting for tomorrow.

"Hey."

I wanted the voice to be talking to someone else, but I would have settled for it not being McDaniel.

"Amelia," he called.

I didn't turn around. "I've had a long day and it's hardly the afternoon. I beg you."

"Where's Nath?"

"I left him with you." We'd reached the door to my building.

"Has he been looking into that group, the hotline?"

"He's all yours. I have no idea."

McDaniel ran his fingers through his hair and made a noise in his throat. "Something's not right. This business with the kids who—"

"Not interested. I'm only interested in ending this day. Another stellar day in the life of Amelia Emmet."

"You're only interested in yourself."

I imagined all the people he'd misquoted in his lifetime. But yes. Where was the harm in that? "That's true of most people."

"Maybe." He blinked at me. "Who wants to be most people, though? I won't believe that about you. Look, he's in trouble. He's carrying around this *list*—"

"He's his own man." That was the only way to get at Nath. I didn't understand him. I didn't understand him, and now I didn't have to try.

"He's a kid, and he's digging himself into a bad spot," McDaniel said.

He reminded me of Nath just now. Big eyes wide, always needing something, always hoping that I'll turn out to be a better version of myself. I dug my keys from the depths of my bag. "I don't know what to tell you."

He reached out and grabbed my elbow.

"Tell me that you don't care about what happens to that kid," he said. "Tell me I'm completely wrong about you."

I took a shaking breath and concentrated on not slapping him away. I slipped out from under his touch. A hot spot on my skin in the shape of his hand. "You don't know anything about me."

"I know—dammit, I know enough."

One long step, and he'd reached for me and pressed his mouth hard to mine. He held me tight. Not as though I might break. My hands, held down by his embrace, grabbed at the thighs of his jeans. He held the back of my head, scraping my mouth with his five o'clock shadow. The lightning bolt through me lit up, and my mind zapped blank. When he relaxed his grip, I turned my face and gasped for breath.

"This isn't—" I said.

"It might be."

"You don't have to—" I knew what I meant, but he stared. Big eyes wide. I pictured Joe's face, morphing into horror. Doyle's, turned to apathy. Nath's. "I've resigned myself."

"Are you telling me you've given up sex?" His voice, low and gruff.

"I—I haven't decided. Maybe."

"Decide later."

I took a breath and stood back, shaking the feel of his body off mine. It wouldn't go away. I felt heavy with it, like I knew something about myself now that I hadn't before. "This isn't me. I mean, this isn't who I am. Anymore."

"I like you. This you. Whoever you are right now."

"I'm nobody. Nothing."

"Wow. Nath isn't the only one who needs to be calling the—" He frowned. "Don't pretend like you believe that about yourself."

"I used to believe—" I pictured the manuscript on Doyle's grill, the page edges rolling and turning black. I'd had to poke the title page through the grate. The last thing I'd seen was my name. Amelia Emmet, PhD. Even then, I'd believed I'd find a way back to the person I should have been. Even then. Hadn't I stowed away another draft? "I'll show you," I said.

McDaniel followed me into my apartment. His eyes roved over the place. Picking details for the story, I supposed. "Wait here."

I hobbled past him to my bedroom and threw open the closet. I dropped my cane and dove in. Shoes, purses, a dry-cleaning bag fallen and never picked up. When I finally had the box in my hands, I felt only surprise and pride at how heavy it was, how much work had gone into this doorstop.

I crawled backward out of the closet, my hair pulled by jacket buttons, to find McDaniel in my door. I sat the box on my bed. "This is what I used to be. I had goals. I worked hard. I was on my way."

"On your way where?" He nodded at the name on the box. "Marshall Field's closed a few years ago."

I teased the box top open. I had imagined that I might retrieve my book someday, but not with an audience. Not with this audience. Maybe I'd imagined Doyle, his hand swiping dust from the lid, making a quip about the boot box. He would have understood what the box, hiding it and getting it out again, cost me. What was Rory McDaniel waiting for? Nothing but a headline. Nothing but an *angle*, and maybe a wedge into my unmade bed.

"You can go," I said.

"What's in Geraldo Rivera's vault there?"

"My point," I said. "But I don't feel like making it anymore."

He glanced at the box, at my hands quivering at the lid. "Is that the missing tome? The point was that you used to be great, because you wrote a book that never got published?"

For a wordsmith he often chose the wrong phrasing. How many books had he written? "My point was that—"

That I was damaged goods. That I'd shut a few doors behind me that mattered, doors I didn't have any keys for.

"If you were great before, it probably wasn't because of whatever's in there. Is that a shoe box? You put yourself in a shoe box." He picked a magazine off my bedside table, something sensational Cor had brought me, put it down. "I heard you were a great teacher. You must still be. Nath thinks you're great. But, for my money, that jury's still out because what I've noticed is that one of your students is out there getting into trouble. *Your* trouble."

A great teacher. Maybe I could have said that once. I remembered Nath's face going slack when I told him to go home. When I told him to give up his dreams. What a teacher I was, destroying my most ardent student—so that we matched? So that I somehow gained the upper hand? So that he couldn't crush me with everything he knew? But I was already crushed.

I pushed the box across the bed and sat down. "Tell me then. Why are you so worried about Nath?"

McDaniel didn't know much, really. A list of students, all but one dead by their own hands. Or so it had seemed. I listened until McDaniel had sputtered out of facts.

"Where'd he get the list?" I asked.

"Don't know."

"Shouldn't we worry about the kid on the list who's still alive?"

"Exactly," McDaniel said, lighting up. "Made a call. That kid turns out to be a legacy. A real one—not just a Rothbert student, but a Rothbert kid."

"I don't know what to do with that."

"Are you kidding? That's a story I could write. Front pager. Rothbert heir arrives on campus," he intoned, blocking out the headline with his hand. "Bodies start piling up. Best*seller*. Change a few names, give it a cover with bloody knife—"

"A knife?" I hadn't heard about any blood other than Leo's. And mine, though Leo and I both seemed beside the point.

"You know what I mean."

"If you've already written the tell-all, shouldn't we call the police?"

"My buddy on the campus force would love this collar."

"Collar? You're out of control. Let's go."

I walked him to the door and out into the hall before he realized I was not going with him.

"Wait," he said. "When—what are you doing? Later?"

"No," I said.

He blinked away. "And Nath?"

"I'll see what I can do."

He rolled his head back and looked up at the ceiling. "This is the you that's still you, right? Because I don't want to have to go through this again with the you that isn't still you."

I closed the door on him.

Finally alone, I dragged myself back to my room. That kiss. I couldn't even think about that kiss.

The boot box sat on the edge of the comforter.

I played with the lid. The rituals we prescribed to our everyday lives, the importance we assigned to mere paper and ink. I'd expected a drum roll, a trumpet blast. Something.

I popped the box open.

Gone.

In the place of my manuscript sat a thick dictionary. Embossed title on the cover, gilt pages, a real tome.

For a moment I felt relieved. It was over. I thought I'd stuffed it here, but it was gone. I'd burned the last copy after all. I could start over, just like Dean Perry had suggested.

The moment passed, and another feeling rose. I thought I'd put it here. I thought I'd always have a chance.

And then anger. I *had* put it here.

I pawed at the book. Gold letters pressed into faux leather, the most mocking text I'd ever seen. I opened the cover.

From the library of Nicholas Doyle, it said, in his handwriting.

CHAPTER 43

Fury hurled me out of my place and once again to campus. I found him in his office, behind his desk. So comfortable with himself and his life. So settled and smug.

Doyle looked up as I walked in and closed the door. "Hey, I tried calling you," he said. "Tonight—what's wrong?"

A week ago, maybe even a few days ago, my answer would have been different. Now his office seemed overstuffed, close, hot. Not the warm sanctuary that I'd always thought. The sight of him didn't stir regrets, except for the months of my life I'd pined away.

"Where's my book?"

He leaned back in his chair and smiled. Any other reaction—confusion would have been the best—and I could have given him the benefit of the doubt.

"You took it?"

"You weren't using it."

"Doyle."

"Took it when I moved out. Didn't want you to use it for kindling."

"It's not your job—"

"Yes, it is." He swept his arm to encompass his desk, his office. "It is my job to encourage you, to see you through a bump in the road. That's exactly what my job is. It wasn't my job—the other stuff."

The other stuff. That's what we were calling our love affair now. And my attack we were calling a bump. "I'd like it back."

"I was waiting for you to say that. Over two years, actually, I waited for you to want it back."

"Protecting me from myself? I didn't need a daddy, Doyle."

"You needed a friend." He leaned across his desk and put his hand on my forearm. His touch, which I had enjoyed and then coveted. But his hand was just a hand, heavy, solid—

My memory snapped to the white room, a hand heavy on my chest.

Doyle, of course. Not the attentive nurse who stopped in for game shows but the man who'd tried to love me even when I hadn't let him know who I was.

He hadn't waited weeks, then made an official visit. He'd been there all along. I made it through the darkest hours to find his steady hand holding me to the earth.

And now, again.

He was the best friend I'd ever had.

"Thank you," I said.

He nodded and took his hand away. I remembered the heat of another hand and a kiss, no question in it but desire, hope. McDaniel's hand on the back of my head. But the memory of that night with Nath quickly followed, bringing with it the shame of everything I'd done wrong.

"I'll bring the manuscript in next week," he said. "Nancy packed it away somewhere."

"She'll be glad to see the last of me in her house," I said.

"She's carving a place for herself into my bedrock. Trying to."

"I have no doubt she'll succeed," I said. "She suits you. In the best way."

"Thank you for that." He had a charming smile. All of his smiles had belonged to me, once. Even those he bestowed on other people were the tell on how happy he was with me. Now I could see that he was happy with someone else. The sting was mild.

"As I was trying to say," he said. "Night Sail is tonight. Tradition holds that you'll be on my boat. This'll be Nancy's first year."

"She wouldn't want me there."

"She's an adult, too, Melly. Give her a chance. The others will be there, Joss, Corrine. They were all invited. Benjamin will preside, I'm sure."

I didn't need another chance to see Woo preen and parade. But Cor—I still hadn't asked her about Leo Lehane standing outside our office. Joss would help us sort it out.

If—if I even wanted to sort it out. Either my exhaustion or the pleasure of finding Doyle's office cozy again, his presence a comfort instead of an anxiety, rendered the question of my attack tiny and long ago. Did it matter? The kid was dead, and I was fine.

I was fine.

"We can pick you up at the not-so-secret tie-up at the rocks. Against official protocol, every year, they'll be shuttling people out. You can swim, if I remember correctly."

"No, thanks. To the swimming I mean."

"You'll go?"

I'd been on Doyle's boat every year I'd been at Rothbert. Every year but one. "Last year—"

"We didn't go out last year. We found individual pursuits. I believe I visited a sick friend."

"In the ICU," I said.

He smiled. One last time, just for me.

Leaning on the buzzer for the hotline headquarters, I eyed the doughnuts, yellow with age, in the vending machine. Not exactly an uplifting corner of the university.

I'd given myself every excuse not to bother with this. Nath was his own man, his own problem. I was not his teacher anymore.

But I'd already let the kid down. I'd let him down hard enough that he might actually hit the bottom. *Tell me you're not worried about that kid.* Well, I couldn't worry about him anymore. Time to turn him over to someone else.

I noted the literature rack, filled to the brim with the same brochure, the same plaintive face of need pleading from the front cover. I started tapping out Morse code on the buzzer. S—O—S.

The door opened, a young man in a too-big T-shirt peering out with dread. "Hope Hotline, how can I—" He stared, swallowed hard. "How can I—"

"Help me, maybe?"

"Aren't you—I mean, are you the professor—"

"Are you the sheriff in these parts?"

He stumbled back to let me in. "Take me to your leader, huh?"

He had shoulders so thin they threatened to slice open his shirt. On his face, a goofy, expectant look. These were the kids who were supposed to talk their peers out of rash life-or-death decisions? "Sure, OK."

The inside of the place told a different story than the lobby. Bright, cheerful. Beanbag chairs, really? I could see some lives being saved here. I eyed the coffee station—all the accoutrements, fancy-brand beans. All the budget cut talk around the university must not have filtered down to this little underground enclave.

The kid stood there, watching me. "Phillip's in his office."

I had expected the request to transmit to my alien friend by now, but we'd crossed wires. "Can I see him, then? Phillip?"

"Who is it, Zach?" came a voice.

"Professor, uh," the student tried. "Dr.—"

A door to an internal office stood half-open. Phillip came to the door and had the courtesy to seem unsurprised to see me. I hadn't recognized him the night he'd cornered Nath and I'd nearly talked the poor kid into going undercover as a troubled student. I gazed over the playground in front of me again. What a waste of time that would have been. Or had been—Nath's time, because isn't that what he'd gone ahead and done? And now he was a troubled student.

"Dr. Emmet," he said. "Come right in."

He let the door close behind us.

"Don't you need to listen for the phones?" I hooked a thumb toward the slim window next to the door, through which I could see the pointy kid settling into a bean chair. "They don't call hoping for your voice mail."

"Zach's got it."

"One guy on the phones is enough? I guess that's good news."

"You don't know about our heavy usage hour. Tonight after most of the town is in bed, we'll have a couple more students on duty."

"Did you say hour? Just the one?"

He waved me into a chair and sat opposite. "We don't make light of it. It's the pinnacle on which every day at Rothbert balances. If we get it wrong, if we tip one direction or the other, someone dies, the campus grieves, the town wonders what the hell is going on over here. Not to mention that a family somewhere is shattered. The university lives or dies on our watch."

He seemed to be reading from an awfully dramatic sales brochure. Or a mythic poem he'd written to his own worth. "I don't think I've ever heard that—sentiment."

"You've probably heard other areas of the university claim how important they are," he said. "In our case, it's true."

The guy had a Napoleon complex, but then so did most of the research faculty, the deans, President Wolitzer. Me, some would say. "Here's what I think, Phillip. You're not going to be able to tell me what I want to know."

"Depends on what you want to know. Maybe I'll have all the answers."

Why had a scared and lonely kid brought a gun to my office door? But I wasn't so sure I needed that answer anymore. I thought of Leo's mother in her tidy house in her tidy town, trying to smooth down the things she couldn't understand. The things she had to live with shamed me.

Phillip Carrington-Wells, said the little plaque on his desk. What a mouthful.

"What's your training, Phil?"

The corner of his mouth twitched. "Phillip. Sorry that my diplomas aren't on display as proof of my value."

"I might have set my diplomas on fire last summer, Phillip. I'm not sure. I just meant—what's this place about? I've put your boilerplate invitation to students on my syllabus for seven years, but I don't know what you do."

"It's on your syllabus? That's great."

"Every semester. Call the—" I'd forgotten where I was. I looked around for a clue.

"The Hope Hotline."

No need to call the hope hotline on you? I hardly knew where the memory came from, but it had a daiquiri taste.

"In the age of copy and paste, it's pretty easy to do," I said, but time had passed. What was I thinking of?

At last I placed it: Corrine, my first day back, worried that I'd pill and swill myself back into the hospital. A day that seemed so long ago, and yet I still felt as though I hadn't fully stepped back onto campus. Still hadn't moved back into my office. Still hadn't crawled back into my life. I was truly misshapen, unable to fit back into the place I'd left.

"Thank you for spreading the word," Phillip said. "Our goal is to make sure students know about us. Before they need us, of course. By that time—well, it's too late."

"You've made a nice go of it. Not to sound gauche, but you must run a busy operation." I glanced toward the narrow window, catching the kid named Zach watching me. He popped up out of the beanbag chair and disappeared. "The university has been cutting to the bone on expenses, but it looks like Munchkinland down here."

Phillip rolled his desk chair back a few inches. "University priority should be to keep the students *alive*, surely, before anything else."

I hadn't realized Rothbert students were so volatile. On the back shelf of my memory, I could barely reach a few big headlines from the *Rothbert Reader* over the years. Students who had problems they hadn't been able to live with. Problems they didn't know yet they could live with, if they just held on. I said, "I thought the joke was that our students came with their own entourage of servants for home, health, and happiness."

His jaw loosened, the hint of a genuine smile. "They're—insulated, aren't they? They hardly know what they need until they need it."

Phillip's eyes flicked past me. I looked to see what had caught his attention. Another student nested in the bean chair, turned in profile with a coffee mug to his lips. He looked like the exact student Phillip had in mind: cocky, self-sure.

"Must be difficult to teach them anything," Phillip said. I turned back to him to find him leaning over his desk on his elbows. "And soci-ology, especially. Rather esoteric. I heard one of your colleagues got a Rothbert Medal, though. That's excellent news."

Excellent news for Woo. I nodded, not sure what to say. Pretty sure I'd never get one of those now.

"I'm sure you were missed last year," he said. "How long were you laid up?"

"Ten—" The fact caught in my throat. I still hated the time, gone. "Ten months, all told."

"Well, I'm sure it was nice to hear from all your family and friends."

The question of Phillip's education hadn't been resolved, and now I wondered if he'd been trained to throw knives by a blind circus per-former. He was either a very bad or a very good shot. "A few novelty greeting cards weren't worth the pain," I said.

"No, of course. Of course not. I'm sorry." His eyes cut to my lower body, my hand on the cane. His gaze was heavy, slow, methodical. "This may not be my place, but I hope you're handling the pain meds care-fully. They can be quite dangerous. A student just this week—"

"I'm fine." Loud, final. I caught movement out of the corner of my eye and looked. The guy outside the window had turned at the sound of my voice. He wasn't another gape-mouthed alien but a smooth, smartly dressed young man. Someone who seemed like he had saved a few lives and might save more, given the chance. A young guy leaning over me—

The back shelf of my memory collapsed.

A hand, rising from the dark. A gun.

An explosion, the world rent in half. I'm off my feet, falling.

Then I'm a pile on the ground, the taste of metal in the back of my throat. Voices nearby, a scream, maybe my own. Gasping breath and a moan. Not mine. In a flutter of movement, the boy's dark face, eyes behind glasses.

Oh no. Oh no.

The voices go quiet.

He's next to me. Oh no, oh no, no, no. *A long minute. A long forever.* Help—*but it doesn't sound like any word.*

A whisper. I'm so sorry.

Nothing but sound and light and burning. When I open my eyes, a hand is next to mine, open like a flower.

She stands in the doorway, hand to her mouth. Her voice far away.

Is she dead?

The young man leans over me.

Let's get out of here, *he says.*

Cor.

Let's get out of here, Cor.

I stood up, reaching for the desk for help. Phillip watched with raised eyebrows. "Are you OK?"

Thoughts detonated, one after another.

I was fine, and not fine. I didn't know what had changed, but I could reach everything on that far back shelf. How had this happened?

The student.

I stepped into view of the bean chair again, but no one was in it. I went to the door and flung it open. He was gone.

Is she dead?

Let's get out of here, Cor.

I crossed the room and pulled at the other door, leaving the hotline behind. The shelf was clear. I remembered everything.

CHAPTER 44
NATH

By the time I started for the tie-up, hundreds of people—maybe a thousand—had encamped along the shore. They'd spread out blankets, drawn up beach chairs. Picnicking families, the student radio station blaring strange, thrumming music. A few students had brought their books. Some sunbathers tried to entice the sun, but the sky rolled by, low and gray.

Poor weather for sailing, I would have guessed, but the lake was already decorated in bright sails. Students clung with bare feet on the painted rocks, dangling their legs into the water, laughing, chasing each other, leaping from boulder to boulder.

Watching them, I felt a hundred years old.

I hardly knew why I'd come. My first Night Sail, my last. I should have been back in my room, picking through the mess the cops had left. Packing, buying a bus ticket.

I'd never made it to the jazz club that Capone used to frequent, or the speakeasy they'd turned into a neighborhood pub, or to the museums to see how the city treated its dark corners of history. Which all seemed so silly to me now. All of this. I'd wasted a lot of time.

In the daylight I had no trouble finding the right spot, the outcropping of rocks on the other side of the no swimming sign. An extra-thick group waited here while a series of dinghies, rowboats, and canoes collected and deposited passengers to boats waiting out a few hundred feet past the buoys. I got an idea of Rothbert tradition by how seriously the rowers took their duty.

Phillip hurried along the shore toward me. He looked flustered.

"Surely it's not a busy day at the office," I said, gesturing at the tableau.

"Depression doesn't take sunny days off." We both glanced up at the roiling clouds. "Anyway," he said. "We'll be busy tonight when all these fools crash."

"Win told me about the black hour."

"It's not a joke."

"I'm not making a joke." I tried to imagine the last time I'd been out at that time of the night, the morning. Whatever you called that between-time when normal people were asleep. I knew what that hour felt like: like the rest of the world had spun on without you. How little could tip someone over? Being awake too long? Being alone too long? How many nights back in my dad's house did I have before I started thinking about the dull knives in the kitchen again? "Is that—from drinking too much?"

"From pretending that the day is sunny when it's creepy and cold, from pretending to like the people they're with all day, day in and out. Pretending to be happy when they're not. It's tiring being this age, this time, this place in the world." He snorted, studying the crowds behind us as though he might pick out people he knew. "Not that the students here even know that. Everything's fine in their narrow little world. It's sunny inside their skulls."

"If that's true, they'd never call."

His head snapped toward me. "They're fine in the daylight. They're fine as long as they're surrounded by commotion and their so-called friends. They're fine until they're not fine. Cracked little vessels that let the bad stuff in, and they hardly know it."

Including me. I was nicked crockery.

"You don't look so good," Phillip said. "Anything I can help you with?"

I'd agreed to go out on gray, choppy water with a guy I didn't like, another guy who didn't like me, and a sea captain who'd already nearly drowned me. A smarter me would have said no. A smarter me might have learned to swim.

"Everything's OK with—" He thought it over, probably crossing out the dead ends he'd already encountered. Father, girlfriend, roommate. "School?"

"I'm dropping out." I hadn't said this to anyone yet, and not only because there'd been no one to tell. Now I knew why. Admitting it felt like a boot to the gut.

"I'm sorry to hear that. I had big plans for you. At the hotline."

"Not sure that would have worked out. More likely I'd have been calling at some point, really."

"What's the plan, then? New place? New job? Get back together with your girl?"

I shrugged. I had no plan.

"If there's anything I could do to talk you out of it," Phillip said. He gave me a flat-palmed slap on the shoulder. "I think you and I could get some work done around this place."

Traction. Everyone seemed to think I could make something happen.

"Is that Win?" he said.

I followed his gaze out to the lake. The boats all seemed the same to me, except Win's, several lengths down the shore, which loomed larger than the others. He flew a bright Rothbert-red banner with a huge white R blazoned across it. At the helm, he could have been a Kennedy. When he saw us, he waved one arm in a wide, slow arc.

"Did you know that he's part of the Rothbert family?" I said. "I didn't even know there was a Rothbert family."

"Not very often we get such an honor."

I couldn't tell by his tone if he was kidding, serious, or writing the next hotline brochure. We watched Win's boat slicing toward us until my unease got the best of me. "I'm not sure this is the best idea I've ever had."

"Me, either." Phillip climbed down the last of the boulders to the line waiting for voyage, and before I'd gotten my bearings and joined him, he'd talked the two of us to the front of the line on the basis of our boat's fast approach. The guy at the oars of the waiting rowboat wore fraternity letters and a sour expression. I knew better than to ask: no life jackets.

We drifted away from the rocks with a shove.

"How—" The boat lurched horribly as one of the others shifted. "How is it that the university posts no swimming and then allows this—this insanity?"

"No swimming allowed," mumbled the oarsman.

"Like with most things, Rothbert students think they're invincible," Phillip said. "The university says it can't stop it, but that's not the truth. The truth is that anything that Rothbert students have been getting away with for a hundred years, they get to keep doing."

"Bitter old dude," the oarsman said.

"A little bit," Phillip said with a chummy smile.

"I'm amazed no one's been hurt," I said.

"There's always this year," Phillip said.

"You guys are assholes," our captain said.

"Fifty thousand a year in tuition and you haven't learned to recognize a joke?" Phillip said.

"Ahoy, landlubbers!" Win cried from above.

He'd thrown *Ladykiller* in reverse to slow her, leaving the helm to help us aboard. Phillip reached for the boat, put one foot up, and leaned into it. He managed to push the rowboat backward. For a moment he was suspended between the two vessels, arms pinwheeling.

Win grabbed his arm and pulled him up.

"Thanks," Phillip said to the deck.

I pulled our little teacup to the boat and launched myself, finding the deck with my feet and not my knees, and considered it progress.

"You lads see Dutch? No? I guess he's facedown somewhere." Win returned to the wheel and saluted the oarsman's retreating back. "Not a man to pass up a facedown-somewhere opportunity, our Dutch."

"Sorry to have missed meeting him," Phillip said. He took one of the bench seats opposite Win—starboard? I would never understand it—and relaxed against the railing. I took the opposite bench, already a little green.

"Nath, as soon as we get out to sea here, you'll need to pop up your seat and find us some liquid fuel. Give us some sea legs. We're all legal here."

"Except you," Phillip said.

"Maritime law, sailor. Anyway. I have—diplomatic immunity."

This seemed to confirm Phillip's worst assumptions. He turned to watch the far city skyline to our backs. Though it was still early evening, the sky was losing light. The wind kicked up. We all watched as the sail snapped loose, then filled.

"Is it supposed to storm?" I asked.

No one answered. I popped the cushion off my seat and fished three beers out of the ice. Tomorrow I'd have to pack and turn in keys and say good-bye to Kendall. Maybe I'd look up Cara's number and leave her a message. I knew I wouldn't do that, but it was OK to think I might. Today I could pretend, as Phillip said, pretend to like the people I was with. Pretend to be a Rothbert student. Pretend that everything would be fine.

Win steered us a few hundred feet out from the buoys, but not so far that we couldn't see the people on shore. A group of girls waved, woo-hooing as though we might stop for them. I saluted.

"A sailor's life for you," Win said.

"Must be that Lake Michigan water still in my lungs, yearning for home."

We crawled along the coast, nothing to say. How long did we have to float around before we called it a night?

"If you don't mind me asking, why did you jump?" Phillip said.

"I didn't—"

"Not everybody has a death wish, Phillip," Win said.

Now I was sorry Dutch wasn't along to tell us all to shut up.

"What's that supposed to mean?" Phillip said.

"Yeah, why not do it out here?" Win said.

All I'd had to do was let Phillip go on this adventure on his own. What did I owe him? They could have pulled some sunbathers off the shore for their regulation number or called in some of the hotline volunteers, made it a team-building exercise. I could be packing now and out the door first thing tomorrow. Surprise my dad, explain in person. Explain as best I could.

I'd have to start with the article about Dr. Emmet. He wouldn't understand that. I'd have to go back further. To that dark night on the porch, the stars wheeling overhead. No. Further back, to Mom's last year and that awful afghan. Or back further still, to that day in Grandpa's barn when I climbed the tractor wheel even though I knew I wasn't big enough for it. I was just a *kid*.

Not everyone had a death wish. But some of us did.

But how far would I take mine? Stop before the trigger pull, I'd told Dr. Emmet. But that wasn't the truth. I had the names of three dead students in my pocket, and I thought I knew who'd put them there.

I'd come onto this boat knowing that my name might get added to the list. Maybe I'd come to Rothbert knowing it.

"Hey, isn't that your professor?" Phillip said, nodding toward land.

Dale Hall sat far back from the shore like a woman pulling her skirts away from the tide. I found Dr. Emmet by her awkward gait. She hurried along the path, bumping through a group of students.

"Shut up, Phillip," Win said.

She wasn't my professor anymore. I watched as she tore her jagged path toward us, moving fast enough that I thought she might leap off the high shore into the lake. She was fast, overtaking the woman ahead of her. But then instead of passing the other woman, she reached out and yanked her arm.

"Uh-oh," Phillip said. "Girlfriend is in trouble."

I stood up. Had she fallen? Had another episode? We sailed on too quickly. "Wait," I said. "Stop the—drop the anchor or something."

The other woman, a blonde, threw her arms around Dr. Emmet's neck, but Dr. Emmet pried her off.

Win finally looked away from them. "Is Emmet going on the boat?"

I didn't know which boat he meant. I watched the receding scene as long as I could see them, then fell back on the bench.

I knew that woman.

Win leaned behind me and fiddled with a rope. The sail let out and grabbed a deeper portion of wind. We were passing beyond campus now, picking up speed. Ahead of us, the lake spread out wide and choppy. And empty. I checked behind us. If we weren't racing, why were we leaving all the other boats behind?

Phillip and I exchanged looks.

"Let's just get some air," Win said.

CHAPTER 45
AMELIA

I raced to Dale Hall only to find the place empty. Reminding me of the night—

The young man at my shoulder.

A small voice at the end of the world. Oh no, oh no, no, no. Then—

Our office was locked. I raced back to the front doors, only then realizing that I'd gone up and come down the stairs under my own power, and quickly. Outside, the general movement of people rolled toward the lake. I followed, clacking along as fast I could.

I doubted the memory. Had it really happened that way? The other student coming before everyone else, then Corrine with her hand over her mouth.

Let's get out of here, Cor.

Then I doubted it all. I doubted this curving path, never going the way I hoped. This gray sky. This next breath.

I hurried through parking lots, over grassy knolls that dragged at my cane. Around slow-moving herds carrying beach towels and lawn chairs. Doubting them all.

I tried to bring back those first few days, the weeks in the hospital or, better yet, my arrival home, and Corrine the only buffer between my sanity and the cliff over Lake Michigan I was nearing now. How had she done it? At my bedside, holding me up as we met with the reality of my apartment, not handicapped-ready. With the reality of the rest of my life and the slim likelihood that I'd ever be able to live it. Bringing me magazines and groceries, taking out my trash. Plumping up pillows and my mood when I started to think about the black room.

Distasteful duties that should have fallen to someone who loved me, but no one did.

Except her.

I saw her ahead on the path and doubted the vision.

But it was. Corrine, dressed for a country picnic, her hair bright against the darkening sky. I bashed my way through a group of students, knocking shins with my cane.

I wouldn't have caught her at all, but she paused to watch a large boat out on the lake. I had the terrible idea that she would run when she saw me. I grabbed her arm.

"What—Mel!" She threw her arms around me as I gasped for air. My fingers raked at her pink skin until she dropped her grip. "What's wrong? Are you OK?"

"What's it all been—" I choked. "What's it all been about?"

"What's going on? Are you going out to Doyle's boat?"

"Why—how could you leave me?"

"Melly, I don't know what you're saying. Should we sit down?"

I looked around. No seats. She meant the ground. I'd moved past pain into the realm of dead weight, but this, from Corrine, still stung. She couldn't acknowledge what was in front of her. She didn't like to mention the cane or the way I moved now. The way I was now. Maybe I'd been in denial, too, in the beginning. But this wasn't something I could wish away.

Except I wasn't sure that I would wish anything back to the way it had been. I felt light, sharp. As though I had burned away all that was unnecessary, as though the attack had torn everything insubstantial from me. I was stronger than I'd ever been.

I raised the cane over my head like a pickax and struck at the path with it. Corrine's eyes slid away. She would rather look to see who was watching than to stay with me, to understand. Why hadn't I noticed the distance she'd put between us? Even nearby, even at the next desk.

"Not a good idea, Cor," I said. I'd finally conquered my breath, just as I'd conquered so much more. I could almost walk away, leave this all here. Almost. "I've remembered some things."

She watched the lake over my shoulder. "That's good, right?"

"That day, Cor. For instance, the young man you had in your office." I had her attention, and my last niggling doubt dashed at the sight of her neck splotching pink. "You left me to die."

"That's not—we called 911—"

No denial, then. They'd been in our office the whole time, then left me and Leo to die. "I can't believe this."

"—we did, Amelia, don't look at me like that. We called and got your ambulance and—"

"Let's get out of here, Cor."

She paled. "What?"

"That's what he said. Have you never heard of first aid? I could have died. Maybe Leo could have made it. We needed your help."

"Leo was *dead*, Mel. We thought you were, too."

"So why the rush? I'm your best friend and you flew out—"

But then I knew why. We, she said. We. "What Corrine did with her summer vacation."

"What?"

"He's—isn't he at least fifteen years younger than you?"

She gave another glance out to the water. "I didn't hear you worrying about fifteen years when you were with Doyle."

"That's—"

"It's no different. No different than you and Doyle and your smug, gooey romance. God, the devotion he gave you, and you couldn't appreciate it. I could have killed for—there's no difference. Except now that I have someone, if I brought him out in public, people would stare. You can date *your boss*—twenty years older, actually—and no one says a word. They all keep your secrets. But if I so much as took Win to a department mixer, I know how it would go. I know what you'd all say."

What would we all say? That she could do better than date a twenty-year-old? She hadn't dated anyone in the time I'd known her. No one-night stands, no friends with benefits, like Joe, no one like Doyle. Men seemed to have written her off. Which I understood. We all had. Corrine was a soft, sincere woman—sexless in her baggy clothes, ageless in her schoolgirl ponytail. Invisible. But I could see her clearly now.

"Did your boyfriend mention that he knew Leo Lehane?" I said.

Her eyes shuttered closed. "We couldn't get mixed up in it. His dad—"

"A better question—how did I get mixed up in it?"

"You don't understand. His family—"

"I'm beginning to wonder who was meant to take that bullet, aren't you?"

Her eyes popped open. She shook her head at me as though I were a child who'd just stuck my fingers in a spinning fan. "Me, you think."

"The kid tried to kill a female professor outside our office, Cor. I didn't know him, but your boyfriend did. What did you think, that if you ran away, none of it would stick? That it wouldn't eventually—"

"It's a year," she said. "Today."

"No—"

But it was. The date crept up like another attack. "Happy anniversary to me, I guess." I wondered what the student paper would do to mark the milestone. "Did it ever occur to you that your boyfriend might know something about this?"

"You don't know him. First of all, we're in love—"

I groaned.

"—and second, he's one of the Rothberts. *The* Rothberts. He's not going to come here and start some crazy scheme—"

Rory's story that could write itself was writing itself. "That's exactly who would come in and drop shenanigans," I said. "Because he can get away with it."

"That's not who he is—if you could only get to know him. And his family—"

"You've met them?" I remembered her standing at the edge of a group, hedging in at the periphery and hoping that someone would include her. And the young man wearing the expensive suit. Of course. "No, no, you wouldn't exactly be allowed at the family reunion, would you?"

"They're upstanding people, Mel. His father is in Congress, and his mother does charity work. The grandmother—one of the Rothbert *granddaughters*—I met her at the faculty reception and she was so proper and sweet, really delighted to hear about the renovations at Dale Hall—it was named for her—and that her portrait is still on the wall."

The pretty co-ed I'd been sharing my secrets with. Spies watching me all year. "Still. You mean *again*, after the blood—"

"Stop it!" Corrine's hands flew into the air to push my words away. "I don't want to hear it—over and over, you won't leave it alone. I saw it, OK? I saw that kid and his face—"

She covered her eyes. The things she'd seen. I could imagine the nightmares, what visions had come to her as she sat by my hospital bed. All the doubts she'd had to swallow. If she'd given into them, what would she have had to believe about herself?

The problem with that: The worst thing that had happened to her had actually happened to me. She didn't see it. She wouldn't see it. I felt as though we hung in a delicate balance, that our friendship might tip in any direction if the barest feather dropped.

"Are you sure," I said, "he didn't try to have you killed?"

She dropped her hand and showed me her raging eyes, then turned on her heel and started down the shore. "There's no truth unless it's your truth, is there, Amelia?" she called over her shoulder. "You have to bulldoze through it, no matter who it hurts."

I watched her go, putting real distance between us.

No matter who it hurts? It hurt me. That she didn't understand told me everything about the friendship we'd had.

She'd left me when I'd needed her most. Now I stood and watched her do it again.

CHAPTER 46

I found a bench along the shore and collapsed on one end, ignoring the couple snuggled at the other. My age or so. They might have wanted to be alone.

I caught the man staring at my cane.

If I could give Corrine her fair share of this, I would. The shooting hadn't just happened to me. It had consumed me. How could I make her understand the many lives that had been cut short? Leo's, but also mine as I knew it. A host of other Amelia Emmets, gone.

The couple on the bench stood and hurried away. They'd caught the stench of the rotting meat I'd turned out to be.

"Now is that you, or is that the you that isn't you?" McDaniel scooted into the place the couple had left. "You all look alike."

"I can't believe you're still following me."

"You leave an interesting trail," he said. "But, alas. I'm here for the paper. For mediocre photos and ambivalent quotes. What do you think Night Sail adds to the personality of our fair city? What do you think the lack of safety measures means for Night Sail's future?"

"Rothbert's First Lady's lap dog can't get a better assignment than that?"

"Aha," he said.

"What?"

"Lap dog. Ouch." He gazed over the lake. "So that's what you think of me."

He couldn't be serious. "Listen—this is your fault. I went to the hotline to get Nath some help. That place turned out to be, well, maybe a cult. But I ran into a kid there I recognized, a student. And my office-mate is, oh, God. They're in love."

"Yuck."

The image of Nath, sleepy eyes and swollen lips. I felt sick. "They were in our office the night of the shooting. That kid knew Leo Lehane."

His mouth opened and closed like a fish. "You're sure? That's—wow. That's it, then. The connection. Leo meant to shoot her, not you."

I had to admit: I enjoyed watching the fish-face turn to admiration. "Jealousy, maybe?" I said. "Maybe Leo had a crush."

"I wonder—"

"Maybe she had a thing with Leo and tossed him for this kid." It could be anything. "Who knows what the relationship was between Leo and Win."

"Win," he said.

"The student, the—yuck."

"Win Harlan," he said.

"I don't know. Oh, he's—"

"The Rothbert crown prince." He gave me a sad smile. "Sometimes it's not good news when the stories write themselves." He stood and walked several feet toward the cliff's edge and studied the scene. "He knew Leo through the hotline."

"That was my guess." My left leg was dead numb. To shift it, I had to lift my thigh with my hands. I realized I'd done this in front of an audience. When I looked up, there was no trace of disgust.

"And Nath knows him, too," he said. "He was cagey about that name earlier."

Nath. My stomach lurched. I'd begun to lose track of Nath the student. He'd become something else: Nath the black hole, Nath the shameful incident.

"Let's call this a weather delay," I said. "Don't you have some contacts on the university police? We should offer him this chance at glory." I managed to stand. I'd have to take it slow back home or find a cab. Or Joss. If only Joss would happen by now. But she was on Doyle's boat or soon would be. I checked the time. This one I couldn't win. I'd have to give Mrs. Doyle a chance to grow fond of me another time. "I'm ready to go to bed for about three days."

I realized what I'd said and cringed, waiting for McDaniel to make an invitation out of it. Waiting to see if I minded what he said.

"Miles to go before we sleep, Amelia. Do you know where Nath is?"

On a bus to the Indiana cornfields? I felt bad about that, about almost everything. "Do you?"

"I saw your man Nathaniel get on a boat not a half hour ago."

I looked past him to the lake. Not as many boats as prior years, but still plenty. Good for him. One last hurrah before he packed. "OK?"

"Win's boat, Amelia. That boat."

He pointed to the north, past the lighthouse, past all the other sails. A single vessel, stark white against the dark sky, sails down. Drifting and alone.

We hurried along the coast trail dodging coolers and dogs. The worst of the storm still gathered, but the people on shore had gotten the message. They peeled up their picnics, carted lawn chairs on their backs toward the parking lot. I stumbled and corrected, fighting my own dead weight while McDaniel tried not to seem impatient.

"Whose boat is this?" he said.

"My boss. And his wife."

He knew Doyle from the faculty reception, would have known who he was with the barest scratch of research. The question he wanted to ask hung in the air.

"His very new wife," I said. "And the faculty, the people I work with. There."

I spotted them, the boat's Rothbert-red hull an easy target. Doyle at the helm, Nancy and Joss. Woo, looking seasick. We called and waved until Joss caught sight of me and pointed us toward the tie-up so that Doyle could execute a turnabout to come for us. I grabbed McDaniel by the elbow and directed him, and out on the rocks, let him return the favor. The crowd for passage out to the boats was thin and hesitant. The boys in the shuttle boats talked to one another as they waited for anyone to take them up on a voyage. "We're next," I said. "That boat there?"

The kid in the inflatable dinghy I'd commandeered turned to see which I meant. "He's already going out there," he said, hitching his thumb.

He meant the rowboat behind him, the student at the oars readying to go. His passenger: Corrine.

The low boat bumped against the rocks with a scrape. I considered the power I had left in each leg, the flat but uneven surface of the boulder. Thousands of Rothbert youth had shimmied off this shelf into waiting crafts, but how many of them were recovering from bullet wounds? I tried for discreet, easing down to the rock's surface with the cane for leverage and sliding into the boat from this lower vantage. Falling the last few inches into the boat, I landed gracelessly, my leg hooked under me.

"You OK?" the kid at the oars said without real interest.

I pulled myself up and laid my cane across my knees with as much ladylike dignity as I'd ever had. "Rory, get in."

"That's it, buddy," the kid said. "Two at a time."

"Only so many life jackets," Corrine said with an icy smile.

I felt waves of something old and animal coming off Corrine. The space between us now narrow and tight. Our fraternity ferryman pushed off. I turned over my shoulder to find McDaniel. "Call him," I said. "Call your friend. And—his friends."

"Be careful," he said, with a glance at Cor.

I knew what he meant, felt it deep in the knot of my reconfigured gut.

Be careful of everything, he meant, and everyone.

CHAPTER 47
NATH

"**Y**ou want to steer, Nath?"

I didn't. The lake churned under us, the boat heaving. I watched the empty horizon ahead. If I took my eyes off that line—dark blue where the sky slammed into it—I'd vomit everything I'd ever eaten. I'd formulated a backup plan to jump overboard. Inside this rocking tin can, the water looked calm, inviting. Less dangerous.

"Just hold the wheel while I trim a bit." Win waited for me to move, but I couldn't. I hoped to learn to swim spontaneously as I leapt over. I would never again convince anyone that I hadn't jumped the first time. "It will help with the seasickness," he said. "I swear."

He pulled me up, stood me in front of the helm, and placed my hands at ten and two. I stared at my hands until he grabbed my chin and pointed me out to sea. "Keep your eyes on the horizon, Captain."

If I was captain, then I had a different voyage mapped out. The wheel turned of its own volition as I let up on my grip. We began to spin in the wind. "Woah, woah," Win said. "No mutinies, all right? Hold steady. There. If you let this swing on its own—we might find some trouble."

I held fast to the wheel and ventured a peek at Phillip. He lounged against the slim rail like a man of leisure, his bets already placed and his pony in the lead.

A wave of nausea swept over me. I hooked my future to the horizon.

I couldn't find it. The water mirrored the gray sky. I thought of the old-time sailors who believed the earth was flat, that somewhere out at the edge of sight, ships tumbled over and into the mouths of monsters. We'd reached that point, our vessel tipping, gray over gray, into the next life, into the void.

"Hold steady, Nath."

I gripped the wheel. Win went back to cranking. In a minute, he had the main sails down and fastened to the boom, the boom tightened. The boat swung with the waves.

"Are we battening down?" Phillip said, his hands tucked behind his head.

"Someone took his seasick remedy this morning," Win said. "You have a stock of those?"

"I'm pretty resourceful."

"More so than us mere humans."

"Don't sell yourself short, Win," Phillip said. "You're the god."

My stomach churned along with the boat. In desperation, I fiddled with the wheel until I found a sweet spot with the rudder. The bucking eased. A god. I felt like the only human in a Greek tragedy, two vengeful deities talking over my head as they shoved me from side to side.

"Not as immortal as all that," Win said.

"So few are. Marilyn Monroe. Vincent van Gogh. Hemingway."

Win turned a sly smile on him. "Hitler."

Phillip thought that one over. "Hitler? Oh, right."

"Some say. An easy way out, considering."

"I'll have to look that one up. Sylvia Plath," Phillip said. "The other one. Anne Sexton. No future in poetry."

"James Dean," I said.

They both looked at me. "Nath—" Win started.

"No, wait," Phillip said. "He might be onto something."

I didn't think I was onto anything. Certainly not the thing that mattered. "Let's please take the boat in," I said.

"Fast car, young corpse," Phillip said. "Immortality like that doesn't come around every day."

"That's the going thing now. Immortality," Win said, reaching for the helm. I held tight. As long as I kept my knuckles white on the wheel, I didn't want to turn myself inside out. I didn't want to leap into the churning water. Eyes on the horizon, I could think. Sylvia Plath. Marilyn Monroe. I chanced a look. Win stood in the center of the deck, feet wide and stable, rolling with the waves. A drop of rain hit my arm.

"People like yourself think they have immortality already," Phillip said.

Ernest Hemingway.

Vincent van Gogh.

"Are you sure it's people like me?" Win said. "Or people like you?"

Vincent van Gogh?

Suicides. Famous suicides, not to mention the thousands and thousands of not-famous ones that must happen every year. Not to mention the three in my pocket. The water seemed like better odds.

Another splat of water hit me. "It's starting to rain." Why were we still out here, letting a Great Lakes squall roll over us? We were going to die out here. Capsize and drown or get struck by lightning where we bobbed. I had wanted to die not so long ago, but not like this. Not with my eyes wide open, like Leo. I'd need something soft for my head, something slow and easy. Something nice and gentle. Pills. Pills, like Marilyn Monroe. Pills, like—

"Jazz Starling," I said.

They both turned on me.

Win let his crossed arms drop. "What do you know about it?"

"Probably not as much as you," I said.

"That's right," he said. "So let me—"

"Let him make his case," Phillip said.

Win considered, then found a perch on the side of the boat. I watched the edge of existence, sailing toward an abyss I hoped was still there.

"I don't have a case," I said. But I did: The woman on shore. I'd found her in my memory, tucked up against Win's chest on the cover of the *Willetson Courier* the day after Dr. Emmet was shot. And she was the teacher I'd met at Dr. Emmet's door, hair mussed and cheeks red while someone cowered in the office behind her. "I have ideas, though."

"Let's hear them," Phillip said.

"By all means," Win said.

Dr. Emmet had sent me home. I should be home.

What did it matter? I hadn't remembered my dad's straight razor that dark night after Bryn, but I would the next time.

I swallowed hard, glancing away from the horizon to see how far from the shore we were. Another boat had ventured out our direction. Surely they couldn't be the fools we were. "You asked him to kill her," I said. "The other teacher, your girlfriend. I don't know why. But he got it wrong."

We all sat with this, the wind whipping their hair and blasting my eyes. "What do you know about Jazz Starling?" Win said.

"Not much. He's—he's not the only one. You gave them poison. Pills. Or talked them into taking something. Replaced their aspirin like you did to Kendall or talked them into it instead of helping them. I don't know why—you got off on the power or something."

Win was silent long enough that I looked to see how he'd taken it. Head hanging over his boat shoes, elbows on his knees. "You've been busy," he said. "It looks bad for me. Who else knows all this?"

Phillip smiled sadly at me. Had he known all along? Suspected? I thought of the lists in his office, the names of the dead marked off.

Dr. Emmet didn't know anything. Rory McDaniel might put things together for his big story, but only after my body and Phillip's were dragged from the water. My stomach lurched at the thought of my dad having to come all this way to identify my waterlogged corpse. My dad. I wanted to do things differently. I wanted—another chance.

"No one," I said. "I didn't tell anyone."

"That's too bad," Win said. "Good thing I did."

I thought I hadn't heard right. Win bumped himself off the rail, hands heavy in his pockets. "Evidence to be opened on the occurrence of my death," he said. "Soon, I think. Unless you brought that gun to shoot fish."

Gun—

Phillip stood, his hand at his waist. I could see the bulge at his hip, now that I knew to look. "Fish in a barrel is my specialty," he said.

My mind raced—*gungungun*—stopping when I reached the hotline room underground, underfunded, under a spotlight, my nerves raw and exposed. Phillip across from me. *This is the training.* But the training was a fishing expedition for how badly damaged I might be. Bad lighting, bad coffee. All the comforts of the room removed. The call log in his bag, the names checked off as though on a shopping list. Jazz Starling, collected. Summer Hightower, check. I pulled the list out of my pocket. William Kanowski. And Win Harlan, the list not yet complete.

"You talked Leo into shooting Win," I said, my voice barely audible over the wind. I looked up, found Phillip watching me with his head tilted. "She surprised him—or maybe he just wanted the night to end. It was never her he was supposed to shoot."

"The winner," Phillip said. The prize, anyone could see, not worth having.

Win looked stricken. "I thought—"

"You thought I was trying to take down your girlfriend. Why bother? Politicians can bed anyone they like, isn't that right? Your dad certainly does. Who cares? If Leo had even half a testicle—"

"Leave Leo alone," I said.

They both turned my way. I'd surprised myself by finding a spark of rage under the fear.

"He was weak," Phillip said.

"Which made him the perfect prey for you." I held onto the wheel—*gungungun*—and swallowed the bile that rose in the back of my throat. But the ember flamed. "Good thing there are people like Leo, people ready to trust, or you might have to do your own dirty work."

Phillip shot out of his seat, a finger poking into my chest. "You have no idea how hard I work for this place and for these people—these spoiled brats. All their fissures, courtesy of mommy and daddy, and I'm supposed to patch them up so they can go on to rule the world." Spit collected at the corner of his mouth. "Leo was just like the rest of them. Spoon-fed senators' sons—"

"Congressmen's," Win and I said in unison.

"—Fifth Avenue royalty and celebrity kids who'll never amount to anything but gossip and credit card bills for their parents. Meanwhile there are people on this campus who fight to be here, who need my help. But you know who cares about them? No one. The university would cut our budget to the bone, if—"

"If rich kids didn't kill themselves once in a while," I said. "Or go crazy and kill a Rothbert heir."

Phillip looked to Win with bright eyes, his hand still on the bulge under his shirt. "They call all the time, but then they're whisked away to—treatment facilities, to Aspen for ski therapy—"

"Hey," Win said. "That's really effective."

"—or to Malibu for surfing and hot-rock massages and anyone who can't afford luxury rescue can go to hell? No, thank you. Let mommy and daddy buy them a nice funeral."

"And then give a big memorial donation to the Hope Hotline," Win said. "To save the rest. To save your job. To keep your empire intact."

Phillip stepped back, smirking. "Just like you to follow the money, Win. Maybe someday there'll be a statue of *you* on campus, along with Great-Great-Grandpa's. Oh, wait. Probably not."

I sneaked a glance at Win. He'd been working on this, too, checking the call logs, looking into the hotline's donors. And then I'd arrived, sniffing around, asking questions. What did he think of me? That night on the boat, when he'd thrown me into the lake, what had I done to inspire the lesson, the hand on my shoulder for a second too long? I'd said—I'd said what had happened to Leo, what Leo had done wasn't his fault. But he hadn't believed it. In a way he was right. It was his fault—he was the prize. Not Dr. Emmet. Not Dr. Talbot. Not Leo. Only Win and his privilege. It hadn't cost him anything, not yet.

Something from Phillip's manifesto stuck in my side. A piece of me knew what he meant. A cold, dark place, deep, that understood the world spun too fast for the likes of me. The ember was out. I sagged over the helm. The rudder reacted, and the boat gave a small leap in the wind. I steadied and corrected, noticing the wall of storm to our north, then Win watching me, his eyes sharp over my shoulder. He gave me the barest nod, as Dr. Emmet had, once, over our table at the Mill. A thousand years ago, that night, when I thought I might have to pretend to be a guy who wanted to die. I didn't want to die.

"I followed the histrionics, Phillip," Win said. "Your weird empire doesn't make any sense. You don't make any sense. I hope—oh, look what I did there—I *hope* you had a better plan than shooting us. Messy. Direct. By your own hand. Not your style."

I swallowed hard and watched the horizon. "I'm going to guess pills."

"That's standard issue," Win said. "Not very ambitious for a last stand."

Phillip shook his head, smiling. "It's not *my* last stand."

Win's bravado, his gallows humor, gave me a pinch of courage. "Pills seemed to work for everyone else," I said. "Except the kid in the car. I always forget his name."

"William," Win said. "But I believe he had a little something in the bloodstream, after all."

"True to form," Phillip said. "His parents got that covered up." He reached into his back pocket—I flinched—and took out a slim flask. "Present for you, Win." He pitched it.

Win caught it. I saw scratches, lacy etchings that could only be a monogram. Win's monogram. Win turned it this way and that, admiring it. "Do you have a crush on me, Phil?"

"Have a drink." Phillip pulled the gun out of the front of his waistband. I'd been expecting it so long, the weapon, at last, almost seemed like a prop.

"This is supposed to be mine, and then they'll find you afloat out here with two dead bodies. 'I don't know what happened, officers. Good thing I stuck to beer.' Nice work, really," Win said, thumbing the etching. "I have a much nicer one than this at home." He leaned back and threw a Hail Mary. The flask splashed into the dark water, somewhere to our east. To our north, a bolt of lightning. "All my chips are on you not having the guts for the alternate route. It would put an end to all your hard work."

"It would. Except I tried to stop you, Win." Phillip put on a look of fear and shuddered. "You were a wild man, depressed, textbook case. Waving the gun all around until Nath tried to disarm you. To your credit, you were broken up over killing your friend, and before I could stop you—"

"No one would believe that," Win said.

I saw Phillip's opening. It was wide. "But your calls."

"What do you mean?"

Phillip grinned. Rain started to patter against the deck.

"Your calls, to the hotline. Before you were—" I saw the problem, had seen it long ago. How did a hotline caller become a trusted volunteer, stable enough for the training and the black hour, week in and week out? He didn't. "You faked those," I said to Phillip. "He never called."

"Oh, but he did. The long hours we talked over his problems. His dad's infidelity, his mother's indifference, the weight of being a Rothbert—"

The roar started low, and then Win leapt at him. He bumped the helm as he flew by. The wheel spun in my hands. We listed steep and fast in time to catch Phillip low and surprised, Win flaring and flying, both of them tumbling into the rail—

And over.

A gunshot split the wind.

They were gone.

I couldn't move. The wind rose, howling, and the rain started in earnest. Below that, the silence was deafening. I fought the wheel back to stable, then left it to spin and stumbled against the choppy water to the rail.

My eyes raked the surface, every white-capped wave hiding a body. I ran, slipping, the length of the boat and back, checked the other side.

No one.

Again: up and down the length, the other side, port and starboard whichwaswhich, back to the rail. "Win!"

Out of the corner of my eye—no, a boat. The one I'd seen earlier, closer. The only other idiots to stay out on the rough water. I waved my arms frantically at them. Their sails up, they rose and fell with the waves like a child's toy.

I heard something hit the side of our boat. Win, swimming and splashing—and then Phillip. They'd risen together, fighting. *Gungungun.* I flipped open the seats looking for something to use as a weapon but only found the elusive life jackets and the last of our beer. When I looked over the side, Phillip was above water, struggling to keep Win under the surface. Succeeding.

I threw a beer bottle at Phillip's head, missing. Another. It splashed lazily, wide. *Gungungun.* Win was still under. I crouched, knuckles white on the rail. I couldn't think, couldn't see any other way.

I stood, found the horizon.

And jumped.

Another gunshot, and the world turned inside out.

CHAPTER 48
AMELIA

"**W**hat's wrong with that one?" Joss asked in low tones as she and Doyle helped me out of the rowboat. She meant Corrine, who'd refused all help, arriving on Doyle's boat much as a royal personage might alight on the *QEII*.

I didn't want help either. My legs had turned to lead, stiff and unbending, but I wanted to come aboard on my own power. I wouldn't be carried on or helped, not in front of Corrine.

"I can't begin to explain," I said.

Corrine had seen me at my worst. She'd helped me through my worst, but I couldn't touch that tender spot without a sharp intake of breath. I'd felt abandoned through all this, friendless except for Cor. I'd gotten it wrong: Doyle, Joss, even Woo, pale with seasickness, managed to flap a hand at me. I'd gotten a lot wrong.

I dropped into the first open spot, next to Doyle's wife, who wore a life vest and sat forward on the bench with her hands on her knees. She glowered at me. "Sorry to—you know," I said. I'd forgotten her name. "Sorry."

"Nancy's not got her sea legs yet," Doyle said. He placed an orange vest at my feet. I'd been on the boat plenty of times and had never actually seen the vests.

Nancy. Right.

"It gets better," I said. "The more time you spend—"

The look on her face, and Doyle's, stopped me. I had a feeling we could be talking about more than sailing.

"Look," I said. "I hate to skip the pleasantries, but I need to yacht-jack you guys. That vessel—" I pointed, Win's boat impossibly far away—"has some potentially noir shit going down."

Even Nancy turned to consider the request. "Out there?"

"There's a stiff breeze—"

"That's an understatement," Doyle said.

"—good company—"

Corrine scoffed.

"—good . . . OK, look," I said. "This might be life and death for one of our students."

Joss pushed her glasses up her nose. "Unpack it for us, Melly."

Even the short version was too long. When I got to Win's participation, Corrine stood and flung herself at me. "He's not like that!" Doyle pulled her away and sat her back down.

"I don't know what he's like," I admitted to the rest of them. Woo's face had become a mask of terror. He didn't have the heart for real trouble of any kind. "But I truly believe Nathaniel Barber is in danger."

"And you want to go get him?" Joss said. There were looks exchanged I was probably not supposed to read.

"I'm not the one in love with a student here," I said. "But that kid— Nath deserves better than I've given him. I want to make sure he hasn't got himself into something he can't handle. That—I haven't gotten him into something he can't handle."

"I would like to be let off at shore," Woo said. "Before you become a taxi service."

No one paid him any attention, except Joss, who shushed him like a child.

"I owe him this," I said. I looked at Nancy. I knew I had to convince her. I wasn't the person Doyle listened to anymore. "He's just a kid."

Her eyes were serious. She nodded slowly and squeezed my arm. She turned to Doyle. "Nick, we have to do something."

"I've never heard such bullshit," Corrine said. "But what else is new? Dr. Emmet needs this, Dr. Emmet needs—"

"Dr. Talbot," Doyle said.

"If she's up for tenure, we all throw our support behind her. If she's sick, we all pitch in to cover her classes—"

"If she's shot, we sit at her bedside to allay our own guilt," I said.

Corrine's look was steel. "When we reach the other boat," she said. "I'll be joining their party."

"And when we reach shore, you'll turn in your letter of resignation," Doyle said.

"You can't ask me—"

"I don't think the Rothbert code of ethics covers relationships between matriculating undergraduates and faculty members, Dr. Talbot. Particularly those who have yet to prove themselves through the tenure process. I'll have to ask Jim."

We all had a moment to imagine the dean's reaction to such a question. Joss gave me a supportive nod, but I looked away. What a narrow ledge I'd walked out on.

Doyle reached behind Nancy and let out a knot holding the mainsail. The sail loosened and filled with the billowing wind. "She's a slow little washtub, you know," he said. "Luckily it looks like they've pulled their sails."

"If I'm following this correctly," Woo said, "one of the students on that boat might be responsible for a fatality as well as Amelia's—disability, and we're going to *hurry*?"

"Wear your Rothbert medal over your heart, Ben," I said. "You'll be fine."

He glanced around like a rabbit and dashed for the back of the boat. I took his spot, and Corrine took the one next to Nancy to get away from me.

Over her shoulder I could see that most of the other crafts had turned south for the marina. Any other year, the lake would have been choked with boats by now, sails down to bob in the cool evening air, a few fireworks set off on shore, the campus golden and regal in the background.

In good weather, some boats draped their rigging with battery-powered twinkle lights or hung lanterns from bow and stern. Enough boats, enough light, and the little section of the lake around Rothbert glowed as a beacon, brighter than any lighthouse.

I'd never seen the Night Sail from the shore, I realized. All that opulence, and somehow I'd become a part of it, forgetting that some—many—had to see this show from afar. This wealth, this privilege. I thought I'd known what it felt like to stand outside, but I didn't. Not as well as Leo Lehane, who watched all of life from a distant shore. Not as well as Corrine, forced to witness me and Doyle and who knows how many other friends over her lifetime find the thing she wanted most. A bit of understanding might have wrenched open my heart, but I couldn't let the cracks show now. Nath didn't have anyone else. He needed me.

They hardly know what they need until they need it.

Who had said that? I sorted the words from the long day I'd had until I heard them from Phillip Carrington-Wells's mouth. He could have been talking about anyone, about me.

Pompous, though, now that I realized he meant he could supply the need when it finally came. Save anybody who came his way, oh, except at least a handful of students whose names Nath had on a list somewhere.

To be in the business of saving lives, though, a bit of ego might be requisite. The same for teaching, really. To be in the business of imparting knowledge, you needed to feel pretty strongly that you had knowledge to give. When this was over, I wondered if I'd ever command a classroom again.

The boat we chased was far larger than Doyle's. At this distance I could see only a few people, two or three, one in a dark shirt, standing on the deck. We were getting close. I turned to give Doyle a grateful smile—

An explosion cut through the wail of wind.

Corrine screamed.

We all stood. A gunshot.

"Oh, shit, oh, shit." This from Joss.

Corrine fought past us to the front, her screams so loud that I couldn't tell what syllables they contained.

"Did you see someone go overboard?" I yelled. Rain began to pelt us. I couldn't see anyone on the boat, but then I did—just one person, the dark shirt gone. Doyle turned the wheel and let the wind out of the sails. "Wait," I said.

"Are you crazy?" Woo yelled. He squatted in the back. "Turn us the hell around."

"We can't leave," I said. "Cor, *shut up*. Doyle, man overboard."

"Man *shot*," Woo said. "I, for one, would like never to know what that feels like."

Corrine wailed so that we all had to talk over her. Joss and Woo bickered. Nancy tried to ask me something I could barely hear and probably couldn't answer. "What?" I said. "Cor, try to—"

"That's enough," Doyle said, an ax cutting through the chaos and silencing us all.

In the absence, I heard the last of Corrine's sniffles and the rising wind under the patter of rain.

"I—" He looked at each of us, landing on Nancy. "I don't know what to do."

Joss, Corrine, Woo—they all turned to me. I opened my mouth, but nothing came out. I couldn't lead them into this. Couldn't ask everything of them. Nancy reached out and took Doyle's hand.

I pushed past Corrine to the bow. On the other boat, one crew member raced forward and aft, again and again, calling into the water. "What is he saying?" Corrine said, finally quiet. I couldn't quite hear. Where was the gun? As we watched, the lone sailor climbed to the gunwale—Nath, oh, God. He crouched there, stood, dove—

—another gunshot.

We all ducked, watching Nath hit the water. Graceless, flat.

"Nath!" I crawled onto the splashboard, kicking as hands tried to pull me back.

"Amelia, don't," Doyle bellowed.

I paused at the point of the bow, my fist wrapped around a cleat. Over at the other boat, nothing moved. I stood.

"Amelia, for the love of God," Doyle said.

I jumped.

I understood my mistake right away. One leg wooden, the other maxed out after the day's excursions—I felt the water rush past as I sank, kicking for the surface but sure that I'd already seen it for the last time.

Above me a white flotation ring dropped. Then one of the orange vests. Still under, I kicked off my boots and used my arms and a dolphin kick, the only thing I could think of, my hip and gut crying out. When I hit the surface, I was beyond the life preservers. Raindrops bounced off the lake and up into my face.

"There she is!"

"Melly, please."

"Oh, no, Corrine. You're staying right here—"

A scuffle rose up behind me as I paddled toward the other boat. A hundred yards I might have guessed on deck, but what did a hundred yards feel like in the water, in heavy clothes and half my body dead weight—

Nath, hitting the water like a stone.

I paddled harder, stretched my strokes, tried the dolphin kick again, and ignored the white-hot rage of my gut.

This is why.

The words came to me. This is why.

Why I—survived.

Why they'd stitched me back together around the lightning bolt, why I'd escaped the black room and then the white, a leaner, sharper tool by which to cut this black spot away—for this, for this alone and to hell with what happened to me.

Nath—young, earnest Nath deserved better than this, than me. But what came to me was McDaniel, idiot McDaniel and his kiss like its own lightning, its own light and heat and fire racing through me and striking, striking home like nothing else had in months, in years, in my lifetime.

I wanted more of it, and I wanted it for everyone I knew: Doyle and Joss and Joe and Nath—most of all young, young Nath, at the beginning, only just the very beginning.

I was almost to the boat when it made a turn in the wind. *Lady-*

killer. I reached up and grabbed the low area near the engine. Somewhere near, a cough.

I let go, sinking until I got control of myself, rising to the surface with my own cough. I hung from the back of the boat again and, hand over hand, dragged myself to port. Someone clung to the side of the boat with both hands, gasping.

"Nath," I choked.

He turned, eyes familiar and wide. Not Nath. I couldn't see him well in the fading light. "I'm hurt," he said. "My shoulder."

"Where's Nath?"

He checked over his shoulders, panicking, coughing. Rivulets of rain ran down his face. "I think—I think he shot him."

He shot *him.* "How many of you?"

"He went crazy. Oh, Christ. I should have seen the signs."

"Phillip? Is that—what are you doing here?"

"Nath had a bad feeling, and I came along. Oh, God. I wish—"

"OK, OK. Win shot Nath—" My voice caught. "Is that what you're saying?"

"And me. I couldn't stop him—"

"You're hit?"

"My shoulder, the pain—"

"Familiar with it. Do you think you can climb into the boat?"

He considered his hands, high above his head. "Not from here."

"Can you come this way? Don't let go. There's a ladder in the back. Hand over—just like that, just like that."

He slid closer, one hand then the other, inch by inch, his face contorted in agony every time he had to move his left arm. He reached my side, a groan coming through clenched teeth. I watched for Nath and Win over his shoulder.

"You're going to have to go around me. Don't let go. Here, I'll move my hand. One hand between mine—exactly. Now the other and cross over—"

We faced each other, hanging like meat in a butcher's window, and at the last minute before he passed, our eyes met—

Maybe I'll have all the answers.

—and I saw that he had only one answer, and it looked like bottomless loathing and disgust. Not just for me—but especially me, right now. He was impatient to be breathing the same air as someone as useless, someone as pathetic. For just a blink, I saw the vast black room that Phillip lived in, always and every day.

I hardly had the time to wonder how I'd ever missed it. He put his hands on mine and held me there. His fingers ground into mine. A whimper escaped me. My fingers already slipping in the rain, I couldn't hold on.

"Professor," he said.

One chance at a breath. I took it and sank into the dark water. A hand cupped the top of my head, fingers encircling like a crown.

I flailed and kicked and scratched. Even with his injury—did he really have an injury?—I had so little left to me.

I realized I had stopped kicking and jacked at him with both legs again, my lungs bursting. The last thing—

I thought of my parents, long gone, the old house and that long driveway with the woods and the pond I should be a better swimmer and a roomful of students waiting to hear what I'll say and that kiss that kiss that kiss.

I reached up, finding air with my hands, and felt for Phillip's face, his neck, alighting here and there but not grasping, not yet, until I found the shoulder the bullet wound the weakness and dug in deep with two fingers and everything I had and anything I could borrow from the lightning bolt inside me.

The scream, underwater, satisfied.

He let go, and I surfaced, gasping and heaving.

"Help! Doyle, Joss. Over here."

I clawed at his shoulder with everything I had, wrapping one leg around his waist to better dig in. He grabbed a handful of flesh with his good hand—my left leg, numbness had its benefits—and pushed me away with the elbow of his injured arm.

He had me. He reached with his good hand around to my good

leg, letting me burrow at his wound, until I realized that I felt, in the crook of my knee, the object that would end this all, one way or the other.

In my next breath, I had the gun. I had it, horrible, black, gun rising from the dark, only this time it's my hand, my gun. He reached for it and pulled it and me down with it.

Trigger.

Trigger. He grabbed my wrist and forced my arm down. My other fingers remembered their job and mined deep into his flesh. He crowed in pain and loosened up on me.

Trigger, gunshot.

A scream, close.

"Amelia, stop—please stop waving that around."

Someone grabbed my wrist and pried the gun away.

"Now what do I do with this?" Joss said. Someone, Woo, probably, wretched over the side of the boat.

I felt a whisper of a breath against my face as hands, so many hands, brought me out of the water, cradled me in something soft. A beach towel. I heard Doyle speaking roughly to Phillip, still hanging on the side of the boat.

When I opened my eyes, Corrine searched my face, then the water. "Where is he? Where's Win?"

I had no idea what she meant, and then I remembered—

I scrambled to my feet, throwing off the towel. "Nath!"

CHAPTER 49
NATH

I hit the water, already forgetting.

Under. I remembered.

I remembered this dark, this midnight.

Nothing else—

But a man. I remembered the man. The man would want me to hold my breath.

I held my breath.

The man would want me to open my eyes.

I opened my eyes.

A boat, like a whale, a giant white whale sat belly-deep in the water above me. Capone's men, sitting on rum, guns cocked. What would the man want me to do?

Dad. The man's name was Dad.

He would want me to swim to the boat and grab on. He wanted me to take my chances, grab the boat and hang on for dear life.

He never grabbed for a thing, never tried, never let himself try. Not in the cards. But the man would want me to try.

He wanted me to try.

The man would want me to breathe.

I fumbled at the boat until I found a spot to clutch with slippery hands. Hang on, breathe in. Hang on, breathe out.

I heard voices. The ghosts of a hundred of Capone's men and enemies lying beneath the black lake. I didn't want to be one of them.

Voices and splashing—

An explosion that might have torn through the boat. I held on. So slippery. I lost track of the surface, water everywhere. I was underwater again, but found the air and the boat and held on.

"Nath," someone screamed.

Me. My name was Nath.

The man would want me to say something. Dad. Dad would want me to say—

"Here."

"Here, he's up here!" They'd spotted me, a castaway.

I held on. Rough hands pulled me in. Everything hurt. I thought of the man who survived the St. Valentine's Day Massacre, only to die off the postcard. Poor bastard, and just as dead.

"He's hurt, too."

Hands pressed me down to the earth. I didn't want to be on the postcard. I didn't want to look at the postcard.

"How many bullets were fired total?"

"Win," I said. The man didn't know anything about this, but I did. "Win didn't."

The woman. The woman's name was Amelia.

I didn't remember why, but I was glad to see her. So glad.

"I know, Nath," she said. "Hold on."

The man would want me to say thank you.

Thank you to Amelia for her voice and the name she called me. Thank you to the people who covered me in warm things and said my name. Thank you to the rain. I licked my lips. Thank you to the lighthouse that lit us. Except the lights were all over, and red and white, and they caught me in a spotlight. A fish, hooked through the gut.

"Phillip," I said.

"We know, Nath, hold on. Here they come."

CHAPTER 50
AMELIA

On the first day of the new semester, I arrived early and sat at my desk with a Smith Hall coffee cup warming my hands. The old windows leaked horribly. I could see my breath. Out on the lake, the waves had frozen the shoreline into odd shapes.

It was still early when someone knocked on my door.

It could be anyone—exactly who I didn't want to see.

"*Rothbert Reader*." A fist pounded on the glass. I heard laughs.

I went to the door and tugged. Always tight, but I would get someone in to sand it down a millimeter, I truly would.

Doyle stood in the door, laden with a box. Joss waved a newspaper over his head. "You're top news again," she said. "If you get a Rothbert Medal out of this, I'm totally getting myself shot *and* drowned next year."

I snatched the paper from her.

Three months later, and they were still running the same grainy enlargement of me, hair wet and stringy across my face, being carted away from the tie-up and into the back of an ambulance. Again. "I'd been waiting for a picture like this to start online dating."

"Come on," Joss said. "I saw the photos of you that Scottish lad put into his paper. You don't need to start online dating anytime soon."

Doyle pretended not to hear. "Where do you want this?"

Today's top headline featured Win, actually, the story writing itself, though not the way McDaniel had predicted. The Rothbert heir, barely escaping with his life, had transferred to another university.

"Poor kid."

"Maybe it's not a bad idea to study somewhere they didn't try to kill you," Joss said, shrugging. "And where your dead ancestor's statue doesn't wave at you every day."

At the bottom of the page, they'd included the same line-up of campus ID photos they'd been shuffling and replaying since the incident: Nath, Phillip, Win, the students we'd long come to know as the sacrificial lambs of Phillip's early career. The snapshot of Leo, this time the photo his mother had protected so carefully.

Here was an action shot of Corrine, carrying a box out of Dale Hall with a scowl. It still hurt.

Doyle cleared his throat. "This is rather heavy."

I looked up. "Good grief, Doyle, I really don't need the whole series. I'm not making a scrapbook here."

"These aren't newspapers." He duck-walked the box to the nearest flat surface. Corrine's desk, empty. Doyle glanced over his shoulder. "This OK?"

"Nothing had better jump out at me."

"It's not a stripper in a cake, Mel. It's your book."

My book. I tipped the box flaps open and peered inside. The manuscript, yellowed at the edges, seemed otherwise pristine. *Silent Witness: The Sociology of Violence in the American Midwest.* Maybe a little on the dramatic side, but still—a viable title, a viable book. Just in time, because the editor who'd called wanted to see anything I had. An updated edition, he'd said, as though there'd already been a first. I imagined a nice foreword that would explain a few things or some small notation in my author's bio. Or maybe no mention of any of it would be best.

The sight of the title made me want to light the barbecue grill. This time, I didn't fear starting over; I welcomed it. I already had another book idea. Ideas came at me as fast as I could jot them down. I'd never live long enough to see them all through, even if I planned on a long life. And I did.

"If you're going to burn it," Joss said, "at least this time invite us to the cookout."

She flicked a wave over her shoulder and passed through the doorway, bangles clacking together.

"Do not burn this, Amelia," Doyle said. Maybe he'd always known me better than I knew myself. "Swear to me."

"I'm not the promise-making type. As you remember." I waited until he met my eyes. "I'm—sorry for that. I never meant to waste your time."

"Well. Time with you was never wasted, Amelia. Just—don't tell Nancy I said so or you'll have to worry for your life again. And mine."

"It's a deal."

"The new semester begins, then. Ready for it?" He glanced at Corrine's empty desk. I missed her, despite everything. I'd been past her parents' home up the shore, but the house was as good as shuttered. No one had heard from her, and none of us expected to.

"I'm ready."

He looked like he might give me a brotherly pat but resisted. "Good, good. I'll see you at the faculty meeting, then."

"There's a faculty meeting?"

"Mel, please tell me—"

"I'm kidding. I've got it together, Doyle. This time, I mean it." And I did. On my desk sat the stacks of class plans I'd need to see through this first day. I wasn't fooling myself, though. It was going to be hard. The students still stared. The *Rothbert Reader* photographers still hung out in the ivy near Dale Hall's front door. But the two a.m. phone calls had stopped. It felt, at last, as though I'd come through the other side.

I saw Doyle to the door and stood there, watching his back retreat up the stairs. Across the hall, my personal silent witness smiled with pastel lips at the twists our lives had taken together.

Downstairs, I heard the commotion of footsteps. The first class session of the semester had just let out. In fifteen minutes, they'd all be in other seats in other rooms or headed into the next stage of their schedules, and the halls would quiet. It had been too quiet since Night Sail and over the winter break. I craved this, this lovely, lively noise all the time now. I wanted to be near them, surrounded by them.

I dropped the newspaper onto my desk, closed my door, and took the stairs, leaving the cane behind. I needed the practice. Twenty-five steps, plus the one before the landing, but if I took my time and gripped the rail, I could get there. I would get there.

By the time I'd reached the bottom stair, the middle worn by generations of Rothbert students, the halls were empty.

I turned, with patience, on the last step and started back. I would do one more round of stairs before I left for the day. But later.

Behind me came the soft throat-clearing of someone in the passing lane. I waved him on, but no one appeared.

I looked back. Nath, his hair hanging in his eyes, leaned crookedly over a dark wooden walking stick. "Good morning, Dr. Emmet."

"There you are, Nath. How are you feeling?"

"Like I got shot in the gut."

"Did they give you the orange pills? You should ask for the orange pills."

"I've seen enough of those. I'm feeling OK. I guess."

I knew what he meant. "Any news?"

"Win is seeing some specialist out in Colorado. Aspen ski therapy, he calls it." A shadow passed across his face. "Actually, I wish he wouldn't call it that. Did you hear that he's transferring?"

What I wanted to know was if Corrine would be going with him— but that seemed unlikely. No matter what she'd thought about their relationship, the kid was just a kid. He had his entire, golden life ahead of him. "I meant, news about you? What do the doctors say?"

"Oh. Probably won't be eating steak for a while. Steak that doesn't go through a blender first. I'm in the club now." He picked up his walking stick, shifting his weight to be able to show me the elegant carved handle, the tapered tip.

"*Nice*, Nath."

"My dad brought it to me. He says it was my grandpa's."

"He wants you to come home?"

He tilted the stick this way and that in the light. "He wanted me to come home months ago. Now he wants me to stay. He sold off a bunch of stuff from my grandpa's estate and put the money into an account to help me finish school."

"Quite a guy. I can see what you inherited from him."

"Probably not."

"Thoughtfulness. If you weren't such a thoughtful guy, you wouldn't be in half the mess you're in."

"That's a nice way of putting it."

"You know what I mean. Nightmares. Doubts, at the very least. How many times have you considered changing your major?"

"Like, seven." He let his hair hide his eyes, then brushed it out of the way. "I have the same nightmare every night. I wake up screaming. My roommate wants me to move out. Which is practically the nicest thing he's ever said to me."

"That you should move out?"

"That I might survive on my own without him."

I felt a smile sneak onto my face. "So you saw the paper—"

"Yeah—again."

"Going to be a little noisy for a while yet, Nath, but I swear, it will get better. It has to, someday."

"Your boyfriend sure got a lot of ink out of it."

I wasn't sure what to say to that. "Well, we can't say he didn't do his part. And mine, at some points." I hated to think what would have happened if Rory hadn't stayed curious and concerned. He tried not to say he told me so. He'd had a smug, new photo taken for his new job at the *Tribune*. In his newly tailored tweed jacket. Insufferable, really, but in a way that I found I enjoyed. "What's your nightmare like?"

Nath studied the floor of Dale Hall as though he'd never seen it before.

"Mine is that I didn't get to you in time," I said. "Over and over, I dream that you're at the bottom of Lake Michigan. Every night."

Nath squinted up at me. "I dream that I'm at the top of these stairs, holding a gun."

I took a deep breath. "Maybe we could use some ski therapy. Or the regular kind."

"Why, though? Why did Leo—you startled him, right? He was there for Win, but you just came up the stairs at the wrong moment. But he didn't have to pull the trigger. He didn't have to shoot you or himself. Or anyone. I mean—not like I don't understand what goes through someone's mind. I've had that day."

"How many of those days have you had since—" I gestured at his walking stick.

He looked away. A few, then.

"Well, you have to put yourself in Leo's shoes." I remembered the boy's panicked face over mine in the hall that night. *Oh no, oh no.* His last words of regret, and then that deep, quiet moment when he must have contemplated what he could live with and what he couldn't. I had finally been able to tell his mother something that might help her sleep, and between him and Win and now Nath, I knew that Rothbert wasn't just a proving ground for the elite's offspring. It was also a place that attracted good people, smart people, and lots of them. People who thought Rothbert was a chance for a new life.

I finally understood the kid behind that shaking gun rising from the dark. "You know what I think about Leo that night? I think he was stretched so far beyond reason—" A pair of students, giggling at competing cell phones, came down the stairs and passed us. Nath watched after them with the impatience of a curmudgeon. He'd have to be careful, or he'd grow into that cane.

"So far beyond reason, that none of his options made sense. I think that we all have chances to be different versions of ourselves," I said. "Phillip won't say how he got Leo to the hallway, but here's what I think: Another Leo Lehane might not have been there. Another Leo Lehane might not have pulled the trigger. Do you understand what I mean?"

If the events of the prior semester had given me one thing, it was that I had finally let go of the other Amelia Emmets. They'd gone their way, and I'd gone mine. I hadn't won every point, but I was who I was. I thought Nath might know about that. He was too young to see that crooked paths often still led where you wanted to go. But he'd also left some of himself behind—in the lake, and along the way. We were all slightly different versions of ourselves now.

"That's what I think," I said. "But we'll never know for sure."

He looked at me in silence, then nodded.

I turned back to the stairs. Only twenty-three more to go and one after the landing. "The kind of therapy I've been doing is a combination of work, work, teaching—which is work, of course—a few less pain pills than the week before, and a beer or two with a friend at the Mill." And sleep. And Rory McDaniel therapy, but Nath didn't need to hear about that. "I can advise you on your own regimen, if you like. Come on up, and take your time."

He was still silent behind me. I glanced back. He slumped against his walking stick, weary and pale.

"What?" I said.

"Dr. Emmet, I'm not ashamed to tell you that I need to take the elevator."

"Well, then," I said. "You're already ahead of me."

He smiled. Good man.

ACKNOWLEDGMENTS

Since this is my first novel, I have many people to thank for making this book—and this writing life—possible.

First thanks go to Sharon Bowers of Miller Bowers Griffin Literary Management and to Dan Mayer, Jill Maxick, Nicole Sommer-Lecht, Meghan Quinn, Julia DeGraf, Brian McMahon, and all the good people at Seventh Street Books/Prometheus Books for making all this possible and being so fun to work with, besides.

Thanks to my mystery writing family, the Mystery Writers of America Midwest Chapter, especially Clare O'Donohue. Thanks also to writers-slash-moral-support artists Lynne Raimondo, Hank Phillippi Ryan, Julie Hyzy, Catriona McPherson, Terry Shames, Susan Froetschel, Jincy Willett, Jamie Freveletti, Lee Reilly, Ellen Blum Barrish, and Holly Montague.

I owe more than thanks to the librarians who put books in my hands back in Boone County, Indiana, and to the writing teachers who have cheered me on through the years, especially Scott Blackwood, Lisa Stolley, Boman Desai, Lawrence Howe, Ann Brigham, Peggy Shinner, and Janet Wondra at Roosevelt University; Michael Price, Mark Massé, and Margaret Kingery at Ball State University (and, of course, Chip Jaggers, who taught me not writing but everything else); Denise Beck, Janet Dingman, and Margaret Keene at Western Boone (and Beverly Parker, who never forgot me, and Jan Coake, of course); Greg Fallis, at Gotham Writers Workshop; and Terence Faherty at Midwest Writers Workshop, for telling me I was a mystery writer in the first place.

Thanks to *Big Muddy* for the first yes and to those who published me afterward, especially *Good Housekeeping*, Laura Matthews, and Jodi Picoult; and *TimeOut Chicago*, Jonathan Messinger, and Michael Harvey for my first crime story publication. Thanks for additional encouragement from Midwest Writers Workshop, Jama Kehoe Bigger and the late Earl Conn; the R. Karl Largent family and my fellow gravedigger Matthew Clemens; Chris Roerden and the Helen McCloy Scholarship committee; Gotham Writers' Workshop; Friends of American Writers; Amy Davis, Pat Cronin, and the Writers Work-Space; Jill Pollack and StoryStudio Chicago.

Special thanks to my partner in crime, Kim Rader, and to Kristi Brenock-Leduc and Meghan Eagan for e-mails with exclamation marks.

Also Tricia David, Emily Lobdell, and Lauren MacIntyre for not needing me during crucial lunch-hour writing time; Denise, Beth, JoAnna, Rebecca, Kate, Meredith, Laurie, Viv, Tricia-O, Sharada, and Erin for encouraging me to leap; Kelly, Michi, Danny, Kelli, Gil, Lauren, Kim, Adam, Becky, Sam, and the entire Roosevelt MFA community past and present; the Lovells for all the cozy murder titles if I ever write one; and all the supportive friends always there, especially Tiffany (yes, Jeff, you, too), Mandee, Melissa, Kirsten, Scoots, and the Schnitzlers.

Tremendous thanks to my first readers, Christopher Coake, Mary Anne Mohanraj, Yvonne Strumecki, and James Burford, who gave time, feedback, advice, and therapy.

The biggest appreciation goes to my family, of course, especially Paula and Danny Dodson; Mel and Janie Rader; Jill, Scott, Jesse, and Addison Bryan; and all of the Days. Also Annie Ellen Rader, who always liked to hear my version of events.

And to Greg, last but most.

ABOUT THE AUTHOR

Lori Rader-Day has published fiction in *Good Housekeeping*, where she won first place in the magazine's first short-story contest; the Madison Review, which awarded her the 2008 Chris O'Malley Prize in Fiction; *Ellery Queen Mystery Magazine*; *TimeOut Chicago*; *Southern Indiana Review*; *Crab Orchard Review*; *Oyez Review*; and other journals and magazines. She lives with her husband and dog in Chicago, where she is active in the Mystery Writers of America Midwest Chapter, Sisters in Crime Chicagoland Chapter, and International Thriller Writers. Author Website: www.LoriRaderDay.com.